3,50

A COMMODORE OF ERRORS

A NOVEL

JOHN JACOBSEN

Arcade Publishing
New York

Copyright © 2011 by John Jacobsen

Arcade Publishing books may be purchased in bulk at special discounts for sales promotion, corporate gifts, fund-raising, or educational purposes. Special editions can also be created to specifications. For details, contact the Special Sales Department, Arcade Publishing, 307 West 36th Street, 11th Floor, New York, NY 10018 or info@skyhorsepublishing.com.

Arcade Publishing® is a registered trademark of Skyhorse Publishing, Inc.®, a Delaware corporation.

Visit our website at www.arcadepub.com.

10 9 8 7 6 5 4 3 2 1

Library of Congress Cataloging-in-Publication Data

Jacobsen, John G.
  A commodore of errors : a novel / John Jacobsen.
    p. cm.
  ISBN 978-1-61145-338-6 (hardcover : alk. paper)
  1. United States Merchant Marine Academy--Fiction. I. Title.
  PS3610.A35665C66 2011
  813'.6--dc22
                          2011020627

Printed in the United States of America

CONTENTS

BOOK II:

The MV *God is Able*, at Sea

BOOK III:
The United States Merchant Marine Academy

For Silvana, who actually believed me when I told her I was going to write a novel.

PROLOGUE

Midshipman Jones stood on the uneven porch of Mrs. Tannenbaume's house and stared at the wooden cross that leaned against the porch rail. The cross was enormous. It was bigger than he—a rough-hewed Midwest farm boy—and made of rough wood beams pegged together with wood dowels. A life-size papier-mâché replica of a bloody Jesus lay on the burnt grass next to the porch.

He'd been wondering what his work order meant as soon as he picked it out of the job box at the MOD's office. He'd also been wondering whether Mrs. Tannenbaume was crazy. Now he knew.

Midshipman Jones rang the ship's bell that served as Mrs. Tannenbaume's doorbell. When Mrs. Tannenbaume arrived at the door in her housedress—she was old, which he sort of expected, based on the rundown condition of the house's exterior—Midshipman Jones waived the piece of scrap paper he held in his hand.

"Good morning, Mrs. Tannenbaume," he said. "I'm here for the job you called in."

"Oh, yes, come in, love."

Wow. What a raspy voice. She must have been a smoker when she was young. Or a drinker. Probably both.

He opened the screen door—half-painted and peeling—and stepped into the small entrance off the porch. Stacks of yellowed newspapers filled the vestibule. He sidestepped his way through them and entered Mrs. Tannenbaume's living room.

The room was a shrine to the Holy Roman Catholic Church—or at least that's how it appeared. Little replicas of the Stations of the Cross were placed in every corner. A leather-bound Holy Bible took up most of the coffee table. Rosary beads were strewn about on the card table in the corner, crammed between the cushions on the sofa and love seats, and hanging off the shade of the floor lamp in the other corner of the peculiar room. Over the fireplace hung a crucifix, also wrapped in rosary beads. The only nonreligious decorations in the room were three framed photographs on the fireplace mantle. Midshipman Jones stared at the photos. They were dark and grainy and appeared to portray three young men. He wondered why these terrible photos were so prominent in the old lady's home.

Mrs. Tannenbaume looked up expectantly at him. "I forget why I wanted you here, love."

Midshipman Jones did not know what to make of this old lady. Her wrinkled skin—*God, she must have been a real sun worshipper when she was young*—made her look pretty old but then she seemed so spry, almost youthful, nothing like his grandmother back in Ohio, who was probably the same age.

He looked at the slip of paper in his hand, then back to Mrs. Tannenbaume. "Let me read it to you, Mrs. Tannenbaume. I want to make sure I get it right." He paused. "It says here, 'Need one midshipman to nail Jesus to the cross.'"

Mrs. Tannenbaume slapped her hand against her forehead. "Oh yes, my papier-mâché Jesus. I got him at the annual yard sale at the St. Aloysius, my church in Great Neck. He was a leftover from a play put on by the kids. Nobody else wanted him. I got him for five bucks, can you believe it? The nuns wanted to know what I planned to do with my Jesus. I told them I was going to find a big cross and nail him to it. When I went to pick him up—one of your classmates helped me, he owns a pickup truck—Sister Mahoney tried to keep me from taking him. I told her, 'No way, Sister, a deal is a deal, I have the receipt to prove it.' She's some kind of *meshuggener,* that Sister Mahoney."

"*Meshuggener?*"

"She's crazy."

A couple of years of dealing with superior officers had taught Midshipman Jones how to bite back a smart remark. He called upon his training at that moment.

Mrs. Tannenbaume led Midshipman Jones back out to the dilapidated front porch and pointed at the cross. "I got this from my tenant upstairs, Mr. Schwartz. We used to go together, you know. When he found out I was Catholic, he broke the whole thing off. He said he could not believe Sylvia Tannenbaume was a Catholic, as if he didn't already know. I said to him, 'Schwartzie, how many times did I tell you? It's Tannenbaume with an *E*. I'm not Jewish.' But he don't listen, that Schwartzie. He said to me, 'I'm sorry, Sylvia, but if my mother knew, she'd disown me.' So I said to him, 'We're both seventy-six years old, love. Does it really matter?'" Mrs. Tannenbaume paused for a moment to admire her wooden cross. "But I think he musta felt bad about breaking up with me because he made me this cross to hang my Jesus on."

To Midshipman Jones, this old lady was a hoot. He really didn't know what to make of her. He wanted to be sure to mind his manners so he just nodded his head while he brushed his hand on the rough wood of the cross and searched for an appropriate remark. "It must be hard for a widow to find a good man," he blurted out.

Mrs. Tannenbaume jerked her head toward him. "What makes you think I'm a widow?"

Midshipman Jones averted Mrs. Tannenbaume's gaze. "I'm sorry, Mrs. Tannenbaume. I don't know, really, I guess I just figured . . ."

"Come here, young man." Mrs. Tannenbaume grabbed him by the elbow. "I want to show you something."

Mrs. Tannenbaume dragged him inside the house once again and stopped in front of the fireplace. She pointed to the nicely framed photographs. "Eddie, Teddy, and Freddie."

Midshipman Jones stepped closer and peered at the photos. Yes, they were photographs of three young men about his age. Mrs. Tannenbaume was lost in her thoughts, so he just looked at the photos and didn't say a word.

"Eddie, Teddy, and Freddie." Mrs. Tannenbaume turned to face him, her hands still clutched to her heart. "One of these boys is my son's father."

Once again, Midshipman Jones had the opportuntity to practice biting back a remark.

"Oh, I was a wild one when I was young," Mrs. Tannenbaume confessed, pointing at the picture on the left. "That's Eddie. He was a sailor. His ship pulled into port during the war. My father was a tailor and he made uniforms for the merchant marine. Ships from all over the world would stop in Durban—that's where we lived, Durban, in South Africa—to pick up uniforms made by my father. I brought a bunch of uniforms down to the ships one afternoon. Eddie was the youngest sailor on the ship, and oh, I tell you, that Eddie was something to look at."

Mrs. Tannenbaume's gaze remained fixed on the photographs on the mantle. She pointed at the middle one. "And that's Teddy. He was a tailor. An apprentice tailor, really. My father agreed to teach him the trade as a favor to Teddy's father. He wasn't very good, though, poor Teddy. All his uniforms had too many buttonholes. To tell you the truth," Mrs. Tannenbaume whispered to Midshipman Jones, "I think I distracted the poor fella whenever I was in the shop. Not for nothing, but I was something to look at, too, when I was seventeen." Mrs. Tannenbaume turned back to the photographs with a wistful look in her eyes.

Midshipman Jones pointed to the last photograph. "And him?"

"Freddie was a jailor," Mrs. Tannenbaume said. "He worked in the Durban jail as a guard. I guess these days he'd be called a prison guard, but in those days he was just a jailor. Freddie was a nice guy. Dumb as a bag of hammers, though. My father made the uniforms for the jailors is how I met him."

"So. Eddie, Teddy, and Freddie. A sailor, a tailor, and a jailor. Wow."

"What's the far-off look for?"

"Oh nothing, I guess," Midshipman Jones said. "It's just that there's something vaguely familiar about this story. Probably just déjà vu."

"It's no story." Mrs. Tannenbaume smoothed her hands on her housedress. "One of those boys is my son's father. Since I'm not exactly sure which one it is, I kind of think of them all as his father."

Mrs. Tannenbaume turned and walked out onto the porch. Midshipman Jones followed along. This assignment was turning out to be a lot more interesting than he'd thought it would be. He pointed at the ship's bell serving as Mrs. Tannenbaume's doorbell. "Where'd you get the ship's bell, Mrs. Tannenbaume?"

"That's from my son's ship, the *God is Able*. My sonny boy is the captain." Midshipman Jones bent over for a closer look at the ship's bell. The *God is Able*? Where had he—

And then it hit him.

"That's it! I knew I had heard the story before. Captain Tannenbaume is your son? He's, like, a legend. The stories about the *God is Able* are the best! I can't wait to tell the guys."

Mrs. Tannenbaume beamed. "You just made my day, young man." Then together Mrs. Tannenbaume and Midshipman Jones turned and faced the wooden cross and the papier-mâché Jesus.

"So what do you think?" Mrs. Tannenbaume asked. "Should we put up the cross first and then nail the Jesus to it, or would it be easier to nail the Jesus to the cross while it's lying on the ground?"

BOOK I

The United States Merchant Marine Academy, Kings Point, New York

Chapter 1

SECOND IN COMMAND

Commodore Robert S. Dickey marched across Barney Square in full view of the regiment of midshipmen. The midshipmen had just finished mustering for Morning Colors and were standing at attention in formation. The Commodore felt them follow his every step with their eyes and basked in their adoration.

Dressed in his summer whites, he knew that he was the very essence of "the officer and the gentleman." The crease in his pant leg was a knife's edge. His shined brass belt buckle glinted off the morning sun. The Filipino Martinizer at the Great Neck Martinizing Dry Cleaners knew that the Commodore liked his shirts pressed crisp, and this morning his shirt was so crisp it audibly crackled as he walked. And even though his hair was mostly covered by his gold-braided white hat, it, too, was perfect. The Commodore took great pride in his hair. His hair was patrician white and possessed a natural luster that needed no mousse, gel, oil, or spray. He looked forward to his semi-weekly visits to the academy barbershop. He liked the compliments he received as he sat, erect and smiling, in the barber's chair. His hair was gorgeous, the barber would say, gorgeous, and so thick and white. When the barber finished trimming his hair this morning, the Commodore asked if he needed any mousse or gel. He knew what the barber would say, but he liked to hear him say it anyway.

"Mousse? In your hair?" The barber placed his hand to his mouth in mock horror. "Commodore, please, your hair is so thick, so gorgeous. A good barber would never soil your hair with such junk."

As the Commodore strode across Barney Square—taking care to avoid the bigger cracks in the black asphalt—three regimental drummers began beating bass drums with mallets that looked like long sticks with marshmallows stuck on the end. *Boom! Boom! Ba-boom, boom, boom! Boom! Boom! Ba-boom, boom, boom!* The Commodore timed his walk across Barney Square to coincide with the beating of the drums. The sound of the big bass drums stirred his heart with pride. How he loved the United States Merchant Marine Academy!

Boom! Boom! Ba-boom, boom, boom!

The Commodore pursed his lips and sucked in his cheeks. The effect on the midshipmen, he surmised, must be overwhelming. As he made his way toward Wiley Hall, the academy's main administrative building (and former summer home to a wealthy automobile magnate), he smiled up at Admiral Johnson, who stood at attention on Wiley Hall's balcony. The balcony overlooked Powell Oval and the flagpole, which stood at the epicenter of the academy's grounds.

Admiral John J. Johnson, the academy's superintendent, did not return the smile.

The Commodore entered the cool marble foyer of Wiley Hall, doffed his cap with a flick of his wrist, and tucked it beneath his left arm. He greeted the secretaries gathered inside the foyer—it was the only place in Wiley Hall, built before the advent of air-conditioning, that provided a natural respite from the oppressive heat—by pulling up with a click of his heels and then bowing like a butler. The secretaries responded as they usually did, by covering their mouths to muffle their giggles and comments, presumably about his beautiful white hair.

"Good morning, ladies," the Commodore said.

"Good morning, Commodore," the women sang in unison.

The Commodore walked toward the staircase to the left of the foyer. "And what kind of day is it today?"

"It's another day to excel, sir," the women said together, before collapsing again into giggles.

"That's right, ladies. Today is just another day in which to excel."

The Commodore took the stairs two at a time. He did this out of habit, not because he was in a hurry. Indeed, he intended to join Admiral Johnson on the balcony at the precise moment the regimental band struck its first note of the "Star-Spangled Banner" and not a moment sooner. So the Commodore waited in the alcove until he heard the regimental band strike a few extraneous notes preparatory to playing the song. Then he stepped onto the balcony, whipped his hand to the brim of his cap, and saluted the flag.

Johnson stiffened. "Late again, I see." Even though they were alone on the balcony, Johnson spoke out of the side of his mouth. "Is the humidity messing up your hair this morning, Bobby?"

The Commodore angled his head toward Johnson and spoke above the din of the band.

"No, sir. The hair's just fine, thank you. I'm just not a morning person, as you know."

The regimental band fumbled through the National Anthem the best they could. Staying up half the night drinking coffee and smoking cigarettes while hitting the books was poor preparation for blowing on a trumpet first thing in the morning. More often than not, Morning Colors featured what sounded like the Star-*Mangled* Banner.

The Commodore winced. "Isn't there something we can do about the band, sir? They are hopeless."

Johnson looked straight ahead at the American flag lying limp against the flagpole in the still air. "The band is fine. At least they show up on time."

"This new bandleader—where did we get him? Is the man not tone-deaf?"

The song was coming to its familiar close now. Try as they might, the stressed-out band jocks simply could not muster the energy to finish the song with the flourish the Commodore craved. This day, like every other in July on Long Island, was shaping up to be hazy, hot, and humid, the kind of weather that can sap the spirit, making it all the more imperative that the regimental band kick off the day with gusto. Couldn't Johnson see that? As the anthem died with a whimper, the Commodore dropped his salute and turned to Johnson. "Surely the United States Merchant Marine Academy can afford a proper bandleader. Might you want me to look into the matter, old boy?"

"Old boy? Enough with the Gatsby bit, Bobby. And no, I don't want you looking for a new bandleader. I like the band just the way it is."

"Yes, of course, sir. The band is perfectly fine. Fine indeed. I just wish they'd end the 'Star-Spangled Banner' with the flourish it deserves. What a wonderful reminder it would be that today is just another day in which—"

Johnson put his hand up.

"Spare me, please."

An awkward moment passed between the two before Johnson broke the silence. "So what's on your agenda today, Bobby? Anything special?"

The Commodore grinned, his mood brightening. "I thought I'd work on my Recognition Day speech, sir. It's coming up, you know."

"It's two months away, for Chrissakes."

"You never can be too prepared. It's an important speech, sir."

"You planning on giving them the 'Back End' speech, Bobby?"

"Well, I do think it is my best speech, sir. It does seem to get the best response from the midshipmen anyway."

"Whatever. Work on your speech, if that's what you want."

Johnson turned to leave the balcony but stopped and turned back when he got to the door. "Oh, and, Bobby . . . don't think your cute little trick went unnoticed by me. The next time you join me for Colors, enter the building through the rear like you're supposed to. If anyone parades across Barney Square in front of the regiment, it'll be me, okay?"

The Commodore sought to reassure Johnson by clicking his heels and bowing—his butler's bow. The gesture was ignored.

"And by the way," Johnson said, "did I hear you say yesterday that someone is joining us for lunch today?"

"Yes indeed, sir. A Miss Conrad from the public relations firm I told you about."

The Commodore saw Johnson perk up. "Miss Conrad? You know anything about her?"

"Yes, sir. I've met with her before. She's smart as a whip, I dare say. And she's quite charming, as well."

The Commodore held back what he knew Johnson really wanted to know. He wanted to make the old horn-dog grovel for it.

"Is she good looking?" Johnson asked.

"That depends on what you consider good looking, sir. Miss Conrad is blonde, has piercing blue eyes, and a rather shapely pair of legs."

Johnson could not hide a lascivious grin. "I look forward to meeting her. See you at lunch."

The Commodore waited until Johnson left the balcony before he turned to face the flagpole and the rest of the academy grounds. He gripped the stone balustrade with both hands and spread his stance wide, devouring all that stood before him—the neat flower beds, the pathways bordered by white painted stones, the shined brass bell at the center of the oval. Yes, the asphalt-covered oval was just as badly cracked and splintered as Barney Square, but the Commodore chose, on this fine morning, to look past the unsightly aspects of the campus. He knew the physical plant of the Merchant Marine Academy fell far short of the other federal service academies, with their elegant brick and granite pavers, but he also knew that with the proper leadership, his alma mater could one day be as pristine as the others.

A group of midshipmen marched by, and one of them looked up toward the balcony and said, "Good morning, Admiral."

The Commodore did not bother to correct the midshipman. "Good morning, boys," he said, sounding, for all the world, like an admiral himself.

Chapter 2

JOHNSON'S JOHNSON

The Commodore departed Wiley Hall with a spring in his step and started off across the academy's grounds to Bowditch Hall to practice his speech. Along the way he greeted still more midshipmen marching to class, only now, up close, they called him Commodore. He had to admit that hearing the midshipmen call him "Admiral" when he stood atop Johnson's balcony was music to his ears. Admiral Dickey had a ring to it, and he so desired to hear it again. But there was room for only one admiral at the academy, and if it was going to be him, Admiral Johnson would have to be taken out of the way first. The Commodore thought of Miss Conrad. She certainly seemed to be Johnson's type—not that he needed a specific type, of course. Any port in a storm would do for "Johnson's Johnson."

Commodore Dickey had dubbed the admiral "Johnson's Johnson" over thirty years ago, back when he and Johnson were brand-new ensigns working in the United States Merchant Marine Academy's Office of External Affairs.

Ensign Dickey happened to be in the right place at the right time to hear Ensign Johnson seduce a young secretary on her first day on the job. Johnson was so preoccupied looking for the beautiful secretary he had heard about from the navy chaplain at their Morning Prayer meeting that he failed to notice Dickey working quietly at his desk when he squeezed into the new secretary's cubicle. Johnson asked her if she was the efficient new secretary he had heard so much about and then promptly invited her to join him for a drink in the officers' club after work. When the young secretary demurred, sighting the strict fraternization rule outlined in her employment package, Johnson assured her that some rules were made to be broken.

When the new secretary explained that she was married, Johnson assured her that there would be other married women at the officers' club enjoying an after-work cocktail with their colleagues. "Why, even the visiting navy chaplain would be joining in on the wholesome fun," Johnson had said, quite smoothly.

Still, the secretary was not sure about having a drink after work with one of her bosses. It just did not feel right, she told him. It was then that Dickey heard Johnson clear his throat, lower his voice, and say, "If size matters to you, young lady, I can assure you that I am the biggest the academy has to offer."

"The biggest? You mean you're the biggest ranking officer here?"

"Well, no, not exactly, although one day I will be," Johnson said. "No, what I really mean is, of all the, ah, *johnsons* here, I am the biggest."

"Are there other officers named Johnson here at the academy, sir?"

"Well, no, I am the only officer named Johnson." Dickey heard Johnson lower his voice further, almost to a whisper. "No, dear. What I am trying to say is that I *have* the biggest johnson here."

The next day her coworkers gathered around the new secretary at the watercooler and asked her if she had met Ensign Johnson yet. Indeed she had, the new secretary said. "So?" her coworkers asked. The new secretary nodded her head over sips of coffee. "He's quite impressive," she said. The ladies collapsed into giggles around the watercooler and reminded each other how lucky they were to be working at the Merchant Marine Academy. Ensign Dickey listened in on this exchange as well. Yes, he was happy to be working at the academy, too. Ever on the lookout for an advantage over his colleagues, Dickey wasted little time in doing what he did best: damaging his adversaries through gossip and innuendo. That's when he decided to give his archrival Johnson a new moniker, Johnson's Johnson. By days' end, the nickname had stuck for good.

As the years raced by and Johnson and Dickey climbed the ladder at the Merchant Marine Academy, Johnson's Johnson's reputation as a lady-killer grew legendary. When visiting heads of state heard about Johnson's Johnson, they were eager to see if they measured up. Indeed, none other than Henry Kissinger himself came calling, anxious to find out if what he had heard was true. In the locker room after a game of squash, Kissinger saw for himself what all the fuss was about.

He didn't measure up. It wasn't even close.

To keep Johnson's Johnson quiet, Kissinger took a personal interest in Johnson and saw to it that he was promoted earlier than his peers at each juncture of his career. As one of the youngest admirals in the United States Maritime Service, Johnson's Johnson became a shoe-in for the position of superintendent at the United States Merchant Marine Academy when the long-serving Admiral Queen died from severe head injuries he sustained when his sailboat, *Queenie*, went aground off City Island. Admiral Queen had been showing a group of midshipmen just how close they could get to the shoals without going aground. What sad irony.

Commodore Dickey envied Johnson's Johnson's meteoric rise to the top— envied it mightily. After he turned fifty, his own career stalled. For seven long years now he had been stuck at Commodore which, as everyone knew, was not even an official rank in the United States Maritime Service—it was an honorific, a title, not a rank. The Commodore himself demanded the title as he liked the ring of it and it differentiated him from the other officers stuck at the rank of Captain, although he wasn't unaware that the other officers at the academy laughed at him behind his back for wanting to be called Commodore.

All of this played on the Commodore's mind as he crossed the academy grounds on his way to Bowditch Hall. He had high hopes that Miss Conrad would be of help in getting Johnson's Johnson into the hot water he deserved. If there was anyone who would not stand for an unasked-for peek at Johnson's Johnson's johnson, it would be Miss Conrad.

Chapter 3

IT'S ALL ABOUT
THE TEMPO

The Commodore swept into Bowditch Hall only to find the bandleader using the same auditorium in which the Commodore wanted to practice his speech. It felt like a slap in the face to be inconvenienced like this by a subordinate. The bandleader was busy lecturing several band members on stage. Why were they not in class by now? The Commodore took a seat in the last row of the darkened auditorium.

"Mr. Gillard," the bandleader said, "tell us how you think we can improve our rendition of the 'Star-Spangled Banner.'"

Midshipman Gillard stared at the floor in front of him. After a long silence, he said, "You play your Walkman too loud. It really throws me off."

The bandleader held up his hand to cut off a chorus of "Yeah, what's up with that?"

"Now, Mr. Gillard," he said, "you know we've been through this before. I suffer from dyslexia and I have trouble keeping the song straight in my head. I know my headphones are a crutch but I need them."

The Commodore writhed. A conductor who wore headphones while conducting? He could not contain himself any longer and flung himself out of his seat, marching down the aisle toward the stage. "Boys! Boys, that'll be all. Run on to class now, boys."

The Commodore did not have to tell them twice. While the boys hurried off the stage, the Commodore marched directly up to the bandleader and came to a halt within a nose of his face. The bandleader shrunk back.

"Those boys have classes to attend, my dear sir!" The Commodore's voice thundered across the stage. "They most assuredly do not have time to coddle you and your neuroses. We've hired a neurotic bandleader, have we? Well what's been done can surely be undone."

The bandleader froze.

"Who hired you? Was it that skirt-chasing ruffian of a superintendent? Or was it our vacuous Commandant, that philistine who thinks God's gift to music is Jimmy Buffett?"

The Commodore took a deep breath. He was winded by his rush to the stage, and a vigorous tongue lashing always left him breathless. He inhaled deeply through his nose. *Wait. Is that Herrera I smell?*

He took a step back and focused on the bandleader's attire. *Could this cretin really be wearing a Paul Stuart bow tie?* The Commodore recognized it from his own collection of fine ties. *Might the man possess some refinement after all?*

"What cologne are you wearing?" the Commodore said.

"Carolina Herrera for Men."

"And your tie. That wouldn't be a Paul Stuart, would it?"

"Yes, in fact it is."

The Commodore suddenly looked at the bandleader with newfound respect. Surely a man who wore Paul Stuart couldn't be all that bad. Like a tornado that rips through a prairie town and clears the city limits without so much as a goodbye, the Commodore's outburst was over.

"Shall we take a seat over here, sir?" The Commodore motioned to a couple of stools off to the side of the stage.

When they sat down, the Commodore crossed his legs and stroked his chin. "I have an idea. Perhaps you wouldn't mind commenting on the speech I'm here to practice? After all, as a musician you must know a thing or two about rhythm, tone, tempo—the essential elements of a well-delivered speech."

"I'd be pleased to help in any way I can, sir."

The bandleader moved the lectern to the center of the stage while the Commodore stood up and began his preparations. He meditated for a moment then breathed in from the diaphragm, held it for a second, and exhaled slowly. His yoga instructor called this the Infinity Breath. He then did the quick stretching routine he learned from his personal trainer. Next, the Commodore exercised his voice—his voice coach recommended that he do his voice exercises every day to maintain his stentorian tone. Next he practiced the hand gestures and slow sweeping arm movements he learned from his acting coach, and the "pause, scan, and nod" technique imparted by his homiletics instructor. He performed the relaxation routine taught to him by his mental therapist, the finger flexes he learned from his physical therapist, and the self-administered neck massage he learned from his massage therapist. After breathing, flexing, and relaxing; exercising, stretching, and massaging, the Commodore was ready. He told the bandleader to take a seat in the front row, then he took his place behind the lectern. After a dramatic pause, scan, and nod, he launched into his speech:

Good morning, ladies and gentlemen. My name is Commodore Robert S. Dickey. I am the United States Merchant Marine Academy's Officer of External Affairs and one of the most influential members of this administration. Today, what we call Recognition Day, is a great day for your sons and daughters. Recognition Day is the day upon which the academy officially inducts its plebes, your sons and daughters, as members of the regiment of midshipmen. I myself graduated from this august institution nearly thirty years ago—I know I don't look my age—and I can clearly recall the feelings of accomplishment that I felt on my own day of recognition. Your sons and daughters have come a long way since you dropped them off at the front gate some months ago and you should be rightfully proud of them. I know that my parents were proud of me that day, and they continue to be proud of me as I climb the ladder of success to its highest rungs.

Before we talk about the importance of Recognition Day to your sons and daughters, please, if you will indulge me, I would like to spend a few minutes talking about the stupendous work done by the Office of External Affairs, lead by yours truly. As Officer of External Affairs, I like to say that I take care of the "Back End" of things at the academy. The little things done behind the scenes that are so critically important to running this institution. The things that people do not see but, if left undone, would sink the academy into ruin. Yes, I, your humble servant, preside over the monstrously intricate machinations that allow this institution to run like a well-oiled machine. I have never been one who needs to be the marquee attraction—I truly prefer the "Back End" of things. In fact, it is the hard work done by my office that has enabled this day, what I like to call Your Day—because it is not about me—to be such a success. Your sons and daughters are to be congratulated, as I myself was congratulated so many years ago—with this head of hair, I know it's hard to believe. You're welcome.

The Commodore stood at the lectern and waited for his audience of one to burst into applause. When the applause was not forthcoming, the Commodore made a show of clearing his throat.

His audience of one clapped modestly.

The Commodore seethed.

"You are awfully quiet. Is that the best you can do?"

The bandleader shifted about in his first-row seat without saying a word.

"Come, come. Out with it, man!"

"Well," the bandleader said, exhaling forcefully. "As bandleader, I naturally focused on the tempo of the speech." The bandleader began to say something more but then stopped. Looking as if he was going to regret what he was about to say, he continued, "I think the parts where you transitioned to talking about yourself, which were frequent, upset the tempo of the speech. Consequently, you never really found a pleasing rhythm."

The Commodore held the sides of the lectern with both hands and squeezed so hard his knuckles turned white.

"If I talked about myself," the Commodore said deliberately, "it was only to give the parents context so that they could understand the importance of the day. Do you know what context is?" The Commodore paused, daring a response from the bandleader. "It is absolutely essential to a good speech!"

"Yes, sir, I understand. But the tempo, the tempo."

"Why you tone-deaf cretin! Don't you tell me about tempo. I know tempo!"

With that the Commodore marched down to the front row, grabbed the bandleader by the scruff of the neck, and walked him toward the door.

"You are through, Mr. Tone-Deaf Bandleader," the Commodore said. "End of assignment and on to the next job for you, if you can find one. I'll be sure to tell Admiral Johnson the good news."

The Commodore practically frog-marched the bandleader to the main entranceway of Bowditch Hall, all the while spouting pleasantries to the academy personnel he came across in the hallways.

"Good morning, Miss Goodson," he said to an administrative assistant in the Marine Transportation Department. "And what kind of day is it today?"

Miss Goodson smiled back and said, "Why, it's just another day in which to excel, sir."

The Commodore marched his charge all the way to the main gate, greeting midshipmen, colleagues, workers—everyone he came across—on this muggy mid-summer day.

"Good morning, Morris," he shouted to the one-armed groundskeeper who was busy butchering a hedge. "I do admire the way you trim a hedge, Morris!"

Morris waved the hedge trimmer at the Commodore and thanked him for noticing.

When the Commodore reached Vickery Gate, he thrust the bandleader toward the guard stationed there, smiling all the time.

"Good morning, Mr. Thompson, you're looking sharp as usual." The Commodore clicked his heels and bowed. "Please use your uncommon abilities as a uniformed guardsman to see to it that this man does not step foot on academy grounds again." The Commodore's voice resonated off the thick stone walls of the old guardhouse at Vickery Gate.

Mr. Thompson, alcoholic and lucky to have a job, hurriedly turned off his mini TV set and ushered the bandleader out the gate.

The Commodore left the guardhouse and stepped back into the hazy sunshine. He took notice of the trees, the clouds, the sky. He smelled the freshly mowed grass and the evergreen bushes trimmed by one-armed Morris. He heard the birds chirping and the squirrels calling to one another.

Yes, indeed, the Commodore thought as he strode confidently in the direction of his dreams, *today truly is just another day in which to excel*.

Chapter 4

S & M

The Commodore spent the rest of the morning the way he spent most mornings: practicing his hand gestures, exercising his voice, and combing his hair in front of his huge office mirror in Wiley Hall. He had made certain to call Miss Conrad earlier that morning to cancel their luncheon date with Johnson. He wanted to make old Johnson's Johnson salivate at the prospect of meeting the leggy Miss Conrad. The Commodore wrapped up his morning by lecturing his secretary, Miss Lambright, on the importance of time management.

When it was time for lunch, the Commodore figured he better not push his luck with Johnson by crossing Barney Square during the Noon Formation. Instead, he ducked out the back of Wiley Hall and walked along the waterfront to the rear entrance of Delano Hall. This allowed him to stop at what he hoped would be the future site of the Mariners Monument, his pet project. In a few days, the Board of Governors were to hold a meeting to determine whether to proceed with the monument, and rumor had it that Johnson was making noises about derailing the project. The meeting loomed large in the Commodore's mind. If necessary, he would retell the entire heroic story of fallen cadet-midshipman Edwin J. O'Hara, and the imperatives for why the academy should erect a statue in his likeness. If the Commodore succeeded, the monument would be finished in time for a dedication ceremony to take place in mid-October, three months from now. The Commodore wanted to be the one to make the dedication speech, wanted it more than anything in the world, but he knew that, as admiral, Johnson's Johnson would be the one to do the honors. The old horn-dog would undoubtedly give his stock speech, replete with sexual innuendos and gratuitous references to the role of women in the merchant marine.

The Commodore looked out toward the Long Island Sound. Not a ripple disturbed its black waters on this windless day. Where he stood on the hill overlooking the boat basin was the perfect location for the Mariners Monument. Posterior to the Memorial Arbors (which the Commodore considered deaf and mute) and anterior to the War Memorial (faceless and inarticulate), and set at a rakish angle, the Mariners Monument would dominate its neighbors. To position the monument askew of the geometric lines of the academy's architecture would send the Board of Governors into spasms. To a person, they lacked subtlety and nuance. Everything with these boors had to be geometrical: straight lines, hard corners, squares, triangles. The Commodore, who considered himself classically trained and broadly experienced, had the confidence to step outside the lines of classicism. But first he would have to overcome Johnson's objections. He would take care of that well enough at the meeting of the Board of Governors.

The Commodore heard the beating of the bass drums over in Barney Square and resumed his walk toward Delano Hall. The sound of the drums carried to the waterfront, but the effect was not the same if one was not in the thick of it. He walked along with his head up but without the usual spring in his step. When he entered Delano Hall through the commissary, the Caribbean cooks and dishwashers sang out greetings, "Today is another day to excel, mon." The Commodore responded in kind, and his mood brightened. He took a seat at the center of the long and narrow table on the dais as the regiment filed in for the noon meal.

The orderly procession of midshipmen marching across Barney Square collapsed into chaos the moment they crossed the threshold of the dining hall. People immediately began talking among themselves, and the pent-up frustrations of a thousand midshipmen filled the cavernous mess hall with the roar of Niagara Falls. The noon meal hour was a time for letting go. By this time, the regiment had been up and running nonstop since 0530 hours. Every minute of their time had been consumed by musters, room inspections, classes, and lectures. And there never seemed to be enough time to get from one place to another, from class back to the barracks in time for a personal appearance inspection, or from the waterfront all the way to O'Hara Hall for PT. When the plebes walked anywhere on campus, they did so by squaring corners, which made their commute even longer. The upperclassmen did not have to square corners but they did have to stay constantly on guard in case they happened across an officer as they made their way about the campus. A proper salute was de rigueur, as well as a proper greeting. Saying "Good morning, sir," instead of "Good afternoon" was enough to earn a stern reprimand. And springtime was the toughest for the regiment. One could not smell the roses, as it were, as one walked across the beautifully manicured grounds. One had to be alert to following the rules and regulations every step of the way. When walking together, a group of upperclassmen must not be too loud or walk too casually. They must always be on their best behavior. But the meal hour was different. The meal hour was loud—loud with the sounds of young men letting their guard down for the briefest of respites.

The Commodore let the cacophony wash over him. To him it was akin to the sound of children at a playground—it was music, a symphony, and it had a steady, resounding tempo.

Johnson's cologne preceded him as he approached the table from behind the Commodore. The cologne nauseated the Commodore—it was the same kind of bottom-shelf toilet water that wafted through the Seafarers' Union Hall in Brooklyn. The Commodore smiled, however, knowing that he wore it in anticipation of meeting Miss Conrad. The Commodore pushed back his seat and stood up to greet Johnson.

"Hello, old boy. Fancy meeting you here," the Commodore said.

"Don't 'old boy' me, Bobby." Johnson looked around the dais. "Where's Miss Conrad?"

"Oh, didn't you get my message?" the Commodore said. "Miss Conrad had to cancel. She had a conflict of some sort. I told her we'd reschedule."

Johnson looked crushed, just as the Commodore had planned. In fact, the only problem with the plan of stalling the appearance of Miss Conrad, as far as the Commodore could tell, was that he had to sit through one more meal smelling Johnson's rancid cologne.

Johnson's disappointment quickly gave way to anger. "What the hell kind of move is that? Canceling on short notice? Sounds unprofessional to me, Bobby. I'm not sure I want to meet with her now."

The others at the table—the commandant, the assistant commandant, and several company officers—took their seats shortly after Johnson took his seat. They listened in on the conversation while a line of plebes filed past them carrying overstuffed platters of food.

"She's no flake, I can assure you, sir," the Commodore said. "In fact, she's a rising star in her firm."

"What's the name of the firm anyway?" Johnson said, as an anonymous plebe delivered a platter of steaming corned beef and cabbage to the table.

"She is with Smith and McClellan Public Relations, a PR firm out of Port Washington."

Johnson placed his fork on his plate and turned to the Commodore. "Smith and McClellan? Wouldn't that be S and M for short? If Miss Conrad is a rising star in S and M, then, yes, Bobby, I do want to meet her."

The others at the table burst out laughing. The Commodore pretended to join in on the raunchy joke.

"Isn't a public relations firm supposed to keep you politically correct?" the commandant asked, sitting directly across the table from the Commodore. "Don't they realize the name of their own company is not PC?"

"Maybe they can help dream up an offensive slogan for our campaign to raise funds for that monument of yours," the assistant commandant chimed in.

Ah, yes, once again having a good time at the Commodore's expense. The Commodore did his best to steer the conversation back to academy business. Finally, he mentioned the trouble they were having with the Town of Great Neck—the town that neighbored Kings Point, home of the United States Merchant Marine Academy.

"Great Neck?" Johnson said. "Don't tell me Mogie's complaining again. I thought we resolved our differences after our last dustup."

Mogie Mogelefsky was the mayor of Great Neck. He had been complaining for years about midshipmen from the academy who sometimes made a nuisance of themselves in "his" town. According to Mogie, they drank at Hick's Lane Bar every weekend, and on the drive back to the academy, they would invariably tear up front lawns, run into trees, or knock down telephone poles. He claimed they drove into fences and gates, parked cars, and front stoops. According to Mogie, the midshipmen were constantly getting stuck in snowbanks in the winter, waking up the neighbors—Mogie's constituents—when they drunkenly tried to extricate themselves. The unhappy constituents always complained to Mogie first thing in the morning. The rowdy midshipmen evidently also frequented various all-night diners in town after a night of drinking where they would throw up on tables, harass the waitresses, and try to pick up whatever stray girl passed their booth. Of course, Mogie had to hear about *that* the next day, too. Mogie frequently called the academy and got the same reasonable response, "Boys will be boys." That did not stop him from calling, though, much to the academy's chagrin. Indeed, it made him a reliable topic of conversation.

The commandant looked across the table at the Commodore. "So, Commodore, tell us, what kind of trouble are we in now?"

"We're not in trouble," the Commodore said. "It's just that the mayor would like us to work on improving our relations with the town of Great Neck. He seems to think that if we had a better image within the community, it would cut down on the number of complaints he's receiving from his constituents."

"His constituents," Johnson said, "are a bunch of whiners."

"Be that as it may, sir, it was Mogie who recommended we use Smith and McClellan. He said they were a nice WASPy firm out of Port Washington and that he knew of Miss Conrad personally."

"Oh, shit." Johnson slammed his fist on the table. "Mogie's not doing her, too, is he? It's bad enough he's banging Mitzi."

The others at the table bobbed their heads. Mitzi Paultz was Johnson's secretary, a forty-ish (on her application she put down that she was thirty-nine) redheaded beauty hired solely for her sultry looks. He doubted she could type a lick, Johnson told his colleagues when he hired her, but what a body! Since she also happened to be Jewish, he figured he would get Mogie, who considered the academy a strange white Anglo-Saxon Protestant enclave, off his back at the same time. He assured his colleagues that hiring Mitzi would be good for business, as it would show Mogie the academy's diversity. But Johnson was disappointed when his usual moves failed to entice Mitzi into joining him for drinks in the officers' club. Mitzi said she liked celebrities as much as the next girl but the answer was no. "Besides," she had said, "Mogie would be furious." Johnson nearly fainted when he heard that Mogie Mogelefsky was banging his beautiful redheaded secretary.

"I'm not privy to his personal life, sir," the Commodore said. "I can only assume that his relationship with Miss Conrad is chaste."

"Mogelefsky doesn't have a chaste bone in his body," Johnson said, gnashing his teeth.

The others at the table bobbed their heads in agreement.

"Nevertheless," the Commodore said, "I do agree with the mayor that it couldn't hurt to hire a PR firm to improve our relations with the outside world. This place can be fairly insular, as you know, sir."

"We like it insular, Bobby. That's the way WASPs are."

The others nodded in perfect synchronization.

"Very well then, sir," the Commodore said. "I'll call Miss Conrad and tell her we're not interested."

"Now hold on a minute." Johnson's Johnson winked at his cronies. "Reschedule the meeting with Miss Conrad anyway. I'd like to have a look at her—what'd you call them?—shapely legs."

The Commodore was thrilled but tried not to show it. "Will do, sir."

The commandant suddenly pushed his ample girth back from the table. "Hey, Commodore, I saw you in the auditorium practicing your speech. I must say, you make beautiful hand gestures."

The others at the table had another good laugh at the Commodore's expense. The Commodore, knowing that his roughneck colleagues were simply jealous of his numerous talents, decided to take the higher road.

"Thank you, Commandant. Coming from a sycophant such as yourself, your praise certainly is expected."

The assistant commandant pushed back from the table now as well, following his boss's lead. "Hey, what's a sycophant anyhow?"

"It means I'm sophisticated, dummy." The commandant slapped his little buddy on the back of the head. "Let's go. We'll leave Mr. Commodore here with Admiral Johnson so he can tell him why he fired our bandleader this morning."

"You did what?" Johnson shouted while the others walked away, laughing.

"I fired the man," the Commodore said. "He was tone-deaf. There is simply no room in this institution for mediocrity."

Johnson's face reddened. "Who died and left you boss, Bobby? You take care of the back end of things here at the academy and don't you forget it. I do the hiring and firing."

"I was merely trying to raise the standards of our dear regimental band, sir. They are truly dreadful and it is for want of a proper leader."

Johnson was about to respond further when he spotted a young woman in a white nurse's uniform enter the mess hall from the galley.

"Who's that?" Johnson was on the edge of his chair.

"Oh her?" The Commodore pretended to look to see who it was. "That's our new nurse. Fresh out of nursing school, I'm afraid. She appears to be a bit wet behind the ears. I'm keeping an eye on her."

"You don't need to do that," Johnson said. "*I'll* keep an eye on her thank you very much. You run along now, Bobby. I think I'll introduce myself to our new inexperienced nurse."

The Commodore breathed a sigh of relief. The poor nurse would have her hands full in a moment, but the Commodore couldn't care less. All he cared about was that she had saved him from Johnson's wrath, for the moment anyhow. The only surprise was that the young thing had followed his orders so well and showed up in the mess hall at the exact time he had asked her to.

Chapter 5

PLEBE KNOWLEDGE

The next morning, Johnson's Johnson gave the new nurse a firm kiss on the cheek and a soft pat on the ass before ducking out the back entrance of the infirmary and walking the short distance across the parking lot to the Superintendent's Residence.

The Superintendent's Residence was the most prominent house on the academy grounds. It stood next to the officers' club on a high bluff overlooking the Sound. Johnson had promised his wife he would stop in during the day to watch her paint a still life of the clay pot he'd bought her for their twenty-fifth wedding anniversary. His wife had never tried a still life before but she had always wanted to paint in their English garden overlooking the Sound.

Yes, twenty-five years they had been married. The last ten or so had not been easy. His wife had developed "nervous trouble," as he called it, out of the blue and for no apparent reason it seemed—at least to him. Anyhow, she was not good for much anymore. It put a strain on their marriage for a time, but things had long ago reached a sort of equilibrium. It was the navy chaplain who had saved Johnson's own sanity. "It's about loyalty, not fidelity," he remembered the chaplain telling him one day. The chaplain's words greatly eased Johnson's conscience.

Johnson entered the quaint garden and found his wife sitting on a wood stool with her back to the water. She faced the clay pot, which was situated on a wrought iron table next to a vine-covered trellis. Johnson sank into an Adirondack chair behind her. Nary a word passed between them for over two hours while his wife mixed her palette of paints until—

"The blue is wrong, don't you think, sweetie?"

"Yeah, I think it is, sweetie. Why don't you work on it some more? I have to go now to meet with the Board of Governors about building this monument the Commodore wants."

"Maybe you're right. Maybe the blue is wrong. And the green as well. Maybe it's the light."

"I think maybe it's the light."

"Okay, sweetie."

"Okay, sweetie."

Johnson patted his wife's shoulder and beat a fast retreat from the garden. He passed through the iron gate in the privacy hedge and nearly bumped into the Commodore, who just happened to be coming out of the officers' club. Of course, the Commodore was on his way to the same meeting as Johnson. The two senior-most officers of the academy cut through the foyer in First Company and crossed Barney Square on the way to Wiley Hall.

"So, Bobby," Johnson said to fill the silence, "how's the incoming class of plebes shaping up? Have you heard any gossip?"

"As I understand it, their two weeks of Indoctrination for Training into the regimental system went smoothly enough. We saw no more plebes than usual show up at the infirmary complaining of the flu. You know—their way of trying to get a breather from the hazing dished out by the upper-classmen."

"Oh, I know, you don't have to tell me," Johnson said. "It's the yelling, Some of them just can't take being yelled at."

Both the Commodore and Johnson, having been plebes themselves once a long time ago, knew that the "gauntlets" were the worst. After an exhausting day that began at dawn; after all the calisthenics, drilling, and marching; after all the room inspections, personal appearance inspections, and duty-station inspections; after a day full of brainwashing and garden-variety hazing, came a specialized form of hazing. A squad of upperclassmen formed a gauntlet by lining up on both sides of the hallway in the barracks with the lights turned off. Another squad of upperclassman would then herd a platoon of plebes through the darkened barracks to the head of the gauntlet. One by one, the upperclassman passed the plebes through the gauntlet in the pitch darkness.

The upperclassmen in the gauntlet would then begin to scream at the plebes:

How many cadet-midshipmen died in the line of duty in WWII? I said how many? You're not sure, you dumb shit? Those poor bastards died so your slutty mother can drive an SUV and you don't know how many died? How high is the flagpole? The United States Merchant Marine Academy has the tallest un-guyed flagpole in the world and you can't be bothered to learn how high it is, you worthless piece of shit? Do you have any pride? You're a worthless piece of shit, do you know that? Oh that you know, but you don't know how many cadet-midshipmen died for your sorry ass? Sound off, dickhead! Midshipman fourth class who? Midshipman Fourth Class Harris? Did your brother go here, Harris? He did? Your brother was an asshole, Harris. He stuck me. Gave me demerits for no good fucking reason. Get out of my sight, you sorry piece of shit.

Back into the gauntlet the sorry piece of shit went. Gauntlets lasted for no more than fifteen minutes, but to the plebes, it seemed an eternity.

"Yes, sir," the Commodore said, "the wonderful cacophony of Indoc—the gauntlets, the cries of plebes sounding off in the barracks, the slapping of hands against the wood stock of parade rifles on Barney Square, all of the wonderful sights and sounds of Indoc have finally given way to the quiet of academic classes. The silence feels kind of eerie to me."

"Suits me just fine," Johnson said. He didn't like Indoc. It pained him to see the upperclassmen hazing the plebes. The official term for the upperclassmen who volunteered to cut their paltry summer vacation even shorter to train the plebes during Indoc was "pusher." Johnson called them "dipshits" and thought they oughta be chasing pussy on some beach somewhere instead of insulting some poor plebe's mother for forgetting a ridiculous bit of plebe knowledge.

"Why the hell do the plebes have to know who Edwin J. O'Hara is, anyway?" Johnson asked.

"Why, old boy," the Commodore said, "O'Hara is the academy's first son, a war hero who died serving his country."

"Bullshit. He was one of one hundred and forty-two cadets who died during World War II. How come the plebes don't know the names of the other one hundred and forty-one poor bastards? And don't old boy me."

"O'Hara is unique, sir, a legitimate hero who deserves a monument."

"Bullshit." Johnson liked the War Memorial, which honored all one hundred and forty-two fallen cadets without singling out any one individual. They were selfless boys who never called attention to themselves and they deserved to be remembered that way. All for one and one for all, wasn't that what it was all about?

In the meeting with the Board of Governors, Johnson explained his tiresome all-for-one-and-one-for-all line of thinking once again. The Commodore seethed. *No, that is not what it was all about. It is about differentiation. All men are decidedly not created equal. Is it not obvious that a rare few of us walk alone? Without the elevating power of the elite, the rest would sink under the weight of their own mediocrity. Who will stand up for the few, the daring few, the difference makers, those willing to stick their neck out for an idea deeply held?*

Granted, the Commodore had not yet developed the unique idea he would someday stand behind with all his might. And until that time, why take chances? If in order to become great one needed to take risks, and if one risked becoming great by not taking any risks, then that in itself was a daring risk, was it not? The dignity of risk! The Commodore first heard the phrase from his life coach. He embraced the phrase from the first and believed it with all his might. It was what set him apart from the risk-averse cowards who needed assurances and handholding. It was what made him special. And it was what made Edwin J. O'Hara special.

Edwin J. O'Hara was a strapping eighteen-year-old from Lindsay, California, who served as engine cadet aboard the liberty ship *SS Stephen Hopkins* during the Second World War. The *Stephen Hopkins* was one of the first liberty ships built and was on its maiden voyage when O'Hara, on his first assignment, joined the ship in San Francisco. The liberty ship's first wartime assignment was to carry a load of war supplies to the South Pacific. After unloading its cargo in Bora Bora, the ship set sail for New Zealand to take on a load of bunker oil. The ship arrived in New Zealand after a long sea passage, loaded the bunkers, and departed for Melbourne, Australia. The voyage plan then called for the *Hopkins* to offload its cargo in Durban, South Africa, and proceed under ballast across the South Atlantic to Paramaribo, Surinam, in Dutch Guyana for a load of bauxite, a raw material vital to the war effort. The ship unloaded its cargo of sugar, took on its ballast, and put to sea once again. But the liberty ship never reached the coast of Dutch Guyana, and cadet O'Hara never again saw the shores of his native California.

A German commerce raider named *Stier* sank the *Stephen Hopkins* in the South Atlantic in one of the most heroic sea battles of the war. The *Hopkins* did not go down without a fight, and cadet-midshipman O'Hara led the charge, risking his life in a vain attempt to save the ship. He was not able to save his ship but he did score five direct hits on the raider *Stier* with the *Hopkins'* four-inch aft-mounted gun, and the *Stier* sank alongside the *Stephen Hopkins* in 2,200 fathoms of water.

The Commodore embraced the heroic image of O'Hara with the fervor of an iconophile. Photos of the sunburned face of the young O'Hara lined the Commodore's office. He admired the young man's square jawline, the imperious gaze, the Roman nose, the erectness of his carriage. O'Hara's image, and the story of his heroic sea battle, was something the academy could and should embody as its own, argued the Commodore. Another faceless war memorial was not what the regiment needed. The boys deserved something more, something mythic. Something that would inspire a desire for greatness. A hero. God knew, the Commodore endeavored to comport himself in a way that would inspire awe in the young boys, but he could not do it all on his own. The boys needed to be in the continual presence of greatness, to be reminded over and over of *potential fulfilled*. The boys desperately needed an icon. Fallen cadet-midshipman Edwin J. O'Hara, if the Commodore had his way, would be that icon.

In the end, the Commodore got his way. It had been a brawl, a real donnybrook as Johnson put it, but somehow the Commodore convinced the Board of Governors to erect a monument honoring Edwin J. O'Hara. In a nod to Johnson, they would call it, not the Edwin J. O'Hara monument, but rather, the Mariners Monument. The Commodore could have cared less, as long as the boys got their icon.

When the meeting ended, Johnson called the chaplain and asked him to meet him down at the boathouse for a cup of coffee. On the way there, he caught up with two plebes who were talking between themselves. Talking out-of-doors was a violation of the fourth-class Regs, and Johnson knew that they were aware of that. Before they realized he was behind them, Johnson had a chance to listen in on their conversation. The bigger kid was talking about how he could've gone to Ohio State to play football. He said how when he visited the academy his senior year in high school he had thought it was so cool. He had never seen a large body of water growing up in Ohio, had never even been to Lake Erie, and the waterfront campus of the academy really made an impression on him. But now that he was here, it was like he couldn't see what it was he had liked so much about it. With all of the regimental bullshit they had to put up with— getting stuck by upperclassmen for no good reason—it felt like they were living in a prison, not some beautiful waterfront estate.

When the two midshipmen realized Johnson was behind them, they stopped, braced, and shouted, "Sir, good morning, sir!" They looked scared, like they were in big trouble. He knew what they were feeling. They were sick to their stomachs, actually, sick because they were thinking, Ugh! After all of our hard work and being so careful to follow the rules we're about to get stuck! That meant demerits, extra duty, and even more scrutiny from upperclassmen. They were scared, indeed.

But Johnson did not stick them. He knew they were good kids. He just smiled and said a quiet good morning as he walked past them.

Chapter 6

BIGGER FISH TO FRY

The Commodore smelled Johnson's Johnson's rancid cologne the moment he stepped foot in Wiley Hall. So did Miss Conrad.

"What's that smell?" Miss Conrad said.

"Smell?" the Commodore said. "I don't smell anything."

In his previous conversations with Miss Conrad, the Commodore mentioned nothing about the legend of Johnson's Johnson. He did not want her to have her guard up when meeting him for the first time.

"You can't smell that?" Miss Conrad said.

The Commodore sniffed the air. "Oh, that. Well, the truth is, Miss Conrad, Admiral Johnson does not have the best sense of smell. Years ago, when he was captain of a chemical tanker, he nearly vaporized his olfactory lobes in a tragic chemical spill. Poor chap never knows if he's wearing too much cologne, I'm afraid."

Miss Conrad seemed genuinely sympathetic. They climbed the marble stairs to Johnson's suite of offices. When the Commodore and Miss Conrad approached the anteroom leading to Johnson's suite, they came upon Mitzi wearing a surgical mask. Mitzi cocked her thumb over her shoulder. "Follow your nose."

The Commodore and Miss Conrad entered Johnson's lair.

Johnson's eyes locked onto Miss Conrad's legs the moment she entered the room. Miss Conrad's business skirt came down to just above her knees and set off her long sinewy calf muscles and slender ankles. Johnson sat back on his red leather couch and never took his eyes off her legs as she walked toward him. The Commodore and Miss Conrad stopped at a respectful distance from the red couch. They waited for Johnson to acknowledge them but he continued to stare at Miss Conrad's legs, never lifting his eyes above her knees. The Commodore cleared his throat. Johnson finally looked up and smiled without saying a word. After an awkward moment, the Commodore spoke up.

"Sir, I'd like to introduce you to Miss Conrad."

Johnson stayed seated. "Hello, Miss Conrad, I'm Admiral Johnson, may I offer you a seat?" He patted the space next to him on the couch. "Unless, of course, you'd prefer to sit on this side." Johnson patted the space to the other side of him.

The meeting could not have gotten off to a better start. The Commodore watched Miss Conrad out of the corner of his eye and waited for her response.

"The red leather clashes with my outfit," Miss Conrad said, looking around for another place to sit. Of course, Johnson did not keep a single chair in what he called his "bachelor pad," nothing but sofas and love seats. Miss Conrad chose the pink velour upholstered love seat to her left and sat in the middle of it. "Here," she said. "This looks comfortable." Unfortunately, she crossed her legs when she sat down and her skirt lifted up, exposing her thigh.

Johnson leapt up from the red couch and squeezed in next to Miss Conrad. "I couldn't agree more. This is my favorite seat!"

Miss Conrad looked up at the Commodore for help. The Commodore ignored her wordless plea. "Well, then, it looks like you two don't need my help here. I'll just leave you alone so you can get down to business." He shook Miss Conrad's hand, struggled to release her grip, and walked out of the room.

Mitzi stood when she heard the intercom buzz, straightened her surgical mask, and strolled into Johnson's Johnson's office.

"Do you have a cold today, Mitzi?" Johnson asked when he saw her.

Mitzi didn't feel like she needed to answer. Besides, with the surgical mask on, she sounded like Darth Vader when she talked.

"Mitzi, it seems that Miss Conrad isn't comfortable here. Would you please show her into my office? I have to make a phone call."

Mitzi had noticed the leggy blond gal on the way in. She certainly looked a lot less comfortable now than when she first walked in.

Johnson turned to Miss Conrad. "This will only take a minute. Mitzi will show you where to sit."

Where to sit. Right. Well, this Conrad looks like a good kid. She deserves a break.

Mitzi motioned for Miss Conrad to follow her. They left the bachelor pad and entered Johnson's office. Mitzi walked over to a floor-to-ceiling bookcase on the right side of the office, looked over her shoulder toward the door for any sign of Johnson, and then pressed a hidden button.

A Murphy bed plopped out of the bookcase.

Mitzi touched the bed. "Satin sheets, babe." She pressed the hidden button again and the Murphy bed sprang up, once more becoming a bookcase. Miss Conrad stared at the bookcase with her hand pressed to her mouth. Mitzi again looked out for Johnson, then pointed at the door next to the bookcase. A brass sign on the door said *Conference Room*. Mitzi pushed open the door so Miss Conrad could peek inside. Miss Conrad saw a hot tub, a wet bar, and a sauna. Mirrors covered the walls and ceiling. Steam wafted from the room.

She stared at Mitzi with her mouth open.

"Have fun, babe," Mitzi said.

They heard Johnson coming. "He'll want you to sit here." Mitzi pointed to one of two rickety director's chairs placed in front of Johnson's desk. "Good luck keeping your legs crossed," she said and walked out of the office, just as Johnson walked in.

Mitzi went back to her desk and pulled up the QVC Channel website that she kept hidden behind a Word document. She kept the corner of her eye on Johnson's door.

Two minutes later, Miss Conrad marched out with Johnson right behind her.

"No!" Miss Conrad said. "I don't want to be in the conference room, or this office with all these bookcases, or that, that, that room back there with all the love seats and sofas."

"But, Miss Conrad." Johnson stamped his foot on the floor. "I so much wanted to meet with you."

Miss Conrad was already out the door. Johnson started running after her but stopped at Mitzi's desk.

"What on earth do you suppose got into her?" he said.

Mitzi snapped her gum behind the surgical mask. She'd been waiting for this. "I guess she has bigger fish to fry."

"Bigger fish?" Johnson said. "Did you say *bigger* fish, Mitzi?"

"Yeah, you know, bigger."

"You do know, Mitzi, that I am the biggest this institution has to offer?"

"Yeah." Mitzi snapped her gum. "So I've heard."

"It sounds to me as if you don't believe it."

"I guess I'd have to see it to believe it." Mitzi, acting as if she did not care either way, discretely slid her hand toward her desk drawer.

Sure enough, Johnson, after a lifetime of obsessing over the size of his johnson, did the only thing he knew to do when challenged. He whipped it out right there in front of Mitzi's desk. Before he realized what was happening, Mitzi had reached into her drawer and pulled out a digital camera.

Johnson froze.

Mitzi snapped a close-up and ran.

Johnson's Johnson stood there with his trousers around his ankles. "Mitzi! Get back here with that camera!"

Johnson chased Mitzi down the marble stairs and out of Wiley Hall. She ran as fast as she could, struggling to breathe through the surgical mask. She ran all the way to the main gate and kept on running down Steamboat Road and did not stop running until she got to the Great Neck Martinizing Dry Cleaners on Middle Neck Road, where Mogie was waiting for her in their secret hideaway upstairs.

Chapter 7

THE LITTLE GUY IS BIGGER

"**W**ell, what do you know," Mogie said, looking at the photo of Johnson's Johnson's johnson. "I'm bigger."

"I knew you had to be, babe," Mitzi said.

"Not when it's down. He may have me beat there, okay? But when it's up, I'm huge. Huge."

"You are, babe." Mitzi stroked Mogie's hair while he obsessed over Johnson's johnson. *Men. If they weren't obsessing over their virility, they were obsessing over money.*

"We've got him," Mogie said. "There's no way they can't fire the guy. After the flap the Air Force Academy had, there's no way the government wants another sex scandal at one of its military academies, see what I mean?"

"I couldn't believe he pulled it out when I was at my desk. One minute I'm working, ya know?" Mitzi snapped her gum. "And the next minute the creep is pulling out his schlong in front of me." Mitzi laughed. "It was pretty big though, I gotta admit."

"I'm bigger, baby. When it's up, I'm bigger."

"I know, babe," Mitzi said. *Bigger. Mogie was always trying to be bigger.* Mitzi knew that Mogie's father called him "Little Guy" and that Mogie hated him for it. When he became mayor, his father went around saying, "Can you believe the little guy is mayor?" Mogie was always reaching for more and it made Mitzi nervous. On the one hand, she was attracted to men like Mogie because they reminded her of her father. But on the other hand, she wanted to turn and run the other way, too . . . because they reminded her of her father. Men were complicated, at least for her they were.

"Anyway," Mitzi said, "it's a good thing my camera was right there."

"It's almost too good to be true, baby," Mogie said. "Think about it. We've got a picture of Johnson in his office holding onto to his johnson."

Mitzi nodded her head. "I think we nailed him, babe."

Mogie got up and stalked around the room. "I'm on to something, Mitzi. I'm on to something, see what I mean?" He stopped pacing and turned to face Mitzi. "I was just thinking. The Commodore didn't help us at all here—you got the picture all on your own—so why should we cut him in on the deal, see what I mean?"

"Who's gonna be the admiral then if not the Commodore? He's next in line ya know, or so he says."

"I don't know," Mogie said. "I just never liked the idea of going into business with a WASP. I'd sure like to get a nice Jew in there as admiral. Someone who talks the same language."

"There aren't too many Jews at the academy," Mitzi said. "Some of the professors are, a few administrators. But most of 'em are dopey WASPs."

"I know," Mogie said. "I gotta think about it some more."

"Oh my god," Mitzi said, "look at the time. We gotta get out of here. Without those damn Martinizing machines going, Putzie'll hear us up here."

Mogie and Mitzi were in their "love shack," an apartment above the Great Neck Martinizing Dry Cleaners. Mogie rented it out from the owner of the dry cleaners, Ira Paultz. They knew each other since they were kids growing up in Great Neck. In fact, Mogie was the one who gave Ira Paultz the nickname Putzie. Putzie, who also happened to be Mitzi's husband, was a creature of habit. He Martinized every day between 10 AM and 1 PM with Raymond, his Filipino helper, a man who Putzie said was the best Martinizer in all of New York. At exactly one o'clock every day, they turned off the Martinizing machines and took a lunch of cucumber sandwiches on white bread. Putzie said the cucumbers were good for his colon. They ate their lunch together, then Putzie took an hour nap on the cot in his office in the back of the cleaners and Raymond took over the cash register so Mrs. Tannenbaume, who worked the register from ten to one every day, could go home. Putzie wanted Mitzi to work the register, but Mitzi hated the goddamn dry cleaning business. It was too hot. She liked being a secretary so she could sit in air-conditioning all day during the hot summer months.

Mogie and Mitzi left by the outside fire escape, their usual route. Mitzi said it was more exciting that way. It felt more like an affair. By the time she and Mogie climbed down the fire escape, the Martinizing machines wound down with a big *clankety-clank*.

After Putzie ate his cucumbers and went to take his nap, Raymond joined Mrs. Tannenbaume behind the counter.

The Great Neck Martinizing Dry Cleaners was in a line of stores built in the Art Deco era. Putzie told everyone who inquired that he hired Mrs. Tannenbaume because she was as Art Deco as the building and that she fit right in. Her wardrobe just kind of went with the look of the place. Putzie said her outfits were gaudy but at least they were consistently gaudy. Even her reading glasses were loud—the kind that swept up at the corners. Raymond called them "cat woman" glasses. Roz, Mrs. Tannenbaume's closest friend, used another word to describe her: kitschy. "What can I tell you?" Roz would say. "My friend is kitschy."

"You know," Mrs. Tannenbaume said, "it sounds like Willie Wonka's chocolate factory in here when the machines shut down."

"This is a bad thing?" Raymond said.

"I didn't spend thirty-five years in education to work in a chocolate factory in retirement. The only reason I work here a few hours a day is because I thought I could be of some help in running the business. You don't spend thirty-five years in education and not learn a thing or two about people, and if you understand people, you'll always have customers. The first thing people want is a clean place to shop. They come into a place that looks like Hogan's Alley and they'll turn around and walk right out. Of course, the product has to be good, mind you. There's nothing more expensive than a cheap product. That's why Putzie hired you. I said to him, 'Putzie, you want a good worker you hire yourself a Filipino. You can teach a good Filipino how to Martinize.' And now look at you. You're the best Martinizer in New York."

A customer entered the shop and cut Mrs. Tannenbaume's monologue short. It was Mr. Goldfarb. He came in every week at this time to pick up his shirts.

"Good afternoon, Mr. Goldfarb," Mrs. Tannenbaume said.

"Good afternoon, Mrs. Tannenbaume with an E," Mr. Goldfarb said. "Have you heard from Captain Tannenbaume lately?"

"My sonny boy is fine. He gets off his ship this October, so he'll be home for Christmas. That'll be nice. He makes a nice eggnog, you know."

"Christmas at the Tannenbaumes," Mr. Goldfarb said. "A one-of-a-kind experience I'm sure. Actually, an eggnog might be in order about now. I was just elected president of the Great Neck Garden Condos."

"*Mozel Tov*! Condo president. Mrs. Goldfarb must be so proud."

"Oh enough about me." Mr. Goldfarb waved his hand at Mrs. Tannenbaume. "Speaking of congratulations, I understand some are in order for Captain Tannenbaume."

"You mean his daring rescue at sea? How'd you hear about that?"

"One of my clients, Mr. Costello, is an official in Captain Tannenbaume's union. I do his taxes. Mr. Costello told me all about it."

"The Coast Guard gave him a commendation. They said the way he maneuvered his ship in rough seas could only be done by someone who knew his stuff. Of course they worded the plaque they gave him a little differently, but that's what they meant, basically."

"Costello says he's the only one out there who practices real seamanship anymore."

"Is that what he said?"

"Costello should know. He's the dispatcher for the union. He tells me he gives Captain Tannenbaume all of the tough jobs. Sends him to the ships no one else wants. The old ones. The ones where you need to know what you're doing."

"Yeah, I've heard my sonny boy mention that. 'Tween-deckers he calls 'em. He hates the new ones—the big container ships. Not enough time in port he says. But he's been on the *God is Able* for years now."

"So I understand." Mr. Goldfarb tried to hide his smile. "I've heard a thing or two about your boy's port visits on the *God is Able*."

"Oh?"

Mr. Goldfarb could no longer hide his smile. He looked down at the floor. Mrs. Tannenbaume sensed he was embarrassed. She thought she knew why. She handed the new condo president his shirts.

"Well, Mr. Goldfarb, you're my last customer for the day. I've got to sashay now." Mrs. Tannenbaume grabbed her pocket book and left.

A minute after Mrs. Tannenbaume left, the Commodore walked in. Raymond came around from behind the counter, and together he and the Commodore sat down in the front of the store, something they did whenever the Commodore came in to pick up his shirts. The sunlight that came through the plate glass window in the middle of the day was pretty harsh, so Raymond swung the curtain partly closed. Maybe it was the curtain, or maybe it was that the Commodore had nobody else to confide in, but something made the Commodore want to sit and talk with Raymond in the front of the store. That was the only explanation Raymond could come up with for why someone like the Commodore would want to talk with him—or talk *to* him, which was more like it. And more often than not—no, always—he talked about himself. But still, Raymond didn't mind. He was flattered that someone as important as the Commodore wanted to talk to him, although he didn't like it so much when the Commodore yelled at him.

When the Commodore told Raymond what had happened with Miss Conrad, he wasn't surprised. He never thought Miss Conrad was the right girl for the job. She sounded like too much of a Miss-Goody-Too-Shoes to be part of a trap like the one the Commodore had set. But Raymond didn't dare tell the Commodore what he really thought. So he just sat and listened, like he always did, and tried not to upset the Commodore.

Chapter 8

EXPERIENCE AT SEA

This time it was the chaplain who called Johnson to suggest they meet for coffee. "Trouble" was all he said before he hung up the phone.

When they settled in with their coffee down at the boathouse, the chaplain spoke first.

"You hear about the bandleader? His wife called early this morning."

"What bandleader? The Commodore fired the poor bastard."

The chaplain shook his head. "His wife says he's missing. She says she thinks the Commodore must be behind it."

"Behind what?" Johnson said.

"Behind the fact he's missing. The police questioned him this morning. They say he was the last one to see the bandleader before he went missing."

"Jesus Christ," Johnson said, coming out of his chair. "You serious?"

"You don't think the Commodore has anything—"

"What? Are you crazy?"

Johnson walked to the big window overlooking the wharf and placed his cup on the sill. The Commodore was unusual, that's for sure, had been forever, but he was harmless, wasn't he?

Wasn't he?

"I want a Jew admiral," Mogie said.

Mogie threw out this tidbit as soon as the Commodore entered his plush office in Great Neck City Hall. Mogie sat in a high-backed chair behind his desk, puffing on a cigar. Smoke swirled around his head. The desk itself was situated on a platform raised a foot off the floor. The combined effect was to make the five-foot-two-and-a-quarter-inch Mogie look more imposing than he really was. Mogie directed the Commodore to take the seat in front of his desk. The Commodore sank into the small stuffed chair and looked up at the cloud of smoke on the platform.

"I am afraid that is impossible," the Commodore said, remaining calm in the face of this outrageous demand.

"What's so impossible about it?"

"Because the superintendent of the United States Merchant Marine Academy needs seagoing experience as master aboard a U.S. merchant vessel. It is a requirement. It is right there in the academy by-laws."

"That wacko Johnson was captain of a ship?"

"For six months, believe it or not," the Commodore said. "A chemical tanker."

"Wow," Mogie said. "What a scary thought."

What was scary was the way this meeting was going.

"There's no reason to be scared," the Commodore said. "I am perfectly capable of assuming the job of superintendent. I was master of the MV *Kings Pointer*, the academy training vessel, so I fully satisfy the academy's requirements for work experience. If we stay together on this, we shall achieve our objectives. It is gut-check time, Mr. Mayor. It's best we remain calm and live up to our prearranged agreement."

"No," Mogie said, his face all but invisible behind by the cigar smoke. "I want a Jew admiral, end of story."

"I was under the distinct impression that we had a deal," the Commodore said as evenly as he could. "You needed me to set up the meeting with Miss Conrad. After the inevitable peccadillo, Johnson would be dismissed, and I would replace him. I thought we were clear on that."

"Yes, but the thing is, Johnson didn't pull out his johnson on Miss Conrad. He pulled it out on Mitzi, see what I mean?"

"No. In fact I do not see what you mean."

Mogie stood up and came out from behind the smoke. "Look, the fact is, the meeting you arranged didn't work. Miss Conrad turned out to be a dud. Mitzi did it all on her own. I don't need you anymore. You're out."

The Commodore was stunned. They had a deal! And Mogie was reneging. The Commodore needed Mogie's help in getting rid of Johnson—he needed an outsider like Mogie to demand the resignation. Otherwise, Johnson's cronies would sweep his shenanigans under the rug and return to business as usual. In return for Mogie's help, the Commodore would cut Mogie in on the business of running the academy. As admiral, he would outsource nonessential services to businesses established by Mogie—landscaping, dry cleaning, plumbing, snow removal. The dry cleaning business alone would be worth millions. For years, the only thing that stood between the Commodore and the superintendent's job was Johnson. Now, with Johnson all but removed, there was yet another obstacle in his path.

The Commodore needed time to think, time to sort out his next move. He would have to placate Mogie the best he could for the time being.

"Very well, then," the Commodore said. "I see I've been bested by a superior adversary." The Commodore extricated himself from the little chair as gracefully as he could. He stood up, clicked his heels, and bowed before Mogie's platform.

"Good day, Mr. Mayor."

With that, the Commodore tucked his hat under his arm and marched out of Mogie's office.

Chapter 9

STICKS, STEPPERS, AND STOOLS

"Not one of them Jew boys went to sea?" Mogie asked. He was lying on the couch in the love shack above the dry cleaners with Mitzi's head in his lap. They were both naked.

"No," Mitzi said. "Commander Katzenberg said Jewish mothers want their boys to grow up and become doctors and lawyers. He says he never heard of a Jewish mother saying, 'If only my boy could be a seaman one day.'"

"He's probably right. But still, we gotta somehow find ourselves a Jew captain. It's in the by-laws."

"We'll keep looking, babe. But ya know, if we don't find one, making the Commodore the admiral wouldn't be such a bad thing. He don't care about the gelt, ya know. All that fruitcake's interested in is the glory."

"That's what scares me. He's got no *Yiddisher kop*, see what I mean? No *Saichel*."

"So what? You've got enough business sense for the both of you."

Mogie didn't respond. For all of his multitasking abilities, whenever a naked woman was around—not to mention one ten years his junior—he lost his train of thought. And this was especially true of Mitzi. Her flaming red hair. Her long legs—sticks, Mogie called them. He was a sucker for a great pair of sticks.

"You're driving me foolish, Mitz." Mogie stroked Mitzi's long, silky thigh. "You've got some pair of sticks, baby. World-class." Mogie slapped her on the side of her rump. "Come on, baby, do your stretching routine for me."

Mitzi pushed herself up off the couch, walked over to the dining table, and standing with her back to Mogie, lifted her left foot up onto the table and pressed her nose down to her ankle.

Mogie groaned.

"Stretch, baby," Mogie said. "Stretch yourself for Mogie."

Mitzi switched legs and stretched some more. Then she spread her legs out wide and bent over so that she looked directly at Mogie through her legs, upside down.

"Oh, baby," Mogie said. "You're driving me foolish. You drive me so foolish when you stretch." Mogie jumped up off the couch. "Hold that stretch, baby, while I get my stool."

Mogie ran into the bedroom and grabbed what he called his "stool." It was one of those plastic steps that Mitzi used in her aerobics class. Mogie placed it behind Mitzi and climbed on top then he grabbed hold of Mitzi's hips and lined himself up. Mitzi liked it from behind but she just couldn't do it on all fours—she had a bum knee from an old gymnastics injury. She'd told Mogie she wanted Putzie to handle her from behind but he was too short—with Mitzi's sticks, he just couldn't reach, not even on his tiptoes. It would never occur to Putzie to use a stool. Mogie, on the other hand, had the ingenuity—that's why he was the mayor. He loved climbing up on his stool to service Mitzi, and Mitzi, bless her, didn't seem to care that he needed her aerobic stepper to do it.

Mogie had long ago stopped trying to get Mitzi to leave Putzie because, deep down, he knew why she stayed, no matter what she said about Mogie leaving his wife first. It all had to do with her father. Mitzi's father went broke when she was in high school. The sucker reached too far. He had made a small fortune selling life insurance and then risked it all on a real estate deal. The building he built in Little Neck stood empty for years. He tried selling insurance again but he was never the same. That's why she married Putzie. His dry cleaning business was safe. People would always need a pressed suit of clothes. Mitzi knew Putzie played it safe and that's why she stayed with him. And that's also why Mogie kept his ever-present money troubles to himself. If Mitzi ever found about his bad debts, she'd drop him in a New York minute. Mogie was always shooting for the moon, even though Mitzi told him he didn't have to own the moon, he just had to take her there once in a while. Hence the stool.

Mitzi was a screamer. She and Mogie only did it when the Martinizing machines were going full bore. Otherwise, Putzie would certainly hear her from downstairs. Mogie, who prided himself on his control, made it a point to hold off as long as he was able. As soon as Mogie heard the Martinizing machines begin to wind down, he told Mitzi to get ready.

"Get ready for Mogie, baby," Mogie said, gasping for air as he went at Mitzi like some kind of Oklahoma oil derrick. "Get ready for Mogie. Here he comes, baby. Here comes Mogie."

Mitzi's screams melded perfectly with the Martinizing machine, and as the machine wound down, so did Mitzi's screams. They both ended simultaneously with a thud. Mogie took his stool back to the bedroom and placed it under the bed—he liked knowing exactly where it was at all times. When he came back into the other room, Mitzi was getting dressed. "We gotta get down the fire escape before Putzie hears us up here," Mitzi said.

When they got to ground level, they went their separate ways, Mitzi to her car that she had parked in the alleyway, and Mogie to his car parked on Middle Neck Road. He normally parked his car to the south of the dry cleaners so that he wouldn't have to walk in front of the store and risk running into Putzie. Today, though, he couldn't find a spot south of the store, so he parked directly in front. Mogie ran to his car and jumped in just as the Commodore pulled up to the dry cleaners.

The Commodore watched Mogie come out of the alley and give a furtive look in both directions before running to his car. *Why would Mogie be coming out of the alley like that?*

The Commodore entered the dry cleaners. Today he did not sit down with Raymond in the front of the store like he usually did. Today he stood up and paced behind the curtain. "I want to be admiral so bad, Raymond, I can taste it. Now this monster Mogelefsky is standing in my way. After everything I've done for the academy, after all the years and years of sacrifice and selflessness, putting others first, never thinking of myself—I never think of myself, you know that. Why is this happening to me?"

"Mr. Commodore," Raymond said, "everything'll work out. You'll see."

"How is it going to work out? Mogie wants a Jew for an admiral. I'm not Jewish."

"But things always have a way of working out, you'll—"

"Raymond, are you listening to me! Have you no empathy, not to mention manners? Look at what I'm going through. Between this and being questioned by the police—"

"What police?"

The Commodore erupted. "Mind your own business, young man!"

The Commodore sat down and put his face in his hands. After several minutes, he looked over at Raymond. He could tell that his outburst hurt the young man's feelings, but surely Raymond understood that he was wrong. He needed to learn to be a better listener. The Commodore was about to apologize, but then didn't. What would be the point?

"I just saw Mogie coming out of the alleyway next door," the Commodore said. "What business does he have around here?"

"Beats me."

"Could it be that he's liaising with Mitzi in the apartment upstairs?"

"How would I know? I'm busy Martinizing all day."

"Imagine that," the Commodore said. "To liaise with a man's wife directly over the man's head."

"The Martinizing machines are really loud. Mogie and Mitzi could be up there and Putzie would never hear them."

Just then the Commodore and Raymond heard Putzie waking up from his nap. Raymond went behind the counter and retrieved the Commodore's crisp shirts. When Putzie walked into the front of the store, he gave the Commodore a grumpy hello.

"Did you have a nice nap, Mr. Paultz?" the Commodore said.

"I always do."

"I'm no good at naps."

Putzie, who had not missed a nap in twenty years, said, "Habits, Commodore. It's all about habits."

"I see." The Commodore glanced toward the apartment above, winked at Raymond, and left the store without another word.

Chapter 10

SHORT AND INADEQUATE

The next day, Putzie strayed from his habits and shut down the Martinizing machines five minutes early. He came to this fateful decision after talking some more with Raymond about the value of sticking with a routine.

Mrs. Tannenbaume, bored by the lack of customers, was hanging around listening in. To her, this talk of routine just sounded sad. She told Putzie that she herself hated routines. It made things go stale, she had said, matter-of-factly.

"What about the hoo-hoo and the ha-ha?" Mrs. Tannenbaume asked. "I hope you're not letting things go stale in the sex department."

Raymond tittered like a schoolboy. "The hoo-hoo and the ha-ha? Sounds kind of fun."

"Well, come to think of it," Putzie said, "Mitzi has been acting kind of cold lately."

"Cold?" Mrs. Tannenbaume said. "How cold?"

Putzie avoided Mrs. Tannenbaume's gaze. A bad sign.

Mrs. Tannenbaume nodded her head. "I know the type. She's as cold as a stepmother's kiss, ain't she?"

Putzie looked down at the floor while the Martinizing machines whirled away. Mrs. Tannenbaume figured Putzie must be uncomfortable talking about his sex life with a seventy-six-year-old woman. She decided to get right to the point.

"Do you ever mix things up a bit?" Mrs. Tannenbaume did not look at Putzie directly so as not to scare the poor fellow. "You know, when you're having a situation?"

"A situation?"

Raymond jumped in. "You know," he said. "The hoo-hoo and the ha-ha."

"Well," Putzie said, his head swiveling from Raymond to Mrs. Tannenbaume, "as a matter of fact, my wife does like a certain position—"

"From behind?"

Putzie winced. "How did you—"

"Most women like it that way," Mrs. Tannenbaume said. "So that the man is breathing on the back of your head and not right smack into your puss. Plus, most women don't like to feel a man's rough beard against their face. It hurts."

Putzie's pained look worsened. "Well, actually, she likes it from behind standing up. She's got a bum knee and can't . . . kneel down, if you know what I mean."

"So why don't you give it to her standing up?"

Putzie really squirmed now. It looked to Mrs. Tannenbaume like he would do anything to get out of the conversation. The poor man. He really did need to let go of these hang-ups. She decided to get to the heart of the matter.

"What don't you like about doing it from behind? Does it smell a bit too French for you back there?"

"No, it's not that. Mitzi's as clean as a whistle."

"So what's the matter?" Mrs. Tannenbaume stood there with her hands on her hips, waiting for an answer. Then she slapped the palm of her hand smack into her forehead. "Oh! I should have guessed it earlier."

Putzie looked up. Mrs. Tannenbaume could tell that he seemed horrified that she might know of his shameful secret. "What?"

"You're too short!" Mrs. Tannenbaume said. "Why didn't you say so earlier, love?"

Putzie slumped down in a chair while the Martinizing machines roared away. Mrs. Tannenbaume felt Putzie's pain. She knew that every woman wants her man to bend her over the kitchen table every now and again. But with Mitzi's long legs—dancer's legs—Putzie simply couldn't reach. The poor man. Too short to take care of his own wife. She knew what that meant—some other man, a man with longer legs, was most likely "servicing" Mitzi.

She reached over and put her hand on Putzie's shoulder. "You need to mix things up a bit, son. You mustn't be so rigid."

Putzie looked up at Mrs. Tannenbaume with moist eyes. "You know something? You're right, Mrs. Tannenbaume. I'm sick and tired of being rigid. It's time to think outside the box, right?" Putzie wiped his eyes, stood up, and faced his Filipino Martinizer. "Shut down the Martinizing machine, Raymond."

Raymond looked at his watch. "But, Mr. Paultz, we still have five minutes to go."

Putzie took off his rubber Martinizing gloves and walked up to Raymond. Like his hero George C. Scott in the movie *Patton*, Putzie slapped Raymond across the face with the rubber gloves.

"Don't be a yellow-belly soldier! The Martinizing machine! Now!"

"But we still have more shirts to press, sir. The Commodore's shirt!"

Putzie ignored Raymond's plea and marched over to the Martinizing machine. With a theatrical flourish, he threw the main switch himself. Shutting the Martinizing machine down five minutes early was the first spontaneous thing Putzie Paultz had done in twenty years.

Putzie thrust his arms over his head to the sound of the Martinizing machine winding down. "I'm free!" Putzie shouted. "I'm free!"

"Not so fast." Mrs. Tannenbaume cupped her ear, straining to hear what was coming from upstairs. "Do you hear what I hear?"

Raymond walked to the front of the store to turn off the loud commercial blower behind the curtain. With the commercial blower turned off and the Martinizing machines silenced, Mrs. Tannenbaume stood with Putzie and Raymond behind the counter with their ears cocked toward the ceiling.

"It sounds like a dog barking," Raymond said.

"It's barking, all right," Putzie said. "But that's no dog."

Mrs. Tannenbaume nodded and put her hand on Putzie's shoulder. *Poor Putzie Paultz. Such a* nebbish. She wished this wasn't happening to him, but it was. Mitzi had found her long-legged lover—and now they all knew about it.

"That's Mitzi," Putzie said. "Years ago, on our honeymoon, Mitzi barked like that. I'd know her bark anywhere." Putzie once again hung his head. "I haven't been able to make her bark since."

"Mitzi barking?" Raymond said. "What would make Mitzi bark like a dog?"

Mrs. Tannenbaume reached over and grabbed a hunk of Raymond's cheek with her clawlike grip. "Don't be such a *shlub*. She's upstairs with her long-legged lover, that's what."

"Oh," Raymond said, rubbing his cheek. "The hoo-hoo and the ha-ha."

"That's right." Mrs. Tannenbaume sighed. "She's having a situation right over Putzie's head."

Putzie slumped into his chair, no longer George C. Scott but the same old Putzie Paultz. He covered his face with his hands and began to weep. His sobs drowned out the barking. In fact, the sobs became so loud they wafted through the ductwork to the upstairs apartment.

Mitzi heard it before Mogie. She stopped barking.

"What's that sound, babe?" Mitzi said over her shoulder to Mogie, still going at it from atop his stool.

Mogie furrowed his brow and listened to the sound coming from the ductwork. "I know what it ain't." Mogie picked up his stool and raced to hide it under the bed. "It ain't the goddamn Martinizing machine. Putzie's onto us. I'm outta here, baby."

Mogie was still putting on his clothes as he half-climbed half-slid down the fire escape to safety. Mitzi stayed put. Putzie's sobbing froze her in her tracks. She cried out in the emptiness of her tawdry love shack. "Why won't you use the stool, you Putz!" Mitzi sobbed. She knew Putzie played it down the middle, that's why she married him, but, God, did he have to be so rigid?

Putzie's sobs collided with Mitzi's sobs and reverberated inside the ductwork. The sobs inside the ductwork undulated back to the store.

"Oh my," Mrs. Tannenbaume said, as they listened to the sheet metal warping. "It sounds like Hogan's Alley up there in the ceiling."

Just then the Commodore strode into the store.

When the Commodore spotted Mrs. Tannenbaume, he doffed his cap with a flick of his wrist and tucked it beneath his left arm. He greeted Mrs. Tannenbaume by pulling up before her with a click of his heels and a deep bow from the waist. He stood there in front of the old woman and waited for the desired effect that his grand entrance had on all women and children—giggles, coos, avoidance of eye contact in the presence of his eminence.

Mrs. Tannenbaume neither giggled nor swooned. Instead, with an irritatingly confident look on her face, she made direct eye contact.

The Commodore fumed at the indignity of it all, the appalling lack of grace on the part of Mrs. Tannenbaume. Yet the old lady persisted with her offensive eye contact. The unseemly standoff ended when Mrs. Tannenbaume broke eye contact and looked the Commodore up and down. She lingered on the Commodore's long legs.

The Commodore shifted his gaze to just over Mrs. Tannenbaume's head, his imperious thousand-yard stare.

Mrs. Tannenbaume turned toward Raymond, rolled her eyes in the direction of the Commodore, and said, "Who's the flouncy?"

"He's . . . he's the Commodore, from the academy. He normally picks up his shirts after you leave."

"Hey, flounce," Mrs. Tannenbaume said to the Commodore. "What's the matter? You think you're too good to say hello?"

The Commodore maintained his thousand-yard stare. He would not be trifled with.

"What's with the glazed-over look?" Mrs. Tannenbaume said to Raymond.

"He's angry."

"He's angry?" Mrs. Tannenbaume said.

The Commodore's posture remained ramrod straight, his bearing regal, his unflinching gaze aimed just above Mrs. Tannenbaume's head. His breathing remained steady, his skin unflushed. At five-foot nothing, Mrs. Tannenbaume was clearly short and inadequate—she simply did not possess the corporeal wherewithal to matter to a man of his stature. He decided to let the matter rest.

"I'm here to pick up my shirts," the Commodore said.

"I'm sorry, sir," Raymond said. "Your shirts have been cleaned but we have not had the chance to—"

"My shirts are not ready?" the Commodore said, his voice rising. "Are you informing me that my shirts have been laundered yet they remain unpressed?"

"That's correct, sir."

The Commodore slammed his fist down on the counter. "This is unacceptable!"

"Smoke screen!" Mrs. Tannenbaume shouted back.

"I want my shirts pressed crisp and I want them now, thank you!"

Mrs. Tannenbaume pointed her finger at the Commodore. "Red herring!"

The Commodore deigned to look down at Mrs.Tannenbaume. After all, the woman was wagging a finger in his face. "My dear woman of unfortunate stature, will you kindly refrain from shouting aloud these inane non sequiturs."

"Don't go changing the subject," Mrs. Tannenbaume scolded. "You're muddying the waters is what you're doing. Trying to get us off the fact that a shamed woman is crying upstairs and her cuckold husband is doing the same down here. Where were you five minutes ago, you long-legged lout?"

"Long-legged?" The Commodore spoke the words clear over Mrs. Tannenbaume's head. "My dear, my legs are neither long nor short."

"Why won't you look at me?" Mrs. Tannenbaume said. "Are you afraid of facing the truth?"

"The truth?" the Commodore said. "The truth is something a person of your unfortunate inadequacy cannot aspire to. You are simply too short to see the truth, madam, for the truth resides on a pedestal—"

"Smoke screen!"

Putzie, who had sat down and stayed down after Mrs. Tannenbaume rightly pointed out that he was not yet free from the bonds of his stifling habits, stood up once again. "No, Mrs. Tannenbaume. I don't think the Commodore is having an affair with my wife. He's not her type."

"Sit down, Mr. Paultz, while I handle this. I mean, look at the long legs on this one. Of course he's your wife's lover."

The Commodore remained calm. "Mrs. Tannenbaume, I assure you, I'm no one's paramour. I am perfectly chaste."

"Well, if you aren't servicing Mitzi, who is?"

"If my guess is right, I believe I know exactly who is liaising with Mitzi," the Commodore said.

Putzie came alive once again. "Who's the yellow belly? I'll have no adulterers in this outfit!"

"I am afraid the man is no yellow belly, Mr. Paultz," the Commodore said, "but a formidable opponent. A lothario of the highest caliber—your very own mayor of Great Neck."

Putzie's head jerked up. "Mogie? But he's only a quarter of an inch taller than me! How can that be?"

The Commodore shook his head in wonder at the audacity of his adversary. "Mogie Mogelefsky always finds a way. The man always finds a way."

Chapter 11

FETISHISMS

When Putzie pushed through the curtain separating the front of the shop from the Martinizing machines and slumped onto a stool by the cash register, the Commodore, Raymond, and Mrs. Tannenbaume were waiting for him. They stared at the black patch on his left eye.

"He uses a stool," Putzie said.

"He hit you with a stool?" Mrs. Tannenbaume said.

"No," Putzie said. "He uses a stool to service Mitzi standing up from behind."

"How . . . clever," Raymond said.

"The man *is* an ingenious adversary," the Commodore said.

"What's with the eye patch?" Mrs. Tannenbaume asked.

"We wrestled right there on the floor in his office."

"Did the lout poke you in the eye?"

"No," Putzie said. "He held me in a headlock on the floor and drooled in my eye. His secretary was nice enough to give me this eye patch."

"My dear man," the Commodore said. "I am sorry for your troubles, but what about our well-conceived plan? Were you not instructed to lure your nemesis into the safe bosom of the Merchant Marine Academy gymnasium for your wrestling match?"

"I tried," Putzie said. "It's that damn chair of his."

"Ah," the Commodore said. "I know the chair. It does place one at a decided disadvantage."

"Stools. Chairs," Mrs. Tannenbaume said. "This loon sounds like some sort of fetishist."

The Commodore did not have time for Mrs. Tannenbaume's crackpot theories. He was too busy thinking of a way to get out of the business deal he had unwittingly made with Mogie. He desperately wanted to lure Mogie into a wrestling match with Putzie at the academy. He figured if Mogie were to lose to Putzie in a highly public way, Mogie would lose face and back off from his demands to replace Admiral Johnson with a Jew. The Commodore fumed at his egregious misstep. He should never have gotten into bed with the likes of Mogie. He could have found his own Miss Conrad to trap Johnson's Johnson.

However, what's done was done. He needed to focus on a way to isolate Mogie so that Mogie's photo of Johnson's Johnson's johnson would be of no value as blackmail.

"Anyway," Putzie said to the Commodore, "in the end, I did lure him into a public rematch. I think he felt sorry for me after Maven put the patch on my eye."

"So then he did agree to a rematch at the academy?" the Commodore said, his pulse quickening.

"Well, I never mentioned the academy," Putzie said, "but Mogie did agree to wrestle anytime, anywhere."

This was good news. Good news indeed. The Commodore felt energized for the first time in days. He now felt sure that if Mogie were humiliated in front of a capacity crowd at the academy gymnasium, Mogie's ego would compel him to leave the academy with his tail between his legs. The Commodore could count on his friends at *Newsday* to spin the story in the academy's favor—"a disgruntled sore loser makes trouble for the academy"—if Mogie insisted on replacing Johnson with a Jew. My goodness, there were things to do, and time was of the essence. At any moment, Mogie could take Mitzi's photograph of Johnson's Johnson's johnson public and the Commodore would lose control of the entire situation.

Prioritize, he must prioritize. The Commodore looked at Putzie. Could this pipsqueak really beat Mogie in a wrestling match?

"How confident are you, Mr. Paultz, in your abilities on the mat?"

"I had him beat in high school before he bit my neck. As long as he doesn't cheat, I know I can beat him."

The Commodore could not form a picture in his mind's eye of Putzie Paultz, athlete. He certainly bore no resemblance to the statuary of Roman-Greco wrestlers the Commodore so favored. But the Commodore was desperate, and lacking another plan to rid himself of Mogie, he was stuck with Putzie and his puny biceps.

"Well now, we won't have to worry about Mogie's chair on our home turf, will we, Mr. Paultz? Nevertheless, you ought to commence a training regimen at once."

Chapter 12

THE *GOYIM* WERE RIGHT?

Raymond drove Putzie's Buick at a crawl down Steam Boat Road. A long line of cars honked their horns behind him, but Raymond didn't care. He had a job to do—to make sure Putzie got his exercise in for the day. Mrs. Tannenbaume sat in the passenger seat. Neither Putzie nor Raymond asked her to come along but she insisted on coming. After all, as she pointed out, you don't spend thirty-five years in education and not learn a thing or two about Phys. Ed.

"Don't forget to breathe, Mr. Paultz," Mrs. Tannenbaume yelled through the passenger window at the small man struggling to jog one block. Mrs. Tannenbaume's regimen called for Putzie to jog a block and walk a block.

"One of Captain Tannenbaume's fathers was a surfer," she said through the window after Putzie pulled up for a breather. "That's the kind of body you want. A surfer's body. Picture a surfer in your mind's eye as you jog."

The long line of cars honked their horns when Raymond put the Buick in park to wait for Putzie, who panted alongside the car. "I don't . . . know any . . . surfer."

"Visualize!" Mrs. Tannenbaume barked at Putzie. "All great athletes use visualization!" She turned to Raymond. "It's all about vision. You gotta have a vision or you'll never succeed at anything."

"I don't have a vision," Raymond said. "I'm just a Martinizer, remember?"

"Not *just* a Martinizer, dear. You're the best Martinizer in all of New York."

Raymond guided the Buick down Steam Boat Road while keeping his eye on the long line of cars in the rearview mirror. The cars were honking their horns more than ever now. Mrs. Tannenbaume kept an eye on Putzie. She watched him trip over a crack in the sidewalk. He was clearly getting tired.

"Look where you're going, Mr. Paultz. The last thing we need now is an accident."

The words were barely out of Mrs. Tannenbaume's mouth when Putzie ran smack into a low-hanging maple branch and crumpled onto the sidewalk. Raymond did not see the crash because he was too busy looking in the mirror. Before Mrs. Tannenbaume could tell Raymond to stop the Buick so that they could rescue Putzie, Raymond drove into the rear end of a parked car.

To make matters worse, the parked car and the tree both belonged to Mrs. Tannenbaume. They had somehow managed to crash directly in front of her home.

The maple tree stood in the middle of Mrs. Tannenbaume's front yard. A long gnarly branch had grown parallel to the ground, out across the front lawn, and dipped down low over the sidewalk. She had meant to do something about it for years but had somehow never gotten around to it. The branch was nine inches in circumference and stood exactly four and a half feet off the ground—face-high if you are Putzie Paultz.

Putzie lay motionless on the sidewalk in front of Mrs. Tannenbaume's house, his face bloody, his black eye patch askew, his Nike Air running shoes gleaming in their newness. Midshipman Jones, busy inspecting the wooden cross he had planted in Mrs. Tannenbaume's front lawn, looked up when he heard Putzie's head hit the pavement and then ran over when the Buick piled into Mrs. Tannenbaume's VW Beetle. The Beetle was in mint condition. Mrs. Tannenbaume rarely drove it—she only took it out of the garage to park it on the street in front of the house every day. Midshipman Jones had told Mrs. Tannenbaume that it was a dangerous place to park her Beetle, but Mrs. Tannenbaume wouldn't listen. She liked to look at it from out of her window, and besides, it kept just anyone from parking in front of her house.

Mrs. Tannenbaume got out of the passenger seat without a word. She stood on the sidewalk with her hands on her hips and surveyed the damage. The Buick had ripped off the Beetle's chrome front bumper. She shook her head in disgust and then walked over to Putzie. She bent over and peeled back the eyelid on his good eye and peered into it. She turned to Midshipman Jones, who did not seem at all surprised that it was Mrs. Tannenbaume who had wrecked her own car.

"He's out cold. You'd better drag him up onto the lawn."

"I told you about that branch, Mrs. Tannenbaume," Midshipman Jones said.

"I know, love. You told me to not park the Beetle on the street, too."

Raymond got out of the driver's seat and joined them on the front lawn. Raymond told Mrs. Tannenbaume how sorry he was for crashing into her Beetle. He told her that he was good with cars and that he would fix the Beetle good as new.

Mrs. Tannenbaume merely nodded. She was inspecting the wooden cross. "You think it's sturdy enough to hold the Jesus?"

"Yes, ma'am. I used two bags of Sakrete." Midshipman Jones grabbed the cross with both hands and shook it hard. "See? It doesn't budge."

"Ahh, excuse me, you two," Raymond said. "Don't you think we should do something with Mr. Paultz?"

Mrs. Tannenbaume looked down at Putzie lying on his back on the grass. "He'll come to soon enough. The fresh air is good for him. In the meantime we might as well hang Jesus."

The first time Midshipman Jones came to Mrs. Tannenbaume's house, he and Mrs. Tannenbaume could not agree on the best way to nail the Jesus to the cross. Midshipman Jones thought it should be done while the cross was on the ground. Mrs. Tannenbaume wanted to plant the cross in the ground first, then nail the Jesus to it—she thought it would be more authentic that way. She did not want to do anything sacrilegious, what with Sister Mahoney acting funny about the papier-mâché Jesus in the first place.

Midshipman Jones had finally agreed to do it Mrs. Tannenbaume's way, but by that time it was late and he needed to get back to the academy. He returned the next day, dug the hole, and planted the cross in the ground. He had come back today to hang Jesus. When she said he was doing more than he needed to, he replied that he was honored to be able to help Captain Tannenbaume's mother. Apparently all the nice midshipmen loved her sonny boy.

Midshipman Jones grabbed the Jesus from under its armpits, hoisted it off the ground, and stood the Jesus up in front of the cross. "You mind giving me a hand?" he asked Raymond. "I'll pick him up and put him in place if you'll grab that hammer and nail him to the cross."

Raymond put both hands to his mouth and stepped backward, tripped over Putzie, and fell flat on his back. He lay there on the ground and looked up at the life-size papier-mâché Jesus, fighting back tears.

"I . . . I . . . I . . . , I . . . I don't think I can do that." He broke down and started to cry.

Mrs. Tannenbaume snatched the hammer herself, stuck a few nails in her mouth, and said through the nails, "Hold him steady, son. I'll nail him up."

Mrs. Tannenbaume started with the feet. She often wondered, whenever she pondered the crucifix at St. Aloysius, why the Romans nailed Jesus's feet to the cross. Was he kicking? Mrs. Tannenbaume asked Father McSorley about it once. "If Jesus died for our sins, then why was he kicking?"

"Jesus went to his death meekly," Father McSorley told her. "A lamb to the slaughter."

"Well, then why did they nail his feet down?"

Father McSorley told her it was for stability reasons, so that Jesus wouldn't fall off the cross, which sort of made sense. Maybe.

Mrs. Tannenbaume grabbed hold of the Jesus's feet. She was about to hammer home a nail when she stopped. "You know, I don't think Jesus needs a nail in his feet."

"Nails in his feet will probably help stabilize him."

"That's what Father McSorley said. I don't buy it. I think the only reason they nailed Jesus's feet was because Jesus was trying to kick them in the teeth. Wouldn't you kick like crazy if a bunch of people were trying to nail you to a cross? Father McSorley has got it all wrong. But then again the Catholics have got a bunch of things wrong." Mrs. Tannenbaume waggled the hammer in Midshipman Jones's face. "Like the fact that Father McSorley says his long-ago church Fathers told him to be celibate. I said to him, 'Father, why would another man want you to be celibate?' I told him I thought it was the typesetter's fault. The church leaders way back when said the priests should celebrate. The knuckleheaded typesetter wrote celibate instead of celebrate, and because of that one simple typo, priests have been celibate for centuries! It makes you question their judgment. If they got duped on the question of whether or not to have sex, it makes you wonder what else they're getting wrong. Father McSorley is a nice man and he tells a good homily but he's got no *saichel*, getting duped like that."

"Seh-kel?" Midshipman Jones said.

"Common sense."

"Where do you get these words anyhow?"

"You hang around this town long enough you pick up a few expressions." Mrs. Tannenbaume motioned for Midshipman Jones to hold the Jesus steady. "If you think nailing the Jesus's feet to the cross will help stabilize him, well then, I'll just put a few nails in his feet."

Mrs. Tannenbaume nailed the Jesus's feet and then held him up around the waist while Midshipman Jones nailed the Jesus's wrists. The papier-mâché Jesus had red paint around the wrists and feet, so, in the end, Mrs. Tannenbaume figured nailing his feet made the whole thing look more authentic. They stood back and admired their handiwork.

"All he needs now is a good coat of varnish," Midshipman Jones said.

"Varnish?"

"I'll get some marine varnish from the shed on Mallory Pier, back at the academy. A few coats of good Spar varnish and the Jesus'll shed rain like water off a duck's back."

Mrs. Tannenbaume looked over at Raymond and noticed that he was unusually quiet. He stared at the ground in front of him before turning his glare toward Mrs. Tannenbaume. He then looked to the heavens and shouted, "I was not a part of this!" and dropped to one knee before the Jesus, crying softly to himself. Mrs. Tannenbaume knelt beside him and patted him on his head. Raymond, it seemed, was just another fearful Catholic. If she'd seen one, she'd seen a hundred—the St. Aloysious was full of them. Putzie, meanwhile, began to stir. Lying flat on his back, he opened his good eye. He heard Raymond crying and saw Mrs. Tannenbaume consoling him. When he moved his head to the right, he saw the mound of dirt. Then he saw the Jesus. His good eye began to blink.

"Oh my goodness, the *goyim* were right after all."

Mrs. Tannenbaume turned toward Putzie. "What did you say, Mr. Paultz?"

"Jesus on the cross. I can't believe it."

"You can't believe what?"

"That when a Jew dies, he sees Jesus in heaven."

"Heaven? You're not in heaven. You've got a little bump on your head. Relax."

"But what's with the mound of dirt? And why is Raymond crying?"

"He's a good Catholic. He's afraid of committing a sacrilege."

"What happens when a Catholic commits a sacrilege?"

"Absolutely nothing," Mrs. Tannenbaume said. "That's what's so great about Catholicism. All you have to do when you commit a sin is go to confession. It's the most convenient religion going."

Putzie looked at Mrs. Tannenbaume absently, then touched his head and looked at the blood on his hand. "The last thing I remember is running like a surfer. How did I end up here?"

"You ran smack into my tree."

"And I ran your car smack into Mrs. Tannenbaume's Beetle," Raymond said. "But I'll fix . . . oh no." Raymond's hand shot up to cover his mouth. "The Commodore!"

Raymond pointed at the maroon Chrysler LeBaron, the standard government car issued to ranking officers of the academy, rolling to a stop across the street from Mrs. Tannenbaume's house.

"We're not at the store to give him his shirts," Raymond said. "He'll be very upset."

⁂

The Commodore got out of the LeBaron on the opposite side of Steamboat Road and waited for the cars to pass. When the traffic cleared, he started to cross then stopped. He looked towards the main entrance to the Merchant Marine Academy, a half a block away. The football team, jogging in tight formation, had just departed Vickery Gate and was heading up Steamboat Road for their afternoon run. He decided to wait for them to pass—he liked the way they sang out a greeting to him as they jogged by. The team, however, took an abrupt turn to the left and ran down Stepping Stone Lane. The Commodore stamped his foot on the ground in disappointment, causing the dust on the side of the road to swirl around his pant leg. He slapped at his leg with his hand to rid his uniform of the dust and, in a fit, started across Steamboat Road without bothering to look for traffic.

A cream-colored 1950 Mercedes convertible, artfully restored and with its top down, came to a screeching halt ten feet in front of the Commodore. The driver honked his horn and shook his fist. The Commodore, in response, stood erect and unflinching and stared imperiously at the driver, not an easy thing to do since the afternoon sun threw a glare on the windshield that hid the driver's face. When a cloud passed overhead, the glare on the windshield faded and he was able to make out the face of the driver.

It was the bandleader.

What was going on here? The bandleader was reported to have been missing. What in God's name was this man up to?

Before the Commodore could accost the bandleader, the convertible lurched into reverse, skidded to a stop, then came ahead again, its wheels screeching as it swerved around the Commodore. The Commodore did not move a muscle as the convertible sped past him. He stood still for a moment longer, long enough for the world to witness his dauntlessness, then crossed to the other side of Steamboat Road and strode up Mrs. Tannenbaume's lawn.

"An assassination attempt," the Commodore said when he reached the others. "You have all borne witness to a brazen attempt on my life."

"Assassination?" Mrs. Tannenbaume said. "Don't you have to be a world leader to be assassinated?"

A leader of little people such as yourself!

"You walked across the street without looking," Mrs. Tannenbaume said. "The driver did everything he could to avoid hitting you."

And I am doing everything I can to avoid accosting you, madam!

"The important thing is that you are OK, sir," Raymond said.

"Indeed I am," the Commodore said, composing himself. "Indeed I am. And you are correct. It *is* important that I have survived this brush with death. For we have work to do. I am reminded of Frost, 'The woods are lovely, dark and deep/But I have promises to keep/And miles to go before I sleep/And miles to go before I sleep.'"

The Commodore swept his hand as gracefully as a jazz singer as he recited the stanza. He was proud of the improvement he had made in his hand gestures—proof that practice makes perfect. The Commodore looked for signs that the others were impressed with his public speaking ability. When they gave no reaction to his gesticulatory flourish—no visible feedback—he deliberately turned his body and looked over at Putzie.

"Just the man I wanted to see—are you ready for combat, Mr. Paultz? You have clearly been training, sustaining injuries along the way it seems. Not to worry, my good man. As far as I am concerned, an unblemished athlete is simply not trying hard enough."

Putzie remained seated on the grass. "I can take Mogie any day of the week, as long as I don't get stuck in that chair of his."

"Well then," the Commodore said, "we ought to schedule the wrestling match ASAP. I'll have my secretary make the necessary arrangements."

The Commodore reached out a helping hand and Putzie took it. The Commodore released his grip when Putzie was standing up, only to watch the poor man's knees buckle when he tried to walk. Oh dear. Were his hopes of ridding himself of his nemesis resting on the slight shoulders of this inadequate man? The Commodore watched Putzie wobble toward the Buick. Short, slight, an eye patch over one eye, Putzie wore the hangdog look of the defeated. Perhaps a pep talk was in order.

"Mr. Paultz." The Commodore called after Putzie. "Do you believe you can defeat Mogie?"

Putzie stopped in his tracks and turned inquisitively toward the Commodore.

"I mean, dear man, at your core, do you believe it? As a core belief? Do you have the desire to defeat Mogie? A burning desire—not some half-baked notion or flimsy wish, but a red-hot burning desire? Because without a deep belief in your abilities and a burning desire to excel, you relegate yourself to the trash heap of mediocrity." The Commodore glanced out of one eye to see if the others were listening. When he saw that they were, he strode over to a spot on the lawn where he was able to face them as a group. Now would be the perfect time to practice his pause, scan, and nod technique.

When he finished nodding, he continued with his speech. "It is never too late to start believing in yourself, Mr. Paultz, and that goes for the rest of you as well. It is never too late to hone your desire for excellence. Because, you see, each day that God gives us is simply another day in which to excel. Yes, today is another day in which to excel. Tomorrow is yet *another* day in which to excel. Do you all want to know the secret to success? Do you? Do you sincerely wish to be a success in life? Here then is the key to success." The Commodore paused, scanned, and nodded, to great effect, he thought. "The secret is 'mental mapping.' Mr. Paultz, you must form a picture in your mind's eye of defeating Mogie in O'Hara Hall in front of a crowd of midshipmen screaming your name. Think of victory! Think of glory! Think of adulation! Everyone will be looking at you, admiring you, wishing they could be you. It happens to me all the time. When I give my speeches, the crowd nearly carries me away on its shoulders, so great is their love for me. Think of how envious others will be of you. Think of how inadequate you will make them feel. When you win, you see, someone else loses. Think of that. Sometimes you do not even have to win. When someone else loses, I feel like I win. If everyone adopted my philosophy, think of how much better off we would all be. We would all be winners. Don't you see? It is so easy. Choose to not be a loser, Mr. Paultz. Think of others as losers, and you will always be a winner."

The Commodore finished his speech with his best hand gesture. He made a loose fist with his right hand and draped his thumb over his lightly clenched index finger and pointed it at Putzie. It was the only polite way to point at someone. He held his thumb point for the perfect amount of time, not too long but not too short either. He was proud of his thumb pointing. He practiced it on his secretary, Miss Lambright, who always jerked her head back whenever he pointed his thumb at her, proof-positive of its effectiveness. Putzie and the others were having a similar reaction as well. They all stood motionless, staring straight at the Commodore, with their heads leaning back ever so slightly. Speechless, in the way that all of the Commodore's audiences fell silent after his leadership speech. The silence of awe. The Commodore allowed the silence to wash over him and cleanse his soul. He always felt healed after his leadership speech, healed of childhood wounds and scars. And he felt affirmed—of not only his greatness, but of the inferiority of others.

Putzie was the first to take his eyes off the Commodore. He looked at Mrs. Tannenbaume, who gave a slight jerk of her head toward the Buick. Putzie nodded and Raymond tiptoed with the two of them to the Buick without so much as a glance at the Commodore.

The Commodore basked in the silence.

After the Buick pulled away, Midshipman Jones gathered his tools. The Commodore tagged along as if he didn't have a thing in the world to do in the middle of a workday. The Commodore was pensive as he watched Midshipman Jones pull Mrs. Tannenbaume's garage door down.

"Midshipman Jones," the Commodore said, "come with me as I drive to the dry cleaners to pick up my shirts. There is something I wish to talk about with you."

Midshipman Jones looked at the Commodore with wide eyes. "Have I done something wrong? I've got a liberty pass. I signed out in the MOD's office, I've—"

"No, no," the Commodore said, "it's nothing like that. I simply want to ask your opinion on a matter."

"My opinion?"

"Don't sound so surprised. Your opinion matters, does it not?"

"Yes, sir, I guess it does."

They walked across Steamboat Road to the LeBaron. The Commodore handed the keys to Midshipman Jones. "Here, you drive, young man." The

Commodore saw that the boy seemed surprised at the offer. Midshipman Jones took the keys and walked over to the driver's side, opened the door, got into the driver's seat, reached over, and unlocked the passenger side door.

The Commodore stood erect outside the car and waited for the midshipman to open the door for him.

"It's unlocked, sir."

The Commodore made a show of clearing his throat.

Midshipman Jones got the message. He got out of the car and scurried around to the other side, where the Commodore graciously allowed the midshipman to open the door for him.

Midshipman Jones drove haltingly down Steamboat Road, over-braking at every stop sign in his nervousness, but the Commodore was too caught up in his own thoughts to reprimand him. Finally, the Commodore shifted in his seat and turned toward Midshipman Jones. He sighed.

Midshipman Jones gripped the steering wheel tighter and shrunk farther down in his seat.

"Midshipman Jones, what did you think of my hand gestures when I recited Frost's poem."

"Hand gestures, sir? What hand gestures?"

The Commodore snapped his head around and faced straight ahead. "You failed to notice my hand gestures?"

"This is about hand gestures?" Midshipman Jones said. "I thought I was in some sort of trouble or something."

"What would give you that idea?"

"I don't know, sir, I guess the way that you're acting."

"And how, exactly, am I acting, young man?" The Commodore said it "ex-act-lee," as if it were three distinct words.

"Like you're displeased with me."

"Indeed, I am," the Commodore thundered, slapping both hands on the dashboard of the LeBaron. "I made perfect hand gestures! Graceful, slow movements that started at the center and swept outward and returned to the center. Hand gestures that elevated the childish musings of Frost to something lofty and ethereal. And you missed it! All of you missed it. That insipid

Mrs. Tannenbaume missed it. Mr. Paultz—Putzie—such as he is, missed it. I can excuse Mrs. Tannenbaume her vulgarity—the poor woman will ever be a philistine—but you, young man! I will not have it. You must open your eyes to notice the finer points of life. You must *discern*. How else will you develop a healthy ego? Do you not wish to excel, young man? My hand gestures were textbook, I say, textbook. They were, dare I say it, gracious. A quality most men avoid, but which I embrace. Graciousness," the Commodore thundered. "You must learn to be gracious!"

The Commodore did not wait for Midshipman Jones to open the door for him when the LeBaron pulled up in front of the dry cleaners. He told Midshipman Jones to wait, that it would only take a minute to pick up his shirts. The Commodore stepped into the dry cleaners and stopped.

Mrs. Tannenbaume was giving a shirtless Putzie a post-workout shoulder massage underneath the commercial blower in the front of the store. The Commodore could not believe his own eyes. He marched over and grabbed his shirts from Raymond.

"You allow this sort of thing in a public place?" The Commodore's words were a harsh whisper. He spun on his heels and strode toward the door.

The Commodore could not recall when in his life he had been more peeved and was relieved that he had Midshipman Jones to vent his feelings to on the ride back to the academy. So while the Commodore lectured his charge, and Raymond manned the register, Mrs. Tannenbaume continued to massage Putzie. Meanwhile, upstairs in the love shack, Mitzi drove Mogie foolish.

Chapter 13

A STANDING OVATION

Johnson sat alone at the mess table in Delano Hall twirling a spoon in his hand. He was waiting on the Commodore. He had hoped to take a few minutes to run down to the ship's store to get a new paint brush for his wife—he had seen an improvement in her mood lately and wanted to do whatever he could to keep her interested in her hobby—but then the Commodore sent word that he was rushing over to speak with him. The plebe who gave him the message said the Commodore said something about a looming crisis, no doubt something about the bandleader. The case of the missing bandleader had been hanging over the academy like a wet sweater for the past three days. So Johnson waited.

When the Commodore arrived, he did not appear to be altogether ruffled. In fact he seemed to be his usual arrogant self. When Johnson heard what it was that was so "looming," he nearly came out of his chair.

"A speech, Bobby? This is about a fucking speech?"

"Yes, sir. A speech, sir. The regiment appears lackluster. Forlorn, almost. A motivational speech will—"

"I thought this was about the bandleader. The regiment is forlorn, Bobby, because their bandleader is missing and word is their Commodore might have something to do with it."

"But the bandleader is no longer missing, sir. And it seems I've gone from suspect to victim—the man tried to run me over."

Johnson stared at the strange man in front of him. He was having difficulty processing what he had just been told, in no small part because of the manner in which it was told to him. The Commodore seemed completely unaware of the effect the missing bandleader had on the academy. Not to mention that he seemed totally unfazed by the fact that he was a suspect in the case. Johnson was beginning to think the man was a true sociopath.

"This place has been on pins and needles for the past three days, Bobby. Are you at all aware of that?"

"Pins and needles, sir?"

"Are you fucking with me, Bobby?"

The sad truth was that the Commodore was not fucking with him. Johnson knew that. The man had his head so far up his own ass that he was incapable of noticing anything or anyone else around him. How the hell did Johnson end up with this lunatic as his second in command?

"If the regiment has been on pins and needles, then maybe a speech is just what they need, sir."

Johnson knew he had to surrender. There was no other way to deal with this man. He put his hands over his face and leaned back in his chair. He stayed this way for what seemed like hours. He eventually removed his hands and let out a long sigh. He looked up at the Commodore standing in front of him. It amazed him how sincere the Commodore could seem when he wanted something.

"What kind of speech, Commodore? Like a pep talk or something?" Johnson's words came out slowly, as if they were being uttered by a man facing defeat.

"Exactly, sir! A pep talk is what our boys need."

"I don't do pep talks." Johnson set down the spoon. "Speaking in public makes me nervous." He looked over his shoulder for the nurse, who usually met him in the mess hall after the noon meal ended. Johnson liked to take a sail with the nurse after lunch—it helped his digestion. His digestion could sure use the help today. "Besides," he added, "the regiment was doing okay until this thing with the bandleader. They're probably just in their usual summer funk, maybe, like they always are in August. It's hotter 'n hell in the barracks—it saps their energy."

"It's not their energy that is sapped, sir. It is their spirit. We give them food to nourish their growing bodies, do we not? They deserve spiritual nourishment as well. Words nourish the spirit, especially when one backs one's words with emotion and delivers them in a stirring oratorical fashion. A well-delivered speech is an intoxicant, sir, an elixir for the masses."

"So who the hell is going to give this stirring speech? The commandant? He can barely string two words together."

"As it happens, sir, I have a speech prepared," the Commodore said.

"Not your 'Back End' speech!"

"No, sir." The Commodore seemed oddly rushed today, in his own pompous, ponderous way. "I'll give a speech on leadership. It's a spellbinding speech, sir. Some have called it evocative."

"I don't know, Bobby. The regiment has enough going on. Academics, regimental training, inspections, parade rehearsals. What the boys need is to get laid. The poor bastards are walking hormones at their age. They need pussy, not some evocative speech. They need entertainment."

"Did I hear somebody say entertainment?" The nurse came up from behind Johnson and cupped her hands around his eyes. "Guess who?"

The Commodore placed his hands on the table. "Before you guess, sir, I need an answer. The regiment needs an answer."

The nurse kept her hands over Johnson's eyes. "This about the bandleader?"

Johnson pulled away from the nurse. "No, the Comm—"

"They found the bandleader. He locked himself in one of the practice rooms in band land. He said he came back to pick up his oboe and accidentally locked himself in the room."

Johnson was dumbstruck. *Why am I always the last to get all the gossip?*

The Commodore, however, was quick to pounce. "What did I tell you, sir? The man is hopeless."

"Right?" the nurse said. "What a loser."

Johnson put up his hands. "Stop it," He felt an intense need to leave the scene immediately. "Okay, Commodore. I give up. Call a special assembly. We'll meet in Dana Hall."

"I thought we'd do it in O'Hara Hall, sir," the Commodore said. "The acoustics are always better in an old gymnasium."

Johnson grabbed the nurse by the hand and pulled her with him. "Let's go sailing, sweetheart. There's a nice breeze today. Now that I don't have a missing bandleader on my hands, maybe I can relax this afternoon." Johnson looked over his shoulder toward the Commodore. "Wherever you want to hold it is fine with me, Bobby. Just tell me where to show up."

A pall fell over the gymnasium when the Commodore finished his speech.

"I thought this was supposed to be a pep rally," the nurse whispered into Johnson's ear. "Pep talks are supposed to be fun."

The Commodore stepped out from behind the podium on the makeshift stage in the gymnasium and walked to the edge of the stage. It looked to Johnson as if his toes might be hanging over the edge.

The nurse elbowed Johnson in the ribs. "What is he doing?"

"The fruitcake is acting as if he's getting a standing ovation," Johnson said.

The nurse elbowed Johnson again. "This is no pep rally. Do something, boss."

Johnson stood and walked across the gymnasium's parquet floor to the stage, his steps echoing in the silence of the cavernous gymnasium. His eyes caught sight of the chaplain sitting among the midshipmen in the first row of bleachers. He signaled for him to get up on the stage. As Johnson and the chaplain climbed the steps to the stage, Johnson said, "Lead the regiment in a prayer or something. Another benediction, anything."

The chaplain walked to the podium and said, "Let us pray." Johnson walked up behind the Commodore, who was still standing with his toes over the edge of the stage. "Your evocative speech is over, Bobby. Let's go." He grabbed the Commodore by the arm and led him off the stage.

"Some speech," Johnson said in disgust when the two were out of sight of the regiment.

"Thank you, sir," the Commodore said. "I told you they would be speechless."

"Yeah. You're gonna wish I was. If you ever talk me into—hey, what the fuck is Mogie doing here?"

Mogie stood with his back against the wall by the rear entrance of the gymnasium talking on a cell phone. His secretary, Maven, wearing a white dress with embroidered red tulips, stood beside him with her first-aid kit. Mogie did not appear to notice Johnson and the Commodore.

"He's part of the entertainment, sir," the Commodore said.

"Entertainment? What entertainment?"

"You specifically said the regiment needed to be entertained. I've arranged for them to be entertained today."

"By Mogie?"

"I've arranged for a wrestling match. Mogie is one of the contestants."

"Wait. Mogie is gonna wrestle here today? In our gymnasium? Have you lost your mind, Bobby?"

"Indeed, I have not, sir. Wrestling is a sport rich in tradition. It goes back to Greco-Roman times. A wrestling match is appropriate entertainment for this august institution."

"I can't believe what I'm hearing. Who's Mogie gonna wrestle?"

"His opponent will be Mr. Paultz."

"Mitzi's husband?"

"That is correct, sir."

"Isn't Mogie banging Mitzi?"

"I am not privy, sir. I do know that the two are adversarial. As to the nature of their dispute, I simply have no way of knowing."

"But, Bobby, a wrestling match? Couldn't we have just gotten Jimmy Buffett for Chrissakes?"

"Please, sir, Jimmy Buffett? The man is tone-deaf."

"Look at him over there." Johnson nodded toward Mogie. "You hear anything more about that picture Mitzi took of me? I thought for sure she'd show it to Mogie. I can't believe the prick isn't demanding my resignation."

The Commodore did not dare make eye contact with Johnson.

"You know something, Bobby? Your little wrestling match just might be a good thing after all. If Mogie gets his ass kicked, he wouldn't dare demand my resignation. He'd look like a sore loser."

"Very astute, sir. I hadn't thought of that."

"What does Mitzi's husband look like? Think he can take Mogie? I mean, look at him over there. Mogie's built like a fire hydrant."

"I am told that Mr. Paultz has been training assiduously. It is a grudge match of a sort, I am told."

Mogie finished his call and handed the phone to Maven without looking at her. Then without hesitating he walked right up to Johnson and got in his face. "I heard you were captain of a boat once, Johnson. That true?"

Johnson made a show of clearing his throat, something he did when he was pissed off.

"Why does the superintendent of a school need to know how to drive a boat?"

"Ship. I was captain of a ship."

"Well, this place ain't a ship or a boat. It's a school, see what I mean? Why do you gotta be a captain to run a school?"

"It's in the by-laws."

"By-laws. You WASPs and your by-laws. You got no common sense but you got by-laws."

The Commodore stepped between Johnson and Mogie. "It is time for you to change into your wrestling gear, Mr. Mayor. The locker rooms are right over here."

Mogie shrugged the Commodore off. "I don't need a locker room. Just take me to the mat."

Johnson watched the Commodore lead Mogie to the wrestling mat. *Why the hell did I agree to all this?*

After he took a seat in the first row of the bleachers, Johnson made eye contact with the chaplain and signaled with his hand for him to end the benediction. The regiment of midshipmen began to stir when they saw Mogie walk out with the Commodore to the center of the gymnasium. Mogie spun around in a small circle and surveyed the crowd. He stripped off his suit jacket like a thug getting ready for a street fight, tossing it to the mat and removing his tie. He stalked the mat and took off his dress shirt and flung it in the air. The regiment ate it up. When someone in the crowd whistled, Mogie pumped his arms up and down to egg them on. He removed his shoes and socks and kicked them aside, spinning around in a tight circle in just his trousers and a white tank top. His shoulders and biceps bulged, but his pecs hung out of the sides of his shirt and flopped up and down when he raised his arms. Dark body hair covered his back like a sweater. His belly hung over his belt and jiggled when he moved.

The regiment was really starting to wake up. They whistled and hollered at the sight of the barefoot mayor of Great Neck in his undershirt and trousers. Mogie searched the bleachers, and when he spotted Mitzi, he flexed his biceps in the classic Charles Atlas pose. The crowd roared.

While Mogie mugged on one end of the mat, Putzie emerged from the locker room in a terry cloth bathrobe too big for his scrawny body. He stepped onto the mat opposite Mogie and removed his bathrobe. He had white tube socks with red stripes pulled up to just below his knees. His gym shorts were baggy and made his skinny legs look even skinnier. He too had a white tank top on. Unlike Mogie, his arms were reeds, and his chest was sunken and hairless.

"He looks like Woody Allen, for Chrissakes," Johnson said to the nurse. "This twerp ain't gonna beat Mogie."

The Commodore took the microphone from the podium and strode to the center of the mat. He then introduced the two wrestlers and explained that the match would consist of three three-minute rounds. When he signaled for the two wrestlers to shake hands before the start of the match, Mogie pulled Putzie's eye patch away from his eye and let it snap back in place. The midshipmen went wild.

The Commodore saw to it that the athletic department had a referee present, along with an official timer and a scorekeeper. The timekeeper pressed the buzzer to signal the start of the match.

Mogie charged like a bull toward Putzie.

Putzie was caught off guard—he was busy adjusting his eye patch—and crumpled like a house of cards when Mogie smashed into him.

The referee slapped his hand down three times on the mat. Pinned! The match was over before it even started.

Mogie jumped up and the referee grabbed his fist and thrust his arm over his head. Johnson fell to his knees and slapped his hand on the wood gymnasium floor. The midshipmen in the first row of the bleachers saw the superintendent do this and so they, too, got on their knees and slapped at the floor. The rest of the regiment stomped their feet on the bleachers. The sound of all the wood slapping and stomping was deafening.

Mogie basked in the pandemonium. Putzie walked over to Mogie and held out his hand, a gentleman in defeat. Mogie gripped Putzie's hand and squeezed. Putzie's knees buckled under the pain of Mogie's viselike grip. The regiment howled. When Mogie loosened his grip, Putzie jerked his hand free and walked away with his head down. Mogie scampered after Putzie and pulled his baggy gym shorts down to his ankles. Putzie stood helpless, his eye patch askew, his baggy shorts around his ankles, his jock strap droopy.

The regiment of midshipmen chanted, "Mogie! Mogie! Mogie!"

Johnson sat on the floor on his haunches, stunned. Mogie was in possession of that damn photograph that Mitzi took. And now this. Did this dumbass wrestling match just seal his fate?

The Commodore stood up and walked across the gymnasium floor with the palms of his hands pressed tight against his ears. He walked ramrod straight, as if he was lord of the manor.

Johnson leapt to his feet and crossed the floor. "Look at what you've done, Bobby. I'm fucked now, thanks to you."

The Commodore did not remove his hands from his ears. "I cannot hear a word you are saying, sir. I must protect my ears."

The Commodore walked away from Johnson and out of the gymnasium.

Mogie, meanwhile, continued to egg on the crowd of midshipmen by thrusting his arms up and down. Putzie pulled his shorts back up and walked off the mat with his head down. Mogie ran up behind him and stole the eye patch off Putzie's head and placed it over his own eye. The bleachers rocked with chants of Mogie! Mogie! Mogie! Putzie did not even bother to try to retrieve the eye patch. He simply walked out of the gymnasium with his head down and his shoulders sagging.

While Mogie jumped up on the stage, Johnson found the commandant. "Get the regiment quieted down and back to class." Johnson walked past Mogie.

"You're finished, Johnson," Mogie yelled. "I've got evidence. Pack your bags."

Johnson continued walking without so much as a glance at Mogie. The chaplain fell in step alongside him. They walked together in silence.

When Johnson and the chaplain exited O'Hara Hall, Mogie followed them, still yelling.

Johnson and the chaplain passed through the arcade joining Jones and Barry Halls and into the confines of the barracks, Mogie right on their heels. When Mogie followed them into the barracks area, Johnson whirled around. "You're in a restricted area, Mogie. Get the hell out of here."

Mogie laughed in Johnson's face. "I've got a picture of you with your schlong—excuse me, whaddya call it? your johnson?—whipped out right smack in front of Mitzi's desk."

A group of midshipmen entered the barracks. The chaplain ushered the boys away, telling them that the admiral was fellowshipping with the mayor.

"I'm telling you for the last time, Mogie. Get the hell out of where you don't belong."

"Boy you just don't get it, do you? I'm in charge now. From now on, I tell you what to do, see what I mean? Mitzi's got pictures."

Johnson stared long and hard at Mogie without saying another word. Finally, he looked over at the chaplain. The chaplain, as good as anyone in the art of stonewalling, nodded toward Wiley Hall, telling Johnson, without words, to retreat. Johnson took a deep breath and looked back at Mogie.

"Good day, Mr. Mayor," Johnson said with a sigh. "Congratulations on your win today."

Johnson and the chaplain turned and entered the barracks. Mogie puffed out his chest and watched them until they turned the corner. When they were out of sight, he spun around and pushed his way through the doors and into the arcade. A shaft of sunlight came through the foliage and blinded Mogie.

He never saw Mitzi coming until she slapped him across the face.

"How dare you humiliate my husband like that," she said. "Putzie trained so hard for that match. You didn't have to pull his shorts down in front of all those people. You're nothing but a bully!"

Mogie stood there in his wrestling getup. His back hair lay dank with dried sweat. Mitzi, in her red pumps, stood a head taller.

"But, Mitz," Mogie said. "I was only doing it for you. It was all for you."

"I'm taking my stepper back. You don't deserve it. You're nothing but a creep."

Mitzi shoved Mogie aside and marched off in her red pumps. Her long sticks carried her to the parking lot outside of the MOD's office in no time flat, where she climbed into her red Mustang convertible and sped off. A group of midshipmen walking past whistled at the sight of the red-haired beauty in the convertible. When they saw Mogie, they shouted, "Mogie!" and high-fived him.

Mogie managed a momentary display of bravado but he was too preoccupied to enjoy his sudden fame. He wasn't thinking about the sticks or even the stool. He was thinking about the camera in Mitzi's possession.

Chapter 14

WOMAN ON TOP

"I'm ready for Putzie, baby," Mitzi said, naked except for her Victoria's Secret bra, and bent over at the waist in her red pumps. "I'm ready for my Putzie."

Putzie stood behind her on top of Mitzi's aerobic stepper, the one that Mogie called his "stool." As soon as he moved, the stepper wobbled, and he slumped over Mitzi's back. He clutched a handful of her hair to steady himself.

Mitzi kept up the encouragement despite the hair pulling.

"I'm ready for Putzie."

The two of them were in Putzie's office at the dry cleaners. A hazy light filtered through the lone dirty window high up near the roof. The dim sunlight was supplemented by a single naked bulb that hung from one of the steam pipes that formed a sort of drop ceiling, and Mitzi's head kept hitting the bulb. What with the humidity and the hair pulling and the scorching-hot lightbulb, Mitzi's beautiful red hair was taking a beating. They had been trying for over an hour to have sex using Mitzi's aerobic stepper. It was not going well.

"My hair, Putz," Mitzi said, over her shoulder. "Let go of my hair."

Putzie held on to her hair like a cowboy holding onto the reins of his horse. "Did you say something, Mitz?" Putzie, after years of working in the dry cleaners, yelled whenever the Martinizing machines were on.

"My hair!"

When Putzie let go of Mitzi's hair, he lost his balance and fell off the stool and crashed onto his cot. Mitzi's head snapped back and hit the lightbulb again.

"When you gonna get a real office, Putz? My head keeps hitting this stupid lightbulb."

Putzie scrambled off the cot. He moved the stepper away from the lightbulb and climbed on top.

"Over here, Mitz," Putzie said. "Let's try again."

Mitzi refused to budge. She stood there in her red pumps and bra with her hands on her hips, snapping her gum and glaring at Putzie. There were worse things in the world than pity sex, but this was getting ridiculous.

"Please, Mitz?"

"It's the humidity, Putz." Mitzi looked away and stroked the frazzled ends of her long beautiful hair. "I hate this dry cleaners, it's too humid in here. When you gonna get air-conditioning in this place?"

"It's too expensive to air-condition a dry cleaners," Putzie said. "Come on, Mitz, one more try."

Mitzi clomped over in her heels and faced Putzie in front of the stepper. Her hands were on her hips again. Without a word, she turned around and bent over at the waist and held on to her ankles.

"I'm stretching for my Putz." She said it without a shred of enthusiasm.

Putzie hesitated on the stepper. "What did you say?" he yelled over the Martinizing machines.

"I said I'm stretching for my Putz!"

Putzie quickly stood up on his tiptoes and placed both hands on the small of her back to steady himself.

"Stop pushing me," Mitzi screamed, through her legs.

"I'm just trying to get a little purchase here."

He grabbed her hair again.

"Let go of my goddamn hair!"

Putzie tried to stay on his tiptoes on the stepper. He pulled on Mitzi's hair and pushed on her back.

"Hold on to my hips," Mitzi ordered.

When Putzie grabbed Mitzi's hips with both hands, he tottered backward and had to slump forward against Mitzi's back to break his fall. When he stood up again, he had his hands around Mitzi's neck.

"Stop choking me!"

"I can't seem to get any purchase here."

"Forget the goddamn purchase, Putz. Are you gonna take care of me or not?"

"I can't concentrate with you yelling at me like that."

Mitzi half straightened up, still bent over at the waist, and put both hands on her knees. Her back was arched, like a weight lifter.

"Okay, Putz." Mitzi let out a huge sigh. "Okay. Here you come, Putzie." She looked up toward the window near the ceiling. She was quiet now, resigned. "Here comes Putzie."

Putzie, however, wasn't going anywhere. The fact was he didn't have the *chutzpah* to service a woman from behind standing up. Instead of wielding his manhood with confidence, he just poked around timidly. Mitzi tried to help him find his way, but as his confidence waned, so did everything else. In the end, it was like trying to open a lock with a rubber key.

Mrs. Tannenbaume sat on top of the store counter with her legs crossed Indian style. Raymond was standing, leaning against the counter. They had heard every bit of Putzie and Mitzi's encounter in the back.

"Poor thing," Mrs. Tannenbaume said.

"It sounds like he's trying too hard," Raymond said. "He's taking it too seriously. He should just think of it as, what you do call it? The 'hoo-hoo and the ha-ha'?"

"That's right, love, the hoo-hoo and the ha-ha. That's what . . . oh no . . ." Mrs. Tannenbaume looked up when she heard the door to the dry cleaners swing open. "Not him again."

The Commodore entered the sweltering storefront. He spotted Mrs. Tannenbaume, scowled, then crossed the room and stood at the counter. Mrs. Tannenbaume waited, but the Commodore just stood there, stone-faced. *What was with this kook? Does he think he's more important and doesn't have to say hello first? This guy really thought he was someone.* Finally, she said, "May I help his majesty?"

"My shirts, please."

Mrs. Tannenbaume looked at Raymond. "Flouncy wants his shirts."

"Raymond," the Commodore said before Raymond could move, "be kind enough to deliver me my shirts now."

"Why do you talk that way?" Mrs. Tannenbaume asked, looking over at Raymond. "Who talks that way?"

The Commodore raised one hand and placed it flat against his temple. He closed his eyes.

"Get a load of this guy!"

The Commodore lowered his hand, opened his eyes, and looked over Mrs. Tannenbaume's head. "Madam, I know not of which you speak."

"Oh you know, buster." Mrs. Tannenbaume bored a hole right through the Commodore, a technique she had learned in her thirty-five years in education. The only way to deal with the class bully was to bully right back. Although, truth to tell, she wasn't sure if this one was the class bully or the class clown. "You know exactly what I'm talking about."

"Authenticity is my watchword, madam. I am who I am. I can be no other."

Authenticity is his watchword? This guy couldn't be more fake if he tried. Mrs. Tannenbaume continued to stare the fake down.

The Commodore slammed his fist on the counter. "Come come, young man. My shirts, please."

Just then Putzie emerged from the back of the dry cleaners. He grabbed the Commodore's shirts off the moving rack and placed them on the hook next to the cash register. He rang up the Commodore himself. Mitzi followed behind Putzie a moment later and pushed open the swinging half-door to the left of the counter. Her heels clip-clopped on the concrete floor as she walked by. She stopped at the full-length mirror next to the front door to flatten her dress against her body. She pulled at her hair and combed it with her fingers, stood straight for one last look at herself in the mirror, flattened her dress some more, and said, "Goddamn humidity." She left without saying hello or goodbye to anyone.

Mrs. Tannenbaume went over and placed her hand on Putzie's arm. "It didn't go so well, did it?"

"I think I blew it." Putzie placed both hands on the counter and blew out a long breath. He stared at his hands. "My big chance."

"Maybe you're trying too hard," Raymond said.

"I just couldn't seem to get any purchase standing on that stool. I don't know how Mogie does it."

"But you don't have to get any purchase," Mrs. Tannenbaume said. "Don't you see? It's more like when you ride backseat on a motorcycle. It's better to lean into the turn than hold on to the driver. It's called rhythm, love."

"I don't know if Mitzi'll give me second chance. She seemed pretty mad at the end. Did you see the way she stormed out of here without so much as a goodbye?"

"We'll work on it, love. We just have to break a few bad habits is all."

While Mrs. Tannenbaume continued to talk with Putzie about technique, the Commodore tried to close his ears. He could not stomach the thought of Mrs. Tannenbaume, the self-proclaimed sex therapist. Better to think about his problems. The wrestling match was, admittedly, a misguided strategy, resulting, quite inadvertently, in an emboldened Mogie. But was he now hearing that Mogie and Mitzi were estranged? What larger implications did this import? And how might this new information favor him? The Commodore needed to find out more.

He once again became aware of the others in the room. He heard Mrs. Tannenbaume saying, "Let's start at the beginning, love. There are three basic positions: missionary, doggie style, and woman on top."

The Commodore put an end to Mrs. Tannenbaume's vulgar musings. "Perhaps Mr. Paultz would benefit from a brief respite." The Commodore smiled at Putzie. "An afternoon nap does wonders for the psyche, so the experts say."

Raymond jumped up. "Yes, Mr. Paultz, your nap, sir. I'll turn off the Martinizing machines so you can sleep." Raymond ushered a weary Putzie to the cot in his office.

"Raymond," the Commodore said when Raymond returned, "am I to understand that Mogie and Mitzi are in some way estranged?"

"Yes, sir. Mitzi is mad at Mogie for the way he embarrassed her husband. She told Mogie she didn't want to be the kind of woman who allowed her boyfriend to disrespect her husband."

"How honorable," the Commodore said. "In a left-handed sort of way, that is."

"But Mr. Paultz told me that Mogie keeps calling Mitzi, bugging her for the camera."

"Camera?" Mrs. Tannenbaume said. "What camera?"

The Commodore put up his hand to silence Mrs. Tannenbaume. "Did you say Mitzi is in possession of the camera?"

"What camera?"

"Mitzi took a picture of her boss, Admiral Johnson, with his pants down," Raymond explained to Mrs. Tannenbaume.

"She's having a situation with him, too?"

"No, no." Raymond laughed. "No, her boss is, shall we say, proud of his . . . his, uh, you know. He calls it Johnson."

"Raymond," the Commodore said, "are you telling me Mogie is not in possession of the camera?"

"That's what he just said, didn't he?" Mrs. Tannenbaume said.

The Commodore continued to ignore Mrs. Tannenbaume. His pulse quickened. If Mogie was not in possession of the camera, then he was in no position to make outrageous demands.

"Mr. Paultz tells me that Mogie wants to replace Admiral Johnson with a Jew," Raymond continued.

"What's he want a Jew for?" Mrs. Tannenbaume asked.

"He says WASPs are dopey."

"He's right, there, you know. They've got no *Yiddisher Kop*."

The Commodore looked at Mrs. Tannenbaume for the first time since he entered the dry cleaners. "*Yiddisher Kop*?"

"It means 'business sense.'"

"I know perfectly well what it means, madam. I am just surprised that Mrs. Tannenbaume *with an E* is so familiar with Yiddish expressions."

Mrs. Tannenbaume waived her hand. "You live in Great Neck long enough . . ."

"I see."

"So why don't you hire a Jew admiral? You got this wacko Johnson who likes to show off his situation, which, P.S., he calls Johnson, but you're afraid of a Jew?"

"We are not afraid, madam. There is simply a shortage of seagoing Jews."

Mrs. Tannenbaume looked at Raymond.

"The academy has by-laws. The admiral has to have been captain of a ship," Raymond said.

"My sonny boy is a captain."

"He is? What kind of captain? Is he captain of a boat or a ship?"

"He's the captain of the MV *God is Able*. Has been for years."

"The *God is* . . . " The Commodore slapped his head. "Your son is Captain Tannenbaume?"

"You say that like it's a bad thing. Have you heard of him?"

"But of course." The Commodore took a step back to have a better look at Mrs. Tannenbaume. He simply could not reconcile the fact that the well-regarded Captain Tannenbaume was related to the woman who stood before him. He was the kind of captain the faculty at the academy liked. He was known to take the job of training Kings Point cadets very seriously—he kept them aboard ship where they belonged and did not set them loose in seamy ports of call the way other captains did. The Commodore heard that some captains even encouraged the cadets to go ashore to sow their wild oats. As far as the Commodore could tell, judging from the fitness reports Captain Tannenbaume wrote, the man was a serious-minded ship's master who kept the Commodore's boys on a short leash.

"My sonny boy would make a terrific admiral, don't you think?"

"He might at that," the Commodore said. "But the fact remains, your son is not Jewish."

Mrs. Tannenbaume looked away. She turned and walked to the end of the counter, grabbed her pocket book, and told Raymond her shift was over and that she was leaving. Raymond and the Commodore watched her walk out. When the door closed behind her, Raymond said, a bit astonished, "That was a fast exit. What got into her?"

"I'm wondering the same thing," the Commodore said.

Chapter 15

WOLF TICKETS

Johnson sailed his Vanguard 420 on a port tack into Hague Basin. The 420 was a nimble boat, and Johnson handled it with ease. He asked the nurse how she liked his boat. She told him she really, really liked it. "It's tippy!" That made Johnson smile.

Approaching the 420, on a starboard tack, was the entire sailing team in a long line of Lasers on their way out to practice Starts for their upcoming race with Fort Schuyler. Johnson held his course. The 420 quickly closed on the entire sailing team.

"Hey!" the nurse said. "We're gonna hit those boats!"

"No need to worry, dear. We have the right-of-way."

The long line of Lasers began to skitter. A rumbling could be heard throughout the team as they all asked each other what the hell the admiral was up to. The midshipman sailing the lead boat called out, "Admiral Johnson! Starboard tack has the right-of-way!"

"Oh, shit."

Johnson pushed on his tiller, but it was too late. The 420 crashed into the Laser. The second boat in the long line of Lasers veered sharply at the last second and missed the lead boat, but that gave the midshipman behind *him* little-to-no reaction time and his boat crashed into the lead boat. In a matter of seconds, it was a fifteen-boat pileup.

The nurse made herself heard through the din. "Hey, dummy. I thought you said we had the right-of-first-refusal?"

The midshipmen scrambled to extricate their boats from one another. No one spoke. Johnson worked to free his boat with his head down. All he could say was, "Sorry, boys. Sorry 'bout that."

It was a good hour before the boats were untangled. By the time Johnson got his boat stowed in the boathouse, he was late for his meeting with the Commodore. Johnson had asked the Commodore to join him in the old Prosser boathouse after his sail to help pick out a new spot for the Mariners Monument. The present location blocked the view from his office to Eldridge Pool, where the nurse liked to sunbathe prior to the noon meal. Watching the nurse sunbathe helped to work up his appetite, and besides, moving the monument might be the last official act of his tenure.

The Commodore witnessed the mishap in Hague Basin from his perch in the Crow's Nest at the end of Crowninshield Pier. The Crow's Nest served as the station for the one midshipman who stood watch on the waterfront at night, a kind of basic training in watch-keeping. The Merchant Marine Academy took great pains to ensure that it graduated junior officers who knew how to stand a professional watch, including how to keep a proper log of the watch. The Commodore took a personal interest in the logbook. Penmanship was altogether critical to good log keeping, and the man who could not be bothered to make his writing legible was more than likely the man who could not be bothered to be faithful to his other watch-keeping duties.

As part of an internal audit a few years back, the senior officers of the administration assigned themselves watch-keeping duties normally assigned to the midshipmen, the better to determine if the midshipmen's activities were relevant to the making of good officers. During the audit, the Commodore relieved the waterfront watch from Johnson and was appalled with the logbook entries of the academy's superintendent. Chicken scratch was what it was. Totally illegible. After taking part in the audit, Johnson wanted to do away with the nighttime waterfront watch altogether. "Who the hell can stay awake in the Crow's Nest all night long?" Johnson wanted to know. Just as the Commodore suspected! The man was incapable of dutifully carrying out even the most sacred of tasks. Falling asleep on watch was the one inviolable rule of watch-keeping, a capital crime if there was one.

And now look at him. Johnson was clearly on a port tack, clearly the give-way vessel, it was obvious to all. Was the man not intimate with the nautical rules of the road? Was it possible that the superintendent of the Merchant Marine Academy did not know port from starboard? Of course it was possible. Was not the entire administration inept? Did not the commandant confirm his ineptness during Indoc when he botched the Manual of Arms in front of the entire plebe class? The commandant—the man expected to know such things—confused preparatory commands with commands of execution. Parade rifles were flying all over Barney Square. Rifles at right shoulder arms collided with rifles at left shoulder arms. Half the platoon was at Parade Rest when the other half was at Order Arms. It was a mess. So why should the Commodore be surprised at further evidence of ineptitude? In the Commodore's mind, the academy was virtually a walled compound of bungling fools.

The Commodore walked down Crowninshield Pier and met up with Johnson outside of the boathouse. The Commodore would not step one foot inside the boathouse, which—everyone knew—served as Johnson's private lair. It disgusted the Commodore that Johnson appropriated the Prosser boathouse for his own licentious purposes. A proper boathouse was more than a storage shed for boats. It was a hangout, a place for the boys to gather after sailing practice, talk about who cut off whom at the start, who had a shot at the nationals, or who had the goods to try for the Olympics. On a wintry day when the wind was fierce and the boats remained nestled in their cradles, the boathouse was a warm bosom, a place where the boys could come to chew the fat, talk about girls, and ward off thoughts of home.

Old Captain Prosser, the longtime waterfront director, knew the importance of a bona fide boathouse. The boathouse on Crowninshield Pier remained unchanged since its construction in 1942. Rowing shells hung from exposed wood rafters, held aloft by three-stranded manila rope and hoisted up by wood blocks and tackle. Prosser kept every assortment of natural fiber rope and cordage in the boathouse: manila for boatfalls and mooring lines; sisal for towlines; hemp for seizing and worming the ends of line, to keep the ends from fraying; cotton for signal halyards. Old Prosser kept synthetic line as well, nylon and dacron and polypropylene, but he wanted his boys to know what a real boathouse *smelled* like, and so the hemp stayed. In the winter months, a fire burned round-the-clock in the wood-burning stove; year-round was the smell of strong coffee.

When the Commodore heard that Johnson took this haven away from the boys and kept it for himself, he nearly wept. Johnson went around telling anyone who would listen that the new "Waterfront Activities Center" was a modern marvel that would serve the same purpose as the old boathouse but without the draftiness and the smell of tarred wood beams. The Commodore mourned for a week.

Now Johnson stood inside the boathouse and held the door open for the Commodore. The Commodore was the first to speak.

"Starboard tack has the right-of-way, old boy."

"Don't old boy me, Bobby. Come in for a cup of coffee?"

The Commodore closed his eyes and breathed in deep. Johnson said he would take that as a no and stepped outside, closing the door behind him. They took the path that led up to the Mariners Chapel then cut across the grass to the War Memorial.

"So what happened out there?"

"The tiller got jammed."

"Of course."

Johnson maneuvered the Commodore to the site of the Mariners Monument. "You see?" Johnson spread his arms out wide and pointed one hand to his office and the other to the pool. "It blocks my view to Eldridge Pool."

"It seems the nurse has distracted you enough, sir. It may not be such a bad idea if the monument blocks your view of the nurse's sunbathing."

"I want the damn thing moved, Bobby. Don't bother me about it."

"You do not want the monument, period. The board has already approved it. Lose graciously."

"Are you selling wolf tickets, Bobby? 'Cause if you're selling wolf tickets, I'm buying!"

"I am not selling wolf tickets. I am merely pointing out the real motivation for your wanting the monument moved."

Johnson broke off and stalked in a circle. "What are you hearing from Mogie? Have you heard anything?" He swung around on his heels. "What do you know?"

The Commodore paused. "I know that Mogie is in possession of the camera. And that he is making noises about using it as blackmail."

"So Mitzi gave Mogie the camera?"

"That is correct."

"Shit."

"I also know that Mogie remains convinced of the need for a Jewish superintendent."

"Oh for God sakes, what—"

"You have agitated an adversary. Now you are paying the price."

Johnson ran up to the Commodore and shook his fist in his face. "I agitated an adversary? If you hadn't put on that damn wrestling match, Mogie wouldn't be feeling so damn sure of himself right now."

"You said yourself the boys needed entertainment."

"I said the boys needed to get laid!"

"The boys shall remain chaste."

"Are you out of your mind, Bobby? These boys spend a year at sea on real ships with real sailors. Real sailors go liquoring and whoring when they hit port and they drag the cadets along with them. Do you think your boy Edwin J. O'Hara remained chaste during his sea year?"

"His sea year was cut short by a German raider, I'll remind you."

"His ship called at a few ports before it went down and you can be damn certain the boy went ashore and did what every other American boy in his shoes would do."

"I will not hear another word. The boys need an icon. A pure and virtuous hero. Edwin was that and more. Please let it be."

"Goddamn it, Bobby. I want that monument moved."

"You want to do away with the monument altogether. The board has spoken. There is nothing you can do about it."

"Bullshit. As superintendent I preside over the board. I can order a special meeting to discuss the matter further. Put the whole question of the monument back in play. Who knows, maybe we'll even vote to undo the whole thing."

The Commodore cupped both hands over his ears and stared wild-eyed at Johnson. *No! This is not happening to me!*

Johnson took one look at the Commodore and backed up a step. "Christ, Bobby. Take it easy. You look possessed. It's only a monument, man. Relax."

The Commodore stalked off. As he walked across the grass, he kept his hands cupped firmly against his ears. He needed to shut it all out. All of it. Johnson and his blasphemy. Mogie and his outrageous demands. The thought of losing the monument. The thought of a defiled Edwin. The thought of a man like Johnson leading his boys—a man so vulgar, so crass. He stole the boathouse, robbing the boys of their idyllic refuge. But he would not steal the monument. He would not do that to the boys.

The Commodore scampered up the white marble staircase that led to the broad plaza behind Wiley Hall. A group of midshipmen descending the staircase greeted him. "Good afternoon, Commodore." The Commodore, his hands still pressed against his ears, brushed past them, entered Wiley Hall, and proceeded straight to his office. When he was in the privacy of his office, he removed his cap and stood in front of the big mirror, running his fingers through his hair.

His hair.

So white. So pure.

The Commodore tried hard to keep Johnson out of his thoughts, but he was unable to do so. The man's crassness had a way of seeping—unbidden—into his mind. And now the one thought he really wanted kept at bay came rising to the surface. Johnson's vulgar phrase, "Loyalty, not fidelity." When he had first heard Johnson use the line, he felt like he had been punched in the gut.

It was the same line he had heard his father use when he was a boy.

He had no idea what it meant until he was older and heard rumors of his father's infidelities. He was devastated when he confronted his father, who told him the truth about betraying his mother. And then his father laughed when the Commodore cried in front of him. This man who was so disciplined, who was so hard on others, had not lived up to his own ideals. And to blithely dismiss it like it was nothing.

The Commodore blocked it out. He breathed in at the count of two and breathed out at the count of four. He let out a long breath, the infinity breath. It felt good. He looked in the mirror and saw the tension drain from his face. His unlined face. He told himself he was stress-free. And why shouldn't he be? He was always in control, wasn't he? Self-possession. *Sangfroid*, the French called it. He had it in spades. Nothing ruffled his feathers. Nothing. He would stop Johnson. He would stop the monster.

Edwin would have his place in the sun. Always.

Chapter 16

PHONE SEX

"My, oh my. Tulips are a favorite of mine."

The Commodore clicked his heels and bowed at the waist. Maven blushed. She shifted in her chair behind her desk and her dress made a rustling sound. Her dress was white, short-sleeved, tight around the biceps, and covered in a profusion of bright yellow tulips from hem to neckline. She finished off her outfit with matching yellow pumps, which the Commodore noticed sticking out from under her desk.

The Commodore cupped his hand to his mouth and whispered, "I am going to steal you away from here, Maven. I am going to be superintendent of the academy soon, and the first thing I am going to do is fire the executive secretary and put you and your classy attire in her place."

The Commodore winked at Maven. Maven looked at her hands.

The Commodore stepped toward Mogie's office. "I know I don't have an appointment, dear, but if you will overlook it just this one time . . . "

Maven looked up in alarm. The Commodore put his hand on her shoulder. "Tulips," he said. "My, my . . . you are one classy woman."

The Commodore saw that Maven could not stop him from doing what he wanted. He put his index finger up to his lips to silence her and entered Mogie's office. Mogie sat in his high-backed leather chair behind his desk up on the platform and spoke in a hushed tone. He was on the phone.

"You're driving me foolish, Mitz. You drive me foolish when you stretch. I can picture you stretching. It's like you're right here. Stretch for Mogie, baby."

The Commodore stepped back into the vestibule when he heard Mogie. *Mogie was having phone sex with Mitzi!* The Commodore had known that it was only a matter of time before Mogie and Mitzi got back together, but he did not think it would happen this fast. He was hoping to come to the mayor's office unannounced, catch Mogie off guard, and reassert himself. Now he felt pressured.

Breathe! Why did he always stop breathing in tight situations?

He stepped back into the office. "Ahem."

Mogie spun around in his chair so fast it nearly toppled off the platform. "Call you right back, Mitz." He hung up. "Commodore? What the hell are you doing here? Where's Maven?"

"Maven said you wouldn't mind."

"Maven knows damn well I mind."

"Be that as it may, I am here. We need to talk."

"What about?"

"It looks like we will not be needing a Jew admiral after all."

"Says who?"

"I have discovered that Mitzi is in possession of the camera. You, therefore, are a blackmailer with no blackmail. You have been rendered impotent."

"Me, Mitzi, same thing. Mitzi does what I tell her."

"I am afraid I know otherwise. Mitzi and Putzie are back together. Your masquerade is over."

"Mitzi's frustrated. Putzie's being a putz—oh, there's a surprise." Mogie opened the humidor on his desk and picked out a cigar.

"Are you able to refrain from smoking until we've finished our business, Mr. Mayor?"

Mogie lit his cigar with his favorite lighter. The flame was a fireball. A billow of smoke enveloped his face. "Please, Commodore. Call me Mogie."

The Commodore would not let Mogie's bullying tactics get to him.

"We have a deal, sir." The Commodore's voice rose. "Don't you remember? I would place Johnson in a compromising situation. You would demand his ouster. I did my part. Miss Conrad did her part. Now it is time for you to do your part." The Commodore's speech coach would not have been pleased to hear the shrillness creeping into his star pupil's voice. "A deal is a deal."

Mogie's response was to puff smoke rings.

"Look." The Commodore hoped he did not sound pleading. "Johnson is on the ropes. I have informed him that you, in fact, are in possession of the camera and that you intend to go public with it. He will fall on his sword. He will walk away. It will be a clean break. Johnson resigns and I take his place. Our plan as we conceived it is brilliant. Why tarnish a good plan?"

"No."

"Mr. Mayor, I beseech you to reconsider." That, sadly, was pleading.

"I said no."

"We had a deal that you would make a public demand for Johnson's resignation. Why is that demand not forthcoming, sir?"

"I'm stalling."

"Stalling?"

"Yeah. I know you're next in line to be admiral. I wanna see if I can't find a Jew first."

"But why is having a Jew so important to you?"

"Because WASPs are schmucks, that's why. You got all these by-laws and rules and restrictions that you place on yourselves. We got a dumb WASP on the city council. He's always bugging us about Robert's Rules of Order. Who cares about Robert's rules? See what I mean? You got all these titles and ranks. What the hell is a Commodore anyway? Isn't he someone who runs a yacht club? You got a fancy title like Commodore but you got no *saichel*. Why should I go into business with some schmuck *goy*? Who needs it?"

"But I'm different. Can you not see that? I am above the rules."

Mogie stood up from his chair. He placed his cigar in the oversized ashtray on his oversized desk and stepped down from the platform. He walked over to the Commodore and stood by his side. Mogie barely came up to the Commodore's chest and had to lean his head back to make eye contact with the Commodore.

"Look. You seem like a nice-enough guy. Why don't you just keep your fancy title and your do-nothing job. Be happy with what you got. See what I mean? Find me a Jew who knows how to drive a boat and let us run things. You'll still be part of the deal. You don't have to worry about that. Look, the Jews have an expression, 'I'll take the gelt, you take the glory.' See what I mean? Don't be a schmuck. Take the gelt."

Mogie led the Commodore by the arm to the vestibule. The Commodore shrugged Mogie off, placed his cap under his arm, and marched out.

When he left Mogie's office, the Commodore spent the rest of the morning driving the streets of Great Neck. He hated himself for it. He hated himself whenever he wandered the streets where the lonely walked. The Commodore thought of himself as a dynamic man. He kept a rigid schedule and held himself accountable for how he spent his time. He earmarked every minute for serious endeavor. Hadn't he just this past week upbraided his secretary for permitting him to dawdle? He had earmarked three hours to rearrange his office to improve its feng shui, and Miss Lambright let him waste an entire day on it. He had been very angry with her that day. Why did she allow him to dawdle? Was it because she herself dawdled? He made a mental note to spend more time accounting for Miss Lambright's time.

That aside, the Commodore's wandering helped to put him in a better mood. As bad as his life was at the moment, he was surely better off than the mass of humanity that passed before him that morning. Did these people not have anything better to do with their lives? Walking, driving, shopping, running needless errands. He felt sorry for them and it made him feel better about himself.

Now the Commodore sat in his LeBaron in front of the Great Neck Martinizing Dry Cleaners and waited for Mrs. Tannenbaume to leave. Mrs. Tannenbaume with an E. If he had heard it once, he heard it a hundred times. He knew for a fact she had been a clerical worker, a typist! She was a flunky, a gal Friday. He was in no mood to deal with that woman this afternoon.

The Commodore wanted to get back to his office where he could think. He needed to come up with a plan B. His attempt that morning to persuade Mogie to stick with their original plan, the plan that would have made him admiral, had failed. Mogie made it clear he thought the Commodore was just another dumb WASP. Well, truth be told, he was another dumb WASP. Dumb like a fox.

This, of course, was the WASP's secret weapon. The Southern WASP hid behind his soft drawl and gentle manner, lulling a helpless "victim" into thinking his intellect was as slow as his speech. Do not be fooled. Behind the drawl was a cunning mind, a chess player's mind, able to think three moves ahead. The Northern WASP hid behind his starchy shirts and lordly mien. It was easy to think of him as an outdated relic, out of touch with the modern world. Again, proceed with caution. Behind the well-worn clothes and high-miles automobile was a fierce competitor, an eager-for-battle warrior. The Northern WASP was not as cunning as his Southern brethren, perhaps, but what he lacked in strategy he made up in doggedness. As a breed, the WASP was easy to underestimate.

The Jew, on the other hand, could not afford to be subtle. When one was surrounded by a hundred million sworn enemies, as were the Jews in Israel, one simply could not afford to ask questions first. It was shoot first and ask questions later. Mogie, who was about as subtle as a miniskirt, was so obviously of this school. So how does a WASP deal with a hard-nosed Jew? Simple. He plays possum with him. He lets him think he is winning. The Commodore knew that this was what he needed to do. But just how could he pull it off?

The Commodore got out of the LeBaron and entered the dry cleaners. Raymond was there to greet him at the door. He had the Commodore's shirts with him.

"I've been waiting for you," Raymond said. "Here are your shirts."

The Commodore refused to take the shirts. Why was Raymond handing him his shirts at the front door? This was highly unusual.

"OK then, Mr. Commodore, I'll take them to your car for you."

Raymond tried to rush out of the store with the shirts. The Commodore grabbed him by his arm just above the elbow and yanked him back in. He held him and looked toward the register. "Where is Mrs. Tannenbaume, young man?"

Raymond made an involuntary, almost imperceptible glance over at the curtain.

"She left early today."

The Commodore let go of Raymond's arm and turned his back to the curtain. He heard Mrs. Tannenbaume and Putzie talking.

He stiffened. "Please do not tell me there is something untoward going on behind that curtain."

Raymond clenched the shirt hanger so hard his knuckles turned white.

The Commodore stomped his foot on the floor, spun around, and pointed his arm at the curtain. He could not bring himself to look in the same direction. He purposefully turned his head ninety degrees away from where his arm remained pointed and closed his eyes. He breathed deeply.

"Raymond . . . this is a public place of business. This type of behavior is reprehensible."

The Commodore wanted Raymond to put a stop to whatever was going on behind the curtain. He did not have to say it. Raymond hung the hangar on the front doorknob and walked over to the curtain. He hesitated.

"Um . . . Mrs. Tannenbaume?" He said it so meekly it went unheard.

The Commodore strained to listen. He heard Mrs. Tannenbaume's gravelly voice but could not make out her words from where he was standing. He did not have time for this. If Raymond could not keep them from using a public space for Putzie's rubdowns, he would have to do it himself. He dropped his arm, marched over, and pulled back the curtain.

He closed the curtain as quickly as he opened it. "Oh, no . . . "

Raymond grabbed the Commodore's arm to steady him and then led him over to a chair, sitting him down gently. The Commodore struggled to breathe. He implored Raymond to help him.

"Why is this happening to me?"

Chapter 17

SEX ED

Mrs. Tannenbaume heard the curtain open and close but she was too involved to notice who it was that had peeked in on her and Putzie.

"Right there, Ira, that's it, right there." Mrs. Tannenbaume knew that Mitzi could be pretty impatient with Putzie. She figured the poor man just needed to hear a few encouraging words when he was in the act to boost his confidence.

Putzie was behind Mrs. Tannenbaume, holding on tight to her waist.

"Oh, yes, that's it. That's the sweet spot." She knew Putzie couldn't find a woman's sweet spot with a Geiger counter, but what else could she do? She had to keep up the encouragement.

The Commodore writhed at the thought of what was happening on the other side of the curtain. So Mrs. Tannenbaume was a talker! "Why is this happening to me?"

"Nothing is happening *to you*," Raymond said.

"Oh, God. You're too good, Ira. Too good."

Putzie was behind Mrs. Tannenbaume with one foot on the aerobic stepper now. "Hoo hoo. That's it, Ira. Ha ha. That's it. Right there."

"So that's where the hoo hoo and the ha ha comes from," Raymond said. "I sort of wondered where she got that."

The Commodore pressed his hands to his ears as tightly as he could, but he could not cover them fully enough to block out the woman's vulgar pillow talk.

"Okay, Sylvia." Putzie climbed up on the aerobic stepper. "Here I come."

Mrs. Tannenbaume felt Putzie struggling behind her. *What a rookie!* "No. Don't do it yet."

"Raymond! Listen to her. Could she be more demanding? Who could be intimate with someone as demanding as her?"

Putzie had Mrs. Tannenbaume by the hair now. When Mrs. Tannenbaume smacked his hand away, Putzie lost his balance.

"Don't forget your rhythm, love."

"Why is she talking about rhythm, Raymond?"

Raymond placed his hand on the Commodore's shoulder. "I think that's how Catholics practice birth control, sir."

"Hold on, Ira."

Putzie was slumped over Mrs. Tannenbaume's back now. "I'm trying."

"We're getting close now, love. Don't stop now."

The Commodore could not stomach being present for the denouement. He pushed himself out of his chair. "I have to leave before it's too late . . . "

Putzie was really wobbling on the aerobic stepper now and Mrs. Tannenbaume could not bear all of Putzie's weight. She screamed out, "Oh, Mr. Paultz!" and they crashed to the floor.

The Commodore had not made it out of the dry cleaners before this incident occured. His hands were at his ears when he turned around to seek out Raymond. "Raymond." His voice was as small as a child's. "Please help me."

"I think I sprained my ankle," Putzie said. "Raymond!"

The Commodore looked at Raymond wide-eyed. *They want Raymond now?*

"Raymond! Help!"

Raymond left the Commodore's side and opened the curtain. Mrs. Tannenbaume and Putzie lay on the floor. Putzie was fully clothed on the floor clutching his ankle. Mrs. Tannenbaume was dressed in a leotard. Raymond helped Mrs. Tannenbaume up off the floor first.

"We were so close, Raymond. The lesson was going so well."

"I know, Mrs. Tannenbaume. We heard."

"He does okay with two feet on the floor, but as soon as he gets on top of that stepper, he loses it. I encouraged him the best I could. It was part of my lesson plan. Did it sound realistic enough?"

"Oh, yes, Mrs. Tannenbaume. It definitely sounded like the hoo hoo and the ha ha."

"Well," Mrs. Tannenbaume blushed. "I know a thing or two about slow learners. They need encouragement most of all, you know."

Raymond told Putzie he would go get some ice. Mrs. Tannenbaume looked at the Commodore with his hands pressed to his ears.

"Oh, don't be such a prude," Mrs. Tannenbaume said. "Haven't you ever heard of sex ed before?"

The Commodore removed his hands from his ears. "I am aware that sex education exists, Madam. I simply have never been privy to an actual—oh, what would one call it?—session. And I certainly have never heard of a private session taking place in a public forum."

"Lesson. It was a lesson and I had a lesson plan. So you learned something?"

"Yes, you might say so."

Mrs. Tannenbaume beamed. "Care to share it with the class?"

"I learned that it will not be long before Mitzi is back in Mogie's arms."

Raymond returned with the ice and rushed to his employer's defense. "He can still get the hang of it. I think you're a good teacher, Mrs. Tannenbaume. You're patient."

"Thank you, Raymond. But much as I hate to admit it, I think Flouncy here is right."

Chapter 18

FLOUNCY

The Commodore was relieved to be back in his office. He lay down on his side on the couch and placed a drop of mineral oil in his ear. The oil was a salve, and he allowed the oil to coat the silica in his ears for over an hour, a half hour in each ear. After his ears were well oiled, he tested his hearing with the machine he "borrowed" from the infirmary. He sat at his desk, pulled out the individually packaged swipes of alcohol that he kept in the top right-hand drawer, and wiped the headphones clean. He placed the headphones over his ears, ran a terry cloth bandana around them, and tied a knot behind his head. He wanted to ensure a tight fit.

His ears tested perfect. That he must protect his hearing was a given. It simply was not possible to produce soaring oratory with tinny ears. A tinny ear gives no feedback, no aural indication as to whether the speaker is producing nasal resonance, and without nasal resonance, one cannot affect a pleasing timbre. The Commodore admired the timbre of his own voice and was certain others admired it as well. It was an inborn quality, to be sure, but that did not mean he did not have to continue with his voice exercises. He stood in front of the mirror and checked to see that his jaw dropped when he opened his mouth wide, that his mouth formed a perfect circle and not an oval, and that his chin remained lifted above the horizontal. He always had trouble with the last part, keeping the chin up.

He called in Miss Lambright and had her stand on a chair by his side to check for the jaw drop and the chin lift. After twenty minutes or so of checking from all angles, he dismissed Miss Lambright. But just before she walked out of the office, he remembered and called back to her.

"Oh, Miss Lambright? Just one more thing." The Commodore gathered his thoughts. "It is about your use of time, dear." He looked toward the ceiling and sighed. He wanted to give the impression that something special was coming— it was a trick he used to get people to lean in closer for more.

"It is a question of values," the Commodore said, "of priorities, is it not? Do you value time, Miss Lambright? Do you guard it jealously? No, we both know you do not. You are profligate with your time, dear, we have talked about this before, have we not? I have noticed that you dawdle. And now you are allowing me to dawdle. We mustn't allow that to happen, dear. There are too many things that I want to accomplish in my lifetime, things of great import, and so you must, always, every minute of every day, ensure that every activity in which I am engaged is truly the highest and best use of my time. I trust you to be a faithful keeper of my time, dear. Am I making myself understood?"

"Sir . . . is practicing your chin lift really the highest and best use of your time?"

The Commodore's chest tightened. He noticed how his breathing became shallow and quick. The Commodore slowly counted to ten. *Breathe!* He stared at Miss Lambright's face. He studied it, noticing the fine lines around her mouth, the result, no doubt, of years of worrying about the inconsequential and the prosaic. Small problems for small people, as the Commodore's father used to say. The Commodore would not allow Miss Lambright to provoke him with her outlandish statements. He did not need her to account for his time. He was an expert in prioritizing and only meant to help the poor woman. The

Miss Lambrights of the world were consigned to the junk pile of mediocrity largely because they lacked time management skills. And what happened when one tried to help the poor souls? They resented it, of course. Resentment. The hallmark of the "victim." It happened to the Commodore every time he tried to help the unfortunate. They slapped him in the face. He resented it himself, but who wouldn't?

He turned his back on Miss Lambright, faced the mirror, and resumed his voice exercises. "You are dismissed, Miss Lambright," he said in his best stentorian tone. "Please try to do something productive with your time for the rest of the afternoon."

No sooner had Miss Lambright returned to her desk than she was on the intercom. "A Mrs. Tannenbaume is on the phone, sir. Probably another Jewish charity. Shall I handle it? I would not want to waste even a moment of your precious time, sir."

Miss Lambright kept talking, but the Commodore was not listening. Of course Miss Lambright thought Mrs. Tannenbaume was Jewish. Didn't everybody? She had a Jewish-sounding name. She used Yiddish expressions. She lived in Great Neck. And if Mrs. Tannenbaume sounded Jewish, how did *Captain Tannenbaume* sound? Why hadn't the Commodore thought of this before? Mogie was so eager for a Jew who knew how to drive a boat that he would never question whether Captain Tannenbaume was a Jew. Tannenbaume with an E? Who ever heard of such a thing? Surely not Mogie.

Miss Lambright's voice again. "Do you want to take the call, sir?"

"Yes, Miss Lambright, put her through." The Commodore lifted the receiver, wiped it quickly with an alcohol wipe, and held it to his ear. "Hello, Mrs. Tannenbaume."

"Are you too busy to talk now?"

"No, I am not busy, not at all, madam."

"I'm sorry I called you Flouncy that time. I hope I didn't offend you."

"Oh, don't be silly. Flouncy is a perfectly fine nickname, you have not offended me."

"I think those loud Martinizing machines at the cleaners hurt my ears. They're ringing like crazy."

"Those loud Martinizing machines hurt my ears as well!"

"Someone told me you have a hearing machine. And that maybe you can test them for me. I hate to waste money on doctors."

"Well, someone is correct. I do possess a hearing machine. And why should you waste good money at the doctor's office? It would be no trouble at all, Mrs. Tannenbaume, to test your ears. Please come right away. I will administer the hearing test myself."

"Thank you. That's awfully nice of you."

"You are quite welcome, madam."

The Commodore hung up the phone. He could not believe his change of fortune. He knew there was a reason he wanted to get back to his office that morning. How else to solve one's problems but to think them through? To think, to really think, was one of the hardest things to do. It came as no surprise that precious few in the world ever did think. Instead of thinking, most people ran around asking, What do *you* think I should do? It drove the Commodore crazy. *What do* I *think? It is* your *problem, fool, do your own thinking.* No, the Commodore did not need others to think for him—he thought for himself.

And today, by simply calming down, by sitting quietly in his office, by thinking, he came up with a brilliant solution to his problem. Mogie wanted a Jew who knew how to drive a boat? Captain Tannenbaume would be that Jew. And with Captain Tannenbaume in hand, the Commodore's nemesis, old Johnson's Johnson, would finally be removed from office. Oh! The thought of a United States Merchant Marine Academy without Johnson made the Commodore's heart sing. The cad had run roughshod over the Commodore's boys long enough.

Getting Johnson out of the way had proved to be more difficult than he first imagined, but the Commodore intuited immediately that pushing Tannenbaume aside would be far easier. Just before the unveiling of the Mariners Monument—oh, delightful irony—the Commodore would simply expose Captain Tannenbaume as a Gentile. Mogie, of course, would be furious at the deception and demand that Tannenbaume step down.

The Commodore's mind raced. He felt he could make a plausible argument that the unveiling of the Mariners Monument was too important to postpone, that a superintendent would have to be in place to preside over such an important ceremony—too many people would be watching—that the only thing to do would be to make the Commodore the new superintendent. The plan was elegant in its simplicity: Tannenbaume would replace Johnson; then, just before the unveiling of the Mariners Monument, the Commodore would replace Tannenbaume. Why had he not thought of this before? Instead of whining to Raymond, he should have been in his office thinking. Instead of listening to Mrs. Tannenbaume give sex lessons to Putzie, he should have been in his office thinking. Instead of wasting his time trying to straighten out Miss Lambright, he should have been thinking.

And, now, instead of beating himself up, he should be thinking. *Think!* What was the next step? Mrs. Tannenbaume, of course. He had to win her over. She, after all, would be an accomplice to his plan. Why had he not been nicer to the woman before? He knew that to win friends and influence people he needed to make genuine and sincere compliments, but what possible virtues did Mrs. Tannenbaume possess that he could dote on? The woman was short and inadequate. She fancied herself a teacher on the strength of her thirty-five years as a typist, which proved she was delusional. How on earth was the Commodore, a man deeply rooted in reality, supposed to deal with a woman as degraded as Mrs. Tannenbaume? The Commodore knew he possessed a real life, but Mrs. Tannenbaume? The woman lived a fairy tale life, the best he could tell. For one thing, she had no idea how others perceived her. Perhaps the Commodore could help her. He would try, if for no other reason than it would be in his best interests.

Miss Lambright's voice came over the intercom. "Mrs. Tannenbaume is here to see you, sir."

Chapter 19

RAISE YOUR RIGHT HAND

The Commodore looked at his desk. It was spotless, a sea of mahogany. He opened the bottom right-hand drawer and took out a sheaf of papers. He divided the sheets—old memorandums and position papers written by others—into neat little stacks and spread the stacks out on his desk before him. He took out a yellow legal pad and fountain pen from the center drawer and began to write. When Mrs. Tannenbaume and Miss Lambright entered the office, he did not look up. Miss Lambright offered Mrs. Tannenbaume a chair in front of the Commodore's desk and left them alone. The Commodore kept his head down and wrote on his legal pad. After about five minutes, he placed the fountain pen down and looked up at Mrs. Tannenbaume.

"Forgive me, madam, I am task-oriented. When I start something, I am simply compelled to finish it. It is said that President Lincoln had the same compulsion."

"You and President Lincoln?" Mrs. Tannenbaume said.

The Commodore spread his hands out to indicate the stacks of paper on his desk. "My work never ends, as you can see."

"I asked your secretary if I was interrupting you. She said you where practicing your chin lift."

"You *are* interrupting me, madam." The Commodore's voice rose when he said it. He caught himself. "But I do try to make time for others. Pro bono, of course."

"Like free hearing tests?"

"Precisely."

"I'm sorry for calling you Flouncy." Mrs. Tannenbaume said it matter-of-factly.

"Never mention another word about it, please. Now, let us check your hearing, madam."

The Commodore retrieved the hearing machine from the credenza behind his desk. He placed the machine on the coffee table and motioned for Mrs. Tannenbaume to take a seat on the couch. The Commodore removed the headphones from their carrying case and handed them to Mrs. Tannenbaume, who placed them on her head.

"They don't fit very well," Mrs. Tannenbaume said.

The Commodore thought of offering her his bandana, but the thought of his headphones pressed tightly against her doubtless waxy ears was more than he could stomach. "We do not require a tight fit for our purposes, madam. The machine is high-fidelity, I assure you."

She took them off and looked at them. "Is there any way to make them tighter around my ears?"

The Commodore grabbed the headphones with both hands and pulled them down on Mrs. Tannenbaume's head.

"Hey, not so rough."

"If you were more compliant, madam, maybe I—"

The Commodore stopped himself. He shoved the headphone jack into the machine. Could the woman be more headstrong? He watched Mrs. Tannenbaume play with the headphones: on her head, off her head, on her head.

"Are you ready, madam?"

"I don't think they fit me. Is there another pair?"

"No there is not." The Commodore struggled to keep his voice from rising. "Hold them in place with your hands."

He sat down on a chair across the table from Mrs. Tannenbaume and watched her hold the headphones in place with her hands. The Commodore fiddled with a few buttons on the machine.

"Are you ready to begin, madam?"

Mrs. Tannenbaume nodded.

"When you hear an audible sound in your left ear, raise your left hand. When you hear an audible sound in your right ear, raise you right hand."

Mrs. Tannenbaume removed the headphones from her ears. "I'm sorry, what'd you say? I was holding the headphones too tight against my ears."

"I said when you hear an audible sound in your left ear, raise your left hand."

"And what if I hear a sound in my right ear?"

"Then raise your right hand!"

"You don't have to yell."

The Commodore glared at Mrs. Tannenbaume.

"Look. If it's too much trouble . . . "

The Commodore paused to take a breath. "Please, Mrs. Tannenbaume. Let us begin again." He lowered his voice but he could not prevent it from quavering.

The Commodore transmitted a high-pitched tone to the left ear. When Mrs. Tannenbaume raised her left hand, the headphone slipped off her ear. It took her a minute to get ready again. The Commodore counted to ten several times. Finally, he transmitted another tone to the left ear.

Mrs. Tannenbaume raised her right hand and then said, "No," and raised her left hand. Now the headphones slipped off both ears. When she tried to catch the headphones, she knocked them off her head entirely. The headphones fell between the coffee table and the couch, and Mrs. Tannenbaume leaned over to pick them up, and when she did, she inadvertently placed her left hand on his hearing machine.

The Commodore slapped her hand off the machine.

Mrs. Tannenbaume, with nothing to hold on to, fell to the floor between the coffee table and the couch. She landed on the headphones. The Commodore heard the hard plastic crunch under Mrs. Tannenbaume's weight. The sound sickened him, like the limb of a great tree snapping under the weight of a late-winter snow.

His headphones! How was he supposed to test his hearing now? And after all the trouble he went through to acquire the hearing machine. The untold number of government requisition orders. The untold hours he spent "justifying" the expenditure of government funds. The Commodore had typed the requisition orders himself—he would never leave the task to Miss Lambright—and attached a separate page with a detailed justification of the requisition. The RO's came back marked "insufficient cause," "lack of justification," and most insulting of all, "totally unnecessary."

Unnecessary? It is unnecessary to check one's hearing on a regular basis? Says who? Dr. Birkhan, the chief medical officer of the infirmary? The man was not even an MD, he was a doctor of osteopathic medicine!

It did not help his cause when he addressed the requisition order to Practitioner Birkhan, the Commodore knew that, but he simply could not bring himself to call the man a doctor. The Commodore had finally asked Johnson to intervene on his behalf, but Practioner Birkhan was having none of it. "Over my dead body is that fruitcake getting a hearing machine, if he wants one so bad, he's going to have to steal one, and then we'll see where we are, heh?"

In the end, the Commodore took the man's advice and simply absconded with the hearing machine.

Of course, this meant that it would be next to impossible to requisition a new pair of headphones and he did not wish to press his luck by stealing another pair. Why had he ever agreed to share his machine with this woman?

Mrs. Tannenbaume pulled herself back up onto the couch. She held the broken headphones in her hand. "Sorry 'bout that."

The Commodore knew he had to keep the upper hand. He knew he had to forgive Mrs. Tannenbaume for breaking his headphones. He got up from his chair and stood in front of the window overlooking the waterfront and the future sight of the Mariners Monument. He thought of Edwin. He absolutely had to control his temper when dealing with this difficult woman. He owed Edwin that.

"My dear Mrs. Tannenbaume, there is nothing to be sorry about. Accidents happen, do they not?"

"You're not mad?"

"Heavens, no. Do I look mad?"

"Well, you look a little stiff is all."

"I am not stiff, madam!"

The Commodore clenched his teeth.

"Mrs. Tannenbaume? Have you ever had a tour of the academy grounds?"

Mrs. Tannenbaume blushed. "Why no, I haven't. I've always wanted to see the academy, but my sonny boy says he'll be furious with me if I ever set foot on the academy grounds. When he was a boy, he applied to the academy but was turned down. I guess he still holds a grudge. But he doesn't have to know that I am here now, I suppose. This is different. I'm just here to get my hearing tested."

"Why was your son not accepted?"

"He failed the physical. He was sickly as a boy."

"I was not aware of that."

"We were both shut out from Kings Point, I guess you could say. When I moved here, I wanted to live in Kings Point but I couldn't afford it. So I bought a house right on the border of Kings Point and Great Neck. My next-door neighbor, Mr. Howells, lives in Kings Point. I don't. Such is life."

"But with a name like Tannenbaume, I should think you would fit right in a town like Great Neck."

"It's Tannenbaume with an E. I'm not Jewish." When she said it, the words lacked her usual defiance.

"Yes, I've heard you say that before."

"I still have to tell people. People just assume I'm Jewish, you know."

"Well, your language is liberally sprinkled with Yiddish expressions. It is an understandable mistake."

"You live in Great Neck long enough, you pick up a few expressions. It's no big *megillah*."

The Commodore smiled. If Captain Tannenbaume sounded anything like his mother, he would have no problem passing as Jewish.

"Come, Mrs. Tannenbaume, allow me to give you a personal tour of the academy."

"Well . . . if my sonny boy found out, he'd be awfully angry with me."

The Commodore clicked his heels and bowed at the waist. Mrs. Tannenbaume blushed.

"Please allow me." The words dripped off the Commodore's tongue. He held out his arm. Mrs. Tannenbaume placed her hand inside of her tall escort's arm and they walked out of his office. Miss Lambright was not at her desk, but the Commodore could not have cared less. He had Mrs. Tannenbaume right where he wanted her.

Chapter 20

CAPTAIN TANNENBAUME
TO THE RESCUE

The Commodore's tour of the academy dazzled Mrs. Tannenbaume, as he knew it would. The oppressive heat and humidity of the summer had miraculously parted for the remainder of the afternoon, thanks to a northwest breeze bringing cool dry air, and their tour of the campus was as enjoyable as a stroll on the Champs-Elysees in springtime. The Commodore showed Mrs. Tannenbaume Amphitrite Pool where, as tradition required, midshipmen tossed coins into the pool of the Greek goddess to bring good luck on exam days. He took her to the Schuyler Otis Bland Memorial Library and showed off the library's seven-foot-high rotating globe, pointing out all of the ports he visited when he was a plebe many years ago. He allowed Mrs. Tannenbaume to ring the ship's bell at the base of the oval in front of Wiley Hall. Together they peered up at the gold eagle perched atop the world's tallest un-guyed flagpole.

The Commodore even walked Mrs. Tannenbaume through the barracks, a restricted area of the campus generally off-limits to visitors, where she saw plebes brace against the wall and sound off when the Commodore passed by.

"Sir, Midshipman Fourth class Russell, sir! Sir, good afternoon, sir!"

"Mr. Russell. How rude of you not to acknowledge my lady friend." The Commodore spoke gently. He knew how nervous the boys became in his presence.

"Ma'am, good afternoon, ma'am!"

Mrs. Tannenbaume turned red. The Commodore patted Midshipman Russell on his shoulder. "Carry on, young man." Midshipman Russell turned on his heels and walked six inches from the wall, as plebes are required to do. When he came to the end of the hall, he "squared" the corner by stopping and turning on his heels before resuming a purposeful stride. Mrs. Tannenbaume watched the plebes square every corner as they made their way through the corridors.

"Why do they walk that way?" she asked.

"Discipline, madam. It teaches the boys discipline."

"The sailors on my sonny boy's ship could sure use some discipline. The way he talks about them, they sound like a bunch of ragamuffins. His ship is a regular Hogan's Alley."

The Commodore wondered about that. Why would a man who clearly ran a tight ship—he had just finished rereading a few of Captain Tannenbaume's Fitness Reports —allow the union hall to dispatch subpar sailors to his vessel? Well, the Commodore would get to the subject of Captain Tannenbaume soon enough. In the meantime, he had more to show Mrs. Tannenbaume—an effective tour is all about pacing and he had to keep up the pace. He took her by Land Hall, the social hall of the academy. The strict regimental regulations of the academy were relaxed in Land Hall and the boys wore their official gym gear—blue athletic shorts, white T-shirts, and white tube socks pulled up to the knee. They still acknowledged the Commodore but were not required to "sound off." "Good afternoon, Mr. Commodore" sufficed in the relaxed atmosphere of Land Hall.

Mrs. Tannenbaume studied the boys' faces while they lounged on sofas and studied.

"One of my sonny boy's fathers was a sailor," Mrs. Tannenbaume said.

"*One* of his fathers? How many does your son have?"

"Well, since we're not sure which one of my boyfriends was the father, we say that he has three."

It was the Commodore's turn to blush. He did not like to hear such talk. And he certainly did not want one of his boys to overhear Mrs. Tannenbaume's blue talk. A change of subject was in order.

"Let us proceed to the chapel, Mrs. Tannenbaume. It is a nondenominational chapel, of course, reflecting the diversity of our boys' backgrounds."

Mrs. Tannenbaume looked up at the whitewashed chapel. "It doesn't look anything like the St. Aloysius."

"We call it the U.S. Merchant Marine Memorial Chapel," the Commodore said. "It was conceived as a national shrine to merchant seafarers lost in both world wars. A Roll of Honor lists all wartime maritime casualties."

Mrs. Tannenbaume gawked at the big white chapel. "You know, I always wondered if one of Captain Tannenbaume's fathers—the one who was a sailor—made it through the war."

The thought of perusing the Honor Roll for the name of a former wartime lover of Mrs. Tannenbaume's made the Commodore's stomach turn. He decided to distract her by taking her by the location of the future Mariners Monument. He would much rather talk about the academy's first son than listen to her reminisce about some long-ago fling. In fact, the idea of listening to Mrs. Tannenbaume at all did not hold much appeal for him. The woman did not converse, rather she launched into monologues—stories that went nowhere, stories about herself, mostly. *Could the woman be more narcissistic?* Whenever he tried to tell Mrs. Tannenbaume about himself, she cut him off and talked about herself.

The Commodore was about to tell her all about his hero, but what, after all, was the point? The woman didn't listen. No, they had been walking the campus long enough and, truth be told, the Commodore had accomplished his mission. His tour of the academy made an indelible impression on Mrs. Tannenbaume, he was sure of that. And how could Mrs. Tannenbaume not be impressed? There was something about the way people looked at him when he strode across the academy grounds in his dress whites. The greetings sung out by entire platoons of midshipmen. The crisp salutes. The Commodore felt satisfied that his POA was working.

They had not gotten very far from the chapel when the Commodore turned toward his guest. "Mrs. Tannenbaume? I should like to return to my office now. I wish for you to join me. There is something I need to discuss with you, something of great importance."

"Do you want me to pay for the headphones?"

"No, no, my dear. Heavens no. No, we have something far greater to discuss."

Mrs. Tannenbaume stopped walking. "Like what?"

The Commodore looked around to make sure nobody was within earshot. "What if I were to say to you that all this"—the Commodore swept his hands in a circle above his head—"could be yours?"

Mrs. Tannenbaume spun her head around to see where the Commodore was pointing. "All of what?"

"All of the academy, that's what."

"Have you been eating Indian food lately?"

"Come, madam. Let's get back to my office where I can explain more fully."

Mrs. Tannenbaume did not budge. "There's nutmeg in Indian food. Nutmeg is a hallucinogenic, did you know that? People say crazy things on nutmeg."

The Commodore started back for his office. He would not stand there another moment and listen to Mrs. Tannenbaume's inanities. She followed him, as he knew she would. More than anything, people like Mrs. Tannenbaume want an audience. Miss Lambright was again nowhere to be found when they reached the Commodore's office, and Mrs. Tannenbaume made herself comfortable on the couch by sitting cross-legged with her shoes off. The Commodore removed the hearing machine from the coffee table, returned it to the credenza, and pulled a chair up to the coffee table across from Mrs. Tannenbaume.

"My dear Mrs. Tannenbaume, I have not had too much nutmeg, I assure you. Please allow me to explain. The superintendent of the academy, Admiral Johnson, has gotten himself into a bit of a jam, recently. A peccadillo one might say."

"You told me. Mitzi took a picture of him with his pants down."

"Yes, correct, I did tell you. Well, the mayor of Great Neck, Mr. Mogelefsky, desires to replace the admiral with a Jew."

"I know. He wants somebody with a *Yiddisher Kop*."

"Yes, of course." The Commodore paused. "When exactly did I tell you this?"

"In the dry cleaners, don't you remember?"

"Oh yes, I remember now." The Commodore breathed a sigh of relief. For a moment he could not fathom how Mrs. Tannenbaume was in the know. "Well, Mrs. Tannenbaume, what you don't know is that the by-laws of the academy specifically state that the superintendent has to have had seagoing experience as master of a merchant vessel. The problem is it is very difficult to find a Jew who goes to sea. Jews own ships, Mrs. Tannenbaume, they don't go to sea on them."

"Tell me about it. I've been telling my sonny boy all these years that if he owned the *God is Able,* he wouldn't have to go to sea all those months of the year, year in and year out. It's plain as day to me. I don't know why he doesn't get it."

"Funny you should mention Captain Tannenbaume." The Commodore stood up, looked down at Mrs. Tannenbaume, and paused for dramatic affect. "I think we have found our Jewish captain."

The Commodore watched Mrs. Tannenbaume's reaction. She did not say anything in response to his statement. She made no visible movement, her breathing remained normal, but her eyes, her eyes gave her away. Mrs. Tannenbaume's dark brown eyes darted up and down from side to side. She appeared trapped, as if she was looking for a way out. Her eyes began to recede in their sockets until they seemed almost lifeless—a blank stare.

"It's Tannenbaume with an E." Her voice was limp. "We're not Jewish."

"Yes, of course," the Commodore said. "But people always assume you are Jewish, you said so yourself."

Mrs. Tannenbaume's eyes slowly came back into focus.

"Mogie is desperate for a Jewish admiral. I am certain that he would not question for a moment whether Captain *Tannenbaume* is Jewish."

"You're saying my sonny boy will be promoted to admiral?"

"That's correct. He will be called Admiral Tannenbaume."

"And he'll be the head honcho? Here?"

"That's right. He will be superintendent of the United States Merchant Marine Academy, the same academy that refused to admit him when he was a boy."

"How ironic."

"The best revenge."

"To think that I spent thirty-five years in education and now my sonny boy will be head honcho of a school himself."

"Indeed he will."

"But sonny's not supposed to get off his ship until the beginning of October."

"That's perfect," the Commodore said. "Just in time for the unveiling of the Mariners Monument."

"And what if Mogie finds out that it is Tannenbaume with an E and that we're not Jewish? What then?"

"I think there is a very low risk of that happening, madam. Mogie does not know you, am I correct?"

"Well, I know that his wife goes to the St. Aloysius. He married a shikseh named Jane. I always see him dropping her off in his big black Mercedes. What if she blows my cover?"

"Hmmm. We'll have to give that some consideration. Why don't you worship at the chapel, in the meantime? Steer clear of St. Aloysius altogether."

"Well, come to think of it, Sister Mahoney is kind of mad at me now, on account of my papier-mâché Jesus. Maybe it wouldn't be so bad to lay low for a while anyhow."

"Perfect. Feel free to use the memorial chapel anytime as my guest. I will instruct the guardsman at Vickery Gate to provide you free gangway."

Mrs. Tannenbaume uncrossed her legs and stretched them out on the couch. She looked at the Commodore. "I can't believe it. I came here to get my hearing checked and now my sonny boy is going to be the admiral. I wanna pinch myself." She averted her eyes from the Commodore. "I'm really sorry I ever called you Flouncy. You don't seem like such a bad guy after all."

The Commodore was not listening. Getting Mrs. Tannenbaume to go along with the POA was easier than he had thought. Something in

Mrs. Tannenbaume's past clearly caused her feel like an outsider, like someone denied admission to an exclusive club. The whole "Tannenbaume with an E" thing, there was something to it that did not meet the eye, the Commodore was sure of that. The woman hungered for acceptance, for a place to call home. She had one foot in Great Neck and one foot in Kings Point and she did not feel at home in either place. She was so proud that her sonny boy was a ship's captain yet she revealed today that she would prefer him to be a shipowner. That the woman had a past was clear enough, but how much did it matter? She spent thirty-five years as a typist, so how clever could the woman be? She would be putty in his self-assured hands, that much was clear.

He could only hope that Mogie would be as pliant. Mogie's eagerness for a Jew was clearly in the Commodore's favor now, but what if Mogie and Mitzi got back together? Mitzi—now there was the fly in the ointment of his POA. Mitzi knew that it was "Tannenbaume with an E," and if she got back with Mogie, the plan would all but blow up in the Commodore's face. Because of Putzie's utter lack of sexual prowess, Mitzi was in all likelihood back in Mogie's arms at this very moment. The Commodore would have to find a way to drive a permanent wedge between Mitzi and Mogie, but how?

Cloying. The Commodore had been trying to think of the one word that described Mrs. Tannenbaume best, and the word just popped into his head. *Yes, cloying, that was the word.*

"I'm so sorry. Did you say something, Mrs. Tannenbaume?"

"I just said, I think my sonny boy could do good here."

"Why I could not agree more, madam. Captain Tannenbaume will make a fine superintendent. And how could it be otherwise? He, after all, has education in his blood, does he not?"

When she got home, Mrs. Tannenbaume lay down on her threadbare couch. She was about to doze off when the phone rang. Upon answering the phone, she thanked the caller and placed the phone back in its cradle. And then Mrs. Tannenbaume let out a bloodcurdling scream.

Chapter 21

MIDNIGHT MUSK

Mitzi pretended to be busy. It wasn't easy with Admiral Johnson standing by the side of her desk with his elbow resting on the filing cabinet. Out of the corner of her eye she saw Johnson shove one hand into his pocket and then cup the back of his head with the other. She knew the filing cabinet had a sharp edge to it, and when she glanced up, she saw it digging into his arm. What was going on here? Why was Johnson trying so hard to act casual?

"So how goes it, Mitz? How's tricks?"

Mitzi did not look up. *Oh gawd. Did he just say "how's tricks"?*

"Hey, what a day, huh? Life's a beach, ain't it babe?"

Oh, no. Please don't tell me this fruitloop's hitting on me.

When Johnson surrendered to the sharp edge of the filing cabinet and sat on the corner of Mitzi's desk, Mitzi opened her drawer and took out her surgical mask. She did not bother to remove the gum from her mouth before she put it on, and when she chewed her gum, the mask moved up and down on her face.

Johnson stood up and paced back and forth in front of Mitzi's desk. He finally stopped and told Mitzi, "Take off the goddamn surgical mask."

"Sorry, no can do."

Johnson slammed his fist down on the filing cabinet, stormed out of the reception area, and retreated back into his bachelor pad.

Mitzi still had her surgical mask on when the Commodore and Miss Lambright entered.

"I'll only be a minute," the Commodore said to Miss Lambright. "Perhaps you and Mitzi might care to talk shop in my absence."

Mitzi was surprised. She kind of felt sorry for Miss Lambright sometimes, but they really didn't have anything to talk about. Or so she thought until she heard what Miss Lambright had to say.

"Jane said that?" Mitzi said. Through the surgical mask the words came out like "Ane ed at."

"That's what she said," Miss Lambright said. "She said the holocaust was exaggerated. I heard it with my own ears, in our Bible study group."

Mitzi flung off her surgical mask, picked up the phone, and dialed Mogie's office.

"Mitzi baby, I've been waiting all morning. Hang on. Okay. You're driving me foolish—"

"No, you're driving *me* foolish, schmuck face. Your little shikseh's been mouthing off again. This time she says the holocaust's exaggerated. I thought you were gonna put a muzzle on that trap of hers."

"What if she's right? How do you know for a fact that it all happened like they say it did?"

"Because my own grandmother's got numbers tattooed on her arm! That's how I know it happened! You're such a self-loather, Moges, you know that? That little bitch has you brainwashed. Wait. Hold on a sec."

Mitzi held the phone under her chin so she could hear Miss Lambright. "What else she say?"

"Well, she once said that Great Neck was nothing but a bunch of bagels."

"She calls us bagels! Oh my gawd!"

"Look, Mitz, I'm sure this is a misunderstanding. We can talk about it on our date."

"No, Moges, the date's off. I've told you before it's either me or your little shikseh. This is the last straw."

The Commodore and Johnson came out of the bachelor pad just as Mitzi hung up on Mogie. Johnson looked pale. "I can't believe Mogie found his Jewish captain. Captain Tannenbaume, I forgot all about him. Well, if it's any consolation to me, I'm being replaced with the best. He's the best, ain't he? That's what they say anyway."

The Commodore cleared his throat and spoke so that Mitzi could hear.

"Captain Tannenbaume is a respected member of the International Brotherhood of American Merchant Marine Officers. His mother, Mrs. Tannenbaume, lives right here in Great Neck, in fact."

Mitzi saw the Commodore look imploringly at her when he said it. She held the Commodore's gaze for a moment and then looked away, snapping her gum.

"I've heard of Mrs. Tannenbaume." Mitzi turned to look directly at the Commodore when she said it. "We go to the same synagogue."

The Commodore was gonna owe her big time. It was high time somebody did.

The Commodore, his back to Johnson, closed his eyes when he heard Mitzi say she went to the same synagogue as Mrs. Tannenbaume. It worked. His POA worked. His heart was in his throat and he did not trust himself to speak or move. Was he really on the cusp of ridding himself of the man who had stood in his way all these years? Johnson had proven to be a staunch nemesis. So many improprieties covered up by his toadies, peccadilloes too numerous to mention glossed over by a chauvinistic board. Well, the board would not be able to cover this one up. Mitzi had a picture of Johnson standing in front of her desk with his trousers around his ankles! If the board did not go along with removing Johnson, the photograph would end up on the front page of *Newsday*.

There clearly were a few more hoops to jump through, but the Commodore would handle them with ease. The best thing he could do was to keep Mogie as far away as possible from Johnson and the board. He would handle the board himself. The Commodore marveled at his continued climb up the ladder of the academy. *It all began with desire. If one desired something, really desired it, it was all but there for the taking. Too many people failed to achieve things of any consequence in life, not for lack of ability, but for lack of desire. The average person looked out at the world and never got past fulfilling his basic needs.* The Commodore's formula for success worked over and over again: first comes desire, then comes a plan, then comes action, what the Commodore called follow-through. The Commodore excelled at following through on his POA.

The Commodore opened his eyes and looked at Mitzi. He mouthed the words "bless you." Mitzi's reaction, her face all but covered by the surgical mask, was difficult to read, though her eyes were definitely cold. But it hardly mattered if Mitzi's reaction did not give the Commodore a warm and fuzzy feeling. She was, after all, his co-conspirator now. They were, for all practical purposes, bedfellows.

The Commodore turned back to face Johnson. He spoke in a hushed tone, as if trying to keep the hired help from overhearing their business. "Well, sir, I am sorry to give you the news. I will endeavor to keep you informed as things progress."

"I'm not waiting for things to progress, Bobby. I'm out of here. Why prolong the agony? Besides, I wouldn't want to give Mogie the satisfaction of kicking me out on my ass. I'll do it my way." Johnson looked at Mitzi with disgust. "You never could type a lick anyhow, Mitzi, not that I would give you the satisfaction of taking down my resignation letter." He looked at Miss Lambright. "Mind if I borrow your secretary, Bobby?"

"Might it be better to write the letter longhand, old boy? Take your time with it?"

"I haven't written my own letters in twenty years and I'm not about to start now. Come, Miss Lambright. This'll only take a minute."

Mitzi opened her drawer and took out a brand-new surgical mask, still in its plastic wrapper. "Take this, babe," Mitzi said to Miss Lambright. "It's never been used. Trust me, you're gonna need it."

Johnson rushed over to Mitzi's desk, ripped the surgical mask out of her hands, and slammed it on top of the metal filing cabinet. "No, she will not need one of your goddamn surgical masks! I paid good money for this cologne. It's *Midnight Musk*. It's advertised in all the sports magazines!"

"What sport? Mud wrestling?"

"Mitzi, you've gone too far. I will not stand for this, this, this insubordination. You're fired!"

Mitzi looked at the Commodore. Her eyes were cold.

"You can't fire me. I need the health benefits. Insurance companies don't like to cover dry cleaners on account of all the chemicals, you know what I'm saying?" Mitzi said it directly to the Commodore.

Now it was the Commodore who turned pale. His plan was falling apart before his very eyes. He nodded his head for Johnson to join him for a tête-à-tête a few feet away from Mitzi. He lowered his voice to a whisper.

"Surely you don't mean it, sir. Things could get awfully sticky for you. She is Mogie's mistress and you know the sway a mistress holds over a man."

Johnson did not bother to lower his voice. He poked his finger in the Commodore's chest. "I do mean it. I'm not working another day with that bitch."

"Shhhh!" The Commodore turned to see if Mitzi heard what Johnson had just called her. If she did hear, it didn't seem to bother her in the least. The Commodore turned back to Johnson. "Look, sir, there must be something—"

Johnson pushed the Commodore away. "Come on, Miss Lambright. I need you to take down a letter for me."

"That's it!" The Commodore swept around on his heels. He held up his hand to stop Miss Lambright. "The perfect solution." He turned back to Johnson. "Why don't we swap secretaries? You take Miss Lambright and I'll take Mitzi."

"Why would you want Mitzi?" Johnson said. "She can't type Cat."

The Commodore ignored Johnson's provocation. His sense about Mitzi —her poor grammar and numerous malapropisms aside—was that she was as capable a woman as he had ever met. "It is an elegant solution, is it not?" The Commodore again pulled Johnson away for a quick word. "Hell hath no fury like the wrath of a woman's scorn, sir. Need I remind you?"

The Commodore saw Johnson's nostrils flare. The man was clearly distracted. "Perhaps you're right, Bobby." Johnson was looking over the Commodore's shoulder when he said it.

The Commodore turned to see what Johnson was looking at. He saw Miss Lambright tuck a single strand of hair behind her ear. She averted her eyes and looked at the floor. Was this former librarian being coquettish? The Commodore heard Johnson breathing behind him, felt old Johnson's Johnson's hot breath on his neck.

The Commodore winced. *Oh, Miss Lambright. What have I done?*

Chapter 22

SUSPECTFULLY REMITTED

"**R**ight this way, my dear," Johnson said over his shoulder to Miss Lambright as he hurried over to the sitting area with the red leather couch and pink velour love seat. He needed to get the indignity of his resignation letter over with as soon as possible.

When Johnson reached his favorite chair, he turned around and was surprised to see his new secretary standing naked before him, her discarded clothes marking a trail back to the door.

The thought occurred to him that she was much shorter without her pumps on. Also, she looked different with her hair down—older, not as cute.

Miss Lambright lunged at him. Johnson's gold buttons popped off his starched polyester summer whites. Miss Lambright tore his shirt open, undid his belt buckle, and unzipped his trousers in a single movement. She then pushed him into the love seat and jumped in his lap.

Johnson arched his back in the love seat. "Down, girl, down."

Miss Lambright pumped up and down on Johnson's lap. After several minutes of pumping with no discernable reaction from Johnson, she stopped, picked up her breasts with both hands, and pushed them into his face. Miss Lambright's ampleness smothered Johnson.

He shoved her away. "Hey, slow down."

Miss Lambright pushed out her lower lip. "What's the matter, big fella?"

"Nothing's the matter!"

"But I've heard so much about you. About how you're the biggest."

"I am. Just not now. We have work to do. I'm trying to resign here."

"Fine. I just heard you were the biggest is all."

Miss Lambright got dressed while Johnson put his uniform back on. They did not talk or look at each other. When Miss Lambright was all buttoned up with her hair in a bun, she turned to leave.

"Please don't leave," Johnson said. He'd never disappointed a woman before. He didn't like how it felt and really wouldn't like how it felt if word got out.

"No, you had your chance."

"Please."

"I thought you wanted to resign."

"I do want to resign."

"I'm ready to take down your letter then."

"Right. Work first, then play. You're so cute with your hair up. Okay. My resignation letter. Here goes. 'Dear Board.'"

"What?"

"I said, 'Dear Board.'"

"Who's bored?"

"The Board of Governors."

"The governors are bored?"

"What are you talking about, Miss Lambright? You're not making sense. Please don't interrupt. And don't repeat what I say, just take it down.

"Dear Board of Governors."

Dear Bored Governors

"I regret to inform you."

I get to reform you

"That I hereby resign."

That I'm here to buy a sign

"A desire to be with my family."

Being tired with my family

"Is at the heart of my decision."

Is the art of indecision

"Respectfully Submitted."

Suspectfully remitted

"You can sign my name for me."

Nine remain for me

"Excellent, Miss Lambright. Type it up on my letterhead. Oh, and title the letter 'Letter of Resignation.' Go ahead and use my computer."

It took Miss Lambright twenty minutes to type the two sentences. Johnson watched in amazement as she pecked at the computer, mumbling over and over about how her computer was different. When she finally handed the resignation letter to Johnson, he did not bother to read it before he signed it.

He placed the signed resignation letter on his desk and then rubbed his hands together. "Now, where were we, dear?"

Johnson reached over and pinched Miss Lambright.

She backed up and placed the love seat between them. "Actually, I'd prefer to go back to the Commodore. I never thought I'd say that but I do."

"The Commodore? But he's a fruitcake."

"At least he's got follow-through. That's what he says anyway."

"But I've got follow-through, too! You never gave me a chance, taking off my clothes like that, jumping in my lap. What man could respond to that kind of pressure? That's the problem with women today, they're too aggressive. But I thought you were different. You looked like a nice librarian. You looked like a woman a man could pursue."

"I don't want to be pursued."

"You don't?"

"No. A real woman wants to get down to business. Maybe a drink or two first, but that's it."

"Oh. Will scotch do?"

"Scotch will do fine, my little hunter." Miss Lambright undid a strand of her hair.

Johnson poured a tumbler full of Dewars for Miss Lambright. When she finished it, he poured another, and then another, matching her drink for drink. He needed to loosen up. Besides, his first chance with Miss Lambright had been too easy. There was no chase, no thrill of the hunt. Johnson liked to be the aggressor—it kept his skills sharp. When a woman made the first move, he got nervous and then he had . . . trouble. That's why he liked younger women—they were meek in his presence. He watched Miss Lambright undo another strand of her hair. Johnson had to strike before she made the first move again. He tickled her ribs.

"No! I'm ticklish."

Johnson moved in for the kill. He chased her around the pink velour love seat. When he caught her, he tickled her some more.

Miss Lambright sprang loose and ran around the red leather couch and then the rickety director's chairs. They played cat and mouse with his big desk, then again around the leather couch until Miss Lambright surrendered. Johnson undid the top button of her blouse. Miss Lambright pretended to put up a fight.

"No, stop."

"You do know I'm the biggest, don't you?"

"So I've heard."

Miss Lambright's tanned skin glowed in the afternoon sunlight streaming through Johnson's office window. Her breasts, supported by her wonder bra, were gorgeous, the color of all that Dewar's scotch they just drank. Miss Lambright undid her bra.

"No," Johnson said. He liked them better pushed up. He put his arms around Miss Lambright and fumbled with the hasp on the back of Miss Lambright's brassiere. He never did get the hang of undoing a woman's bra, not even after all these years, and now he had to figure out how to put the damn thing back on. Miss Lambright fought to take the bra off while Johnson struggled to clip it back together.

"Hey," Miss Lambright said, "what are you doing?"

"Just give me a sec," Johnson said.

He turned Miss Lambright around and peered at the lock and hasp mechanism. It looked easy enough, but his big hands just could not grab the little hasp.

"Hey, it's already off, what are you doing back there?"

Miss Lambright jerked away, causing one of her breasts to fall out of its cup. Johnson scooped it up and tried to stuff it back in place, but the bra strap slipped off Miss Lambright's shoulder, so Johnson grabbed the cup with his other hand, slapped it on Miss Lambright's breast, and held it in place while he tried to get her arm through the strap.

"Hey! Are you trying to take this thing off or put it back on?"

Johnson pushed Miss Lambright's arm through the strap, and instead of dealing with the lock and hasp, he simply tied the two straps in a square knot. This pushed her breasts up even more, which Johnson liked. But in the fight to put her bra back on, Johnson had undone Miss Lambright's tight hair bun.

"Oh no," Johnson said.

Putting Miss Lambright's hair back into a bun proved even more arduous than putting her breasts back into her bra. Miss Lambright's tight little bun was now a beehive.

Johnson grabbed Miss Lambright by the shoulders and held her out at arm's length to have a good look at her. She was all out of focus. He pushed her from side to side to change the way the light fell on her and peered at her with one eye closed.

Miss Lambright allowed herself to be pushed around like a rag doll.

"You like what you see, big boy?" The word "see" came out all slurry and her knees nearly gave way when she said it.

"You'd better come with me, Miss Lambright. I think you've been over-served."

Johnson ushered Miss Lambright into his office and slapped his hand on the secret book in the bookcase. The Murphy bed plopped out of the wall, Johnson plopped onto the bed, and Miss Lambright fell facedown into the silk sheets and curled herself into a ball by his side. Miss Lambright's beehive brushed up against Johnson's nose and made him sneeze one time before he fell asleep as well.

The two sleeping beauties did not notice the Commodore walk in a moment later. The Commodore had his camera with him and wasted no time snapping a few photos of Johnson and Miss Lambright with her messy hair in the Murphy bed. On his way out, the Commodore snatched Johnson's resignation letter off his desk and tucked it under his arm.

His POA was proceeding unimpeded.

Chapter 23

SYLVIA'S MY NAME

Mrs. Tannenbaume got the stepladder out of the garage herself. She couldn't wait a minute longer for Midshipman Jones to show up. Umbriago! The garage looked like Hogan's Alley. She'd been meaning to clean it out, she just hadn't gotten around to it what with everything else going on in her life at the moment.

"I'm crazy busy," she told her friend Roz earlier over coffee. "Crazy busy." First she's told that her son is going to be the next superintendent of the Merchant Marine Academy, and that they're going to make him an admiral, no less. Then she finds out from Florence, the gal who works in the home office of the shipping company that owned the *God is Able*, that her sonny boy just married a Thai bar girl.

Flo didn't use the word "bar girl," but come on, love, who's kidding whom? After sixty years on this earth, her sonny boy finally finds Miss Right and she's a nineteen-year-old Thai girl working in Singapore? Mrs. Tannenbaume told Roz that she didn't just fall off the back of a turnip cart. "I've been around, lovey, and no one is going to tell me that a nineteen-year-old Thai girl working in Singapore is anything but a two-bit tramp."

She was always afraid that her sonny boy would do this. She knew he carried on when he was at sea—she heard him talking on the phone with his other shipping buddies when he was home between voyages. The dispatcher at the Union Hall told her that seamen who stayed on the South American run for too long usually ended up having a girlfriend in every port. The love run, seamen called it. The love run didn't pay spit, but the women more than make up for the lousy pay. Captain Tannenbaume had stayed on the love run from New York to Rio for over twenty years. Her sonny boy was what was known as a "shore hound," the union officials down at the hall told Mrs. Tannenbaume, and that's why he had no money.

If her sonny boy knew she had gone down to the Union Hall to see about him getting on higher-paying ships, he would have threw a fit. But what else could she do? She knew that officers in the merchant marine made good money and she just couldn't understand why her sonny boy sent home such meager allotment checks. He kept telling her that only the captain made any money and everybody else worked for slave wages. But when he finally became captain, he sent home even less. That's because as captain, he was able to spend even more time ashore, whereas as chief mate, he was practically glued to the deck when the ship was in port.

"He spends money like a drunken sailor, is all there is to it," she told Roz. "Not that he's a drunk—he hardly ever touches the stuff—it's the carrying on when he's in port, the hoo hoo and the ha ha, that's where all the money goes." Mrs. Tannenbaume knew it to be true—her sonny boy couldn't hide it from her. But it's not as if the apple fell far from the tree. One of Captain Tannenbaume's fathers was a sailor and look what he did? Carrying on in a South African port with a seventeen-year-old girl. Of course, he himself was only nineteen at the time. That was a little different than being sixty years old and carrying on with a nineteen-year-old bar girl.

Mrs. Tannenbaume lugged the stepladder out of the garage, through the kitchen, and into the hall. She opened the door to the upstairs, Captain

Tannenbaume's room when he was young, before she turned it into an upstairs apartment for Mr. Schwartz. She missed Mr. Schwartz. She always knew the angina would get him in the end. After he'd passed on during the excitement of a canasta game a couple of weeks ago, she took his stuff—clothes mostly, also a clock radio, his TV, his collection of handball gloves—down to the St. Aloysius. The kids had yard sales from time to time and they were always looking for stuff to sell.

Mrs. Tannenbaume dragged the stepladder up the stairs, bouncing its weight on every step. The house was dormerless, so the upstairs apartment had little headroom. It hadn't bothered Mr. Schwartz, who was short, but her sonny boy, who was tall, finally had to move out of the house when he was in his forties—he kept hitting his head on the slope of the ceiling. He told his mother that his stateroom aboard ship was bigger than the entire upstairs of her house. Plus, he had no place to store any of his stuff. The attic was the only storage space in the whole house and Mrs. Tannenbaume kept it padlocked. Whenever her sonny boy asked her what she kept in there, she said, "My past."

When she became pregnant and told her father that the baby's father could have been any one of three boys—Eddie, Teddy, or Freddie—her father disowned her. Her mother told her it was best if she left home to have the baby. America, her mother had insisted. "Find the next ship going to America and get on it." That was so long ago. Mrs. Tannenbaume set up the ladder below the door to the attic. She sat on the bottom rung and took a moment to catch her breath. She wasn't exactly a spring chicken any longer. *Where, oh where, did the years go?*

She had not opened the padlock to the attic in . . . forever. When was the last time? Could it have been when she moved in fifty years ago? Was that possible? She still had the key. She kept it in the drawer in the side table next to her bed, and she'd had the same bed, the same side table, the same lamp for sixty years. When you grow up looking over your shoulder, you tend to want to hold on to things, things that are familiar. You want to keep what you have. Mrs. Tannenbaume's mother always told her that there was nothing more expensive than a cheap product, so Mrs. Tannenbaume bought good stuff and held on to it. Of course, her mother did not subscribe to the buy-and-hold philosophy when

Mrs. Tannenbaume was about to leave her home to have her baby. No, then her mother advised her to leave everything behind. Everything.

Including her faith.

"It's too hard being a Jew," her mother told her. When Mrs. Tannenbaume's father took his family to Durban after Kristallnacht, her mother wanted to live anonymously. "Why do we have to be Jewish here?" her mother asked. "Why can't we tell people that it's Tannenbaume with an E, that we're not Jewish, that we're German? We can join the Reformed Church and act like good Protestants. Our life will be easier, and we won't have to live in fear." Mrs. Tannenbaume's father would not hear of it. They were Jews, he said. There's no running away from that. It's a fact, like being tall or short, it's how you are born. Mrs. Tannenbaume's mother had said, "Fine, you want to be a Jew? Be a Jew. But don't drag me into, I'm tired of being persecuted, tired of running away. I want to live in peace. I don't want to be a Jew anymore."

It was her father who insisted that Mrs. Tannenbaume become a Bat Mitzvah. Oh, the fights her parents had over that. Her father shouted that his only child would become a daughter of the Commandment and no one would stand in his way. In the end, Mrs. Tannenbaume's mother didn't stand in the way, but she surely didn't help either. A Bat Mitzvah must read from the Torah, and Mrs. Tannenbaume's *haftarah* reading was from the book of the prophet Malachi and it was long. Too long. Her father was strict and he made her practice for long hours in preparation for her Bat Mitzvah ceremony. Mrs. Tannenbaume needed help learning Hebrew, but her father was too busy and her mother refused to speak it, so it was left to her father's assistant, who was also the local cantor. He chanted Hebrew along with Mrs. Tannenbaume in the shop. The cantor played the guitar, and when he and Mrs. Tannenbaume were finished practicing, he would sing fun songs, shanties that he learned from the seafarers who came into the shop looking for uniforms and work clothes. They were the same songs her father remembered from the docks of Bremerhaven. He would have preferred that the cantor get back to work, but since it reminded him of home, he let the cantor play on.

When a ship from Edinburgh pulled into port and the sailors could not pay for their uniforms, the ship's agent coerced the captain to give up his bagpipes. Mrs. Tannenbaume's father had no use for a set of bagpipes and was about to give them back to the agent when he saw the cantor fooling with them. He was grateful to the cantor for teaching his daughter Hebrew so he gave the bagpipes to the cantor. Mrs. Tannenbaume loved the sound of the bagpipes, loved the ethereal way the Jewish folk songs sounded on them. When the Scots or the Irish came down to the shop looking for clothes, the cantor would pull out his pipes and play for them. The sailors laughed at the sight of an old Jew and a pretty young girl singing shanties.

Mrs. Tannenbaume remembered the three long years of preparation for her Bat Mitzvah, three years in her father's tailor shop while her friends played at the seaside where it was cool and breezy. When Mrs. Tannenbaume's big day arrived, her mother refused to attend, and when Mrs. Tannenbaume came home, her mother ignored her beaming daughter and didn't offer so much as a *Mazel Tov* to the family's new Jewess.

Mrs. Tannenbaume teetered on the top step of the ladder. The lock would not open. She tried to pull the key out but it was stuck. Mrs. Tannenbaume climbed down the ladder and went downstairs to get some WD-40. She was on the ladder spraying the lubricant into the lock when she heard Midshipman Jones. "Up here, love," she called.

When Midshipman Jones came upstairs and saw Mrs. Tannenbaume sitting on the top step, he grabbed the ladder with both hands.

"What are you doing up there with no one holding the ladder? Why didn't you wait for me?"

"I got tired of waiting, love. I'm anxious to get inside of this attic again. You know I think it may have been sixty years since I last opened this lock?"

"I believe it, by the looks of it."

Mrs. Tannenbaume fiddled with the key.

"Why don't you let me give it a try?" Midshipman Jones said.

When Midshipman Jones inspected the lock, he said, "I better be careful with—oh shoot." He held the key up. It had broken off in his hand. "The other half of the key is stuck in the lock. Sorry about that, Mrs. Tannenbaume. I can run back to the academy and get some tools to pry it off."

Mrs. Tannenbaume sat down on a chair and looked up at Midshipman Jones on the ladder. She sighed. Suddenly, she was very tired.

"Oh the heck with it," she said. "Some other time. I just wanted to look at some old stuff I have up there. We don't have to do it today."

"What kind of stuff do you keep up there anyway?"

The phone rang before Mrs. Tannenbaume had a chance to answer him. She stood up and asked Midshipman Jones to take the ladder back down to the garage for her. She said that she would call him when she felt like getting up there again.

Mrs. Tannenbaume reached the phone on its fifth ring. Most people didn't wait that long these days. She wondered who could be calling.

"Yello?"

"Hello, Mother?"

"Hello, love!"

"Mother, I'm calling on the SATCOM from the ship, so we can't talk long, it's godawful expensive."

"You could afford to call your mother if you didn't carry on the way you do."

"Yes, well, be that as it may, I won't be carrying on anymore. Mother, I got married in Singapore."

Even though Mrs. Tannenbaume had already heard the news from Flo, it still felt like she was hearing it for the first time.

"Mother? Are you there?"

Mrs. Tannenbaume's throat went dry.

"Mother?"

"Yes, love."

"Did you hear what I said? I got married."

"So I've heard."

"You know? Who told you?"

"The gal from your office called. Flo."

"Who told her to call?"

"I figured you did. I figured you were ashamed to call me yourself."

"Ashamed, Mother? I've got nothing to be ashamed about. Sylvia's a nice girl."

"Her name is really Sylvia? A Thai girl named Sylvia?"

"That's what she likes to be called, Mother. You should be flattered she picked the same name as yours."

"I'll never call her Sylvia. Sylvia Tannenbaume is my name. She can't have my name."

They were silent for a few seconds. It was Captain Tannenbaume who spoke up again.

"I thought you would be happy for me, Mother. I know how much you've hated my carrying-on."

"I wait sixty years for you to find your Carmen and you bring me this? A nineteen-year-old Thai girl?"

"She comes from a fine family."

"The same fine family she sends money home to? And exactly how does she earn this money, may I ask?"

Another pause.

"Mother, this call is expensive. I just wanted you to know."

"I have some news as well."

"Oh? What's that?"

"They want to make you superintendent of the academy."

"What academy?"

"The Merchant Marine Academy."

"Kings Point? You must be joking. Who told you this?"

"The Commodore told me himself."

"The Commodore? You act like you know him."

"He comes into the dry cleaners. He likes the way we do his shirts."

Mrs. Tannenbaume sat on the couch and curled her feet under her legs. "Sonny, how can you do this to me?"

"Oh, Mother."

"Don't Oh Mother me. What am I going to tell the Commodore now? That my sonny boy would love to be the superintendent but that he wants to bring his Thai whore with him."

"Mother, don't ever call Sylvia that again. She's my wife."

"What do I tell the Commodore?"

"Tell him anything you like. I don't want to be superintendent anyway. I like being captain."

Mrs. Tannenbaume uncrossed her legs and got up off the couch. "Are you *meshuggener*? Nobody in their right mind would turn down the job. Think of it. The same school that turned you down now wants you to be the head honcho. Why would you say no?"

"I don't know, Mother, I'll have to think about it. I've been on these ships for a long time. It might be nice to get a shoreside gig, come to think of it."

"You call it a gig? Superintendent of the United States Merchant Marine Academy? Please, sonny, please say you'll take the job."

"I'll think about it, Mother. I'll have to talk it over with my wife."

It sounded funny to hear her sonny boy refer to his "wife."

"I won't call her Sylvia," Mrs. Tannenbaume said.

"Okay, Mother, this call has cost enough. My ship gets into New York in mid-October. I'll see you then. We sail from Singapore in a few days. Bye, please."

Mrs. Tannenbaume fell onto the couch. She had been hoping all along that somehow Flo was wrong. What wishful thinking that was. Mrs. Tannenbaume was sick. Sick at the thought of this turn of events. *What on earth would the Commodore say when he heard the news?* Mrs. Tannenbaume had to tell him. She couldn't just let her sonny boy show up as the next superintendent of the academy with a teenager on his arm.

Chapter 24

A HANDSHAKE DEAL

The Commodore was practicing his breathing when Mogie burst into his office. The Commodore preferred to meditate standing up in front of the big mirror, and the unexpected sight of Mogie in the mirror made the Commodore choke on his own Infinity breath, upsetting his whole chakra. Mogie ran up to the Commodore and stopped directly behind him, glaring at him in the mirror.

"Where the hell is Mitzi?" Mogie said.

The Commodore felt dizzy. Too dizzy to respond.

"I looked for her in her office and some librarian was sitting at her desk. She told me Mitzi works for you now. Where the hell is she?"

The Commodore's head reeled. "My chakra!"

"Your what?"

"You've upset my chakra!"

Mogie whirled in place and looked at the floor around him.

"Who's Chakra? Your dog?"

Mogie got on all fours and looked under the Commodore's desk. "Here, Chakra. Come here, girl."

The Commodore saw Mitzi enter the office. They locked eyes in the mirror.

"Am I hearing things?" she said. "I thought I just heard Mogie's voice."

"Come here, Chakra. Where are you, girl?"

Mitzi looked under the Commodore's desk and saw Mogie on his hands and knees. When Mogie crawled out from under the desk, Mitzi stood over him.

"What the hell are you doing down there?"

Mogie looked up at Mitzi. "I'm looking for the Commodore's dog. He says I upset her."

"The Commodore ain't got a dog. What the hell are you talking about, Moges?"

Mogie stood up and brushed off his pants. "He said I upset his Chakra."

"His Chak—" Mitzi slapped Mogie in the back of the head. "He's talking about his *chakra,* you dope. You interrupted him while he was meditating."

"But I found him standing in front of the mirror." Mogie looked at Mitzi and then at the Commodore in the mirror. "Who the hell meditates standing in front of the mirror?"

Mitzi walked over to the Commodore and caressed his face. "Poor, baby. Why don't you finish your breathing here at your desk? It'll be safer."

"Maybe I should." The Commodore glared at Mogie. "But he has to leave."

Mitzi turned around and grabbed Mogie by the elbow. "Come on. The Commodore has to finish his Infinity breath."

"What the hell is an Infinity breath?"

"He learned it in yoga," Mitzi said. "Let's go."

Mogie looked over his shoulder at the Commodore as Mitzi dragged him out of the room. "Sorry to interrupt your yoga breath, Commodore."

Mitzi closed the door behind her. When they were alone in the outer office, Mogie broke free of her grasp.

"What the hell are you doing putting words in Jane's mouth? She says she never said anything about the holocaust."

"Well that's what I heard," Mitzi said.

"Who the hell told you that?"

"None of your business. Besides, if she didn't say it, she easily could have, the Nazi bitch."

"Hey, Jane may be a Catholic, but she's no Nazi."

"Oh yeah? Then why's she got that little fish on the back of her car?"

"What little fish?"

"That little fish symbol on her rear bumper. It's like a modern-day swastika."

"Who told you that?"

"Don't be so naïve, Mog—wait a sec, hold on, I think I hear the Commodore."

The Commodore poked his head around his office door. "Mitzi. Let's do the Toe Hang now."

His Toe Hang. Right. The Commodore used to practice his Toe Hang on the stage in the auditorium until Mitzi suggested he do it in the privacy of his office. *The loony bastard loved the idea.* Mitzi snickered to herself. She had brought in her aerobic stepper—Mogie wasn't using it and Putzie never did get the hang of it—so that he could stand on it in front of the mirror and hang his toes over the edge and really become one with his imaginary audience. Mitzi sat at his desk and critiqued him. What a cake job that was.

She glanced at Mogie. What if Mogie were to hear her critiquing the Commodore on his Toe Hang? This could be fun . . .

"What the hell is a Toe Hang?"

Mitzi didn't answer Mogie. Instead, she closed the door in his face. Then she went and sat on the edge of the Commodore's desk while he set up the stepper.

"A little bit to the side, Commodore," she said, louder than usual.

"How's that?"

"A little louder, Commodore," Mitzi whispered.

"I said how's that?"

"That's it. Right there. No, in a little more. That's it."

"That feels good right there," the Commodore said.

"That's it, baby, right there. You've got my attention now."

"We truly are one, now, are we not, Miss Paultz?"

Mitzi cooed.

In a few minutes, they were done. The Commodore took the stepper and placed it under his desk. He told Mitzi that now was as good a time as ever to tell Mogie about Captain Tannenbaume. He asked her to bring him into his office.

Mitzi found Mogie pacing outside the office door. Beads of sweat ran down his forehead. When he saw Mitzi, he got right in her face. "What the hell was going on in there?"

"None of your business."

Mogie's neck bulged. A knotty vein shot up to his temple like mercury in a thermometer.

Mitzi turned her back on him and said over her shoulder, "Come on in. The Commodore has something to tell you."

Mogie stormed into the office and sat himself in the chair in front of the Commodore's desk. His neck was a forest of gnarly veins. The Commodore, on the other hand, sat at his desk looking quite pleased with himself.

"I must say, Ms. Paultz, that aerobic stepper of yours is a handy device," the Commodore said, as if Mitzi had scripted it. "How clever of you to suggest it."

The Commodore nudged the stepper with his foot and smiled at Mitzi. Mogie looked down at the aerobic stepper under the Commodore's desk and his eyes nearly came out of their sockets. Mitzi, who was standing beside the Commodore's desk, put her hands out in front of her. Maybe the fun had gone a bit too far. "Easy, Moges. It ain't what you're thinking."

The Commodore continued with his sincere compliment. "I mean, what can I say? I'm in heaven when my toes are hanging off that stepper."

Mogie's hands were around Mitzi's neck before she knew what was happening. Mitzi, though, was considerably taller than he and that gave her the leverage to beat him back.

"Get your goddamn paws off me, Moges, it ain't what you think!"

"He was using my stool!"

"He was only practicing his Toe Hang!"

Mogie came at Mitzi again, shoving her up against the wall to get a better hold of her.

"A Toe Hang? You call it a Toe Hang!"

The son of a bitch was hurting her. Mitzi choked right back, digging her nails into Mogie's neck. "It's not what you call it, Moges, it's how you do it that counts!"

The Commodore sat at his desk while Mitzi and Mogie fought. *Remarkable*. He knew his Toe Hang had come a long way, but, still, it surprised him that a man like Mogie could be so insanely jealous of it. Well, to be fair to himself, it *was* an effective technique. And not something that just any man could do. Only the most dexterous of leaders had the wherewithal to become one with an audience of average Joes. The Commodore serenely watched Mitzi and Mogie scratch and claw at each other. It was more than the satisfaction of possessing an enviable Toe Hang. His POA called for him to keep Mitzi and Mogie at odds with each other, and he had obviously touched on a point of contention between the two of them. Mogie kept calling it *his* stool.

But of course! The aerobic stepper. How on earth could the Commodore have forgotten? Mitzi's aerobic stepper was the same stepper that Mogie used to service his paramour and the same stepper that Mrs. Tannenbaume had used in her sex ed class with Putzie. That he utilized the sordid stepper for his own lofty purposes was repugnant, repugnant indeed, but he was also pleased at the result the stepper had unwittingly wrought. Mitzi and Mogie were at each other's throats, quite literally.

The Commodore stood up from his desk and approached Mogie. "Mr. Mayor, pardon me, sir."

The battle went on.

The Commodore finally had to separate Mogie from Mitzi by placing his physical superiority between them.

"Mr. Mayor, I did not call you here to my office, you've come of your own volition. But now that you are here, there is some business for us to discuss." The Commodore led Mogie back to the chair in front of his desk. "Will you please have a seat, sir?"

Mogie took his seat and glared at Mitzi. "The Commodore and I've got business to discuss, Mitzi. Beat it."

Mitzi looked at the Commodore, the Commodore nodded his head, and Mitzi left the room. When Mogie and the Commodore were alone, Mogie spoke up first.

"Boy, you WASPs are too much. Any port in a storm, isn't that your expression? And using another man's stool—is nothing sacred with you people?"

"All's fair in love and war, is it not, Mogie? Do you mind if I call you Mogie?"

"You're acting awfully sure of yourself, Commodore."

"Well, I merely assumed that since we are now business partners, we might want to be on more familiar terms."

"Since when did we become partners?"

"Since I've lived up to my end of our business deal, that's when."

"You found a Jew captain?"

"I have indeed, sir."

Mogie showed no reaction. He reached in his pocket for his cigar. The Commodore wagged his finger at Mogie, but he stuck the cigar in his mouth anyway.

"I think better with a cigar in my mouth."

"What is there to think about? You said to find a Jewish captain. I've found one."

"I'm just thinking is all." Mogie stood up, walked to the window, and looked out at the water. After a moment, he returned to his chair in front of the Commodore's desk. He stared at the Commodore for a long time without saying anything.

The Commodore could tell that Mogie was trying to sniff out a rat. *Well, two can play that game.* The Commodore remained coy.

It was Mogie who spoke next. "So this means we finally get rid of Johnson?"

The Commodore's heart leapt. He tried not to let his excitement show. "Precisely."

"So what do we know about this guy? What's his name?"

"His name is Captain Tannenbaume. He is a respected member of the International Brotherhood of American Merchant Marine Officers. His curriculum vitae is quite impressive."

"Tannenbaume, huh? My dentist's name is Tannenbaume. Yeah, Tannenbaume, that sounds good. So when do we make the switch?"

"Captain Tannenbaume is on a ship presently. The ship is en route to New York as we speak, due to arrive mid-October, just in time for the unveiling of the Mariners Monument."

"And what about Johnson? Is he gonna go quietly or what?"

"In fact, I have in my possession a resignation letter from Johnson. He is all too aware that a superior adversary has bested him."

That was clearly all Mogie needed to hear. It was written all over his face. Yes, the Commodore knew how to play Mogie. *When a man has an ego as large as Mogie's, it is so easy to use it against him.*

"You're goddamn right he's been beat," Mogie said. "Nobody beats Mogie. Nobody. I'm gonna go into business with some *schmuck Goy*—no offense, Commodore. This arrangement is much better for you too. Trust me, you'll be better off in the long run. Look, I know you wanted to be admiral, but just let me and Tannenbaume run things. Okay? I've told you you'll get your cut of the action. The dry cleaning alone'll be worth millions. We're gonna soak the government for all it's worth."

Mogie stood up. He stuck his hand out across the Commodore's desk. The Commodore shook Mogie's hand.

"That's all you'll need, Commodore. A handshake from Mogie is all you'll need. Me and Tannenbaume'll run things. You just keep the WASPs off our backs. What an arrangement, huh? This is gonna be great."

Mogie went on about how he was going to run the Merchant Marine Academy like a business, not like some Moose lodge. The Commodore was not listening. He needed to find a way to end the meeting—the less they talked about Tannenbaume, the better. Fortunately, Mitzi came to the rescue. Her voice broke in over the intercom.

"Commodore, pick up please."

The Commodore reached over and answered the phone.

"You're not going to believe this, sir, but Mrs. Tannenbaume just called. She's on her way over. I tried to tell her that now was not a good time but she wouldn't listen."

The Commodore's fist clenched the phone. Mitzi, bless her, remained calm.

"We gotta get Mogie the hell out of here," Mitzi said. "I'm coming in."

"Very well," the Commodore managed to say.

Mitzi walked into the office carrying a clipboard. She walked up to the Commodore all business. "You asked me to help keep you on schedule, Commodore. Well, we have a meeting with the dean. It's time to go."

The Commodore had not even hung up the phone yet. Mitzi walked over and took the phone out of his hand. She opened his drawer and took out the Commodore's sheaf of phony papers. Then Mitzi took the Commodore by the hand and said, "Let's go."

The Commodore got to his feet and allowed Mitzi to lead him out of the office.

Mitzi said to Mogie on the way out, "Sorry to end your meeting so fast, but we gotta go see the dean."

Mogie jumped to his feet. "You didn't end the meeting, Mitz. The meeting was already over." He followed right behind Mitzi. "The Commodore and I are going to be partners. We found ourselves a Jew captain." Mogie's words came out in a rush, without belligerence.

"Good for you, Moges."

"But, Mitz." Mogie grabbed Mitzi's arm to stop her. Mitzi stopped, but she continued to hold the Commodore by the hand.

"But what?" Mitzi said.

"Don't you see? I told you there was a Jew out there who knew how to drive a boat. We got what we wanted."

"No, Moges. *You* got what you wanted. You and I are no longer a 'we.'" Mitzi shook Mogie off. "We got a meeting with the dean. It's time for you to go. You know the way out."

Chapter 25

A SUPERNUMERARY
AND A CADET

"**Y**our son did what?"

The Commodore was back at his desk with his sheaf of papers spread out before him. Mitzi stood at the side of his desk with both arms wrapped around her clipboard. She looked down at Mrs. Tannenbaume who sat in the chair in front of the Commodore's desk.

"He went and married a Thai bar girl," Mrs. Tannenbaume said.

"He told you she was a bar girl?" Mitzi said.

"Well, he didn't come right out and say it, but who's kidding whom? She's nineteen years old and living on her own in—"

"She's nineteen?" The Commodore and Mitzi responded in unison.

"I know—it's a shock to the system. That's why I wanted you should know."

The Commodore felt his chest tighten. He was meeting with the Board of Governors tomorrow to submit Johnson's resignation letter. What would he tell the board now? That the man he found to replace Johnson was a well-regarded ship's captain who happened to have a teenager for a wife? *My god, the graduating seniors would be older than the superintendent's wife! Do I now have to tell the board that the June Ball would now be presided over by a bar girl? And what of Tannenbaume? The man's morals were flabbier than I had previously surmised.*

"And to think she has the same name as me. Whoever heard of a Thai girl named Sylvia?"

The Commodore snapped out of his stupor. "Her name is Sylvia?"

"I'll never call her that. My name is Sylvia Tannenbaume, not hers."

"You'd think her name would be Joom-Nee or something," Mitzi said.

"I'm not suprised her name is Sylvia," the Commodore said.

Mitzi and Mrs. Tannenbaume looked at each other.

"A Thai girl named Sylvia?" they chorused.

"Um, well, not a Thai girl. A Thai working girl. All ladies of the night in the seaports of the world take on an alias. A *nom de guerre*. Anglo names that the seafarers of the world can pronounce. The name Sylvia is one of the more common."

This changed things considerably. With a name like Sylvia, the Commodore could easily hide from the board the fact that Captain Tannenbaume's wife was Thai. He would merely say that Captain Tannenbaume and his wife, Sylvia, would arrive sometime in mid-October to begin their tenure as First Couple of the Merchant Marine Academy. In fact, the more he thought about it, the more the Commodore liked the idea of Captain Tannenbaume's Thai wife. Springing a nineteen-year-old Thai working girl on the board immediately before the unveiling of the Mariners Monument would make his task of scuttling Captain Tannenbaume that much easier. How could the academy unveil a hero's monument with an impostor for a superintendent and a teenage wife by his side? The Commodore felt much better.

"What's everybody here gonna think when Captain Tannenbaume shows up with a Thai wife?" Mitzi asked. "It's bad enough we have to pass Captain Tannenbaume off as Jewish. How are we gonna pass off his Thai wife as Jewish?"

"That is a good point, Ms. Paultz," the Commodore said.

"What if we tell people she converted?" Mrs. Tannenbaume said.

"The Jews in Great Neck'll see right through that," Mitzi said. "They'll ask a few questions and the girl'll get all tripped up. It'll never work."

"What if we teach her how to act Jewish?" Mrs. Tannenbaume said. "If she acts Jewish, then maybe nobody will think to try and trip her up."

The Commodore liked the way this conversation was going. He was beginning to see some intriguing possibilities.

"You yourself act Jewish, Mrs. Tannenbaume, even though you're not. I know," the Commodore put up his hand to stop Mrs. Tannenbaume's objection, "it's from living in Great Neck all these years."

"I just know a few Yiddish words is all," Mrs. Tannenbaume said.

"I do know that the Thai people are great mimics," the Commodore said. "Perhaps you can teach Sylvia some Yiddish expressions."

"But my sonny boy's ship doesn't get here until the middle of October," Mrs. Tannenbaume said. "You said that would be just in time for the unveiling of that monument of yours. You can't teach someone Yiddish in a day or two."

"What if you joined Captain Tannenbaume's ship now? You can join as a supernumerary. Teach Sylvia some Yiddish." The Commodore's heart raced.

"What?" Mitzi said. "That's the craziest thing I've ever heard. You can't make someone seem Jewish by teaching them a few words of Yiddish. It'll take more than that."

"Like what, Ms. Paultz? Be specific."

"Like . . . a lot of things. Like how to keep kosher, for starters."

"Can you teach someone how to keep kosher, Ms. Paultz?" The Commodore wiped his palm on his pant leg. He hoped Mitzi and Mrs. Tannenbaume could not see that he was sweating. He could barely contain his excitement at the idea forming in his mind.

"Of course. My family has always kept kosher."

"Well what if you joined the ship as a supernumerary as well? Between you and Mrs. Tannenbaume, surely we can turn Sylvia into a nice Jewish girl."

"What kind of ship is it?" Mitzi said. "Like a cruise ship?"

"Well, no," the Commodore said. "It's not exactly a cruise ship . . . "

"It's an old freighter," Mrs. Tannenbaume said. "My sonny boy calls it 'his 'tween decker.'"

"Is it safe?" Mitzi said.

"A 'tween decker is a classic ship design, my dear. Its integrity is beyond reproach. You don't see many of them anymore."

The Commodore knew that classic really meant "old." Mitzi would probably regard the *God is Able* as a rust bucket.

"A 'tween decker," Mitzi said. "It sounds romantic."

"Romantic, indeed, Ms. Paultz. You ought to consider joining the *God is Able* on its voyage back to the States. I'm sure it can be arranged. I have friends—former classmates—in the Maritime Administration. I'm certain we can pull some strings and get you credentialed as a supernumerary."

"Wow," Mitzi said. "A supernumerary. Putzie would be so proud of me."

"I have a standing invitation to join my sonny boy's ship," Mrs. Tannenbaume said. "I wouldn't need any arrangements. My sonny boy is the captain."

The Commodore sensed that Mrs. Tannenbaume was feeling infringed upon, as if she, and only she, had the privilege of being a supernumerary on her son's ship.

"You are correct indeed, madam. Perhaps we can arrange that Mitzi join the ship as an emissary of the academy."

"But not as supernumerary," Mrs. Tannenbaume said. "There can only be one supernumerary."

Mrs. Tannenbaume looked at Mitzi when she said it. Mitzi refused to acknowledge Mrs. Tannenbaume. She turned to the Commodore. "Well then, what would I be?"

The Commodore needed to be certain of his next move. He desperately wanted to rid himself of both Mrs. Tannenbaume and Mitzi for the next month. Mrs. Tannenbaume was too unpredictable to keep around, and he was not at all confident of his tenuous relationship with Mitzi either. Mogie continued to circle Mitzi like a shark and it was only a matter of time before they resumed their affair. And what then? Surely Mitzi would confide in Mogie that Tannenbaume was not Jewish. No, the faster Mitzi and Mrs. Tannenbaume were out of the Commodore's hair, the better. What better place for them to be than in the middle of the ocean on a rusty old ship?

"What if we sent Mitzi to the ship for some professional training? An executive administrative assistant to an important executive at the Merchant Marine Academy surely needs to know the inner workings of a ship. We'll call it 'continuing education.'"

"She can be the ship's cadet," Mrs. Tannenbaume said.

"The cadet?! I don't wanna be no cadet," Mitzi said.

"But what's wrong with being the cadet?" the Commodore said. "I was a cadet once."

"My sonny boy says the ship's cadet is lower than whale shit."

The Commodore slammed his hand down on his desk. "How dare you talk of my boys that way, madam!"

"I'm just telling you what my sonny boy said."

Mrs. Tannenbaume looked at Mitzi when she said it. Mitzi ignored her.

"Well," Mitzi said. "I have heard some of the midshipmen talking about their year at sea. It does sound kind of fun."

"Sea year is a transformative experience." The Commodore spread out his arms towards Mitzi and Mrs. Tannenbaume. "So? Do you two think you can work together to turn Sylvia Tannenbaume into a nice Jewish girl?"

Mrs. Tannenbaume appeared to be mulling it over. She looked the forty-ish Mitzi up and down. "Some cadet. She looks more like a cougar."

"Cadets come in all shapes and sizes, madam," the Commodore said.

"Well, I do want my sonny boy to be admiral. I guess we have to do something about his little Thai girl." Mrs. Tannenbaume looked at Mitzi again. "Are you really a keeper of kosher?"

"My whole life."

The Commodore wanted to bring this thing to a close. The more he thought about it, the more he realized that having Mitzi and Mrs. Tannenbaume hang around the academy for the next month was simply too great a risk. If Mogie found out in the coming weeks that Captain Tannenbaume was not really Jewish, the Commodore's perfect plan would blow up in his face. Mogie would have enough time to replace Tannenbaume with someone else. No, the

Commodore needed to spring the news on Mogie the day before the unveiling of the Mariners Monument. The board would have to appoint a new superintendent immediately or risk grave embarrassment to the academy, and the clear successor to Tannenbaume would be the Commodore. The Commodore's plan was sound. He just needed to protect it.

The Commodore leapt to his feet and clapped his hands together. "Well then, it looks like you two will be shipmates."

Mitzi and Mrs. Tannenbaume still did not look at each other.

"So where do we join the ship?" Mitzi said.

"My sonny boy said his ship departs Singapore the day after tomorrow."

"Singapore? That sounds far. And how long will we be on the ship?"

"The voyage back will be about a month," the Commodore said.

Mitzi looked at the Commodore. "But who's going to help you with your Toe Hang?"

"His what?" Mrs. Tannenbaume said.

The Commodore patted Mitzi's shoulder. "My Toe Hang will be just fine."

"You got a hangnail or something?" Mrs. Tannenbaume said.

"Oh gawd." Mitzi slapped her hand against her thigh. "You see what I mean? How am I going to spend a month on a boat—"

"It's a ship," Mrs. Tannenbaume pointed out.

Mitzi turned her back on Mrs. Tannenbaume. She lowered her voice when she spoke to the Commodore. "She don't even know what a Toe Hang is. She's like—what was that word you used the other day, the one about people that got no culture?"

"Philistine?" the Commodore said.

"Yeah. She's like a Philipine. How am I gonna hang around with a Philipine for the next month?"

"The word is philistine, Ms. Paultz."

"Isn't that what I said?"

The Commodore had to get Mitzi on that plane to Singapore. His very sanity hung in the balance. He pulled Mitzi aside.

"My dear Ms. Paultz, you must recognize that every person of great erudition has a responsibility to pass on his or her knowledge. We—you and I—have a great many things to impart. Now, I grant you, many of the philosophical tenets we embrace will simply be beyond Mrs. Tannenbaume's ken, but, nevertheless, we do feel a certain *noblesse oblige* to pass things down, do we not?"

Mitzi stared at the Commodore. "Who's Ken?"

"Pardon me, Ms. Paultz?"

"You mentioned Mrs. Tannenbaume's Ken. Who's he? I don't even know him and I'm supposed to embrace him?"

The Commodore did not—could not—respond.

"Is there going to be a waiter on this freighter?" Mitzi said.

"My sonny boy gets waited on in the officers' mess," Mrs. Tannenbaume said. "But then, he's the captain. And I'm sure the supernumerary gets waited on. I don't know about the cadet."

Mitzi pointed at Mrs. Tannenbaume. "If she gets waited on, I better get waited on!"

The Commodore held up his hands.

"Ms. Paultz, you will be joining the ship as a cadet from the Merchant Marine Academy. A cadet is an Officer in Training. Cadets are afforded the same privileges as officers aboard ship. The crew will treat you as a lady, I assure you."

Mitzi did not respond.

"You are right to think of it as a cruise, Ms. Paultz—a cruise to a better day."

The Commodore swept Mitzi and Mrs. Tannenbaume out of his office. "You two have some packing to do."

The Commodore walked them to the entrance of Wiley Hall. "Don't forget to pack your suntan lotion, Ms. Paultz. And give my regards to Captain Tannenbaume, the next superintendent of the United States Merchant Marine Academy. How does that sound, Mrs. Tannenbaume?"

Mrs. Tannenbaume let Mitzi walk on ahead of her. When she saw Mitzi head toward her car parked in the MOD parking lot, she spoke to the Commodore.

"Are you sure about this plan of yours, Commodore?"

"My dear Mrs. Tannenbaume, the plan is flawless. It is the execution of the plan that is at stake. You work hard at turning Sylvia into a nice Great Neck wife. Leave everything else to me."

"Well, okay," Mrs. Tannenbaume said. "I must say, I have to pinch myself every time I think about my sonny boy the admiral. I take back everything I thought about you, Commodore. You seem like a real *mentsch*."

The Commodore clicked his heels and bowed at the waist. "Well, with a mother like you, one might say that Captain Tannenbaume was born to be the superintendent of the United States Merchant Marine Academy. One can almost sense an element of destiny in it."

"Yes. I know what you mean. I know that my sailor boy would have been so proud."

"Your sailor boy?"

"One of Captain Tannenbaume's fathers."

"Yes, of course. Very well, Mrs. Tannenbaume. Bon voyage."

The Commodore watched Mrs. Tannenbaume walk down the oval toward the Vickery Gate. The last thing he wanted was to be drawn into a conversation about one of Captain Tannenbaume's fathers. The Commodore was not interested in Mrs. Tannenbaume's lurid past. He only cared about his own future. His future as superintendent of the academy.

Tomorrow he would meet with the Board of Governors to submit Johnson's letter of resignation and seal old Johnson's Johnson's fate.

Chapter 26

BONA FIDE BOARD MEMBERS

Miss Lambright pulled the LeBaron to a stop at the foot of Mallory Pier. The Commodore sat in the passenger seat in his service dress blues and held the door handle in a tight grip. The dress blues were such a dark navy that they contrasted sharply with his white knuckles. September had snuffed out the last of the summer humidity, which was a relief, but even so, the Commodore wore his hat in the car to hide the bead of sweat that appeared, despite the coolness, on his forehead. He had woken up that morning feeling a little nervous and had asked Miss Lambright to drive him the short distance down to the pier. It would give him time to gather his thoughts, he told her.

"It's really blowing today, Miss Lambright." The Commodore's voice was small.

Miss Lambright peered out from under the visor at the American flag on the mast of the MV *Kings Pointer*. "The flag is hardly moving."

"But look at the white caps."

Miss Lambright looked at the water. "I don't see any white caps."

The Commodore did not care for Miss Lambright's brazenness, but he did not have any fight in him this morning. He felt as if he had a pallet of bricks on his chest. "Look at that pier, Miss Lambright. It is a disgrace."

"What's wrong with it?"

"It's old and splintered! We should tear the thing down. And look how far out it extends over the water."

Miss Lambright laughed. "What's the matter, Commodore? Are you afraid?"

The Commodore slapped at the air. "Don't be ridiculous, Miss Lambright. Of course I'm not afraid. I just don't like walking out over all that water without a life jacket."

"So why don't you wear a life jacket?"

"Well, I do have one with me. It's in the trunk."

Miss Lambright put her hand on the Commodore's forearm. "Do you want me to get it for you?"

"No! I'll be laughed at."

"But how else will you get to the ship?"

"Maybe we should just reschedule. Until this front blows through."

Miss Lambright looked again at the flag. "What front? There isn't a puff of wind." She opened the driver's side door and got out of the car. "I'm getting your life jacket."

"No!"

The Commodore whirled around in his seat. Through the rear window, he saw Johnson walking toward the car.

"Miss Lambright! Get back in the car!"

It was too late. Miss Lambright opened the car trunk and took out the life jacket just as Johnson walked up.

"Miss Lambright," Johnson said, stopping next to the LeBaron. "I've been looking for you. What are you doing here?"

"I drove the Commodore here so he could gather his thoughts this morning."

Johnson pointed at the life jacket in her hand. "Like how's he going to get down that long rickety pier this morning?"

Johnson laughed when he said it. The Commodore fumed. Johnson had done this on purpose. As superintendent, Johnson presided over the board and, as chair, was able to make certain unilateral decisions, such as the venue of board meetings. Johnson had made the decision to hold the board meeting in the wardroom of the MV *Kings Pointer*, the academy's training vessel tied up alongside Mallory Pier. A number of years back, a rumor had taken hold that the Commodore was afraid of the water. He always suspected that Johnson was the one who had started the preposterous rumor. The Commodore knew that it was time to put an end to the lie. His very credibility was at stake.

He got out of the car and took the life jacket from Miss Lambright. "Thank you, Miss Lambright. You may go now."

The Commodore ushered Miss Lambright to the driver's side and shoved her into the car. He then turned and faced Johnson. He made a great show of putting on his life jacket. He looked Johnson in the eye as he buckled the last buckle.

"I'm making a point, do you see? Mallory Pier should be condemned. The life jacket symbolizes how unsafe I deem the pier to be."

"Sure," Johnson said.

"Shall we go?" The Commodore's voice cracked ever so slightly.

"No, you go ahead." Johnson slapped the Commodore on the back of his life jacket. "Great idea. The life jacket as a form of protest. I like that."

The Commodore started off for the pier then stopped. He turned around to Johnson. "You sure you don't . . . " The Commodore heard his voice crack again and stopped to clear his throat. "Ah, you sure you don't want me to wait for you, old boy?"

"No, no. You go on ahead by yourself."

Miss Lambright called out from the front seat of the LeBaron. "You want me to walk with you, sir?"

The Commodore waved his hand. "Nonsense, Miss Lambright. I am certainly able to walk down the pier myself."

The Commodore turned around and steeled himself. It was only a pier, after all. He took one step forward and froze. He did not want to look down but he couldn't help himself. He saw the water through the cracks in the pier—it slapped the undersides of the stringers and made a frightful sound. The Commodore looked up at the flags on the yardarm of the *Kings Pointer*. The flags were moving in the breeze, he was sure of it.

Get moving! And don't look down, he told himself.

The Commodore took a hesitant first step. He had to move. Johnson was looking! He forced himself to take a second step. His legs obeyed but were also convulsing uncontrollably. The Commodore managed another step, and then another. He wanted to run toward the gangway but his legs shook so hard that it prevented him from walking as fast as he would have liked. The gangway of the *Kings Pointer* loomed in the distance. As he got closer, he thought he saw two gangways. He lunged for the gangway on the left.

A midshipman standing watch at the head of the gangway caught the Commodore just in time, preventing him from going straight over the side of the pier.

"Commodore, are you okay?"

The Commodore leaned his entire weight on the young midshipman.

"I'm fine, young man," the Commodore said. "It's the heat."

The midshipman led the Commodore onto the gangway. When they reached the part that extended over the water, the Commodore stopped and gripped the handrail. The midshipman held the Commodore's free arm with both hands and pulled, the way a farmer pulls a milk cow. The Commodore let go of the handrail and the two of them fell forward onto the main deck. Another midshipman came over and helped the Commodore to his feet. The Commodore's face was ashen.

"Sir, you don't look so good," the second midshipman said. "Why don't you have a seat over here?"

The Commodore pushed the boy away.

"I'm fine."

The Commodore steadied himself. *May God damn you, Johnson! How dare he do this to me! And Miss Lambright. Embarrassing me with the life jacket.*

The Commodore was fuming—he didn't need the life jacket, he wasn't afraid of the water, it was that damn pier. If it were up to him, he'd do away with Mallory Pier once and for all.

Just then a gang of midshipman rushed up to him. A chorus of "Is everything okay, Mr. Commodore?" sprang from their lips when they stopped in front of him. The Commodore bulled past them.

"You are sycophants, all of you. Have you no pride?"

The Commodore said it in a harsh whisper. He did not want any of the board members to overhear and think that he was in need of help of any kind. It was imperative that he project a strong image today. When one of the midshipmen tried to take the Commodore's life jacket from him, the Commodore chastised the young man, a blistering attack that made the others shrink away. The Commodore took a moment to compose himself, clutched the life jacket under his arm, and entered the wardroom.

The varnished wood bulkheads, brass handrails, and high-backed leather club chairs of the wardroom exuded power and exclusivity. A dark hardwood floor covered the steel deck and a navy blue rug with a gold anchor lay beneath the polished mahogany conference table. The wardroom on the MV *Kings Pointer* was one of the Commodore's favorite rooms. He just wished it were not on a ship. When he became admiral, he would have the academy's fine cadre of carpenters build a replica of the wardroom on terra firma, in Wiley Hall, and not on some hulk floating at the end of a deep-water pier.

The Commodore took a seat against the bulkhead in the back of the wardroom. He could have sworn he felt the little ship roll. Perhaps the wind was increasing. The Commodore decided to put his life jacket on, for safety's sake. The secretary of the board, Mrs. Coffee, took roll call and announced that they had a quorum and that Commodore Dickey was the only scheduled guest speaker on the agenda.

Johnson flipped though his copy of the agenda. "Ah, my dear, it says here that Mayor Mogclefsky will be addressing the board today."

"Yes, sir, that's correct. However, the mayor's office called this morning and said that the mayor had to cancel."

"But it was my understanding that the mayor had business before the board. Are we striking that business altogether?"

Mrs. Coffee looked around for help.

"Mrs. Coffee," Johnson said, "I want to know. Are we striking that business from the agenda?"

"Well, ah, sir," Mrs. Coffee said, "the business does remain before the board. Parliamentary procedure requires we address the business."

Mrs. Coffee was the octogenarian widow of Commandant Coffee, the second commandant of the Merchant Marine Academy and the acknowledged architect of its regimental system. The Board of Governors had invited Mrs. Coffee to join the board after her husband died an accidental death at the hands of Morris, the academy's landscaper. Morris had inadvertently severed the wrist of Commandant Coffee when the commandant insisted on showing Morris the correct way—the regimental way—to trim a hedge. No one suggested Morris severed the commandant's wrist on purpose, but still the same, the board deemed it prudent to keep the widow Coffee close to the vest. Mrs. Coffee, like most widows, liked to keep busy, and she jumped at the opportunity for more busy work.

To Mrs. Coffee's left sat Mrs. Willowsby, widow of the academy's great benefactor, Ashord Willowsby, Class of '46, who went on to found Willowsby Plastic of Dakron, Ohio, a maker of plastic bath toys. Ash made a fortune with his bath toys and bestowed his millions on his dear alma mater. The academy had been sucking at the tit of Ash Willowsby for a long time, and when that sweet mother's milk stopped flowing with Ash's death, the Board of Governors wailed like a baby. Mrs. Willowsby, although childless, just could not bear to hear a baby cry, and she let it be known that in exchange for a seat on the board, the academy could latch onto her breast in perpetuity. The childless woman finally experienced the warm glow of motherhood.

To the widow Willowsby's left sat Captain Cooper Thompkins, known to everyone as Captain Cooper. A graduate of the Merchant Marine Academy and a classmate of Johnson's, Captain Cooper was an ex Exxon captain whose career came to an abrupt halt when he inadvertently dropped his ship's sixty-ton stockless anchor on top of a tugboat, killing the tugboat's skipper, Frank Beebee. Captain Cooper went to great lengths to console Beebee's wife, Marge, and over time, they became close, so close that the two ended up getting married in the chapel at the academy. Cooper made Johnson his best man and Johnson, in return, offered Cooper a seat on the board. The disgraced captain was grateful for the chance to restore his reputation, but Frank Beebee's family cried foul. How, they wanted to know, could a criminally negligent sea captain become a board member of the country's finest maritime institution? Beebee's sister, a sixty-year-old mining company spokesperson from West Virginia known as Miss Beebee, acted as the family spokesperson. She so impressed the academy with her deliberate language that they made her a member of the board as well, ensuring that the Beebee family spokesperson forever remained mum on the appointment of Captain Cooper to the Board of Governors.

The widows Willowsby and Coffee were impressed with Miss Beebee's direct manner as well. They were amazed when Miss Beebee spoke up and asked a question at the very first meeting she attended as a new board member. My, the widows could scarcely believe their ears but there it was, Miss Beebee challenging Johnson on a rule of order. And she was right, wouldn't you know it. There *was* a spelling error in the minutes of the last meeting. When the chair announced that the minutes of the meeting were approved subject to the corrections per Board Member Beebee, the widows sat back in awe. In all their years on the board, the widows had not once opened their mouths, at least not about business before the board. Captain Cooper—he really was a nice man after all—often changed seats with Miss Beebee so that she would not have to talk over him. And the nice chairman, Admiral Johnson, did not seem to mind their chatting at all; in fact, he seemed to encourage it. They repaid his kindness with their votes. Miss Beebee told the widows that in West Virginia a lady dances with the one who brung her. The widows thought Miss Beebee a sage and followed her every move.

The charter for the board specified that it be comprised of seven board members, but the board could legally function with a minimum of five at the discretion of the board's chair. Johnson, as chair, liked the makeup of the board just the way it stood. The meetings ran like clockwork. He and Cooper discussed the various items, and when they came to an agreement, as they always did, Johnson interrupted the widows to procure their votes and move on. When business came before the board regarding Johnson's various peccadilloes, as it often did, Johnson simply explained that the allegations were unfounded and that, for the sake of the august institution they served, the matter could best be handled with a vote of confidence in the job he was doing as superintendent. Miss Beebee told the widows that to get along you have to go along, and the geriatric widows overlooked Johnson's "youthful" indiscretions. That is, except for the time the widow Coffee summoned the nerve to say she'd heard there were pictures of the tryst that Johnson allegedly had with a female midshipman. Miss Beebee's and the widow Willowsby's ears picked up at the mention of photographs. Johnson, who had destroyed the licentious photographs, steadfastly informed the widow Coffee that no such pictures ever existed. Miss Beebee, especially, seemed disappointed.

Johnson called the meeting to order. He suggested they handle Mayor Mogelefsky's business first. The widows were quick to agree. Johnson assured the board that the allegations brought by Mayor Mogelefsky were unfounded and that in the best interests of the institution they so proudly served, the matter could best be handled with a simple vote.

Miss Beebee raised her hand. "I hate to be a bother, sir, but it has come to my attention that there might be a photo of the allegedly alleged allegation? You all know how I am. I like to go along so that we can all get along. But what better way to clear your good name than with photographic evidence? How's that saying go? A picture—"

"A picture is worth a—" the widow Coffee continued.

"A thousand words," the widow Willowsby said, looking proud to have finally spoken up in a board meeting.

Johnson glanced at his buddy Cooper. They'd talked about this before the meeting, and it was at least possible he could bull his way through this.

"I make a motion," Captain Cooper said, "that the board extend a vote of confidence in the job—"

"It is my understanding that there are pictures?" Miss Beebee said again. She looked in the direction of the widows. Mrs. Coffee lowered her eyes.

"I heard it as well," Mrs. Coffee said into her hand.

Johnson conferred with Cooper. Cooper just gave him a shrug, as if to say, "What else can we do but call their bluff?"

"Well, Miss Beebee?" Johnson said. "Can someone produce these photographs?"

Miss Beebee looked at Mrs. Coffee who looked at the Commodore. When the Commodore did not speak up, Mrs. Coffee cleared her throat. After another awkward moment of silence, Miss Beebee turned around in her seat. "Would the Commodore like to address the board this morning?"

The Commodore stood up.

"I am a stickler for parliamentary procedure, as you all know." The Commodore pulled out a plain brown envelope and smiled at Mrs. Coffee when he said it. "Do I have permission to address the chair, sir?"

Johnson looked at Cooper and threw up his hands. The Commodore had done it. He'd gotten Mogie's picture. "Go ahead," he said.

"Mr. Chair, ladies and gentlemen of the board, I have been asked by Mayor Mogelefsky to bring his business before the board."

"Did you bring the pictures?" Miss Beebee said. Johnson sighed audibly.

"The mayor brings serious charges of improper conduct—"

"Of a sexual nature," Miss Beebee pointed out.

The Commodore glared at Miss Beebee. "Correct, Miss Beebee. Now if I may proceed uninterrupted?"

Miss Beebee folded her hands primly and nodded her assent.

"As I was saying, the mayor has decided, in effect, to hold us hostage. If the board does not take consequential action against Admiral Johnson, the mayor has threatened to take the lurid photograph public. It would be a stain on this great academy's reputation. This board cannot allow that to happen."

The widow Willowsby winked at the widow Coffee. "He said 'lurid.'"

"The photograph must stay in-house," Miss Beebee pronounced. She held out her hand to the Commodore and indicated that he hand over the photograph to her.

The Commodore held on to the photo.

"The mayor has one more demand. As you know, the academy and the town of Great Neck have been at odds for quite some time. Our boys have been known to get a tad rambunctious when they are in town on liberty. To us they are good boys blowing off a little steam, but to the mayor's constituents they are ruffians. Because the mayor's constituents are predominantly Jewish, the mayor believes we can greatly improve our relations with the town by installing a Jewish superintendent."

The widows gasped.

"But we like the academy just the way it is," Mrs. Willowsby protested.

"We don't like to make changes for changes' sake," Mrs. Coffee agreed.

Miss Beebee leaned forward and spread her hands on the table. "We may be accused of being restrictive, you know."

"But we are not restrictive," Mrs. Coffee said. "We get a Jewish boy almost every year."

"The spotlight will be on each one of us," Miss Beebee cautioned. "The highly-paid executives of West Virginia Mining came under scrutiny when they tried to cut the wages of the miners. Their country club memberships, their fancy cars. It was all brought out in the papers. The same can happen to us."

"Ash didn't leave me a fancy car," Mrs. Willowsby said.

"But how about your country club?" Miss Beebee said. "How many members are Jews?"

"Well," the widow Willowsby said, "I'm not sure. Surely we have at least one Jewish family at the club."

"Not one," Miss Beebee said. "Silver Oaks was restrictive when Ash joined. Still is. It's been in the papers."

"Oh my. I had no idea."

"The mayor has a hold over us," the Commodore said, looking at the others. "Our best course of action is to capitulate. For the good of the academy." The

Commodore braced himself and turned to Johnson. "Sir, you have served this academy with distinction. However, the time has come to step down."

Johnson put his hands up in surrender. At least he could go gracefully. "Members of the board, I figured the mayor would do something like this. I am prepared to resign. To fall on my sword. For the sake of my alma mater, I have prepared a letter of resignation. I would have brought it with me but I seem to have misplaced it."

"We believe it is important to be on record with the photograph," Miss Beebee said. "We should make it part of the minutes of the meeting. For safekeeping."

"I don't think that's necessary, Miss Beebee," Johnson said. "I've already tendered my—"

Miss Beebee slammed her fist on the conference table. "I want that photo!"

She stood up and faced the Commodore. West Virginia Mining did not hire Miss Beebee for her deliberate language only. Miss Beebee stood six feet tall and was not embarrassed to use her stature when necessary. She had famously stared down a gang of angry miners in the wildcat strike of '77. The Commodore was no match for her withering stare. She again held out her hand for the photo. The Commodore complied.

The widows jumped out of their seats and snatched the photo from Miss Beebee. They all looked at the photo together, each of them holding a corner of it with their fingers. They stared at the photo for a long time. Then they raised their heads and looked at Johnson.

"That's it?" the ladies said.

Blood rushed to Johnson's face.

"I did not know Ms. Paultz had a camera in her desk drawer," Johnson said. "I was caught off guard. That's not my normal self you see there." Johnson was stammering. "I'm . . . I'm . . . I'm bigger than that."

The ladies studied the picture intently.

"We were expecting more," Mrs. Coffee said.

"Perhaps there's a magnifying glass?" Mrs. Willowsby asked.

Johnson jumped up from the table. "A magnifying glass!" Johnson looked to his good friend Cooper.

Cooper put up his hands. "Hey, buddy, you've been telling everybody you're the biggest all these years. The ladies do not appear to agree with you, big guy."

Johnson threw his agenda down on the table. "But I am the biggest. Besides, I've already resigned. This isn't fair."

The Commodore reached in to take the photo back from the ladies. The ladies did not try to keep it. The Commodore placed the photo in his breast pocket.

"What a disappointment," Mrs. Coffee said.

Johnson turned again to Cooper. Cooper turned his back on him. Just then the door to the wardroom opened.

It was the nurse.

"May I ask what business you have with the board?" Mrs. Coffee asked.

"Why, I'm here as character witness for the admiral." The nurse looked at Johnson. "Surprise."

Johnson smiled weakly. *Could this get any worse?*

"And how do you know the admiral?" Mrs. Coffee asked.

"I'm his girlfriend."

The widows clucked their tongues.

Johnson didn't have to take any more of this. He walked over to the bulkhead behind him and yanked his hat off the hook. He pulled the hat low over his eyes and walked past the ladies with his head down.

"What's going on?" the nurse said. Johnson said nothing and they left the wardroom.

"The poor thing," the widows said.

Miss Beebee agreed. "All this time he thought he was the biggest."

"If I heard it once, I heard it a thousand times," Cooper said.

Mrs. Coffee brought them back to business. "Well, we need a formal letter of resignation to make it official."

"I have it right here." The Commodore reached into his pocket, past the "lurid" photo he'd taken of Johnson and Miss Lambright, fully clothed on the

Murphy bed, and withdrew the resignation letter Miss Lambright had typed. He laid it on the table. The ladies gathered around the letter and read it aloud:

Dear Bored Governors:

I get to reform you I'm here to buy a sign. Being tired with my family is the art of indecision. Just nine remain suspectfully remitted.

Admiral Johnson

The ladies looked at one another.

"The poor thing," they said again.

The Commodore spoke up. "In my opinion, the stress of being 'the biggest' took a toll on our dear admiral."

"Judging from the photograph, I really can't see what all the fuss was about," Mrs. Coffee said again.

The widow Willowsby and Miss Beebee shook their heads, agreeing with their colleague.

"Be that as it may," the Commodore said, "judging by the resignation letter, the man has suffered some sort of breakdown. He deserves our pity. Well, enough about him. Back to the business at hand." The Commodore walked around the conference table to Johnson's chair. "May I take a seat?"

The Commodore did not wait for a response. He sat in the chairman's seat and smoothed his hands over the mahogany table. A shiver went up his spine. How long had he waited for this, and now it was within his grasp.

"Ladies and gentleman," the Commodore said, "the mayor wants a Jewish superintendent. I have found just the man. His name is Captain Tannenbaume. He is a respected member of the maritime community. He and his lovely wife, Sylvia, will be available to join our team in time for the unveiling of the Mariners Monument. So you see? The all-important business of the United States Merchant Marine Academy will continue uninterrupted."

Miss Beebee was the first to respond. "This Captain Tannenbaume, is he a good talker? I mean, can he verbalize?"

"Captain Tannenbaume is a superb speaker," the Commodore said. "Any other questions about the captain's qualifications?"

"Is he a good dancer?" Mrs. Willowsby asked.

"He is a superb dancer," the Commodore said.

"Is he tall?" Mrs. Coffee asked.

"My understanding is that he is above average in height."

The ladies nodded their heads.

"He sounds perfect," Mrs. Willowsby stated.

"Yes, indeed," the Commodore said. "Now, do we have a motion to make Captain Tannenbaume the next superintendent of the United States Merchant Marine Academy?"

Miss Beebee made the motion. Mrs. Coffee seconded. The motion passed unanimously. The Commodore stood up.

"I am not a member of the board," the Commodore said. "Far be for me to interject. However, it has been a trying meeting. Perhaps now would be a good time to adjourn?"

Miss Beebee made a motion to adjourn. She asked Mrs. Willowsby if she would second the motion. Mrs. Willowsby blushed.

"Why, I suppose I could," Mrs. Willowsby said.

When Mrs. Coffee read the motion to adjourn by Miss Beebee as seconded by Mrs. Willowsby, the ladies could not keep from smiling.

The Commodore read their minds. "My, my, ladies, you are acting like bona fide board members."

"We *are* bona fide board members!" the ladies chanted in unison.

"And fearless," the Commodore said. "Quite like myself."

"Is that why you are wearing your life jacket?" Captain Cooper asked dryly.

The ladies looked toward the Commodore at Captain Cooper's remark. Mrs. Willowsby reached across the table and patted the Commodore's hand. "Ash was afraid of the water, too."

The Commodore was too close to realizing his dream to care that others might be grossly mischaracterizing him.

"By hiring Captain Tannenbaume," the Commodore said, "you have gone where no board members have gone before. You have impressed me with your boldness."

"Here's to Captain Tannenbaume!" the ladies cheered.

Yes indeed, the Commodore thought. Here is to Captain Tannenbaume.

BOOK II

The MV *God is Able,*
at Sea

Chapter 27

COFFEEPOTS
AND PAPERWEIGHTS

Captain Tannenbaume stood in the doorway to the radio room on the MV *God is Able* and waited for the radio officer to look up from what he was doing. Captain Tannenbaume shook his head—he just could not understand how Sparks managed to keep his space so tidy. A torrent of paperwork flooded the radio room each day, inbound and outbound, yet there was not a scrap of paper in sight.

Whenever Captain Tannenbaume asked, Sparks just said he had a system. "Everything in its place," he said. "That's the key." Captain Tannenbaume could have used a system—his own office was a mess. His desk was a mountain of loose papers, and he was constantly working to make a dent in it. "Working on his desk" he called it. He would even skip coffee time, a union-mandated twice-a-day twenty-minute coffee break, to work on his desk. Of course, he made certain to not skip coffee time entirely. The chief engineer, Paul Magnusson, a hefty Midwestern Swede, didn't like it whenever anyone skipped out on coffee time. So Captain Tannenbaume would show up in the officer's wardroom at eighteen minutes past ten o'clock, two minutes before coffee time broke up, and pour himself a conspicuous cup of joe. This last-minute arrival never fooled the chief.

The chief was a union man, like his father and his father before him, and as he noted, "the union was what got 'em these fine wages they enjoyed, and it's the union what fought tooth and nail to get 'em coffee time, too, and to miss coffee time was to slap the union in the face." The chief did not exactly say all that to captain Tannenbaume. He said it to the others after the captain left, but he might've said it. And he might've told the man another thing or two if the man did not bug out of there to go work on his desk. When the chief said, "Work on his desk," he held up both hands and clawed the air twice with his fingers. The chief was fond of his air quotes. He rarely made it through a sentence without using them. The others gave the air quotes right back to the chief, but the chances were good the chief failed to notice that they were making fun of him because the chief, like most engineers, was slow on the uptake with subtleties like that.

Captain Tannenbaume stepped back into the passageway outside the radio room and looked at his watch. What was so wrong with the GPS that it was taking this long to fix it? If the noon position report didn't go out soon, the home office would be telexing to find out where it was, but without the GPS, how in the world where they going to fix the noon position? The deck officers on the *God is Able* hadn't practiced celestial navigation in years, and Captain Tannenbaume doubted that any of them even knew where the ship's sextant was stowed. *No, his officers needed their GPS and they needed it now.*

Captain Tannenbaume wanted to interrupt Sparks but . . . Sparks became agitated whenever he had to fix stuff. Most radio officers were whizzes at repairing electronics, but Sparks was an "old school" radio officer. Give him a wireless with tubes and filaments and he'd have it repaired in no time. Anything solid-state, however, gave him the willies. When the microchip came out, Sparks predicted it would be a flash in the pan. That microchips powered the personal computer, and hence the entire world, did nothing to dispel Sparks of his conviction that the microchip was *en-passant*.

"You can't work on them," Sparks would say whenever anyone challenged his position on the personal computer. "When people have to throw away their precious PCs because no one can fix them, you'll see them clamoring again for something with a tube in it."

If Captain Tannenbaume heard it once, he heard it a hundred times.

Captain Tannenbaume peeked in on Sparks again. It was plain that Sparks was becoming frustrated, and when Sparks was frustrated, his stutter, which was normally pretty bad, became intolerable. Captain Tannenbaume did not feel like sitting through one of Sparks's stuttering explanations so he decided to go to the bridge to see if the ship's sextant had turned up.

When Captain Tannenbaume got to the bridge, one deck up from the radio room, he found Swifty, the ship's third mate, in the chart room with his head over the chart. The chart room wasn't much of a room—it was really just a big table with large narrow drawers for holding nautical charts separated from the rest of the bridge by a heavy curtain.

"Afternoon, Swifty," Captain Tannenbaume said. "Any luck finding that sextant?"

It was the chief who gave the third mate the moniker Swifty, the very first day the brand-new third mate joined the ship. The young man had decided to make the coffee during coffee time to show the others he was a team player, only he had a heck of a time figuring out how to work the damn coffee machine. The chief was dying for a cup of coffee, but since he knew there was always a fresh pot brewing in the control room down below, he decided to see just how long it would take the young man to make a fresh pot. When coffee time ended, the new third mate was still working on getting the pot brewed.

Later, in the control room—the air-conditioned space within the furnace-like engine room where the engineers liked to hang out to escape the oppressive heat—the chief held court in front of the second engineer, two oilers, and a wiper. The chief's chair was a swivel chair that had lost its swivel, and to keep from tilting dangerously to one side, he had to sit hunched over with his legs spread wide and with his hands clamped onto his knees. The chief sat like this and told the others he might've showed the man how to make a pot of coffee if the man had asked for help. The chief also said that he might've known the man could not make a pot of coffee. "One look," the chief had said, "is all it took to know that this one was no brain surgeon. He's a real 'Swifty,' this one." When the chief removed his hands from his knees to make his air quotes, the chair heeled over. He caught himself and tried again but the chair would not cooperate and the chief was forced to make the quotation mark sign with one hand. Even with a one-handed quotation mark, the name "Swifty" had stuck for good.

Captain Tannenbaume looked at the chart over Swifty's shoulder. The ocean plotting chart was a clean white expanse with a diagonal drawn on it for a course line. There was no noon position on the chart.

"No luck finding the sextant?" Captain Tannenbaume asked again.

Before Swifty could answer, the door to the navigation bridge opened and in walked the chief.

"Good morning, Maggie," Captain Tannenbaume said. "What can I do for you?"

Captain Tannenbaume was the only one who called the chief "Maggie." Captain Tannenbaume knew that it burned the chief's ass, but he didn't care. The big blowhard ran roughshod over the entire crew, always pontificating about the union this and the union that. The captain was the one guy the chief could not steamroll and captain Tannenbaume let him know it every chance he got. Oh, he would never confront the man, never. The risk was too great—the Swede would be insufferable if he felt he got the best of the captain. No, Captain Tannenbaume just took subtle jabs, like calling the big oaf Maggie.

"I haven't received my noon report yet," the chief said. "I just figured I'd ease on up to the bridge to see what's up."

"Easing on up to the bridge to see what's up is my job, Maggie. I don't ease down below to see what's up down there."

The chief acted as if he had not heard a word Captain Tannenbaume had said. He walked over toward the chart table and stood next to Swifty. He didn't look at Swifty when he spoke to him. The chief rarely looked at the person he was speaking to. Instead, the chief rocked on his heels and looked up at the overhead when he said, "Trouble figuring the noon position, Mr. Mate? I heard the GPS bought the farm."

Captain Tannenbaume stepped between the chief and Swifty. "Maggie, that's enough. Swifty here is plotting the ship's position as we speak. You'll get your report."

"Oh, is that so?" the chief said. "And just how is the young man going to fix the ship's position without the GPS?"

"The old-fashioned way. We're professional navigators. We don't need a GPS to know where we are at sea."

"Oh, is that so?" the chief said. "Don't you fellas need a—what's that thing called again? The thing you use to"—air quotes—"'shoot' the stars?"

Captain Tannenbaume sighed. "It's called a sextant, Maggie. Now if you don't mind, there are a couple of navigators here who would like to do some navigating."

The chief held up his hands. "Don't let me get in the way." A broad smile creased the chief's face as he sauntered off toward the coffee machine, poured himself a cup, and walked off the bridge.

"I told that big Swede not to come up to the bridge to drink our coffee. I don't go down below to drink their coffee."

Swifty shrugged. "The coffee's old, if that's any consolation. I haven't had a chance to make a fresh pot yet."

"Serves him right." Captain Tannenbaume looked at his watch again. "Ah, look at the time. We've got to get out a noon position report or the damn office'll start breathing down our necks." Captain Tannenbaume looked down at the chart. "Where abouts are we, Swifty?"

Swifty gazed at the chart. After a minute or so, he said, "Well, I think we're somewhere on this chart."

The small-scale ocean-plotting chart Swifty was referring to covered an area of some half a million square miles. Captain Tannenbaume appraised his young third mate carefully. Was Swifty playing him for the fool? Unfortunately, Captain Tannenbaume guessed not.

"Swifty?" Captain Tannenbaume said. "What ocean are we in, son?"

Swifty tried to cheat by glancing down at the chart, which, of course, was of no use, since a plotting chart is a generic chart for use when the ship crosses great bodies of open water. There were no landmasses on the blank ocean chart.

"The Med?" he said.

Captain Tannenbaume shook his head.

"We're not in the Mediterranean?" Swifty asked.

"Swifty, we left Singapore yesterday, transiting the Straits of Malacca. We're in the Indian Ocean, a couple hundred miles off the coast of Sumatra."

"Oh."

"Oh is right." Captain Tannenbaume smoothed his hands over the ocean chart. "To hell with it. We'll just DR it."

Captain Tannenbaume picked a pair of dividers out of the chart table drawer, did some quick math in his head based on their course and speed, and walked off the number of miles the ship had run on its course line since leaving Singapore. Navigators call it Dead Reckoning, or DR for short. It was an approximate position, but what else could he do? Have the office, not to mention the chief, bust his balls because his officers couldn't navigate without a GPS? He grabbed the noon position form and wrote out a noon slip in triplicate: one for him, one for Sparks, and one for the chief. He told Swifty he was going down below anyhow, so he'd just deliver it to Sparks and the chief himself.

"And, Swifty, find the damn sextant. It has to be up on the bridge somewhere."

The chief engineer's office on the *God is Able* looked like every other chief's office on a merchant ship. Even though the bulkheads were sheathed in Formica, they were not clean and shiny like they were elsewhere on board. They were smudged with black grease from the coveralls of the engineers and wipers who came and went from the chief's office throughout the day. Even the leather-bound reference manuals lining one entire bulkhead were smudgy from the grimy hands that referenced them.

Captain Tannenbaume could not remember the last time he'd entered the chief's office. If he ever needed to speak to the chief, he just picked up the phone and called him, or he'd wait until mealtime as he knew he'd see him in the officers' mess. The chief always had two or three guys from the engine department in his office sucking up to him, laughing at his jokes, listening to him spout off, and Captain Tannenbaume would just as soon not subject himself to it. The chief's blather made Captain Tannenbaume's stomach turn. Sure enough, when Captain Tannenbaume got to the chief's office, one deck below the wheelhouse on the starboard side, he found the chief having a cup of coffee with the second engineer and the electrician. The three men were laughing among themselves, but when Captain Tannenbaume entered the office, they stopped. The second and the electrician did not look at Captain Tannenbaume. A sign of disrespect is what it was.

"I've got your noon slip, Maggie," Captain Tannenbaume said. "I can't say I know what all the rush is about."

The chief looked at the second, who covered his mouth with his hand.

"You got the GPS working?" The chief looked not at Captain Tannenbaume but at the second when he said it.

"No, Maggie. I've got Sparks looking into it." Captain Tannenbaume dropped the noon slip on the chief's desk. "I look at it as a good thing. The mates need to practice celestial every once in a while. Just to stay sharp, you know what I mean?"

The chief picked the noon slip off his desk and handed it to the second.

"I know exactly what you mean, Cap." The chief looked at the electrician this time when he said it. Still looking at the electrician, he said, "Hey, Second, will you put that noon slip under my paperweight there."

Captain Tannenbaume saw it before the words were out of the chief's mouth. The second picked up the sextant and placed the noon slip under it. Then he and the electrician broke out laughing, covering their mouths with their hands and avoiding Captain Tannenbaume's woeful glare. Captain Tannenbaume's face turned red.

The chief looked Captain Tannenbaume directly in the eye when he spoke to him. "It seemed like it would make a good paperweight. I've had it for years. No sense in letting a heavy piece of brass go to waste."

Captain Tannenbaume felt weak in the knees. God, he hated to have the big Swede get the best of him like that. He grabbed the sextant off the chief's desk. He wanted to say something clever, but what could he say? An awkward moment passed before he said, "Thanks a lot, Maggie," and left the room.

Captain Tannenbaume heard the three of them laughing as he walked down the passageway. He had egg on his face, Captain Tannenbaume knew it. There was no escaping that fact. God almighty, how could he have let the chief get the upper hand on him this early in the voyage? And to have the electrician laugh at him that way? It was bad enough to have a junior officer laugh at him, but an unlicensed crewmember? Well, the electrician did not know what he had in store for himself. The long voyage home just got a little longer for him, the captain thought.

Captain Tannenbaume walked the rest of the passageway toward the radio shack with his head hanging low. He was so caught up thinking about what the chief had just done to him that he failed to see the GPS fly out of the radio room. He did hear it strike the bulkhead, though, and he turned in time to see it smash into little plastic pieces.

Captain Tannenbaume looked into the radio room and saw Sparks at his desk with his arms folded across his chest. He picked up a sliver of plastic from the shattered GPS, a little piece that bore the name of the manufacturer Garmin, rushed into the radio room, and shook the piece of plastic in Sparks's face.

"What the hell do you call this! Have you lost your mind!"

Sparks was calm. Serene almost. "See what I muh—muh—muh—mean about ssssssolid-state?" Sparks said. "What good is—is it if you can't fuh—can't fuh—can't fuh—fuh—fuh—fix it?"

Captain Tannenbaume stared at the man who sat before him. For the life of him, he could not figure what made Sparks tick. Most radio officers wanted nothing more than to fiddle around with electronics. As boys, they built erector sets and elaborate electric train sets and homemade ham radios. Aboard ship, they were known to be able to fix anything. If the chief steward needed a cake mixer repaired, he'd bring it, not to the electrician but to the radio officer. Yet Captain Tannenbaume had somehow ended up with a radio officer who did not like to fix things.

He slumped in the chair by Sparks's desk and held the sextant in his lap with both hands. He stared at the sextant a long while before looking up at Sparks.

"You think this is easy?" he said.

When Sparks did not respond, Captain Tannenbaume continued. "You think it's easy being captain of this ship? I've got a Third Mate who doesn't know what ocean we're in. I've got a Chief Engineer who's been using the ship's sextant as a paperweight. I've got a brand new wife who won't get out of bed because she's afraid of my mother. I've got a mother who won't get out of bed until my wife gets out of bed. I've got a so-called cadet who thinks she's on a cruise ship. And last but not least, I've got you, a radio officer who not only doesn't fix things, he *breaks* things."

Sparks just sat there, impassive as a grapefruit.

Captain Tannenbaume held up the plastic sliver. "This is the one and only GPS we've got, Sparks!"

Sparks shrugged. "It was all . . . all . . . already broke."

Captain Tannenbaume suddenly felt very tired. He pushed himself up out of his chair and stood before Sparks.

"Look," he said. "When you send out the noon report, send along a telex to the office saying that my mother and Ms. Paultz joined in Singapore." Captain Tannenbaume turned to leave. When he got to the door he turned around. "Hey, do you think we should send a SITCASREP on the GPS?"

Captain Tannenbaume was a stickler for reports. Aboard ship, there was an official report for every occurrence and an acronym for every report. A SITCASREP was a Situation Casualty Report, used whenever a primary piece of navigation equipment failed. On the *God is Able*, it was becoming apparent to Captain Tannenbaume that the GPS was not the primary piece of navigation—it was the *only* piece of navigation equipment, given the incompetence of his mates with the more traditional navigation instruments like a sextant.

"I'll take care of it," Sparks said.

Captain Tannenbaume was starting to feel bad for yelling at Sparks and figured he'd make it up to him. "Stay at your desk. Where do you keep the SIT-CASREPS? I'll get 'em for you."

"No, please. I'll get it out of the locker in a minute."

"Don't be silly."

When Captain Tannenbaume turned around to open the clean metal filing cabinet behind him, Sparks came flying out of his chair. "No!" he said.

It was too late. Captain Tannenbaume opened the door to the cabinet and an avalanche of papers crashed down around his feet. Then a shelf broke loose and more papers and manila folders and bound forms of every description that had been crammed into the locker came pouring out as well. Captain Tannenbaume bent down and picked up a scrap of paper. It was a noon position report—from four years earlier. He dropped his hand to his side and let the piece of paper slip from his fingers.

Captain Tannenbaume turned around and faced Sparks. He cradled the sextant like a baby in his arms. He and Sparks held each other's gaze for a long while. It was Captain Tannenbaume who broke the silence.

"Everything in its place, hey Sparks?"

Captain Tannenbaume stepped over the pile of garbage and walked out of the radio room. He needed a nap.

Chapter 28

INDIAN OCEAN FOG

The hoarse sound of the ship's foghorn woke Captain Tannenbaume. He looked at his watch and groaned. He'd only been asleep for twenty minutes. He was hoping to settle in for the rest of the afternoon. He needed the rest, considering everything he'd been through that morning. Captain Tannenbaume felt the silky skin of his young Thai wife brush against his thigh. The foghorn didn't wake her, she was still sound asleep. How could the girl sleep so much? She hadn't been out of bed since the ship departed Singapore.

She'd told him yesterday that if she didn't get out of bed she would not have to deal with his mother. He had to admit that his mother did not exactly make a good first impression. When Captain Tannenbaume introduced the two, the first thing his mother had said was, "Get your own name."

"Mother," Captain Tannenbaume said, "her name is Sylvia, too. Deal with it like an adult please."

"Why should I?" she said. "I had the name Sylvia Tannenbaume first."

Sylvia, who was more world-worn than your average nineteen-year-old, simply turned on her heels and walked away. She couldn't be bothered and had decided just to go to bed. She had not gotten out since.

Wait a second. Fog was not a weather phenomenon mariners had to deal with in the Indian Ocean. What was going on?

He called the bridge. "Swifty, what's going on up there? Why are you blowing the foghorn for Chrissakes? You woke me up."

"Well, sir, it's just that some fog has rolled in."

"Fog doesn't 'roll in' in the Indian Ocean, son."

"No, really, sir, the bridge is completely socked in. I can't see a thing out the windows."

Captain Tannenbaume started to get out of bed for a look out his porthole but remembered that Sylvia had cardboarded and duct-taped the portholes so that she could sleep during the day. He put on his khakis and went up to the bridge. When he got there, he felt bad for doubting Swifty. The fog was so thick he couldn't see out of the windows. He walked over to the coffee machine and poured himself a cup. He liked to be on the bridge when fog set in, and one never knew how long the fog would last, so he poured himself an extra big cup and climbed up onto the captain's chair. From his chair he saw that the fog was so heavy it caused condensation to form on the windows. Swifty had his nose pressed up to the forward window.

"You should have your nose pressed into the radar, young man, not the window," Captain Tannenbaume said.

Swifty, turning bright red, walked over to the radar and fiddled with the knobs to bring up a better picture.

"Second Mate's already tuned it up," the helmsman, an able-bodied seaman named Ski, said. "Better not mess with it."

Swifty ignored the helpful suggestion and continued to press buttons and turn knobs.

Captain Tannenbaume heard Swifty mutter something under his breath about a missing target. "What do you see in there, Swifty? Anything?"

"Not a thing." Swifty looked to Ski for help. Ski gave him a look that said, "I told you so."

Captain Tannenbaume sunk down into the big leather captain's chair and held the mug of coffee with both hands. *God almighty, Swifty really likes a cold bridge. Here we are in the Indian Ocean and it felt more like the North Sea.*

"Ski, see if you can turn the AC down a bit," Captain Tannenbaume said. "It's so cold you can hang meat in here."

"We can't," Ski said. "It's stuck."

"Stuck? What are you talking about stuck?"

"The thermostat's stuck," Ski said. "The chief himself was up here messing with it. He said it's stuck and we'd just have to live with it. He told me to open the window in the back if it got too cold."

"The chief was up here?"

"Yeah. Just a little while ago."

"Why the hell didn't he send the electrician?"

"He said the electrician was on break."

Captain Tannenbaume suddenly had a visual of the electrician with his hand over his mouth, snickering at him in the chief's office.

"Swifty," Captain Tannenbaume said. "Get a hold of the electrician and tell him he's wanted on the bridge."

Swifty walked over to the phone and called the crew lounge. "Who's this? The chief steward? Have you seen the electrician? He's wanted on the bridge . . . He is? Doing what? Would you like to get rid of him?"

"What's up, Swifty?" Captain Tannenbaume asked.

"The steward says he's trying to watch *The Outlaw Josie Wales* and every time Clint has a line in the movie, the electrician's saying it before Clint does. The steward is asking if we don't have any lightbulbs that need changing."

Captain Tannenbaume smiled. "Indeed we do, young man, indeed we do."

"Get him up here," Swifty said into the phone, "and pronto."

Captain Tannenbaume looked at his watch when the electrician finally arrived on the bridge. The little shit sure took his sweet time. The electrician stood about five foot four and wore enormous workboots in a pathetic effort to give himself a little extra height. *If he wanted to look taller, he oughta think about getting rid of that damn ponytail.* In addition to his enormous boots he wore an enormous moustache, the kind that puffed up around his nose and covered most of his cheeks. Captain Tannenbaume did not care for facial hair. He'd always thought that people with facial hair were trying to hide something.

The electrician walked up to Swifty. "Someone was looking for me?"

"That would be me," Captain Tannenbaume called out from his chair. He waited until the electrician came over to the chair before addressing him again. "We've got some stale lightbulbs that I'd like changed out. Why don't you start with the masthead light."

"I don't know, sir. With all the, ah, fog, and all, maybe I'd better not go aloft right now."

Captain Tannenbaume noticed that when the electrician said "fog," he covered his mouth with his hand to hide the smile on his face. He'd wipe that smile off his face.

"Don't play Philadelphia lawyer with me, Electrician. I ordered you aloft."

"Union rules forbid going aloft in precipitation."

It was the chief engineer. Captain Tannenbaume hadn't heard him come in through the chart room. Captain Tannenbaume's head rolled back and he let it rest on the headrest. He looked up at the overhead and let out a big sigh. *What the hell is Maggie doing up here?*

The chief walked up to the front window and pressed his nose up against it. He turned to Captain Tannenbaume. "Fog counts as precipitation, don't it?"

"Don't fight me on this, Maggie, I want that masthead light replaced."

"But what about the fog?" The chief said it to Captain Tannenbaume, but he looked at the electrician when he said it. Captain Tannenbaume saw the electrician's hand go to his mouth again.

"What the hell is so goddamn funny!"

"Now, now," the chief said. "Let's remember to mind our manners."

"Manners my ass, Maggie. If Miss Manners here had any manners, he wouldn't be covering his mouth with his hand all the time!"

The chief was about to say something when the phone rang. Swifty answered it. "Captain," he said, "it's . . . your mother."

As Captain Tannenbaume got down from his chair, he pointed his finger at the electrician. "Don't go anywhere. You're going to be changing lightbulbs up here whether you like it or not." He grabbed the receiver. "Yes, Mother."

"What's all the racket about up there? I'm trying to sleep."

"It's the foghorn, Mother. And anyway, it's time for you to get out of bed."

"Oh, no. I'm not getting out of bed until Syl—until that girl gets out of bed first."

"That girl has a name, Mother. I'd like for you to use it."

Captain Tannenbaume suddenly became aware that the others were listening in on his conversation. He decided to get back to business.

"Anyway, Mother, I'm busy now. We're socked in up here and I've got a job to do."

When Captain Tannenbaume hung up the phone, the chief asked, "Isn't it unusual to experience fog in the Indian Ocean?"

"You can get fog anywhere, Maggie, if the conditions are right."

"Oh? What conditions would those be?"

"Look, Maggie, I can't teach you meteorology over a cup of coffee. It took me years to master the subject."

"I've just never heard of fog in the Indian Ocean, that's all. The North Atlantic, yes, but never the Indian Ocean."

Captain Tannenbaume felt slightly unsure of himself whenever he debated with the chief. He had to admit that the big Swede was smart and knew a lot about a lot of things. But still, weather was the captain's bailiwick, not the chief engineer's.

"Just keep the plant turning and leave the weather to me, Maggie. Now if you'll excuse me, I've got work to do."

Captain Tannenbaume turned his back on the chief. "Swifty, give me an update on traffic. Ski, check the magnetic compass against the gyro."

"No traffic in the radar, sir."

"Use the forty-eight-mile scale. I want early warning of any closing traffic."

Captain Tannenbaume liked the way his rapid-fire commands sounded. He'd show the chief a thing or two about being in charge. What did the chief know about the responsibilities of command? The chief engineer was only in charge of one department aboard ship. Captain Tannenbaume got down from his chair and paced back and forth on the bridge with his head down. He'd show the chief and his little sidekick what it was to bear the heavy weight of command. The deep forlorn sound of the foghorn only served to heighten the sense of drama. As he paced back and forth, Captain Tannenbaume tried to think of another command that he could give. He whirled around. "Swifty, have you posted a lookout on the wing?"

"Um . . . no, sir. I didn't think of it."

"Goddamnit! I want a lookout on that wing now!" He was putting on a real show for the chief now. By the time the fog lifted, the chief would have a newfound respect for him. Maybe he was finally getting through to the chief. *Maybe it's a good thing that he's up here seeing firsthand what it is that captains do.*

The door to the bridge opened and the lookout, an ordinary seaman named Thibodeaux, walked in. Tibby was from Massachusetts. Both of his parents were Harvard PhDs, and although he himself barely made it out of high school for profound lack of interest, he clearly possessed an IQ that was off the charts. At nineteen he still had a chip on his shoulder and went around telling everyone that on his next ship he was going to Africa. "Joseph Conrad country," he called it. That no one on board had ever read Joseph Conrad gave Tibby a sense of superiority. The little shit even had the audacity to ask the captain if he had ever read Conrad. When Captain Tannenbaume said he had never heard of Conrad, Tibby told him Conrad was the greatest chronicler of the sea, ever. Captain Tannenbaume told the little shit that he preferred Patrick O'Brien. Tibby said O'Brien was inauthentic. When Captain Tannenbaume saw Tibby enter the bridge, he felt a tinge of uneasiness. The little know-it-all had better not embarrass him in front of the chief with any more questions about books.

"Tibby, get out to the wing. We need a lookout."

"Why do you want a lookout?" Tibby said.

"Don't question me, OS! Just get out there on the wing. Can't you see we're in fog?"

Tibby looked toward the back of the bridge and saw the open window. "Why's the window open if you have the air-conditioning blasting away?"

"The AC's stuck," Swifty said. "We opened the window so it wouldn't be so cold."

"Well that's where your fog is coming from," Tibby said.

"What are you talking about?" Swifty asked.

"What happens when you take a glass of cold water outside on a hot day?" Captain Tannenbaume felt the color drain from his face.

"It's not foggy outside," Tibby said. "The windows are full of condensation."

Tibby rolled open the large sliding door to the bridge wing with one swift pull on the handle. The intense Indian Ocean sun inundated the bridge in white light. The sun was so strong Captain Tannenbaume had to shield his eyes from the glare.

"Will you still want a lookout?" Tibby asked, but Captain Tannenbaume could not make out the young man's words over the laughter coming from the chief and the electrician. His head felt gauzy and all he heard was static.

Captain Tannenbaume walked off the bridge like a blind man, with one arm covering his eyes and the other arm out in front of him feeling for the bulkhead and the door. His cabin was dark and it made his head feel better and he took off his clothes and crawled into bed with his young wife. Captain Tannenbaume fell into a deep sleep the second his head hit the pillow and he did not hear the danger signal sounded by the supertanker off the starboard bow of the *God is Able*. Everybody on the bridge sure heard it and, ironically, it was the chief who saved the day when he took the wheel away from Ski—who froze when he saw the huge supertanker bearing down on them—and swung the ship hard to starboard. The supertanker captain stood on the bridge wing waving his fist and yelling at the *God is Able* as it slid past the side of his ship, close aboard.

When they woke up, Sylvia told Captain Tannenbaume she was tired of lying in bed all day and that she might as well start dealing with his mother now. She asked Captain Tannenbaume if he wanted to go to breakfast with her but he said that he was waiting for an apology from the chief first.

Now it was Captain Tannenbaume who refused to get out of bed.

Chapter 29

SAFETY FIRST

It was Mitzi who got everybody out of bed. It was her first cruise and she wasn't going to let anybody spoil it.

Her mother told her before she left that if she had any issues aboard ship, anything at all, all she had to do was call the purser's office. Her mother had been on over one hundred cruises, so if anybody would know about these things, it was her mother. Mitzi woke up on the third day with the sun streaming through her porthole and decided to have breakfast served in her room—her mother told her that at least once on her cruise she had to have breakfast in bed and Mitzi figured today was as good a day as any. She looked at the ship's phone directory taped to the bulkhead next to the phone in the cadet's cabin and found the number for the galley. The chief cook answered the phone, and Mitzi told him she wanted breakfast served in her room.

The cook hung up on her.

When Mitzi called back, she overheard the second cook tell the chief cook to "tell that bitch to get her ass down here like everyone else and what the fuck makes her so special." That infuriated Mitzi. She didn't think she was special—she just wanted breakfast in bed. It looked like it was time to call the purser's office. She got the number off the phone list and dialed it as fast as she could. The phone just rang and rang. She checked the phone list to make sure she had the right number and dialed again. Again no one answered. Mitzi let it ring.

She, of course, had no way of knowing that not only was there no purser aboard the *God is Able*, but the purser's office was now a storeroom used by the chief engineer.

At one time, every ship had a purser. The purser's main job was paymaster, but he was also responsible for signing the crew on and off the ship, maintaining the ship's articles, keeping track of their Mariners documents, and issuing shore passes. It was a big job when ships carried a big crew, but when the size of the crew on cargo ships began to dwindle with the advent of container ships, the purser's job became obsolete. The *God is Able* was over forty years old, and her purser's office was centrally located on the main deck so that the crew had room to form a line when the ship hit port and the purser paid out draws, an advance of money subtracted from a sailor's earned wages. This meant the purser's office was prime real estate, and when the purser became a thing of the past, a battle royale ensued as to which department aboard ship would get the office. The chief steward complained that he did not have enough space to store all the sheets and towels and tablecloths, not to mention all of the precious foodstuffs. Also, if he had the use of the purser's office, he'd be able to keep mops and buckets handy and maybe the main deck wouldn't look so grimy all the time. The chief mate said he'd be damned if the purser's office became a glorified slop chest. The mate needed a new ship's office, the one he had was tiny and located on the upper deck. The ship's office needed to be centrally located so that when the ship was working cargo, the cargo bosses could find him. "Why do you think longshoremen never follow the stowage plan?" the mate wanted to know. The chief steward told the mate that if he was out on deck where he belonged, maybe the cargo boss could find his ass. The mate ignored this and repeated that he'd be goddamned if the purser's office became a fucking slop chest.

The chief engineer stayed quiet and let the steward and the mate duke it out for a while. When he finally weighed in, the chief intoned that the question of who got the use of the purser's office was strictly a safety issue. The ship did not have a safe space to store spare lube oil, and he always felt the purser's office would be the perfect place to keep it. It was an air-conditioned space, and the lube oil needed to be kept in a cool place because of the "flammability thing." Captain Tannenbaume, who was judge and jury, said, "Safety first," and that was that. That lube oil had a flash point equal to that of water apparently went over the heads of the chief mate and the steward, but Captain Tannenbaume did not bother to let them in on the chief's secret. The truth was, if the chief didn't get his way on this, he'd be a royal pain in the ass, and Captain Tannenbaume just wanted the power struggle over the purser's office to go away. In the end, the chief used the purser's office to store beer for the engine department. The office was stacked to the overhead with cases of Heineken. That the chief never did keep the dangerous lube oil in there burned all of their asses, but what could they do? The chief had the key to the office and that, as Captain Tannenbaume said, was that.

When the chief had his guys clean out the purser's office, they took out every stick of furniture, including the shelving. The only thing left in the office was the wall-mounted telephone. The phone worked and the engineers just could not bring themselves to rip a perfectly good phone off the bulkhead. The phone was in the back of the office, completely blocked by cases of Heineken. Until now, no one had ever bothered to ring the office, so it was never a problem.

The purser's office sat adjacent to the crew lounge, where the chief steward was watching *Dirty Harry* for the umpteenth time. The crew lounge was the one place on the ship that was not spic and span. The lounge was off limits to Captain Tannenbaume and the other officers, so the crew was free to keep their little clubhouse any way they saw fit. "Loungy" is how the chief described it. "A goddamned mess" is how the chief mate saw it, but then again, it didn't matter because neither one was allowed to set foot in there.

Between the ringing phone and the electrician jumping on Clint's lines, the steward couldn't hear a thing Clint said. Finally, he hauled himself off of the lounge's worn davenport and called the chief. "Someone's ringing the phone in your storeroom."

"What do you want me to do about it?" the chief said.

"I want you to answer it. It's driving me crazy," the steward said. "How I'm supposed to hear what Clint's saying?"

"Clint doesn't say much anyway," the chief said.

"Don't you go making fun of Clint now!"

"Now, now, don't get your shorts bunched up, Stew."

"Look," the steward said. "Get someone in there to answer that phone or else."

The chief laughed out loud. "Or else what?"

The steward hung up the phone and lay down again. After a moment, he slapped the side of the dusty davenport with his ham-sized hand. His favorite part in the movie was coming up and he couldn't concentrate. He got up again and called the bridge.

"Wheelhouse, Third Mate here."

"Who the hell's calling the purser's office?"

"Who's this?" Swifty said.

"It's the steward!"

"How am I supposed to know who's calling the purser's office? I didn't even know we carried a purser on board."

"We don't! Man, you're an idiot." The steward hung up the phone then called the radio room. "Sparks? This is the Steward here. Are you calling the purser's office?"

"We don't carry a purser on board," Sparks said.

"I know we don't, you idiot!"

"Duh-Duh-Don't call me an id-id-idiot," Sparks said. "You're the wuh-one who—"

The steward hung up the phone and called Captain Tannenbaume. "Cap this is the steward. I hate to bother—"

"Oh it's no bother, Stew," Captain Tannenbaume said. "What can I do for you?"

"Someone's calling the purser's office and—"

"We don't have a purser on board, Stew."

The steward did not respond.

"Stew? You still there?"

The steward waited another moment before he answered. "Yes, sir, I'm still here. And yeah, I know that we do not have a fucking purser on board—"

"Now, Stew, don't get fresh with me. You know where that got you on your last ship."

The steward took a deep breath. "Captain, I am trying to mind my own business. All I wanna did this morning is watch *Dirty Harry* but between the electrician running his yap and the phone ringing—"

"That electrician's running his yap again?"

"Yeah, but it's the phone in the purser's office that's—"

"You tell that electrician I said to get back to work," Captain Tannenbaume said. "Alright stew, go back to your movie."

Captain Tannenbaume had no sooner hung up the phone than it rang again. He clearly was not going to get the sleep he needed.

"Sonny, I'm trying to ring—"

"Good morning, Mother," Captain Tannenbaume said.

"Good morning, Sonny. I'm trying to ring the purser's office but it's been busy for the last ten minutes."

"We don't carry a purser, Mother."

It took Mrs. Tannenbaume a minute for that to sink in. "No purser? But my friend Roz said if I had any complaints not to bother you but to call the purser's office instead."

"Which would be good advice if we actually had a purser," Captain Tannenbaume said. "If you have a complaint, I'll call whichever department head can best handle it. Now, what exactly is wrong?"

"Nevermind," Mrs. Tannenbaume said. "I'll handle it myself. But you should really look into why the purser's office phone is busy."

"I told you we don't have a purser, Mother."

"Oh yeah?" Mrs. Tannenbaume said. "Then why is his phone busy?"

Captain Tannenbaume had to admit he didn't have an answer for that one. He hung up and rested his head on his pillow.

Sylvia saw him thinking hard and asked him what was going on.

"We've got a crank caller," he said. "I've heard of this happening on other ships before. We've got a deranged crew member on board." Captain Tannenbaume picked up the phone and dialed the purser's office. It was still busy.

"Yup." He swung his legs over the side of the bunk and got out of bed.

"Wow," Sylvia said. "A deranged crew member!"

Captain Tannenbaume got dressed and then called the chief engineer. Unlike most chief engineers, the chief was a late sleeper, which meant Captain Tannenbaume had the pleasure of waking him. An added benefit. "Maggie, we've got someone on board with a loose screw. Get someone in that storeroom of yours to answer that phone."

"What storeroom?" the chief said.

"The purser's office storeroom, that's what storeroom."

"Someone's calling the old purser's phone?"

"That's right," Captain Tannenbaume said.

"Oh boy." Captain Tannenbaume heard him groan. "We've got an awful lot of bee—uh, lube oil—to move."

"Well, start moving it."

The chief put the entire engine department on it. The men complained that it was a Sunday and that they'd better get paid double time for it. The chief said since they were moving—air quotes—"lube oil," he'd consider it hazardous work and give them all hazardous pay. When the deck department found out that their counterparts were getting haz pay for moving beer, they wanted in on the deal, but the chief mate said, "Haz pay my ass. If anybody puts in for haz pay I'm redlining it." The mate was so stingy with overtime that the deck gang figured they might as well take what they could get but they'd be goddamned if they were going to bust their asses for it. Especially since it wasn't even their beer.

So when the boatswain, the foreman of the deck gang, saw Tibby grab two cases at once, he nearly had a conniption. The bosun told the OS, "Safety first, son, safety first." He wasn't going to have any back injuries in his department, he said. He turned and winked at the older seamen in the deck department. "Take it one case at a time, son," he said. "And bend those knees," the bosun said. The older seamen showed the bosun just how safe *they* could be by moving the beer, not one case at a time, but *one six-pack* at a time.

By the time Captain Tannenbaume came down to see how things were going, the engine department had followed the deck department's lead, and they, too, were moving the beer one six-pack at a time. Captain Tannenbaume stood next to his chief mate and watched. He was all too familiar with how the unlicensed crew manipulated the union pay scale: the higher the hourly rate, the slower they worked.

The mate read his mind. "This thing would have to happen on a Sunday."

Captain Tannenbaume was watching the electrician whispering to one of the oilers. The oiler glanced over at Captain Tannenbaume and whispered back to the electrician. Then the electrician removed a can of beer from the plastic ring and walked out of the purser's office. He was about to place it alongside the rest of the beer being staged in the passageway when Captain Tannenbaume ran over to him and grabbed the can of beer out of his hand. "Knock off."

"He can't knock off."

It was the chief. Captain Tannenbaume spun around and faced him.

"He's gone too far with this slow bell thing, Maggie," Captain Tannenbaume said. "I mean, come on, one can at a time?"

"Okay," the chief said, "maybe he has gone too far but you can't knock him off. All hands means all hands. If everybody else is working, the man has the right to work. It's right there in the union contract."

Captain Tannenbaume saw the electrician's hand go up to his mouth. He threw his hands up and walked over to the mate. "God almighty it just burns my ass."

The mate just stood at parade rest with his hands behind his back and watched the slow bell brigade. "It burns my ass, too. They're going to pay for this though. I'm going to redline the shit out of their overtime sheets the rest of the voyage."

Sparks joined Captain Tannenbaume, the chief, and the mate to watch the men move the cases of beer. "It's like, like watching firefight-fight-fight—"

"Try"—air quotes—"'firemen,' Sparks," the chief said. "It's only got two syllables, not three."

"Fight-fighters retrieve a kitten from up a tree."

A few minutes later, the second engineer joined the crowd of onlookers. Before long, nearly the entire crew, officers and unlicensed, gathered outside the old purser's office, listening to the phone ring and ring, and watching the beer moved one six-pack at a time.

"Actually," Tibby said, "since nearly the entire ship's crew is present and accounted for, we could figure out who the crank caller is by process of elimination."

"That's a good idea." Sylvia turned to Captain Tannenbaume. "Why didn't you think of that?"

Captain Tannenbaume seethed. "Tibby, knock off." The words were not out of his mouth before he regretted saying them.

"All Hands means—"

"I know, Maggie, it's All Hands."

"Well if you know it's All Hands, why do you keep trying to knock the sailors off?"

Captain Tannenbaume looked at the mate, mostly for commiseration, but the mate remained at parade rest, his attention absorbed by the spectacle before him.

The work continued all morning, right up until coffee time. By then, only a few stacks of beer stood between Captain Tannenbaume and the phone on the bulkhead.

"Don't let them knock off for coffee now," he told the mate. "There's only a couple of more stacks to move and we can get to the phone."

"Union rules," the chief said. "Coffee time is"—air quotes—"'coffee time.'"

And so the crew knocked off for coffee, along with the rest of the onlookers, including Captain Tannenbaume, who didn't want to, but what else was he going to do? When Captain Tannenbaume turned to go, he saw that the mate had not budged from his parade rest.

"You coming?" he asked.

"No."

When everyone returned from coffee time, the mate was right where everyone left him, still at parade rest, still staring straight ahead, still seething, smoke practically coming out of his ears.

The crew removed the last of the beer from in front of the phone. Captain Tannenbaume went to answer the phone himself but the electrician beat him to it.

"Hello," the electrician said into the phone. "Purser's office."

"Oh, give me that phone." Captain Tannenbaume tried to take the phone away from the electrician but he turned his back and kept the phone for himself.

"Breakfast in bed?" The electrician rolled his eyes at the crew. "Coming right up."

The electrician hung up the phone. "The new cadet, Mitzi, wants breakfast in bed."

"I already told her," the steward said. "If she wants breakfast, she has to come to the mess like the rest of them."

"Are you nuts?" the electrician said. "If that redhead wants breakfast in bed, I'm going to give it to her."

It did not take long for the other sailors to see what he meant by that. They all made a mad dash for the galley. Even the chief jumped at the chance to bring Mitzi her breakfast. Only Captain Tannenbaume, Sylvia, and the mate stayed behind.

"I knew that redhead was going to be trouble the moment I set eyes on her," the Mate said.

"I didn't know I could have breakfast in bed," Sylvia said.

"You can't, dear," Captain Tannenbaume said. "This is a 'tween decker, not a cruise ship. Ms. Paultz will soon find that out. She's in for quite a surprise if she thinks—"

"Hello! Anybody home? Hello!"

Sylvia rolled her eyes when she heard Mrs. Tannenbaume's gravelly voice. Mrs. Tannenbaume came around the corner of the passageway and stopped when she saw her son.

"Oh, there you are. Beat-me-Daddy-eight-to-the-bar," Mrs. Tannenbaume said. "Is there a fire on board?"

"No, Mother," Captain Tannenbaume said, "the crew wants to bring Mitzi breakfast in bed."

"Breakfast in bed? You told me this wasn't a cruise ship. Why does she get breakfast in bed? She's only the cadet. I'm the supernumerary. Why can't I have breakfast in bed?"

"Yeah," Sylvia said, "why can't she have breakfast in bed? She's the supernumerary."

Mrs. Tannenbaume looked at Sylvia, held her gaze for a moment, and nodded.

Captain Tannenbaume read his mother's mind. She felt she just won their first power struggle—Sylvia had acknowledged Mrs. Tannenbaume's position on board the *God is Able*. Captain Tannenbaume looked around at the cases of beer in the passageway and smiled. If that's what it took to get his mother and Sylvia talking, then so be it.

He put one arm around his wife and one around his mother. "Let's go to the officer's lounge and talk about it."

The only one remaining at the scene of that morning's events was the mate. He was still at parade rest. Finally, he, too, left.

"God almighty," he said aloud to himself as he walked away, "it just burns my ass."

That evening, Captain Tannenbaume gathered his officers on the bridge at sunset so that he could reacquaint them all with the art of celestial navigation. There was no way he was going to let the chief think that his deck officers didn't know how to handle a sextant—not to mention, of course, the matter of it being the ship's only means of navigation at the present time. The truth was, Captain Tannenbaume cared about what the chief thought of his mates, but he could care less what the chief thought of him. Actually, he already knew where he stood with the engineers. The engineers, the chief included, thought he was a buffoon, but then again, every engineer on every ship in the merchant fleet thought the captain was a know-nothing. That's how engineers were. It was a jealousy thing, of course, how could it not be? The engineers were stuck down in that inferno of an engine room while the captain sat on his high horse on a sunlit bridge deck all day. Who wouldn't be jealous?

When he got to the bridge, Captain Tannenbaume saw Swifty fiddling with the ship's old but reconditioned *Cassens & Plath*. It was clear Swifty didn't know how to handle a sextant.

"You're a Kings Pointer, aren't you Swifty?"

"Yes, sir."

"They teach celestial at that school?"

"Sort of." Swifty looked at the sextant inquisitively. "We spent part of one class on it. We passed a sextant around the room. It was a plastic thing, made in Japan. It didn't look anything like this heavy German one. Our professor told us what all the parts were for, but he never really showed us how to use it. All we did was practice the computations so that we could pass our Third Mates exam."

"So you know how to use the sight reduction tables? H.O. 229? Or do you guys go with H.O. 249, the air almanac?"

The mates just stared at him.

"Does any of this sound familiar?" Captain Tannenbaume looked around at the second mate and the chief mate when he said it. The mates nodded their heads. "Yeah," they said. "229. We used H.O. 229 on our license exams."

Well maybe they weren't as useless as he thought. And when he began showing them the different parts of the sextant, it looked to him like they were picking it all up pretty readily. *The academy must have taught them something about what it is to be a ship's officer, after all. The place could not be all about marching in straight lines, could it?* he thought. Captain Tannenbaume remembered what old Captain Holmes—the man who taught him everything he knew about celestial, and everything else about ships for that matter—used to say. Captain Holmes was a hawse piper himself, who'd learned everything *he* knew from an old salt as well. He said the idea was to pass down the stuff that mattered—such as how to navigate by the heavenly bodies. Or how to tie a stopper on a hawser that was under a heavy strain, or sweep a lee for the pilot. He used to say that the United States Merchant Marine Academy ought to teach its students less about marching a straight line and more about following a rhumb line. Captain Tannenbaume could not agree more, although, he had to admit, he had been teaching the new kids less and less in recent years. They just weren't interested in learning. By the time they got out of the academy, they figured they knew it all. And how could he argue? With GPS, and Automatic Radar Plotting Aids, Chart Plotters, and Moving Maps, what did they need with an old sextant?

Captain Tannenbaume showed the mates how to use the sextant. He shot six stars in six minutes, an unheard-of feat. And then he reduced each sight to an LOP, a line of position, and plotted them on the chart. His plot was a perfect pinwheel, the sign of a real pro.

"And, look." He pointed at the horizon. "You can still see the horizon. A good mate ought to be able to plot his position before darkness falls."

The mates' heads just bobbed. Captain Tannenbaume thought he detected a slackness in their jaws, along with their head bobbing. He knew that only an absolute expert could get his position charted as fast as he just had.

He hoped he hadn't intimidated the poor fellows.

While Captain Tannenbaume was on the bridge shooting stars, Sparks was in the radio shack reading the evening telexes. The telexes came out in one long ream of paper that folded up on itself when it hit the floor, and Sparks sat in front of the machine holding the scroll-like paper between his legs while he read. Sparks knew that the *God is Able* would have to pass close aboard the Somali coast on the way to the Red Sea so he was not the least bit surprised to read telex after telex from the state department warning ships in the area to keep a sharp lookout for pirates. When the redundant telexes finally stopped coming, Sparks tore the long ream of paper off and stuffed it in the metal filing cabinet across from his desk.

Chapter 30

BREAKFAST IN BED

A crowd of sailors stood outside of Mitzi's stateroom with plates of runny eggs and untoasted white bread, jostling for position. The electrician declared that he was the one who was going to serve Mitzi in bed. He'd answered the phone, not them, and they could all just kiss his ass. Before entering her room, he took a moment to balance the plate of eggs with one hand so that he could fix his ponytail with the other.

It was the steward who knocked the plate out of the electrician's hand, sending the runny yolk down his pant leg and on to his boots.

The sight of yellow egg yolk on the electrician's nubuck leather workboots sent him into a dither, and he spun on the crowd behind him, demanding to know who did it. Ski stepped in front of the steward and said he was the one who did it. "What are you planning on doing about it?" he asked.

Somewhere during his response, the electrician made the unfortunate mistake of calling Ski a dumb Pollack, and it went downhill from there. The mate, writing up the scene later in the deck log, described what he saw taking place outside Mitzi's stateroom as "pell-mell."

Mitzi got out of bed when she heard the plates smashing on the deck. She opened her door to find a full-blown food fight right outside her stateroom.

"Hey!"

The sound of Mitzi's voice silenced the crew. They all turned and stared at her. The deck was a mess with broken plates and egg yolks and not one sailor had anything to offer Mitzi for breakfast.

"You call this room service?" Mitzi said.

"Yes, as matter of fact, I do."

The voice came from behind them. Mitzi saw that it was the big Swede, the guy they called the chief. The sailors all turned to see him walking up with a breakfast tray of fresh fruit, yogurt, a bagel, a glass of freshly squeezed orange juice, and one of those tin metal covers over a plate. When the chief stopped in front of Mitzi, he lifted the cover to reveal an impressive display of steaming eggs Benedict smothered in Hollandaise sauce. And it wasn't just the breakfast that was impressive. The chief was in a brand-new white boilersuit, with an ascot wrapped around his neck.

Mitzi took the polyester ascot in her fingers and pulled it slowly off the chief's neck. "You look like Elvis in this getup."

Mitzi then wrapped the ascot around her own neck and led the chief into her stateroom. The chief gave a big wink to the crew, who moaned as the door closed.

Inside, the chief set the tray on the metal side table attached to the metal bunk, and lowered the shade over the porthole to keep out the white-hot Indian Ocean sun. Mitzi got in bed and sat up against the bulkhead. She pulled the covers up to her waist.

"I'm ready," Mitzi said.

That afternoon, at coffee time, the chief regaled the others with the story of his breakfast with Mitzi.

"She's something else," he said. "Something else altogether. She did things to me I've never even read about. It was the eggs Benedict, is what did it. Mitzi loves eggs Benedict. And the Hollandaise sauce? The things that woman does with Hollandaise sauce. I'm having"—air quotes—"'breakfast' with Mitzi every day."

Captain Tannenbaume watched as the others hung on every word of the chief's story. Captain Tannenbaume shook his head. He'd already heard Mitzi's side of the story from Mitzi herself. She said the chief had acted like a perfect gentleman, served her breakfast in bed, and waited on her hand and foot. Mitzi thought the big Swede looked pretty sexy in his Elvis getup, and she gave him an obvious green light to make a move, but he never did. He seemed a little nervous, she told Captain Tannenbaume. And now here was the chief talking shit about Mitzi. That's why Captain Tannenbaume didn't like to attend coffee time. He'd realized long ago that, when sailors are aboard ship, all they do is talk about women, but when a ship arrives in port and they're surrounded by women in the dockside bars, all they do is talk about the ship.

He grabbed a cup of coffee and sat down on the brand-new couch across from the chief. The officer's lounge, unlike the crew lounge, was neat and clean at all times. "So is she a real redhead, Maggie?"

Captain Tannenbaume's question caught the chief off guard. He did not respond.

The others in the officer's lounge waited for an answer.

"What do you mean?" the chief said, looking at his feet.

The second engineer jumped in. "Come on, Chief, you know what he means." The second looked around at the others. "Is she, you know, a *real* redhead?"

The chief, of course, had no way of knowing, and Captain Tannenbaume got more satisfaction than he probably should have watching the chief squirm. But it served the bastard right. The guy held court every day at coffee time as if he was God's gift to women, and Captain Tannenbaume knew damn well that most of it was bullshit. The chief was fifty-five years old and still living with his mother back home in Minnesota. How much of a Casanova could he be?

"So?" he said, "What color is she below decks, Maggie?"

The chief's eyes glazed over.

Captain Tannenbaume was enjoying this interrogation far too much, but then he remembered the cute little trick with the air-conditioning on the bridge. Not to mention the sextant. He looked around the lounge and saw the others looking at the chief, as well, and Captain Tannenbaume knew that he would finally get his revenge.

Ironically, it was Mitzi herself who saved him.

"So how's my big Swede?" Mitzi said it as she breezed into the lounge. The whole room turned to see Mitzi at the coffee urn in her red miniskirt with the red pumps and the frilly white socks. Mitzi poured herself a cup of coffee and then went over and sat on the chief's lap. She wore the ascot around her neck and playfully took it off and placed it around the chief's neck.

"You left your scarf in my cabin," she said.

The chief beamed—the lucky bastard. Captain Tannenbaume knew that Mitzi was playing him for the fool, but to the others, it sure looked like the chief had scored big time. He had seen enough. He drained his coffee and rinsed out his cup—the cup that had "Master" printed on it—and placed the cup on the rack. He walked over to Mitzi and held out his hand. "Come with me, young lady. Coffee time is over."

Captain Tannenbaume heard the entire lounge groan, but he didn't give a rat's ass what they thought.

"Aw," Mitzi said. "I just got here."

"Now, now Mitzi," he said. "You've been assigned to this ship as a cadet and cadets work aboard ship. My wife is very eager to learn how to be a good Great Neck wife and you are here to teach her. At least that's what I've been told by Commodore what's-his-name."

Mitzi got down off the chief's lap. She held the chief's face in both hands and then pinched his cheek. "See you tomorrow at breakfast time, Chief."

The others in the lounge groaned again, this time louder than before. When Captain Tannenbaume and Mitzi were at the doorway, the chief called after Captain Tannenbaume.

"Hey, Cap, I heard from Sparks we've got pirates along our route of travel. Want me to fire up the Fire Main?"

It was the first Captain Tannenbaume had heard about pirates this trip but he didn't let on. "I'm on top of it, Maggie," Captain Tannenbaume said over his shoulder as he guided Mitzi out of the lounge. "You just worry about keeping the plant turning and let me worry about the pirates."

The chief and the others listened to Captain Tannenbaume explain to Mitzi as they walked down the passageway that pirate sightings were commonplace along their route of travel but that they presented no real threat. They could tell that Mitzi was not buying it. When Captain Tannenbaume and Mitzi were finally out of earshot, the chief told the others he wasn't buying it either. Pirates *were* cause for concern and he and the other engineers knew it. They were all too aware that they were down below completely blind to what was going on topside while there were pirates lurking around. Trusting the mates to keep them safe did not give them a warm and fuzzy feeling, especially since the *God is Able* still used the same old method of deterring pirates—running out fire hoses on deck and blasting the pirates with water as they tried to climb up on deck. Fighting pirates—armed with AK-47s—with water hoses did not inspire the engineers with confidence, especially since the deck department was responsible for manning the hoses.

"We oughta be armed with a few good hunting rifles is what I think," the chief told the others. "Something with a scope on it would do the trick. Relying on the mates armed with nothing but fire hoses makes me nervous."

"Why can't we be the ones to man the hoses?" the second asked.

"Union rules," the chief said. "The deck department works the deck, plain and simple."

"Isn't there anything else we could do?" the electrician asked. "Shouldn't we at least have sea marshalls on board?"

"The company's too cheap to pay for security," the chief said. "I asked. They said to run out the fire hoses."

"But there's gotta be something else we could do," the electrician said.

"It wouldn't matter if we could," the chief said. "Like I said, it ain't our bailiwick. Union rules forbid us from working the deck."

The others just nodded their heads, agreeing with the chief that there probably was nothing else they could do but hope the mates would protect them in case of a pirate attack.

"We're in the Hope business," the chief announced. "And that's all there is to it."

Chapter 31

A THREE-STEP PLAN

Captain Tannenbaume made it a habit to check in on Swifty at least once during the morning eight-to-twelve watch. Discovering that Swifty was unaware of what ocean they were in earlier in the voyage had been a bit unsettling to say the least. He normally gave his mates free reign to run their navigation watch as they saw fit but he knew he'd have to keep a closer eye on Swifty. And even though he had come to expect the unexpected whenever he popped in on Swifty, he never imagined that he'd find what he found today.

He'd entered the navigation bridge from the starboard wing as he was fond of the surprise entrance—the better to keep his deck officers on their toes—but with the sun in his eyes, he didn't see the chunk of plywood hanging from the overhead just inside the bridge wing door until it was too late.

When the wooziness wore off, he could see that the plywood was actually a sign that read *Mitzi's*. Whoever made it didn't take the time to sand the rough edges where the plywood was cut with a handsaw, so now Captain

Tannenbaume had a nasty gash on his head. It became immediately obvious to him what the plywood sign was for. In the space of a single day, Mitzi had turned the navigation bridge of the *God is Able* into a beauty salon.

Captain Tannenbaume did not recognize his own bridge. Someone had rigged a makeshift hair dryer behind the captain's chair using heat guns and aluminum paint trays bent and shaped in the form of a human head. *Probably that little shit of an electrician.* Captain Tannenbaume had to admit that the heat gun/paint tray gizmo was an ingenious idea, but he did not appreciate how the captain's chair had been fashioned into a perfect barber's chair. As the captain's chair was only for the use of the captain, it was assumed that no crew member in his right mind would dare risk the captain's wrath by taking the liberty of sitting in his chair. Captain Tannenbaume, who otherwise ruled his ship with a light hand, had once found a young AB by the name of Carlyle sitting in his chair at night, in the middle of the twelve-to-four watch. A number of years back, Carlyle's father happened to be the head of Marad, the Maritime Administration, and no doubt because of his father's position, the young AB acted as if he were untouchable. Captain Tannenbaume fired the boy on the spot. About three months later, he received a letter on official Marad stationery from old Tanner Carlyle thanking him for firing his son.

Next to the captain's chair was a table, another rough-cut job made of two-by-fours and plywood, with an assortment of nail polishes, polish removers, nail cutters, files, scissors, hairbrushes, combs, teasers, curlers, and an old Olympia curling iron he recognized as his mother's. As his head cleared, the odor of nail polish, acetone, and hairspray hit him like a brick.

Captain Tannenbaume became aware of Swifty for the first time and overheard him on the phone. "No, she's all booked up today. Try back tomorrow." Swifty hung up the receiver. "I tried to call you, sir, but the phone has been ringing off the hook. The entire ship wants a pedicure from Mitzi."

"Where the hell is Mitzi anyhow?" Captain Tannenbaume asked.

"Coffee time."

"Well, call down to the lounge and get her ass up here." Captain Tannenbaume looked like a gunslinger with his feet planted firmly into the deck and his hands at his sides. "I want my bridge back."

Before Swifty had a chance to pick up the phone, Mitzi, his mother, and Sylvia sauntered onto the bridge.

"Whew," his mother said as she reached the top of the stairs. "That nail polish remover is honking."

"It smells just like a beauty salon," Mitzi said, with obvious pride.

Captain Tannenbaume nearly pushed his mother aside to get at Mitzi when she reached the top of the stairs. "What the hell do you call this?" Captain Tannenbaume pointed toward the captain's chair and the heat guns.

"You told me to get to work." Mitzi pointed at Sylvia, who stood shyly on the top step behind her. "You want me to turn her into a Great Neck wife or don't you?"

Captain Tannenbaume simply could not allow Mitzi to speak to him that way in front of his crew. Yet, standing there in front of Mitzi, he had the absolute sense that he was no match for her. He glanced over his shoulder and saw that, sure enough, Swifty and Ski were waiting to hear his response.

"Oh, I see," he said. "Yes, I did order you to get to work on your sea project. And I see now that you are simply following my orders." He turned and looked at Ski when he said the bit about following orders, as if to say, "Make sure the crew gets the message."

Mitzi ushered Sylvia to the captain's-cum-barber's chair and pushed her down in it. Sylvia didn't seem to mind, which surprised Captain Tannenbaume, who knew his wife to be a tad headstrong like most teenagers. Mitzi then motioned for him to stand a few feet in front of the chair.

"Look at her," Mitzi said. "Do you see what I'm seeing? The flat hair. The boring fingernails. Do you see what I'm talking about?"

Captain Tannenbaume looked at his young wife and liked what he saw.

"No," Mitzi said. "I can tell that you have no idea what I'm talking about."

"What *are* you talking about?"

"Does she look like a Great Neck girl to you?"

Captain Tannenbaume did not respond. He agreed that she didn't look anything like a Great Neck girl but that was precisely what he liked about her.

"She don't even wear makeup for God's sake!"

"Do we . . . have to make her look like a Great Neck girl?"

"The Commodore said it's important she fits in right away," Mitzi said. "He's really concerned that she look good at the unveiling of that monument he's so excited about."

"What monument?"

"The monument for that idol of his, what's his name," Mitzi said. "The cadet who died in World War II."

"Never heard of him."

"But, he's, like, the hero of the academy," Mitzi said.

"I never went to the academy." Captain Tannenbaume waved his hand dismissively. "They turned me down when I was a kid. I sometimes wonder why I want to be superintendent of that place anyway."

"But, sonny," his mother said. "Think about it. What great revenge."

Captain Tannenbaume sighed. He looked at Sylvia. "You sure you want to go through with all this, sweetie?"

"In my country, the headmaster of a school is a very prestigious position."

Captain Tannenbaume didn't give a rat's ass about the prestige. All he knew was that he had been on these ships for too damn long and that the thought of never having to see the likes of the chief again was more than enough reason to take the job.

"Oh, what the hell. Let's just go through with it." He looked at Mitzi. "So what do you propose to do with my wife?"

"Well, actually," Mitzi said, "we do have a plan."

"A lesson plan," Mrs. Tannenbaume said.

"It's a three-step plan," Mitzi said.

"Sylvia has to *look* the part, *act* the part, and *talk* the part," Mrs. Tannenbaume said.

"The first thing is to make her look the part," Mitzi said.

"Hence the beauty parlor." Captain Tannenbaume's voice dripped with resignation.

"You think this is easy? Look at her." Mrs. Tannenbaume pointed at Sylvia, sitting primly in the chair.

While Mrs. Tannenbaume and her son continued to talk, Mitzi walked over to the captain's chair, straddled Sylvia's legs, and began to push up Sylvia's hair with her hands. Sylvia's limp hair fell down the second Mitzi let go.

"Hair spray!" Mitzi called out.

Mrs. Tannenbaume jumped into action.

"Hair spray!" Mrs. Tannenbaume thrust the oversized can into Mitzi's hand.

Mitzi worked fast, pushing up Sylvia's hair with one hand while she sprayed with the other. Captain Tannenbaume could only take a step back and marvel at what was unfolding in front of him. Mitzi sprayed with the ferocity of a crop duster. After a minute of nonstop spraying, a cloud of aerosol enveloped Sylvia's head, and she began to gasp for air, trying to fight off the crazy woman with the big can of aerosol. But the slightly built Sylvia was no match for Mitzi, who continued to primp and spray while deftly parrying Sylvia's blows with her forearms and elbows. It was a virtuoso performance.

Captain Tannenbaume naturally felt the impulse to come to the aid of his wife, who was very clearly on the losing end of a hairdresser catfight, but then again, Mitzi's dexterity downright awed him. Captain Tannenbaume did not have a dexterous bone in his body and he felt inferior to the more adroit Mitzi. In the end, it was Mrs. Tannenbaume who hip-checked Mitzi out of the way when she saw Sylvia go limp.

It took a moment for the aerosol cloud to dissipate, and when it did, the others on the bridge gasped at Sylvia's transformation. Her hair stood straight up on her head like a castle with peaks and turrets and gargoyley-looking wisps of hair locked in place by the big can of hairspray.

"Now that's what I'm talking about!" Mitzi said.

Captain Tannenbaume looked at Mitzi in disbelief. "She looks ridiculous."

"Maybe to you," Mitzi said. "But not to the women of Great Neck. With that head of hair, she'll be the envy of the *shul*."

Captain Tannenbaume looked to his mother for confirmation. She nodded.

"The women in Great Neck like to wear their hair high," she said agreed.

Captain Tannenbaume walked over to his wife. "Do you have any idea what you look like?"

Sylvia shook her head.

"I thought so. Mother, could you hand me the mirror, please?"

When Sylvia looked in the mirror, her entire countenance changed. Just like that. Gone was the teenaged child. In its place was a self-assured young woman. The others noticed the change, as well.

"You see?" Mitzi said. "The higher the hair, the more confidence you have. I don't know why it's true, but it is."

Captain Tannenbaume could not believe his eyes. "Are you telling me that high hair makes a woman feel more confident?"

Mrs. Tannenbaume nodded. "The women in Great Neck are pretty darn confident."

"They're more than confident." Mitzi straddled Sylvia's legs again and pointed her finger right in Sylvia's face. "They're assertive."

"Damn right," Sylvia said.

Sylvia's words stunned Captain Tannenbaume. It was true that Sylvia could at times be a difficult teenager, but by and large she was a sweet young lady. *What on earth is happening to my humble wife?*

"Nail polish remover!"

Mrs. Tannenbaume handed Mitzi the bottle and Mitzi, still straddling Sylvia's legs, grabbed Sylvia's hand and rubbed the cafe-au-lait colored nail polish off with the palm of her hand. Mrs. Tannenbaume gave Mitzi a rag, and Mitzi removed the last bit of old polish. Captain Tannenbaume had never seen a woman work so fast with her hands.

"Nail polish!"

Mrs. Tannenbaume was right there with the nail polish, a bright, garish, glossy red.

Mitzi had the nail polish on Sylvia's finger nails so fast it was as if she'd dipped them in the bottle. When Mitzi was finished, she pushed Sylvia's hands up over her head so that the heat guns could dry the wet polish. To Captain Tannenbaume, Sylvia looked like a poodle standing on her hind legs with her paws in the air. Mitzi swung her leg over Sylvia's legs and stood with her hands on her hips, panting from the exertion. After a moment, she shook her head.

"The bracelets have to go," she said, more to herself than to anyone else.

On each wrist, Sylvia wore the cotton woven bracelets that were popular in Thailand. Mitzi called out for scissors and quickly snipped the bracelets off. And, ominously, Sylvia did not try to stop Mitzi from removing them. Mitzi took off her own gaudy gold bangles and slipped them on Sylvia's wrists. Mrs. Tannenbaume added a few of her own fake gold bracelets and Sylvia rotated her wrists so that they clanged. She seemed to like the sound of that.

While Sylvia played with her bangles, Mitzi applied makeup to her face. First came thick layers of dark foundation, then gobs of ghoulish rouge. Black eyeliner followed blue eye shadow. Mitzi finished Sylvia off with black lip liner and glossy, blood-red lipstick. When she was done, she ordered Sylvia to stand up. Sylvia got out of the captain's chair and stood before Mitzi with perfect youthful posture.

"Posture's gotta go," Mitzi said. "You look like a cadet on parade. Push out your butt."

Sylvia did.

"Now push out your chest."

Again Sylvia did as she was told.

"Now walk."

Sylvia walked to the other side of the bridge and back. Gone was the graceful glide that Captain Tannenbaume so admired, and in its place was the gait of a goose.

What had they done to his sweetie? He, of course, knew that he had only himself to blame. Mitzi would have been happy to play the femme fatale for the entire voyage, but it was he who insisted that she get to work on her "seaproject." He only did that because he knew from experience the havoc to be wreaked by an idle crew member, especially when the idle crew member happened to be female and put together the way Mitzi was. And since he had agreed to this crazy plan of having his mother and Mitzi join the ship in the first place, he figured it was wiser to keep them both occupied.

He, however, had never imagined that the two of them would transform his wife into such a creature. Captain Tannenbaume thought back to the memo he received from Commodore what's-his-name. The Commodore wrote that he had Sylvia's interests in mind—and only Sylvia's interests—when he conceived of the plan to have Mitzi and Mrs. Tannenbaume join the ship, as he put it, "To prepare Sylvia for life under the microscope." Sylvia would feel so much more at ease, the Commodore wrote, if she "fit in" with the other wives. Captain Tannenbaume didn't know the Commodore, but from the tone of his memo, he seemed like a man who put others before himself. And maybe he was right—maybe Sylvia *would* feel more confident if she fit in with the other wives. Captain Tannenbaume could see that Sylvia already looked more confident and this after a change of hairdo and makeup. What else did Mitzi and his mother have in store for his young bride?

After several forays around the bridge, Mitzi told Sylvia to sit down in the captain's chair again.

"Swifty," she said, "fetch Sylvia here a cup of coffee. Milk, two sugars."

"I don't really want—"

Mitzi put up her hand to silence Sylvia. The moment Swifty placed the coffee in Sylvia's hands, Mitzi whispered something in her ear. Sylvia took a moment to compose herself, and then she handed the coffee back to Swifty. "It needs more milk."

Swifty took the cup from Sylvia's hands and looked at Captain Tannenbaume, as if to say, "Do I have to be your wife's coffee boy?" Captain Tannenbaume thought he understood what Mitzi was doing. He recognized it as something that he first took notice of as a kid growing up in Great Neck. Whenever he ate in restaurants in Great Neck, he noticed that the women always sent stuff back to the kitchen—the soup was too cold, the coffee too hot—something was always wrong with their order.

Captain Tannenbaume could not bring himself to look Swifty in the eye. He just waved his arm at the coffee station. He knew what Mitzi was up to, and there was no sense in trying to prevent her from doing what she was on a mission to accomplish.

All Captain Tannenbaume could do was let out a long, tired sigh. *Good God, what have I wrought?*

On his way down to his cabin, Captain Tannenbaume stopped in on Sparks and gave him a good ass chewing for being kept out of the loop on the pirate thing.

Sparks told him if he'd seen one pirate warning, he'd seen a thousand. Besides, Sparks said, the reports just mentioned pirate sightings—they said nothing about an actual pirate attack.

Captain Tannenbaume agreed that the reports looked pretty cookie-cutter but he told Sparks to keep him better informed in the future.

"The last thing I need is the chief sniffing around the radio shack checking up on us," Captain Tannenbaume said. "The more he stays down below, the better off we'll all be."

Chapter 32

SEND IT BACK

At breakfast in the officers' mess the next morning, Sylvia practiced sending stuff back. She sent back the scrambled eggs because they were too runny, the grits because they were too watery, and the toast because it wasn't dark enough.

Mitzi was there to coach her along. "Tell the messman you just want the cook to tighten up the eggs a little bit. And tell him the grits are looking a little soupy."

Sylvia was a fast learner. She sent back the oatmeal on her own, telling the messman that it was too oaty.

"Is that a word?" Sylvia asked Mitzi. "Oaty?"

"Doesn't matter. Send them back if you think they're too oaty," Mitzi said. "Don't let them take advantage of you."

The "oaty" bit, evidently, was too much for the steward. He stormed into the officers' mess wanting to know what the hell "too oaty" meant.

"Oh, I meant no offense," Sylvia said. "I just thought the oatmeal had, well, too many oats in it."

"So order the goddamned cream of wheat."

When the cream of wheat came, it was too creamy.

Captain Tannenbaume, who had been sitting next to his wife without saying a word, decided to draw the line there. He took the bowl of cream of wheat out of the messman's hands and said he would eat it.

"Why do you let people push you around like that?" Sylvia asked.

Captain Tannenbaume shrugged. "I don't like to impose on people."

Sylvia looked at Mitzi and nodded toward him. "He's got no *chutzpah*."

Captain Tannenbaume dropped his spoon of cream of wheat. "*Chutzpah*?"

"She's right, Sonny," his mother said. "A little *chutzpah* would do you good."

"My wife uses the word '*chutzpah*' now?"

"Oy, would you listen to this schmuck?" Sylvia leaned over the table and put her hand on Mitzi's arm. "'My wife uses the word *chutzpah*?'" Sylvia had a knack for mimicry—she sounded just like her husband, and she and Mitzi laughed.

Captain Tannenbaume ignored his wife's needling. He was more interested in her new vocabulary. He was familiar with the words—his mother used them all the time—but they just sounded so foreign coming out of his Thai wife's mouth.

"Is this part of my wife's makeover?" he asked Mitzi.

Mitzi shrugged. "The Commodore wants her to fit in. She needs to speak the lingo."

"It wouldn't hurt if you spoke the language a little yourself, sonny," his mother said.

"Oh," Captain Tannenbaume said through a mouthful of cream of wheat. "Does the Commodore want me to speak the language too?"

Captain Tannenbaume noticed the look Mitzi and his mother gave one another. It was a look that did not bode well.

"Look, if you think I'm changing how I talk for that Commodore, you've got another thing coming. I'm not changing for anybody."

"No, sonny," his mother said, "nobody wants you to change for anybody, either, but would it be such a bad idea to use your *Yiddisha Kop* once in a while?"

"My *Yiddisha Kop*? Since when do I have a *Yiddisha Kop*?"

"But, sonny boy, I've always told you you have a *Yiddisha Kop*."

"You should be happy you have a *Yiddisha Kop*," Mitzi said. "Would you rather be a dopey WASP?"

The messman interrupted them when he brought Captain Tannenbaume his usual breakfast of bacon and eggs with white toast. When Captain Tannenbaume picked up his fork and pierced a slice of bacon, Mitzi slapped his hand.

"Stop that. You got yourself a young wife now," Mitzi said. "Think about your health." Mitzi took the bacon off his plate. "Like you need all that cholesterol!"

Captain Tannenbaume looked at his young wife sitting next to him. "Well, maybe you're right." He reached over and squeezed Sylvia's hand. "Maybe I'll give up the bacon."

"Mitzi's right, sonny." His mother's words came out in a rush. "In fact, maybe you should give up pork altogether."

"What is it with you and pork, Mother? You've been trying to get me to give it up my whole life."

"Pork comes from the pig," Mitzi said. "Pigs are the only animals that shit where they eat. Did you know that?"

Captain Tannenbaume had to admit that he did not and told his mother if he knew that about pigs he would have given up pork a long time ago. Mitzi smiled at Mrs. Tannenbaume, as if she had just won some prize.

"I was a little girl when my mother taught me not to eat pork," his mother said. "I guess I forgot the reason . . ."

Now it was the Steward who interrupted them, barking at the cook for coming into the galley on his day off.

"Captain, could I talk to you?" the cook said. "Right away?"

"If you need to see the captain when he's in the officers' mess, you come to me first," the Steward said. "I told you for the last time, I am the only one in the steward's department that's allowed to interrupt—"

"What can I do for you, Cookie?" Captain Tannenbaume said.

The steward slapped his hand against the side of his own head, something he did whenever something or someone exasperated him. "Captain, what I just said? Didn't you hear me just tell the man that I am the only one that can interrupt you?"

"Oh, yes," Captain Tannenbaume said. "Okay, Stew, what is it I can do for the cook?"

The steward turned to the cook. "Okay. Tell me what it is you want me to tell the captain."

"We're supposed to be in the middle of the Indian Ocean," the cook said. "I was having a smoke on the fantail when I noticed that we're hugging the coast of somewhere."

Captain Tannenbaume looked directly at the cook. "We're hugging a coast?"

"Captain, please," the steward said. "I'm trying to school the man."

"Oh. Sorry, Stew. Well, uh, can you ask him how close to land we are?"

The cook waved his arms up and down in front of Captain Tannenbaume. "We're really fucking —"

The steward cuffed the cook upside the head.

The cook turned and waved his arms in front of the steward. "Tell him we're really close. Tell him we're really fucking close!"

The steward turned slowly toward Captain Tannenbaume. "The cook says we're really fucking close to land now, Captain."

Captain Tannenbaume stood up.

"Which side—Sorry, Stew. Can you ask him which side of the ship?"

The cook was too excited to point. He waved his arms over his head and said, "The . . . "

"Hey!" The steward really slapped the cook upside his head now. "How many times? Huh? How many times I gotta said it? Only department heads talk to the captain."

"Well then, how come the messman gets to talk to the captain?" the cook pointed out. "He's no department head."

"He is the only—"

"Uh, Stew." Captain Tannenbaume put his hand on the steward's shoulder. "This is pretty important."

The steward took a deep breath and counted to ten. "Captain, please. You want me to run a tight department, and then you do not let me school my men."

"Of course, Stew." Captain Tannenbaume struggled to keep patient. "Go ahead and school your man here."

The Steward counted to ten again. He gave the cook a hard look. "Okay, Cook. Now. Tell *me*. Which side of the ship the land is on?"

"The port side!"

Captain Tannenbaume did not wait for the steward to pass on what the cook said. He tore out of the officers' mess, leaving the steward furious.

"How I'm supposed to school my men!" he shouted after him.

Captain Tannenbaume turned right out of the officers' mess and raced through the passageway on the port side of the ship to the watertight door leading to the main deck. Mitzi, his mother, Sylvia, and the cook followed close behind. He opened the door and they all fell out onto the main deck.

Sure enough, there was land, about a hundred yards off the port beam. Captain Tannenbaume recognized the mahogany brown cliffs surrounding the ancient city of Muscat, on the Arabian Peninsula. Somehow, the *God is Able* had found its way into the Gulf of Oman and was steaming right for the Straights of Hormuz. Years ago, as a junior officer, Captain Tannenbaume had worked on a tanker that made regular runs to the Persian Gulf, and Muscat was an oasis in an otherwise desolate landscape. He'd recognize it anywhere. He also knew that the ship had good water right up to the shoreline, and the best he could tell, the *God is Able* was running directly parallel, so he relaxed some.

Mitzi, however, was not relaxed. She punched the cook in the shoulder.

"Hey," she said. "Are you telling me we're supposed to be in the middle of the ocean right now?"

"Yup," the cook said. "That's what Tibby told me. And he said we were running way too close to shore with all the pirate warnings we've gotten lately, especially with no fire hoses laid out on deck."

Captain Tannenbaume went stiff at the sound of Tibby's name.

"Oh, that's what Tibby told you? Well tell Mr. Tibby he is wrong. It just so happens that I ordered a change of course so that Mitzi here could have a look at the ancient city of Muscat." Captain Tannenbaume pointed at the shimmering mirage. "There, Mitz, all for you. I wanted this trip to feel more like a cruise for you."

"You did that for me?"

Captain Tannenbaume saw the hurt look on his mother's face.

"And for you, too, Mother." He fake-punched his mother in the arm. "My little supernumerary."

Captain Tannenbaume noticed that Sylvia did not seem to be feeling left out, so he did not say anything to her. Instead, he put his arms around all of them and ushered them back inside. "Let's go on up to the bridge for a better look."

When they got to the bridge, they found half the crew there, jostling for a position around the chart table. Swifty seemed to be the object of their attention. Captain Tannenbaume assumed they were all trying to get a good look at the chart, to figure out where the hell they were.

"Hey!" Swifty shouted. "Give me some space. How am I supposed to book you when you're ripping the appointment book out of my hands?"

"Attention on deck!" Ski yelled.

The sailors ignored him. It was Mitzi who got their attention. She calmly walked over to the captain's chair, dismantled the makeshift hair dryer, and then attacked the scrum of sailors gathered around the chart table with the heat gun. One by one, she peeled the scrum back until she got to Swifty. He remained hunched over the appointment book, guarding it with his life, and did not turn around until the heat gun singed the back of his shirt.

When Captain Tannenbaume snatched the book out of his hands and threw it to the deck, the sailors were on it like a dog on a bone.

He grabbed Swifty by the elbow and walked him out to the port bridge wing. He pointed at Muscat. "Do you know where we are, young man?"

"I . . . sir, I've been so busy . . . "

Captain Tannenbaume got up into Swifty's face. "What about all those positions on the chart? All those perfect sunlines of yours, perfectly matching the ship's Dead Reckoning track."

"Sir . . . I . . . we . . . the truth is, none of us knows how to use H.O. 229. We can't make heads or tails of the nautical almanac, or the air almanac, or the sight reduction tables, or any of those mathematical tables."

"So why didn't you ask?"

"We were reluctant to, sir. I guess we were a little awed by what you did the other night."

"And the noon position reports?"

"Sparks has been making them up," Swifty said. "He feels bad about smashing the GPS."

Captain Tannenbaume's head fell to his chest. He suddenly felt very tired, dog tired. He had been going to sea for too long. He lifted his head and looked at the young junior officer standing before him.

It seemed like just yesterday that he himself was a third mate, happy to be an officer after spending years as an unlicensed crew member. He had taken his time working his way to the top of the unlicensed deck department, to the job of boatswain, a job that he liked. He liked running the deck gang, liked organizing the boatswain's locker, liked the neatness of his life aboard ship. Mostly he liked being the boss so that he could go ashore the minute the gangway hit the dock. As boss of the unlicensed deck department, he set the port watches for his men, and he always gave himself the most shore leave. But whenever he overreached, the chief mate would be right there to rein him in. That's when he set his sights on making captain, where there would be no one left to tell him what to do.

When he finally became captain, he realized he could not have been more wrong—there is always someone to tell you what to do. Now it was the home office, usually some dumb-ass manager who had never been to sea in his life. No, he'd been on these damn ships far too long.

Captain Tannenbaume let go of Swifty's shoulder. "Go back inside."

When he was alone, he leaned against the bulwark to catch his breath, and it occurred to him that this really might be his last voyage. Yes, he'd accepted the offer to be superintendent of the academy, but in his heart, he had not been 100 percent certain he was actually going to go through with it. With each passing day, however, the idea of becoming superintendent seemed more and more appealing. But first, of course, he had to get this old 'tween decker home.

He called up a chart of the world in his mind's eye. To get to the Suez Canal, all they had to do was turn around and keep the Arabian Peninsula on their starboard side until they hit the Red Sea, then it was straight up the Red Sea to the canal. They'd pick up the new GPS that Sparks had requisitioned in Suez, and from there it was a short jaunt across the Med and then across the Pond to New York. Surely his deck officers could manage that. *They could at least do that, couldn't they?*

Captain Tannenbaume looked into the wheelhouse. It seemed Mitzi had straightened everyone out. The sailors were lined up single file, patiently waiting to book their appointments. She was some woman, that Mitzi. Not only was she drop-dead gorgeous, she was a real go-getter to boot. Although he didn't necessarily like the changes Mitzi had wrought, both to his ship and to his wife, he had to admit they were impressive in scope.

The love of a dexterous woman, that's all he ever wanted, really. Seeing Mitzi in action made him realize that Sylvia was anything but dexterous. Keeping their stateroom in order was beyond her capability—how was she ever going to keep their home in order? Of course, keeping a home was not why Captain Tannenbaume married her. He married her because she was young and nubile. What was it his mother called it? The hoo hoo and the ha ha?

"Two times," Captain Tannenbaume had bragged to the chief earlier in the voyage, after the chief had humiliated him with the whole sextant thing. Two times a day he had sex with his wife: once at night and once again when they woke up in the morning. That was the way Captain Tannenbaume liked it, and for Sylvia, after spending three years in a Singapore cat house, two times a day was like being on vacation.

Swifty walked out onto the wing. "Sir, would it be all right if Mitzi gave me a pedicure tomorrow?"

"This would be during your watch, I take it?"

"Sir, it's just that the chief mate runs me ragged with overtime work when I'm off watch, and the only chance I have to get one of Mitzi's pedicures is when I'm on. Everyone else is getting a pedicure, why can't I get one too?"

Captain Tannenbaume just stared off, his eyes fixed on the horizon. *So this was what life at sea had come to. Third mates demanding pedicures on the bridge.*

Captain Tannenbaume waved Swifty away. "Whatever. You're no good to me on the bridge anyway, son."

On the way down to his cabin, Captain Tannenbaume bumped into Sparks. He was about to bring up the fictitious noon position reports, but then thought it wasn't worth the bother.

"Any word from the agent about whether or not we're getting a GPS in Suez?"

"I still haven't heard from the agent," Sparks said. "But don't worry. We'll get the GPS in Suez if I have to go ashore and get it myself."

Captain Tannenbaume waved off Sparks the same way he had waved off Swifty. He closed the door to his cabin and sat down on the settee in his office. Jesus. He hadn't worked on his desk in days. Just the thought of it made him exhausted. He wondered about the superintendent's job. Since there would be nobody above him—there was no home office he'd have to answer to as far as he knew—he wondered if he'd even need a desk at the academy.

Chapter 33

RIGHT-OF-WAY

Captain Tannenbaume woke up on the settee a little after dawn with the side of his face covered in drool and immediately wondered why his wife went to bed without him. When he crawled into bed and tried to spoon her, Sylvia pushed him away.

Captain Tannenbaume shot up in bed. "Sylvia, what the hell is going on?"

"Oh, didn't I tell you? From now on, we *schtup* once a week, on Saturday night."

"*Schtup*?" Captain Tannenbaume said.

"Yeah," Sylvia said. "You know—the hoo hoo and the ha ha."

"Once a week?"

"But you have to take me out to dinner first. And it better be a fancy place."

"What the hell has gotten into you? And where the hell did you come up with '*schtup*'?"

"The women in Great Neck *schtup*," Sylvia said matter-of-factly. "But only once a week." Sylvia sat up in bed and inspected her nails. They were getting longer, and Mitzi's garish nail polish gleamed in the early morning light. "And one other thing. There will be no more hand jobs, either."

"What!"

"Mitzi says it will ruin my nails."

"Oh, is that what Mitzi says?"

Captain Tannenbaume threw off the covers from his side of the bed, grabbed the phone off the bulkhead, and dialed the bridge. When his mother answered, he told her to put Mitzi on the phone.

"She's in the middle of giving Swifty a pedicure."

"Finish pedicuring Swifty yourself, Mother, and send Mitzi down to my cabin, pronto."

"Is something wrong, sonny?"

"Yes, Mother, something is wrong," Captain Tannenbaume said. "I quit. Tell that Commodore of yours to find himself another superintendent."

Mitzi and his mother were in Captain Tannenbaume's cabin before he had a chance to hang up the phone.

"Okay," Mitzi said without prompting, "forget the Saturday night–only thing. Have sex as often as you'd like. Just don't let it get out that you have sex twice a day, or the women in Great Neck'll think you're Irish or something."

"And the hand jobs?" Captain Tannenbaume asked.

"As far as the hand jobs are concerned," Mitzi said, "we can go with fake nails, so maybe Sylvia could just remove the fake nails for the hand jobs and put them back on for formal functions."

His mother raised her eyebrows.

"What?" Mitzi said.

"I don't get this business about the hand jobs. Aren't they messy, sonny?"

Captain Tannenbaume didn't want to have this conversation with his mother, but there was no way around it. "A regular hand job keeps my prostate nice and limber, mess or no mess."

"Oh, yeah," Mitzi said. "Mogie swears by them."

Captain Tannenbaume's ears perked up. "Mogie?"

Mitzi waved her hand. "An old boyfriend."

Captain Tannenbaume looked away. *So Mogie's her boyfriend?* He ran his fingers slowly through his hair. He did not want to let on that he knew about the reams of telexes that Sparks had been intercepting from some guy named Mogie. Mostly, he didn't want to let on about the reams of telexes that Sparks had been sending back.

"So that's settled then?" his mother said. "You're back on board, sonny?"

Captain Tannenbaume did not respond. He was thinking about the telex he had picked up off Sparks's desk a few days back—it was the very first time Captain Tannenbaume had read a telex not meant for him. There was something in it about a stool. Some fellow named Mogie had wanted to know if Mitzi missed his stool. Knowing Mogie was an old boyfriend changed the complexion of that question.

"Sonny boy? You're not really going to quit are you?"

Captain Tannenbaume could not take his eyes off Mitzi. So Mitzi gave hand jobs. Was that what the stool was for? Captain Tannenbaume pictured a farmer milking a cow. The dexterity of it all sent his heart racing.

"Sonny?"

Mitzi. You farmer's daughter you.

"Sonny!"

"Yes, Mother. Yes. I mean, no. No, mother, I won't quit. As long as Sylvia continues to take care of me."

Captain Tannenbaume did not look at his mother when he said it. He only had eyes for Mitzi, the farmer's daughter with the special stool.

The *God is Able* managed to make its way into the Red Sea unscathed. Swifty and his fellow deck officers simply followed the other ships that were steaming in the same direction. They were all going to the same place, of course—the Suez Canal—and there was only one way to get there. At the same time, Swifty managed to keep out of Captain Tannenbaume's hair. Having been relieved of the burden of celestial navigation, not to mention the stress of having to fake the noon position reports, Swifty and his fellow navigation officers actually enjoyed the journey up the Red Sea. The mates basked in the collegial atmosphere of

Mitzi's salon, using the engineers and cooks and stewards—who gathered on the bridge waiting their turn for Mitzi's services—as lookouts and helmsmen while they, the mates, received their manicures and pedicures. Swifty had become so enamored of his daily pedicure that he handed over more and more of his watch-keeping duties to the others so that he could enjoy his time in the captain's-cum-barber's chair without the tedious interruptions of navigating a ship in a congested waterway.

As the ship proceeded northbound toward the canal, ship traffic increased significantly, and Swifty had the others answer the incessant VHF calls from ships bearing down on the *God is Able* from every direction. He taught the engineers to make meeting arrangements with oncoming ships. He taught the cooks how to make overtaking arrangements with ships that were overtaking them. And he taught Mrs. Tannenbaume how to deal with crossing traffic. Mrs. Tannenbaume had a hard time with the rules for crossing vessels. She could not abide having to change course for a ship just because it was on her starboard side. Why couldn't the other guy change course, she had asked Swifty. Why did she have to be the one?

Swifty told her that's what the Rules of the Road stated: a vessel that has another vessel on its starboard side is the give-way vessel. Period.

Mrs. Tannenbaume did not agree with the Rules of the Road. She called them arbitrary. "Fine," Swifty said. "If you do not want to alter course, then hold your course and speed. You'll see what happens."

Within the hour, an enormous tanker in semi-ballasted condition was crossing the path of the *God is Able* from right to left. Swifty was getting his nails done in "the chair," and Mrs. Tannenbaume, acting as lookout, told him that there was a ship on their starboard bow. Swifty told her to alter course to starboard to pass under the other ship's stern.

"No way, José," Mrs. Tannenbaume said, peering through a pair of binoculars. "That sucker's going to have to alter course for us."

"Fine," Swifty said. "Do it your way. Mitzi, do we have any more of the clear polish? My pedicure lasts longer that way."

Mrs. Tannenbaume ignored the urgent calls coming in over the VHF radio. A half-hour later, the tanker was within a half-mile of the *God is Able*. The other ship blew the danger signal, five short and angry blasts on the steam whistle, in an effort to get Mrs. Tannenbaume to alter course, but Mrs. Tannenbaume was not budging. The tanker passed ahead of them by no more than a hundred yards.

"Okay, that was too close for comfort," Swifty said. "Captain Tannenbaume's standing orders call for a Closest Point of Approach of one nautical mile."

"Standing orders my tush," Mrs. Tannenbaume said. "A miss is as good as a mile."

"But the standing orders—"

"Show me these standing orders."

The phone rang. It was the chief wanting to know who was blowing the danger signal.

"It's all under control," Mrs. Tannenbaume assured him.

"It doesn't sound like it's under control. We don't exactly feel so comfortable down here relying on you mates to keep us safe," the chief growled. "By the way, you guys keeping a good lookout for pirates?"

"Oh, pirates, schmirates."

"If it was my department, I'd have run out some fire hoses."

"You worry about your department and let me worry about mine."

"Oh, and now it's your department?" the chief said. "From supernumerary to captain? And speaking of captains, where is that son of yours anyway? I haven't seen him for days."

"He needs his rest, leave him out of this," Mrs. Tannenbaume said. "Besides, we're doing just fine up here without him."

"Well it sure doesn't sound like you're doing fine," the chief said, and hung up the phone.

Mrs. Tannenbaume turned to Swifty. "Tell me more about this danger signal."

"Get the Nautical Rules of the Road off the bookshelf. It's the blue book on the end. You can see it in black and white for yourself."

When Mrs. Tannenbaume brought the book over to him—Mitzi was blowing his nails dry with the heat gun—Swifty told her to open the book and turn to Rule Thirty-four, Maneuvering and Warning Signals. He read subsection (d) aloud.

"When vessels in sight of one another are approaching each other and from any cause either vessel fails to understand the actions or intentions of the other, or is in doubt whether sufficient action is being taken by the other to avoid collision, the vessel in doubt shall immediately indicate such doubt by giving five short and rapid blasts on the whistle."

"So you blow the danger signal when you don't know what the other ship wants?"

"Well, rule 34 refers to 'doubt,' but mariners call five short and rapid blasts the 'danger signal.' But the danger signal is sounded not so much to convey actual danger, as to say, in effect, 'Get the hell out of my way.' Of course—"

"I've heard enough," Mrs. Tannenbaume said and put the rule book back up on the shelf where it belonged. "I know exactly what to do now."

The danger signal became Mrs. Tannenbaume's favorite new whistle signal. She blew it morning, noon, and night, and with Mrs. Tannenbaume at the conn, the *God is Able* barreled its way up the Red Sea, a trail of angry ships in her wake.

Chapter 34

DOING FOR OTHERS

M ogie had sent his first telex to the *God is Able* before the ship even departed Singapore. He was evidently desperate to know if Mitzi had any trouble with the Malaysian taxi drivers in Singapore who, Mogie heard, liked redheads. The next telex from Mogie came when the ship was still in the straits of Malacca, and then there was nothing for several days. Then the one about the stool arrived, and after Sparks wrote back, pretending to be Mitzi, the telexes began to arrive in bunches —two, three, sometimes four or five in a day.

When Captain Tannenbaume first discovered, years before on a long voyage around the Cape of Good Hope and across the South Atlantic to Brazil, that Sparks was reading other people's mail, he was mortified. He told Sparks it was an invasion of privacy and that he would not stand for it. But time after time during that voyage, he entered the radio shack only to find Sparks's nose buried in a telex meant for someone else. Captain Tannenbaume knew that he could not stop Sparks from reading other people's telexes, and it eventually dawned on him that it might be better, in the end, if Sparks did read them. Radio officers had a tendency to get squirrelly on the long sea passages, what with all that time on their hands, and if reading other people's mail provided some degree of respite for Sparks, then perhaps Captain Tannenbaume ought to turn a blind eye to the questionable practice.

It wasn't until later, on another long sea passage, that Captain Tannenbaume realized that not only did Sparks read telexes that were not meant for him, but he responded to them as well. Again Captain Tannenbaume tried to stop him, and again he found his efforts frustrated by the ever-persistent Sparks. Although he did not approve of what Sparks was doing, he had to admit that every once in a while he found his curiosity piqued whenever Sparks was deep in a back-and-forth with an unsuspecting pen pal. But until this voyage, he had resisted the urge to find out what exactly it was that Sparks wrote in his telexes.

Maybe it was the stress of having his mother and wife on board. Maybe he was feeling restless over his impending life change, but something had made Captain Tannenbaume pick up and read a telex that he well knew was not addressed to him.

The telex was from a man named Mogie, and it was about a stool.

Captain Tannenbaume was disgusted by his lack of discipline. How could he read something that he knew was meant for someone else? And after all of his lecturing about invading another's privacy? Although he was indeed curious about the nature of the telex—who Mogie was, and what this business was about a stool—Captain Tannenbaume quickly got a hold of himself, walked out of the radio shack, and banished from his mind all thoughts of reading any more telexes.

Until he heard Mitzi say that Mogie was her boyfriend.

He didn't know why that affected him so much. Was Captain Tannenbaume so naïve as to think that a woman like Mitzi did not have a long trail of suitors? That a woman so dexterous, so capable, so *in charge* did not have a boyfriend on the side? For all he knew, maybe it wasn't just one. Maybe there were others, lots of others. She was, after all, carrying on with the chief. Oh, Captain Tannenbaume knew that the big Swede was all talk when it came to women but who really knew what went on in her cabin after the chief let himself in with the breakfast tray every morning. And what about that electrician? The little shit was probably changing out her lightbulbs this very moment. Well, Captain Tannenbaume could not very well snoop around on Mitzi and the chief, and he didn't want to look silly by ordering the electrician to stay away from Mitzi's cabin, but he could find out about this Mogie character. He could, if he wanted, just sneak into the radio shack and read the telexes from Mogie himself. He could.

And in the end, he did.

When Sparks was at coffee time one morning, Captain Tannenbaume snooped around the radio shack until he found the telexes in the top left-hand drawer of Sparks's desk. Sure enough, Sparks had written back that he (she) did not miss Mogie's stool, that there were plenty of stools aboard the *God is Able*. Sparks, pretending that he was Mitzi, said he (she) was in stool heaven.

Sparks's response produced an outpouring from Mogie. A new telex was on the wires before the last had printed. Sparks answered each one. He clearly had a way—born of long practice, Captain Tannenbaume was afraid—of pushing Mogie's buttons with one word. The telexes from Mogie kept coming until the top left-hand drawer was crammed full.

When Sparks came back from coffee time that day, he found Captain Tannenbaume at his desk. Captain Tannenbaume didn't even try to hide the fact that he'd read the telexes.

"So what exactly does Mogie do with this stool of his?" Captain Tannenbaume blurted out.

"I . . . I don't know. I'm still trying to guh . . . get it out of Mogie. When you're pruh . . . pruh . . . pretending to be someone else, you can't ask any obvious questions."

"Right, well . . . keep me in the loop regarding this Mogie. It's a matter of security."

Sparks did keep Captain Tannenbaume in the loop. He showed him every telex he received from Mogie the moment it arrived. Soon Captain Tannenbaume huddled with Sparks every morning so that he would be there when the first telex arrived. Together he and Sparks crafted a response.

Mogie wrote that the thought of so many stools on board was driving him foolish. He wanted to know what the sailors' stools looked like. Sparks wrote back that they were handcrafted of exotic hardwoods and covered in Spanish leather. Sparks wrote to Mogie that the ship's carpenter was making a new stool just for him (her). Mogie was furious and wanted to know why Sparks (Mitzi) needed a new stool.

Captain Tannenbaume was so preoccupied with the telexes that he holed himself up in his cabin and shut out the world. He did not hear the danger signal his mother blew at every passing ship. He was unaware that Swifty had abdicated all of his watch-keeping duties to the sailors and engineers who crowded the bridge every day. He no longer joined his shipmates for coffee time. He even replaced his own lightbulbs for fear the electrician would say or do something to get his goat. He simply could not afford the break in concentration.

Captain Tannenbaume became desperate to know what exactly Mogie did with his stool. But he and Sparks just couldn't figure it out.

"Tell me again what you like best about the stool?" Sparks asked. Mogie wrote back that it made him feel like a king.

"What else?" Sparks asked. Mogie said it made him feel tall.

Captain Tannenbaume couldn't understand that one. How could Mitzi sitting on a stool milking Mogie make him feel tall?

Mogie wrote long telexes reminiscing about the many times—and places—he and Mitzi used the stool, but still he did not give a glimpse as to what the stool was *for*.

Captain Tannenbaume became convinced that Sparks should be more direct in his questioning. Sparks told Captain Tannenbaume that one had to be careful when playing this game. One false move would blow their identity. "Patience," Sparks counseled. "Patience."

Patience my ass. And so without thinking too much about it, when the ship was in the Suez Canal and Sparks was on the bridge sightseeing, Captain Tannenbaume fired off a telex of his own.

Sylvia left the bridge without saying goodbye to anyone, not that anyone on the bridge even noticed that she left. Things were beginning to get a little crazy up there, what with Mitzi being fully booked and every sailor aboard wanting either a manicure or a pedicure, or both. The sailors, who used to compare the buildup of their varnishing jobs, now compared the buildup on their nails. They even showed Mitzi how to scuff up the first few coats of nail polish so that the final coat would hold better and create a deeper shine.

The engineers, it turned out, were Mitzi's best customers, and the chief did not like it one bit when his engineers began showing off their manicured hands at coffee time. The chief had long prided himself on being the only one in the engine department with clean fingernails, and he wondered aloud if anybody down below was slinging wrenches anymore. The engineers told the chief that slinging wrenches would damage their cuticles, that Mitzi had told them that they should be able to see a—air quotes—"half-moon" in their fingernails, that a—air quotes—"half-moon" was the sign of a healthy cuticle. The engineers used air quotes more than ever, now that their cuticles were healthy.

Sylvia just wanted to lie down. She had spent the entire morning getting her hair blow-dried, her eyebrows tweezed, her nose hairs trimmed, her toes painted, and now she just wanted to get away from Mitzi for a little while. Mitzi had let Sylvia know this morning that she was not happy with the progress she was making in her assertiveness training. But Sylvia could not imagine being any more assertive than she was already. She asserted herself everywhere—on the bridge, in the lounge, not to mention in the officers' mess, where she had never sent back so many things in all her life. Just yesterday in the officers' mess she had sent back her ice water (too icy), chocolate cake (too chocolatey), sweet tea (too sweet), and her ice water again (not icy enough). She bossed her husband around without mercy, meddled in his business, and *kvetched* without letup. Sylvia complained about everything in her life from morning 'til night, but still Mitzi was not satisfied. And on top of the complaining and *kvetching* and meddling, Mitzi now informed Sylvia that she was not doing enough for others! A Great Neck wife feels compelled to "do for others," Mitzi had told her. The first thing Mitzi asked Sylvia when she arrived on the bridge every day for her daily pedicure was "are you doing for others?" So now Sylvia spent what spare moments she had in the day putting together care packages for the needy children back home in Phuket. Sylvia was beginning to feel that the life of a pampered Great Neck wife was not all that it was cracked up to be. Between getting herself made-up every day, not letting anyone push her around, and doing for others, she was exhausted. It was no wonder the women in Great Neck only *schtupped* once a week.

Sylvia opened the door to her cabin and found her husband sprawled on their bunk with pages and pages of telexes all around him. He had his face pressed into one of the telexes and did not notice that Sylvia had entered their cabin. When the phone rang, he didn't notice that either.

Sylvia answered the phone.

"This is the chief. The damned—"

Sylvia shoved the phone against her husband's ear.

"What," Captain Tannenbaume said.

"What?" the chief said. "The damn whistle woke me up from my goddamn nooner again, that's what."

"What whistle?"

"What whistle? The whistle that has been blowing all day every day for the last week. That whistle."

Captain Tannenbaume cupped the phone to his hand. "Have they been blowing the whistle on the bridge lately?"

Sylvia threw her hands up in the air. "Hang up, honey." She moved a pile of telexes out of the way and sat on the edge of the bunk.

"Look," she said after her husband hung up the phone. "Do you mean to tell me you haven't heard the ship's whistle blowing nonstop for the past week?"

Captain Tannenbaume merely stared at Sylvia with an uncomprehending look on his face.

Sylvia threw up her hands. "What has gotten into you? Your ship is going to pot right before your eyes and you act like you could care less."

Captain Tannenbaume could not look his wife in the eye. He gripped a handful of telexes. "I guess I've been busy with these."

"What is it with these telexes?" Sylvia picked one up off the bunk but Captain Tannenbaume snatched it out of her hand before she could read it.

"It's important business from the home office. The company is buying a new ship and they need my help." Captain Tannenbaume gathered the rest of the telexes up off the bunk and clutched them to his chest. "It's a complicated transaction."

Sylvia took advantage of the clean bunk and curled herself up in the fetal position. She reached out for her husband and tried to pull him down to her.

"Come here," she sighed. "Mitzi is running me ragged doing for others all day."

"What others?"

"Oh . . . unfortunate others," Sylvia said. "Mitzi says the women in Great Neck do for others."

"Do what for others?"

"Whatever it is they need."

"I don't understand."

"Me neither. I barely have time to do for myself every day. But Mitzi says in Great Neck you do for yourself *and* you do for others. I don't know how they can do so much."

Captain Tannenbaume shook his head. "That Mitzi is something, huh?"

Sylvia did not answer. Her eyes were closed and her head was resting against Captain Tannenbaume's thigh. Captain Tannenbaume moved her head onto the pillow and put a blanket over her before he slipped off the bunk. Then he stashed the telexes in the top drawer of his bureau and snuck out of his cabin. He was dying to know if Mogie had answered his telex.

Chapter 35

GODSPEED

Captain Tannenbaume knocked on the door to the radio shack and entered without waiting for permission. Sparks was not at his desk and there was no answer when he rapped on the door of the adjoining cabin, so Captain Tannenbaume eased himself into the chair behind the desk and opened the top left-hand drawer. It was empty.

He closed the drawer and sat back with a sinking feeling. This was the first day in over a week that Sparks had not received a telex first thing in the morning from Mogie. That wasn't a good sign.

Before Captain Tannenbaume had a chance to dwell on this bad news, he heard the telex machine come to life. Perhaps his telex to Mogie was not so bad after all—at least Mogie was writing back.

Captain Tannenbaume pulled on the corner of the paper coming out of the printer, as if pulling on it would make it print faster. Turns out it wasn't worth the wait. The telex was not addressed to Mitzi but rather to his mother. It was from the Commodore. As much as he did not want to read his mother's telex, he could not keep his eyes from running down the page as he walked it over to the drawer. When he spotted his name in the middle of the telex, he stopped and read:

My dear Mrs. Tannenbaume:

I do hope you are in receipt of the missive I sent to you by post. The agent for the *God is Able* has informed me that the ship picked up its mail in Suez, so I presume you have received it. If, in fact, you are not in receipt of said missive, please do notify me by telex, as some very important and time-critical information is contained therein. My epistolary to you neglected to inquire about the progress of our two students. Will Sylvia make a good Jewish wife, after all? And what of Captain Tannenbaume? Have we, at least, gotten him to refrain from eating pork? And what of this notion of furnishing him with a Yiddisha Kop? Has Mitzi been able to impart a thing or two about the arcane machinations of the business world? Mr. Mogelefsky possesses an uncanny horse sense when it comes to the murky realm of commerce and I dare say he will rather easily detect any lapses in Captain Tannenbaume's critical thinking along such lines. (He informs me he can spot a dumb Goy from across the room (Mr. Mogelefsky's words).) Now, I am cognizant that one cannot make a silk purse out of a sow's ear, but, nevertheless, I would like to know that you are making an effort. You do know that, at the United States Merchant Marine Academy, it is the effort that counts, never the results, so just do the very best you can.

I wish you God Speed for the remainder of your voyage, my dear.

Submitted respectfully,

Commodore Robert Dickey

Captain Tannenbaume threw the telex into the drawer and slammed it shut. So Mitzi and his mother *were* trying to change him. The "stop eating bacon, the cholesterol is killing you" thing was just a ruse to get him to stop eating pork. All of his mother's talk about wanting him to use his *Yiddisha kop*—it was obvious now that the Commodore was the one behind it all.

Well, if the Commodore thought he was changing for him, he had another thing coming. He was about to get the telex out of the drawer again so that he could throw it in his mother's face when Sparks walked into the radio shack.

"No telexes this morning, Sparks," Captain Tannenbaume said. "Well, not from Mogie anyway."

Sparks did not respond. Captain Tannenbaume could see Sparks's leg rustling under the desk, a nervous tic of his that usually meant he was trying to get up the courage to speak his mind.

"You ruined it for us," Sparks finally said.

"I ruined wh—"

"We were so cl-close and you ruined it."

Captain Tannenbaume's heart leapt. "So Mogie wrote back? What did he say?"

Sparks glared at Captain Tannenbaume. "M-m-my little m-m-milk cow? You really think M-Mitzi calls M-Mogie her little m-milk cow?"

"It was as good a guess as any!"

"It was st-stupid." Sparks reached under his desk saver, pulled out the telex from Mogie, and threw it across the desk. Captain Tannenbaume read it in a flash.

"Who wrote this?" was all the telex from Mogie read.

Captain Tannenbaume threw the telex back onto the desk. "Shit."

"He'll never r-r-write again," Sparks said. "You sc-sc-scared him off."

"Well, you were being too damned timid. We were never going to find out what the stool was for with you in charge."

"You have to be p-p-patient."

"I don't have time to be patient. I've got a ship to run. I haven't been on my own bridge in over a week because of your incompetence."

"My incomp—"

"You couldn't get the simplest little thing out of Mogie! I had to take matters into my own hands!"

Sparks's leg banged uncontrollably against the side of the desk. "G-g-get out."

"I will not get out! This is my ship and I'll be anywhere I damn well please."

"F-fine then. I'll g-g-go to the bridge. That's one place I know I won't f-find you."

"Go to the bridge for all I c-c-c-c-care."

He knew he shouldn't have said it the moment the words were out of his mouth. He wished he could take the words back right then and there. God, how could he be so stupid—he knew how sensitive Sparks was about his stutter.

Sparks went silent and turned his attention back to the telex machine. To Captain Tannenbaume's surprise, a calmness seemed to come over Sparks—his leg stopped shaking, his breathing slowed down. He just stared intently at the telex machine, so intently that it began to make Captain Tannenbaume nervous. He had seen this look before from Sparks.

It was the same sereneness that had come over Sparks after he had flung the GPS against the bulkhead.

"No!"

Captain Tannenbaume bum-rushed him and tried to get his arms around Sparks, but he was too late. Sparks had already sprung, lithe as a cat, and pounced on the telex machine. He picked it up and raised it over his head, yanking the electric cord out of the socket as he did, and ran headlong with it straight into the bulkhead. The telex machine cracked in two, then the two pieces split in half again when they hit the deck. Sparks was not even breathing hard after the exertion, surprisingly, and his back was to Captain Tannenbaume when he grabbed Sparks around the throat with both hands.

It wasn't very long at all before Sparks went limp, out of fear more than anything else, which was a good thing because Captain Tannenbaume was so mad he probably was not going to stop choking him. In contrast to Sparks, Captain Tannenbaume *was* breathing hard and needed a moment to catch his breath before he looked closely at Sparks to see if he could detect the rise and fall of his chest.

When he saw that Sparks was "resting comfortably," Captain Tannenbaume stepped over the wreckage that was the telex machine and headed back to his cabin with absolutely no idea what he was going to do next, now that there would be no more telexes to read.

When Captain Tannenbaume entered his cabin, he found Sylvia fast asleep, so he climbed onto the bunk and snuggled up next to her. The soft rhythm of his young wife's breathing put him into a deep sleep in no time flat, and he dreamed of milk cows getting milked in a green foamy pasture that rolled on a long ocean swell.

Chapter 36

SHALOM!

The telexes that Sparks kept receiving, not the ones from Mogie but the reams of telexes that warned of pirates in the area—the ones Captain Tannenbaume had called "cookie-cutter"—weren't so cookie-cutter after all. The pirates finally showed up and the ship, as the chief had warned, was caught unawares.

The steward was the first one to lay eyes on them. He had been dumping a load of trash over the side when he spotted the pirates hauling themselves up over the gunwhale on the port quarter. There must have been a dozen of them, he figured, and before any of them had seen him, he was able to duck into the slopchest on the main deck, the place where he should have been dumping the trash in the first place. Stew was deathly afraid that the pirates would find him and he silently cursed the chief mate for not having fixed the deadbolt on the slopchest door like he had asked him to do umpteen times. From his vantage point, Stew was able to see the pirates as they huddled on the deck and looked around for the crew. He was happy the deck gang had never laid out the fire hoses because he would have been compelled to use them now to defend the ship, but then what sort of trouble would the chief make about that? Surely the chief would point out that only the deck gang was allowed to work the deck and that the steward had no business fighting off pirates with gear belonging to the deck gang. So Stew was thankful there were no hoses on deck and he wouldn't have to deal with the chief over the damned union rules.

The pirates looked surprised, Stew said later, that the crew was nowhere to be seen. One of them left his comrades to go around the corner for a peek, and when he came back, he was shaking his head with a bewildered look on his face. The steward knew why. It was broad daylight and the ship's crew should have seen them approaching in their wooden dugout canoe with the two outboard engines slung off the back, but instead of finding an angry crew laying in wait to defend their ship, the pirates had the entire deck to themselves.

When the pirates made it down to the engine room they looked even more surprised to find that there was no one to fight off there as well. The only one down there was the chief.

"Well, well, well," the chief said when he looked up from his girlie magazine and saw a bunch of pirates entering the air-conditioned control room. "I've been expecting a visit from you guys."

The pirates rushed into the control room. Two of them grabbed the chief while the others spun around with their rifles looking for the engineers.

The oldest one, the one with the unkempt beard, shouted in the chief's face. "Where is everybody? Where are the engineers?"

"The engineers?" The chief scoffed. "If you're looking for engineers you've come to the wrong place."

A few of the pirates who had gone back out into the engine room were coming back through the door into the control room now. The old pirate—no doubt the leader—looked at them but they shook their heads.

The leader stood in front of the chief. "Where is everybody?"

"They're all on the bridge. Ever since Mitzi started up her salon, I can't keep my engineers down here. They're . . . "

The chief saw one of the younger pirates take a piece of rope out of his pocket. It looked like a piece of old polypropylene.

"Oh, don't use that old stuff to tie me up. Poly's too sharp on the skin. Look over on the control panel there, you'll find some cut-up T-shirts the engineers have been using to clean their hands. It's the only thing that doesn't scuff up the shine on their nails."

The pirate ignored him and began to tie him up.

"No, no," the chief said, getting up from the chair. "Use the other chair. This one lost its swivel. I need to be able to swing around to see the gauges."

The young pirate looked to the leader, who just pointed at the chair the chief had been sitting on.

"Oh, come on," the chief whined. "How am I supposed to see all the gauges from this chair?"

The leader stepped closer to the chief, now tied up in the swivel-less chair with the rough polypro cutting into his wrists. "Where is everybody?" the leader said. "This must be a trick."

"Yeah, right." The chief laughed. "I wish it was a trick. No, my men are all up on the bridge, getting their nails done instead of slinging wrenches. Go on up there, you'll see."

The chief could tell that the pirates did not believe him, that they really thought the crew was playing some kind of trick on them. He watched the pirates file out of the control room, looking over their shoulders.

"Don't expect to cut the line!" the chief called after them. "You'll have to wait your turn like everyone else."

The leader put a halt to the procession out of the control room when he stopped to turn back to the chief. "What line? What are you talking about?"

The chief just laughed. "You'll find out. Go on. Just go on up to the bridge."

Mrs. Tannenbaume was the first one on the bridge to see the pirates. They were standing outside on the wing looking a little unsure of themselves.

She signaled to Mitzi, who was working on Swifty in the chair, to have a look outside. Mitzi, who, Mrs. Tannenbaume knew, was a bit squeamish about pirates, went white when she laid eyes on them. Mrs. Tannenbaume walked calmly over to her and said, "Just follow my lead. Don't look nervous."

When Mitzi's face took on an even more alarmed look, she said, "Trust me. If you get nervous, who knows what Captain Courageous here will do." Mrs. Tannenbaume was talking about Swifty, who was beginning to stir now that Mitzi had stopped pulling on his toes. "Look," Mrs. Tannenbaume whispered, keeping one eye on the pirates still hovering uncertainly on the other side of the bridge wing door. "We're surrounded by nothing but followers up here. So trust me, if we stay calm, the crew'll follow our lead."

Swifty's hand went up to the hot cloth on his face but Mrs. Tannenbaume grabbed it and placed it back on his lap. "We've got some visitors," she said quietly, bending down to Swifty's ear. "Stay under that cloth and everything'll be alright."

Swifty must've known who the visitors might be because Mrs. Tannenbaume saw the blanket covering his body go taut. She knew there was no way he'd move a muscle now.

"Well look here," Mrs. Tannenbaume announced in a voice loud enough for everyone on the bridge to hear. "Looks like we've got visitors."

The pirates made their move at the sound of her voice but then stopped suddenly—piling into one another—when Mrs. Tannenbaume swung open the sliding door to the wheelhouse.

"*Shalom!*"

She knew she had them at "hello."

The pirates were a ragtag bunch, that's for sure. Most of them were shoeless and their black feet were callused and knobby from so many protruding, ugly corns. And skinny! The way their bony legs stuck out from their baggy and tattered shorts, Mrs. Tannenbaume wondered what they spent all their ill-gotten booty on. They sure weren't spending it on food. One of them had a gray scrubby beard, but most of them looked like they could be teenagers, their faces were so smooth and clean. All of them wore clothes that were soiled and stained and ill-fitting for the most part, and most had big sunglasses covering their faces and bandanas covering their heads. The rest were bareheaded and squinting in the sun. There was nothing particularly menacing about them—they merely looked "third world," as far as Mrs. Tannenbaume was concerned. The only thing giving them away as "bad guys" was their weapons. They all carried rifles, one or two slung over their backs and one that each carried in his arms. The rifles looked cheap and ill-made, even the ones that weren't rusted and held together with duct tape. Aside from the beat-up weaponry they carried, they didn't look all that evil. But, they were pirates, after all, and they were armed to the teeth. The crew didn't stand a chance fighting them off. What were they going to use for weapons, their heat guns?

Mrs. Tannenbaume knew they wouldn't need heat guns if the crew followed her lead. And so far they were.

"Come in, come in!"

A couple of the engineers were sitting on the chart table waiting for their turn with Mitzi when they saw the pirates. They jumped down to defend their ship but Mrs. Tannenbaume held them back.

"Don't even think about it. These are our guests. They deserve a manicure as much as you do."

Mitzi told Swifty to make way for the pirates and he complied without complaint. With one hand still clutching the hot cloth to his face, he shimmied out of the captain's chair into Ski's waiting arms, which were there to guide his blind shipmate to the stool next to the wheel. When Swifty was seated, he put both hands on the cloth and held it firmly against his face. This display of cowardice disgusted the engineers and they again looked like they were about to make their move against the pirates but this time it was Mitzi who discouraged such a tactic.

"You," she said, pointing to the second engineer. "Make yourself useful and get another towel from the coffeepot." She then walked over to the electrician, who was getting his nails done by Sylvia. "Get up. We need to make room for our friends."

Mrs. Tannenbaume knew that the electrician, who by now had proven to be Mitzi's best customer, would comply with whatever was asked of him in order to keep his favored status in Mitzi's appointment book. He stood right up, brushed the seat clean, and held his arm out to welcome the pirates. "Who's next?" A genuine smile lit up his face. "You guys are gonna love Sylvia's work. She's really come a long way."

The electrician walked toward the pirates with his hands out, palms down, to show off his half-moons. "See?"

The leader spread out his arms to keep his youthful compatriots from getting too close to the half-moons.

Mrs. Tannenbaume could tell from the chief pirate's reaction that he knew he was in uncharted waters with this ship. His eyes darted around the wheelhouse—when he dared to take them off the electrician's hands, that is—and Mrs. Tannenbaume watched him take in all that he surveyed. He appeared to be particularly curious about the heat gun/paint tray getup. His eyes kept coming back to it while he took in the rest of the bridge—the bookshelves lined with bottles of nail polish, the cheesecloth-draped chart table, the hand-painted wood signs advertising Mitzi's daily specials. Surely the man had never seen a bridge like this one. And aside from all the nonstandard bridge equipment he saw, he surely had never seen a crew like this one. The normal attire on the bridge of a ship—at least any ship he would have likely pirated—was khakis, not boilersuits. But here he found engineers in boilersuits and stewards and cooks in white smocks, lounging around with wet hair, waiting on a blow-dry and manicure from a stunning redhead and a cute young Thai girl.

When the second engineer—resplendent in his pressed boilersuit, exquisitely coiffed hair, and gleaming nails—walked over with the Pyrex coffee pot in one hand and a pair of channel locks with a steaming hot towel in the other, the chief pirate had evidently seen enough. He spread out both arms to keep the young ones safely behind him and backed his entire team off the bridge wing. When they got to the ladder at the aft end, they backed down it, never taking their eyes off the bizarre crew.

Mrs. Tannenbaume walked out to the edge of the wing and watched the pirates descend all the way to the main deck. When the last of them climbed down into the waiting pirate boat, she called to the bridge, telling Swifty to put in the log that the pirates were away.

The crew let out a whooping holler.

Captain Tannenbaume, down below in his cabin dreaming of milk cows, never even knew pirates had attacked his ship.

Chapter 37

NIGHT ORDERS

Mrs. Tannenbaume had been looking forward to this day, a day to herself, a day where she would do absolutely nothing. She'd spent the last week on the bridge navigating 24-7 as the ship made its way through the heavily trafficked waters of the Gulf of Suez, and then the canal, and then the Mediterranean.

With her son preoccupied doing who knew what, with Swifty busy with his manicures and pedicures and the other mates with theirs, Mrs. Tannenbaume had become the de facto master of the *God is Able*. She was certainly the one who made the final call on meeting arrangements with other ships—whether to alter course or hold course and speed, that all-important calculus that keeps ships from colliding with one another. She told the mates that she did not like this business of always being the give-way vessel. She had been giving way her entire life, and she was tired of it. "Let the other guy move," she told the mates. "Don't let him—or the Rules of the Road—bully you into changing course." Mrs. Tannenbaume saw the leviathan ships that plied the world's oceans as nothing more than bullies scaring the smaller boats into keeping out of their way so that they could pass unimpeded. Well, Mrs. Tannenbaume would not let the bastards intimidate her.

In the odd moments when Mrs. Tannenbaume was not navigating or lending a hand in Mitzi's salon, not to mention quelling a pirate attack (such as it was), she had her nose in one of the various logbooks she discovered on the bridge—a nod, perhaps, to her thirty-five years in education as a data entry clerk. She read the various logbooks with a critical eye and found herself second-guessing some of the orders her son had given over the years. And since she was the supernumerary, she felt it was her right to make her own log entries. Also, after only a quick perusal of the Captain's standing orders book, she decided to make a few changes. Captain Tannenbaume's Standing Orders called for the deck officers to, among other things, keep a one nautical mile Closest Point of Approach with all ship traffic, to call the master if the CPA dropped to less than a mile, and to blow five short and rapid blasts of the whistle if in doubt as to the intentions of the other vessel—in that order. Mrs. Tannenbaume wanted the mates to blow the danger signal first, notify her second, and to forget about keeping the one nautical mile CPA altogether. The mates, however, knew better, which is how it fell upon Mrs. Tannenbaume to do all of the navigating. She made it sound like navigating 24-7 was a burden, but in truth, she preferred to do it all herself—at least that way she knew it would be done to her liking.

By far, Mrs. Tannenbaume's favorite logbook was the Captain's Night Orders book, orders issued by the captain on a nightly basis that supplemented his standing orders. They were sometimes explicit orders, such as an order to call the master when the ship came near a known shoal area, or perhaps just a simple reminder to keep an extra special lookout for small fishing vessels if the ship was expected to be in the vicinity of a fishing fleet overnight. Mrs. Tannenbaume saw the Night Orders book differently. She saw it as a way to harp on her pet subject night after night, and since the mates were required to place their initials next to the night orders when they came on watch each night, Mrs. Tannenbaume knew she had a captive audience. "Hold your course and speed" became her nightly entry in the Captain's Night Orders book. The mates dutifully initialed the new orders, as did the engineers and cooks. In fact, everyone who stepped foot on the bridge placed their initials next to her night orders, something that greatly pleased Mrs. Tannenbaume. She felt like she was putting her stamp on things and everyone treated her like the head honcho.

Everyone except the Suez Canal pilot.

The pilot had presented a distinct problem for Mrs. Tannenbaume. When he first came aboard, she figured him to be some sort of flunky, someone to be coddled but not taken seriously. As far as Mrs. Tannenbaume could tell, the man only seemed to be interested in extracting from the crew a stash of cigarettes. Marlboro reds, evidently, were his brand, because Mrs. Tannenbaume noticed how indignant he became when Swifty offered him a carton of Lucky Strikes. She was mortified when Swifty gave in and coughed up a carton of Reds. She, for one, would not kowtow to the man.

As it turned out, the cigarettes were the least of her worries. Not only did Swifty turn over the cigarettes to the pilot, but to Mrs. Tannenbaume's utter amazement, he also turned over the ship to him. "Okay, Mr. Pilot," Swifty said the morning the pilot came aboard and the flap over the cigarettes had ended. "She's all yours."

"What?" Mrs. Tannenbaume pulled Swifty aside. "What the hell is going on here? Who is this guy we just gave the ship to?"

"He's the pilot," Swifty said. "He's in charge of navigation now. We can just sit back and enjoy the view."

Mrs. Tannenbaume looked out at the scrub desert on either side of the Suez Canal. "You call this a view?"

"Look," Swifty said, "I have an appointment to get my face wrapped. You do what you want. Just . . . the pilot has the conn now, all right?"

Mrs. Tannenbaume would have none of it. She walked over and stood beside the pilot, a smallish man in rumpled linen pants and shirt, with dark sweaty hair that he wore matted down over his head. When he didn't acknowledge her, Mrs. Tannenbaume nudged the pilot's forearm.

"Give it back," she said.

The pilot looked past Mrs. Tannenbaume to Swifty, but Swifty was already in the chair with a hot cloth on his face.

"Give me back the ship," Mrs. Tannenbaume repeated.

"Who are you?"

"The supernumerary, that's who."

"Well I'm the pilot. I answer to no one, not even the captain." The pilot lit up a Marlboro and blew smoke rings. "I certainly do not answer to any supernumerary."

"Well I'm not just any supernumerary. I'm the captain's mother and I'm making the decisions up here, not you. And the first decision I'm making is no smoking on the bridge."

Mrs. Tannenbaume yanked the dangling cigarette from the pilot's mouth and handed it to Ski at the wheel. Ski, who was smoking himself, extinguished the pilot's cigarette in the remains of his coffee.

In a voice far stronger than anyone imagined the little man might possess, the pilot thundered, "I want to see the captain on the bridge right now!"

No one else on the bridge wanted to see the captain right then, judging by the way they all sprung into action to isolate the pilot from Mrs. Tannenbaume. Swifty threw off his hot towel and escorted Mrs. Tannenbaume to the wing while the second engineer showed the pilot to the captain's chair. Mitzi had the pilot's shoes off before he knew what was happening and she went to work on his feet like nobody's business. Ski, meanwhile, got another hot towel out of the spare Pyrex coffeepot and placed it over the pilot's face. Ski told the pilot that he had been driving ships through the canal for twenty years and that all that he, the pilot, had to do was relax in the chair while they took care of things. Ski knew that pilots, as a rule, enjoy a little pampering, and this pilot was no different. After a minute with the soothing hot towel on his face, the pilot was sleeping peacefully. Mrs. Tannenbaume was not altogether pleased with having to navigate from the wing, but Swifty convinced her that if she wanted to keep Captain Tannenbaume off the bridge doing who knew what, then she'd have to make the adjustment this one time.

The trip through the canal went smoothly after that, with Ski doing most of the driving. Mrs. Tannenbaume took an occasional turn at the wheel, almost nodding off from time to time from the sheer boredom of steering a dead straight course through the dead straight ditch. She tried to get the pilot's goat by asking him to tell her, again, why they even needed a pilot in the Suez Canal, but Swifty and Ski were there to hurry her off to the wing. With the last of the dreary ditch behind them, the *God is Able* dropped off the pilot just outside the entrance. The pilot, it turns out, was sad to go, seeing as he looked and felt a whole lot better than when he first came aboard. Mitzi had primped-up his matted-down hair, trimmed the profusion of bristling hairs sprouting from his nose and ears, and had given him a gleaming manicure. He had never had a better transit, he told Swifty, as he admired the fresh gloss on his fingernails. Swifty made sure to repay the compliment with a couple more cartons of Marlboro Reds.

Mrs. Tannenbaume noticed the additional cartons of Marlboros in the pilot's arms as they bid each other farewell but she had bigger fish to fry. She had never seen so many ships in all her life. She felt like she was coming out of an overcrowded elevator and that there was an even bigger crowd waiting to get in as soon as the doors opened. Mrs. Tannenbaume took it personally. Couldn't they at least let her get out first? She steered the ship until it pointed at the center of the mass of ships hovering outside the canal, told Ski to steady her up there, ordered the engines ahead full, told the lookout on the bow he might as well knock off, then held her thumb down on the whistle and blasted right through the ships until the *God is Able* was in the clear. Once they got past the ships in the immediate vicinity of the canal, they came upon another set of ships, and then another. Mrs. Tannenbaume discovered she needed to blow the danger signal more than ever in the crowded shipping lanes of the Med.

It wasn't until the ship had passed Tunisia that the traffic abated. Mrs. Tannenbaume scanned the horizon with a pair of binoculars and did not detect a single ship. She handed the binoculars to Swifty, slumped into the chair, and asked Mitzi for a back rub.

"I need a day off," she told Mitzi.

"Somehow, I don't think the crew will mind," Mitzi said.

Mrs. Tannenbaume was too tired to argue. She got up from the chair after Mitzi finished her back rub and said she was going down below to her cabin for the rest of the day and that if they had any questions about traffic they were to blow the danger signal before interrupting her.

Shortly after Mrs. Tannenbaume left, the chief called the bridge to ask why everything was so quiet. He was in the middle of his nooner, lying in his bunk, staring at the overhead, waiting for the whistle to go off. Swifty told him that Mrs. Tannenbaume had left the bridge and that, hopefully, the whistle would not be going off anytime soon. That was not the answer the chief wanted to hear. The chief had gotten used to the sound of the whistle—it had become white noise for him—and he told Swifty to go ahead and blow the damn whistle so that he could get some sleep.

Mrs. Tannenbaume was already stretched out in the easy chair in her cabin with her shoes kicked off when she heard the whistle. It made her feel like things were going smoothly on the bridge and she began to relax. She thought she might take a nap—she certainly could use the rest—but she also needed to catch up on her mail. The agent in Suez had dropped off the ship's mail and Mrs. Tannenbaume had two letters to open, one with the return address of the *Great Neck Martinizing Dry Cleaners* and the other the *United States Merchant Marine Academy*. Mrs. Tannenbaume picked up the letters from the side table next to the easy chair, opened the one from the academy, and saw that it was from the Commodore:

Dear Mrs. Tannenbaume,

It pains me to inform you that as of this instant the regiment of midshipmen is in a state of upheaval. My boys have been unruly and I know that they are merely acting up out of boredom. Ennui prevails for no reason other than a lack of leadership, of course. The board accepted Admiral Johnson's resignation, as you know, but they have steadfastly refused to appoint an interim superintendent. I have proffered my services more than once and have even suggested that I would be amenable to retaining my present rank and pay, but still the board has refused my entreaties. They can be a stubborn lot, that cabal of widows.

Now that Johnson is gone, his cronies have gone missing in action—it should come as no surprise. The commandant does not even bother to keep up the pretense of performing his job. He takes Mondays and Fridays off, and the remainder of the workweek he spends in the gymnasium. His trapezoids are bulging while the regiment's spirit atrophies. For my part, I am doing all that I have always done—comporting myself in such a manner as to inspire others. My carriage is erect as I walk the campus even as my own spirit sags. It pains me to see my boys suffer even one more day.

To wit, my dear, I entreat that you make great haste in bringing Captain Tannenbaume to the academy. The dedication of the Mariners Monument is fast approaching and I want your son to be present and to make a respectable impression on Mayor Mogelefsky and the board. The bronze likeness of Edwin J. O'Hara is now complete. The sculptor captured perfectly the imperious gaze, the Roman nose, and the square chin of our young hero. I was overcome with emotion when I faced Edwin for the first time. I looked into his intelligent eyes and felt him staring back at me. I dare say I felt naked in the presence of such greatness. The workers have affixed the statue to the pedestal and the monument is now in place on the lawn facing the Sound. They tried to place a protective plastic wrap around Edwin to keep him out of the elements until his unveiling on dedication day, but, fortunately for Edwin, I intervened. The thought of wrapping dear Edwin in *plastic* was anathema to me, and I prevailed upon the workers to cover him in a cotton sheet (300 thread count) followed by a canvas tarp. So Edwin is comfortably under wraps until his big day. All that is needed is for the MV *God is Able* to deliver Captain Tannenbaume on time for the unveiling.

And so, Mrs. Tannenbaume, I implore you to do everything in your power to see that the ship makes its best speed for New York. I reiterate my desire for your son to make the biggest impression possible in front of the most people as possible.

I look forward to your return. God Speed.

Yours,
Commodore Robert Dickey

Mrs. Tannenbaume placed the letter back on the side table. She was about to open the other letter when she felt the ship roll—Swifty, changing course for another ship. Well that simply would not do. Anything other than a straight course line would slow down the ship's progress, and they did not have a moment to spare if they were to get back in time for the unveiling. She, too, wanted her sonny boy to make a big splash. When Mrs. Tannenbaume got to the bridge, she saw that, sure enough, Swifty was in the middle of changing course.

Mrs. Tannenbaume did not chastise Swifty for his decision—she knew that making Swifty a take-charge ship's officer was a lost cause. She simply ordered Ski to turn the ship back onto its course and then she blew five short blasts on the whistle at the ship bearing down on them from their starboard side.

Chapter 38

PHILADELPHIA LAWYER

Captain Tannenbaume had not made morning chow in over a week. He had been so consumed reading (and rereading) Mogie's telexes that he had fallen out of sync with the normal rhythms of the ship. He had been eating breakfast mid-morning, skipping lunch altogether, and coming in at the very end of the evening meal hour. But today he arrived in the officers' mess on time for breakfast—and found himself all alone. He sat by himself and stared out the lone porthole, his plate of eggs untouched. Since he had not been on the bridge in so long, he had no way of knowing that the morning was Mitzi's peak time and that the crew had taken to bringing their breakast to the bridge while they waited in line for their back rub or pedicure or scalp massage.

The steward came in. "Everything okay, Captain?"

"Eggs are as tight as ever, Stew, thanks. I'm just not hungry, I guess."

He was waiting on Sparks so that they could have a chat about the new GPS Sparks had picked up in Suez. Since he was not allowed to step foot in the radio shack, he was forced to wait while Sparks took his sweet time getting down to the officers' mess that morning. Oh, he could go into any space on the ship he damn well pleased, but truth be told, he didn't want to get Sparks any more riled up than he already was. The fact was he needed Sparks's help to get his ship back across the pond. Captain Tannenbaume knew from what little interaction he had with his mates—chance meetings in the passageways mostly—that Swifty and the others were having a devil of a time getting the GPS initialized. Sparks could initialize it in his sleep, but he told Captain Tannenbaume that he was too busy, that he had already told Swifty how to initialize the GPS, and that if Swifty couldn't get the thing initialized in a few days, then maybe he'd have time to help then. But Captain Tannenbaume knew they didn't have a few days to wait. The ship was going to be in the Atlantic Ocean in less than twenty-four hours, and seeing as they couldn't simply hug the coast across the Atlantic, the mates needed that GPS. Of course, Captain Tannenbaume could do the navigating himself now that he had his sextant back. Or he could use the crossing as an opportunity to finally teach his mates celestial. But the thought of it made his stomach turn. A, he wanted to spend as little time on that bridge as possible, and B, he figured it was better to start from scratch and teach celestial to a fresh batch of plebes when he became head honcho at the academy. Swifty was already a lost cause.

Captain Tannenbaume heard someone coming from the passageway and he began to unconsciously push plates and cups and saucers around the table in anticipation of his confrontation with Sparks. The rearranging of the tableware came to an abrupt end when the chief walked into the mess.

"The mates get that GPS initialized yet?"

God Almighty, how did stuff get around on this ship so fast? He ignored the chief's question and did not say good morning when the chief joined him at the table. The messman came in and placed a glass of prune juice in front of the chief and told him his breakfast would be out in a minute.

"You waiting on Sparks this morning?" the chief said.

Captain Tannenbaume thought about ignoring him, but he did not wish to be openly hostile. Instead, he waited a good minute before replying, "Yes, as a matter of fact I am."

"He's been coming to breakfast a bit late, lately. He likes to get his cuticles pushed back—you know that half-moon thing?—before the morning rush up at Mitzi's."

Just then Sparks walked into the mess. He sat alone at a four-top across the room from where the chief and Captain Tannenbaume were sitting. The sound of the ship's clock ringing two bells came in loud and clear in the quiet mess room.

The chief broke the awkward silence. "Care to join us over here, Sparks?"

Sparks shook his head.

"You get that GPS initialized yet, Sparks?" Captain Tannenbaume didn't like the way his words came out. He was going for light and breezy but it came out sounding confrontational. He always marveled at how the chief could argue with a smile on his face.

"No," Sparks said.

Captain Tannenbaume did not want to say, in front of the chief, how much his officers needed the GPS to cross the Atlantic.

"The mates don't *need* it, Sparks, but it sure would come in handy." Captain Tannenbaume smiled when he said it. "As a backup, is all."

"It's not my job to initialize the GPS."

"It is *too* your job!" Captain Tannenbaume shouted so violently he scared the messman, who spilled Sparks's glass of orange juice.

"No it's not."

"You're being insubordinate!"

"No he's not." The chief was smiling, of course, when he said it.

"Stay the hell out of this, Maggie."

"Union rules say the radio officer only has to make his best effort at 'repairing' the electronics. Nowhere in the contract does it say he has to"—air quotes—"'initialize' the electronics."

To Captain Tannenbaume, it felt like the chief was scratching his fingers on a chalkboard when he made his goddamn air quotes. He pushed his plate of cold eggs across the table. A glass fell off the edge and broke on the deck.

"Don't play Philadelphia lawyer with me, Maggie. The man is insubordinate."

"Not according to the contract."

"I don't give a damn what the contract says. We need that GPS working!"

This time the chief smiled before he spoke. "I thought we didn't"—air quotes—"'need' it. I thought—"

"I don't give a damn what you think, Maggie. Look, Sparks . . . " Captain Tannenbaume got up from the table wagging his finger and crossed the room to where Sparks was sitting. Just then he heard the faint sound of the ship's whistle.

"Is that our whistle?"

The chief looked at Captain Tannenbaume in amazement. "You can hear the whistle? You haven't heard the whistle in over a week. Now all the way aft in the officers' mess, you can hear the whistle?" The chief shook his head. "I don't understand that at all."

Captain Tannenbaume suddenly realized he needed to get to the bridge immediately.

"Look, Sparks, I don't have time for this now. I want that GPS initialized pronto. If you don't get the thing initialized today, you're fired."

"You can't fire him for that. It's not in the contract."

Captain Tannenbaume could care less about the contract. He wanted to know why the hell Swifty was blowing the danger signal. He walked out of the mess, and as he made his way down the passageway toward the bridge, he heard the chief shouting something about waiting until he took his nooner. It felt funny to be walking toward the bridge at a swift clip and made him aware that it had been a while since he had last been up there. He felt a little self-conscious about that and wondered just what he'd find.

He heard the sound of the whistle again and it made him pick up his pace, and when he got to the stairwell, he took the stairs two at a time.

Chapter 39

MITZI'S

Due to the sound of the blaring whistle, no one on the bridge heard the door squeak open, and so the crew was unaware that Captain Tannenbaume, after over a week's absence, had finally returned to the bridge of the *God is Able*. Not that he stepped very far onto the bridge—he stopped just inside the doorway, unable to move a muscle, so profound was his shock. Mitzi's make-over of the bridge was now complete. The chart table, directly in front of him, which should have had a large-scale chart spread out on it with a proper fix laid down and a DR track plotted, was festooned with massage oils and candles and fluffy pillows. Long sheets of cheesecloth, used by the boatswain to wipe down wood when prepping for varnish, had been sewn together to replace the heavy canvas blackout curtains that surround every chart table. The cheesecloth billowed in the air, blown by the air-conditioning unit from the back of the bridge. Captain Tannenbaume's captain's chair, which he could just make out through the cheesecloth, was all but unrecognizable under the jury-rigged heat guns and paint trays, not to mention the person lying in the chair with a hot towel wrapped around his face and a blanket draped over his body. He thought he recognized Swifty's hush puppies poking out from under the blanket.

Captain Tannenbaume had never before seen so many people on his bridge. He recognized cooks and bedroom stewards and engineers and deck hands. They milled about, drinking coffee, reading magazines, waiting their turn for Mitzi's services and talking about what kind of work they wanted to have done that day. The engineers, who cared so much about their hands, were busy inspecting the different bottles of nail polish—bottles and bottles of nail polish. The ship's agent had misread the requisition that Mitzi made out and dropped off not a box of nail polish, but a pallet full. The bottles of nail polish lined the bookshelves that formerly housed the *Rules of the Road* and *Bowditch* and the *Sight Reduction tables*.

Captain Tannenbaume was having trouble accepting that this was the bridge of a ship he was standing on—*his* bridge. The electrician—the electrician, of all people—was getting a shoulder massage from Mitzi. The second engineer was at the coffee station lazily removing steaming hot towels from the coffeepots with a pair of channel locks. The second engineer, who should have been down in the engine room getting his hands dirty, was instead on the bridge playing barbershop. Even Sylvia was part of the act. Sylvia got the ship's carpenter to turn the slop chest on the bridge into a shampoo station. At the moment, she was giving Ski a scalp massage.

So with Swifty asleep in the captain's chair, and Ski getting a scalp massage, who the hell was steering and keeping a lookout?

It was this thought that finally jarred him awake, and it was only then that he became aware of the sound of the whistle again. He walked around the chart table.

His mother had her hand on the whistle. She was blowing the unorthodox signal at a tanker—a tanker—hard on their starboard bow.

Captain Tannenbaume slapped his mother's hand off the whistle.

Mrs. Tannenbaume shouted, "Sonny boy!" and Ski, from the slop chest, shouted, "Attention on deck!" From under the hot towel came, "Oh, shit."

Oh, shit, indeed.

Captain Tannenbaume was vaguely aware of frantic shuffling behind him as he spun the wheel hard to starboard to go under the tanker's stern. When he turned around, he found that the cooks and stewards had left the bridge without a fight. Only the engineers stayed behind. Apparently, they had come to get their nails done and they were not leaving until they did.

Captain Tannenbaume was about to tell the engineers that they should feel free to join the cooks and stewards, but he stopped himself. He had to get his navigation bridge squared away first. He ordered Ski to the wheel.

"Sonny—"

"Please, Mother," he said. "Don't say a word."

"But we have a schedule to keep. Changing course slows us down."

"I suggest you read the *Rules of the Road*, Mother."

"I read them. And I don't agree with them. Why should we always have to be the one to change course?"

"I suggest you read my standing orders then, Mother."

"I read your standing orders, too. And I have to say, sonny, I wasn't impressed."

Captain Tannenbaume watched the tanker cross slowly in front of them.

"So I changed them."

"You did what!"

Captain Tannenbaume caught himself. He could not very well get upset with his mother. He knew he had only himself to blame. He knew he had to take responsibility for what had happened on his bridge—he had to take it on the chin, and then he had to move on.

With his ship no longer in extremis, Captain Tannenbaume turned his attention to his next most urgent problem. The GPS. He called Swifty over and, without saying a word about the manner in which the man was conducting his watch, gave him back the conn. Then he called Mitzi over. He took her by the arm and walked her out on the wing.

"We've got a problem," Captain Tannenbaume said when they were alone. "I think you can help."

"Shoot," Mitzi said.

"We need that GPS programmed."

"So I've heard."

"I'm getting nowhere with Sparks. Do you think you can convince him to do it?"

Mitzi thought about it for a moment. "He's a strange bird, that Sparks. I don't relate to him."

"You don't have to relate to him. He only has to relate to you. See what I'm driving at?"

"Oh, no." Mitzi put up her hands to stop the conversation. "I've had enough trouble getting the chief to relate to me. You merchant marines are all talk and no action. I don't know if I'm up for being alone in a room with another merchant marine who is scared to death of a woman."

"I think Sparks is different. I've never heard him talk about women. He could be the silent type."

Mitzi looked over Captain Tannenbaume's shoulder into the bridge. "What about my salon? The engineers get awfully cranky when they don't get their nails done as soon as they come off watch."

"What about Sylvia? Can she keep an eye on things while you're away?"

"Yeah. I suppose so. I've been training her. She's got a good work ethic."

"Good," Captain Tannenbaume said. "That settles it. Go to work on Sparks. We need that GPS."

Mitzi shook her head. "You're gonna owe me one for this."

But Captain Tannenbaume did not hear what Mitzi said. The tanker was now passing down the side of the *God is Able* at a range of no more than a quarter mile. The captain of the tanker was out on the wing, waving at the ship that had just nearly cut him in half. It surprised Captain Tannenbaume that the other captain was waving his hand, but after taking a closer look, he saw that he was not using all of his fingers.

Chapter 40

IT'S CALLED LEVERAGE

Mitzi was back on the bridge before noon. She handed the GPS to Captain Tannenbaume. "Go ahead. Fire it up."

Captain Tannenbaume took the GPS from Mitzi. "You're kidding," he said as he took a step back and looked at Mitzi, appraising her. Then they both started laughing.

"You were right about Sparks being the silent type."

"But I never thought—"

Captain Tannenbaume stopped mid-sentence. Ski was waving his arm and nodding toward the door. They all turned when they heard the door open, and sure enough, there was Sparks. Captain Tannenbaume watched Sparks as he walked over to the coffee station. There was something different about the way he was walking. What was it? He nodded toward Sparks. "Are you seeing what I'm seeing?"

Captain Tannenbaume did not need an answer from Mitzi. The answer was all over her face. She was looking at Sparks the way a teacher looks at a student who gets it for the first time.

Sparks poured his coffee and walked to the windowsill at the front of the bridge. That was it. A purposeful stride had replaced his usual stoop-shouldered shuffle. He put his coffee cup down on the sill, pulled his shoulders back, took a battered pack of cigarettes out of his pocket, and lit one. When he blew the smoke out of his mouth, he narrowed his eyes and looked off into the middle distance. To Captain Tannenbaume it looked as if he was thinking about something, and not only that, it looked as if he was sure, absolutely certain, of what he was thinking about.

"There's nothing like a good smoke with a cup of coffee," Sparks said without turning around.

"I didn't know you smoked, Sparks," Ski said.

Sparks held his middle-distance stare. "There's a lot you don't know about me, Ski." Then he turned, slowly, and looked directly at Mitzi. "There's more to this radio officer than most people know."

Captain Tannenbaume realized that Sparks had just made it through the three sentences without missing a beat. He—miraculously—had lost his stutter. Sparks was a new man.

What kind of woman was this Mitzi? What powers did she possess? Captain Tannenbaume knew from the telexes the effect she had on her boyfriend Mogie. And now . . . the woman had cured Stuttering Sparks.

"Mitzi," he said, reaching out to her, as if to take her in his arms.

Mitzi waved him off. "Oh, go on."

Captain Tannenbaume caught himself. He noticed that Mitzi was blushing. He hoped he hadn't been too obvious. He saw her glance over at Sparks, and he spun around in time to catch Sparks grinning at her. *Shit, he* was *too obvious. What was his problem? What was it about Mitzi that made him act so damn obvious?*

"Swifty!"

Swifty came running over.

"Here's your goddamn GPS." Captain Tannenbaume shoved it into his chest. "Fire it up and put a proper fix on that chart."

Swifty took the GPS from Captain Tannenbaume and handed it to Ski, so that Ski could plug it in for him.

"It'll be the first goddamn fix anybody's put down since the Indian Ocean," Captain Tannenbaume muttered, before shouting over his shoulder, "and I want that chart table cleaned up!"

Captain Tannenbaume walked over to the bookshelf and stood before it, glowering at it. The bottles of nail polish on his old bookshelf were too numerous to count. It was a goddamn sacrilege to remove Bowditch's *Epitome of Navigation* from its rightful place to make room for nail polish. How in the hell did he let it all come to this?

He called Ski over. "Where are all my books?"

"I think your mother has them."

"Get her up here. She's probably down in the mess having lunch."

"Yes, sir."

"Swifty!"

"Yes, sir."

"Post a lookout."

"But it—"

"Post a lookout!"

"Yes, sir."

"Ski."

"Yes, sir."

"Put her in hand steering."

"Yes, sir."

"Sparks."

Sparks did not say, "Yes, sir," but Captain Tannenbaume did not let that deter him. "Send a noon slip to the office. Pronto."

There. Now there was no doubt as to who was in charge. Captain Tannenbaume glanced over at Mitzi. If she was impressed, she was wasn't showing it.

He climbed up onto the captain's chair, the only person on the ship allowed that privilege—at least from this point on. When he adjusted the chair, the heat gun fell from its mount, crashing to the floor. Mitzi turned her face away from Captain Tannenbaume. He wasn't sure if he saw anything when she turned her head. He couldn't be sure.

But when the aluminum paint tray came loose, making a soft, muted bang on the deck, he clearly heard her stifle a laugh.

Captain Tannenbaume waited for his mother to get to the bridge. In between dozing off in the captain's chair, he amused himself by reading his mother's night orders from the previous week. He had to admit she had good instincts. In order to make any kind of time at sea, a captain often had to act boldly—resist slowing the ship down in fog or heavy weather, allow closer CPAs, that kind of thing. If a captain took every precaution advised in books on seamanship and company safety regulations, he'd never keep a schedule. So when his mother arrived on the bridge, he had no hesitations about handing her the conn. Hell, her instincts were better than Swifty's. At this point in the voyage, Captain Tannenbaume just wanted to get home.

"Okay, Mother," Captain Tannenbaume said after he got out of his chair and stretched his limbs. "She's all yours."

Mrs. Tannenbaume looked at the chart. The GPS showed them off the coast of Morocco. They'd be in the Straits of Gibraltar in eight hours.

Captain Tannenbaume was already off the bridge, heading down the stairs when he heard, "Are we going to stop in Gibraltar for bunkers, sonny?"

He came back up. "Bunkers, Mother? Since when do you know about bunkers?"

"I've been talking to the engineers. I've taught them a thing or two about command, and they've taught me about their job."

"What else do you know, Mother?"

"Well," Mrs. Tannenbaume said, "I have been thinking about our fuel burn. It'll be close, but I think we can probably stretch the fuel. What with the value of the dollar, why buy bunkers with euros? Why not wait until we get across the Atlantic and buy with good old-fashioned green backs? Also, we don't have time to waste bunkering in Gibraltar. We've got a schedule to keep."

Captain Tannenbaume could not believe his ears. His mother had been at this for a week and she was already talking about bunkers and fuel burn?

"Why don't you let me worry about that, Mother. You have enough on your hands, don't you think? The traffic'll be getting heavy as we approach the Straits."

"I was just thinking is all," Mrs. Tannenbaume said, appearing hurt.

Captain Tannenbaume turned to leave. "And lay off the whistle, Mother. Follow the Rules of the Road. You'll be better off, trust me."

Captain Tannenbaume was halfway down the staircase and did not hear his mother mutter, "Rules, schmules," as she stood at the windowsill and eyed a cruise ship, way off on the horizon on their starboard bow.

Captain Tannenbaume had not been at afternoon coffee time in longer than he could remember. As soon as he walked in the officer's lounge, he remembered why. The chief was in the middle of one of his monologues and the engineers were hanging on his every word.

"Really," the chief said, "the GPS shouldn't be working now. Sparks shouldn't have initialized it. It's right there in the contract. Spells it out,"—air quotes—"'repair.' Says the radio officer shall make his best effort at 'repairing' the electronics. Says nothing about initializing. That's the mates' bailiwick. Not that those dumb bastards could initialize an electric coffeepot if you asked them to. Dumb as a bag of hammers them mates. What'd I say about that third mate when he come aboard? What'd I say? A real"—air quotes—"'Swifty.' And look at him now. Can't even turn on a GPS."

The electrician was the first one to spot Captain Tannenbaume. He immediately straightened up in his chair and cleared his throat. The others, the chief included, got the message that the captain had decided to join them. The chief made a show of staring at Captain Tannenbaume. Captain Tannenbaume knew why. The chief wanted the engineers to think coffee time was his show, that Captain Tannenbaume was a sort of interloper. Well, Captain Tannenbaume could care less what the engineers, especially that little shit of an electrician, thought about him being there.

Then Captain Tannenbaume saw that Mitzi was there, tucked away on the davenport with a magazine, separate from the others. He guessed that the engineers were shunning her. He'd seen this before. It's what happened to every female crew member—the good-looking ones anyway. If she hooked up with one of the senior officers, either the chief or the captain, then even if they broke up, she was permanently off-limits to the rest of the crew. It was just an unwritten rule.

"Got tired of working on your desk, Cap?" The chief, as was his habit, looked at one of the other crew members when he said it.

Captain Tannenbaume would not take the bait. "As a mater of fact I have, Maggie."

"Haven't seen you in a while," the chief said.

Captain Tannenbaume pulled up a chair next to the chief. "Yeah, well, be that as it may, Maggie, I need to talk bunkers with you."

"I was wondering when you were going to get around to that. We're stopping in Gibraltar I presume?"

"Well, that's what I want to talk about. I know we always stop in Gibraltar for fuel, but have you seen the price of the euro lately? I thought we might try to stretch the fuel. Wait 'til we get to the States to take on bunkers. Pay with good old-fashioned green backs."

"Look," the chief said, looking directly at the electrician. "I don't know about foreign currencies and what makes the best sense money-wise. All I know is we need bunkers."

"Well as captain I need to think about the dollars-and-cents of things, Maggie. I'm trying to do the smart thing here."

Captain Tannenbaume made the slightest move of his head to see if Mitzi was listening. He saw that she had put down the magazine she was reading. He didn't dare try to get a better look.

"Look," Captain Tannenbaume said, "we always stop in Gibraltar for bunkers, just because that's what we always do. But other company ships stop in Algeciras. So I thought that if we did take on bunkers now, that maybe we'd stop in Algeciras and buy bunkers from the same outfit. You know, get a better price that way."

The chief looked at him uncomprehendingly.

"It's called leverage, Maggie."

"Leverage?"

"Yeah, leverage."

"I don't know about all that business stuff," the chief said. "I'm an engineer. I know fuel burn. And I know we burn twenty tons a day and at that rate we'll need to take on bunkers in Gibraltar like we always do." The engineers all nodded their heads.

Captain Tannenbaume hitched his pant leg up and leaned forward in his chair. He dared a glance Mitzi's way. He saw that she had her ear cocked in their direction.

"But, on the other hand, what if we pulled her back five or ten RPMs? We'd burn less fuel. And that way we wouldn't have to take on bunkers until we got to New York. That way we'd really save money by buying in dollars instead of euros."

The chief leaned back and folded his arms tightly across his chest. "All I know is we always stop in Gibraltar. I don't see why we'd get a better price in Algeciras. And I sure as hell don't get why we'd be better off buying back home." The chief tightened the grip he had on himself. "I guess I just don't understand currencies."

Mitzi was off the davenport by now. She came over to where everybody was sitting.

"Don't you get it, Chief? Either leverage yourself against the fuel distributor in Algeciras, or buy with cheaper dollars back in the States. Captain Tannenbaume is right."

Mitzi looked at Captain Tannenbaume and he returned the compliment with a nod of the head. He could see that Mitzi was impressed with his line of reasoning.

"Of course," Captain Tannenbaume added, "we can always make a futures contract. That may be the smartest play. It's called *arbitrage*, Maggie."

Actually, Captain Tannenbaume was not sure if it was called arbitrage or not. He wasn't exactly sure what arbitrage was. And he wasn't all that clear on the futures business. But he had read about it once, and he knew that people did those things. He was banking on none of the engineers calling his bluff.

"Arbitrage," Mitzi repeated, and Captain Tannenbaume heard wonder in her voice. And the way she was looking at him made *him* blush, now.

It was so easy. All a guy had to do was not act so obvious. It seemed to him that the easiest way to a woman's heart was to ignore her. Why had it taken him so long to figure that out?

Chapter 41

HANDSOME SMOOTH

Mrs. Tannenbaume felt as if her son had tied her hands behind her back. He had taken away her most important navigational instrument: the ship's whistle. For the last several hours, the *God is Able* maintained a steady bearing/ decreasing range with the cruise ship on its starboard side, the classic scenario for a collision at sea. Mrs. Tannenbaume kept waiting for the cruise ship to change course but the darn ship was being stubborn.

"What would you do, Ski?" she asked.

"Come to starboard to pass under her stern."

"Swifty?"

"Sounds good to me."

Mrs. Tannenbaume looked over at Sparks and raised her eyebrows.

"I say maintain course and speed until we're almost on top of each other and then blow five short blasts."

Mrs. Tannenbaume and the others stared at Sparks in disbelief. Sparks, nonplussed by all of the attention, ignored their staring and went back to his cigarettes.

Of course, that's what Mrs. Tannenbaume wanted to do, but she would need the whistle to scare away the other ship, and she didn't dare go against her son's explicit orders to lay off the whistle. Mrs. Tannenbaume stood at the windowsill and brooded over what to do.

The two ships got closer and closer.

Before long, everyone on the bridge was lined up at the sill with Mrs. Tannenbaume, watching the cruise ship getting bigger and bigger in their sights.

When they were within a half a mile of each other, Ski said, "I can't take it any longer. We need to put her in hand steering."

"Hey. Who has the conn here?" Mrs. Tannenbaume said.

Mrs. Tannenbaume walked out to the wing. She stopped at the far side of the wing and leaned over the side, cupping both hands to her mouth. "Yoo Hoo!"

The cruise ship, at a distance of a quarter of a mile, finally took action to avoid a collision. The ship turned hard to starboard and made a big round turn. The *God is Able* nearly skimmed the port side of the cruise ship as it moved past her. The passengers lined the railing and waved their arms and cheered at the fun maneuver the two ships had just made for their benefit.

When Mrs. Tannenbaume returned to the bridge, the crew gave her a standing ovation.

Mrs. Tannenbaume took their adulation in stride. She had a job to do. She would get the *God is Able* back in time for the unveiling of the Mariners Monument come hell or high water. And if she could not use the whistle, she would have to use her wits.

The ringing telephone silenced the cheering crew. Swifty walked over to answer it, but before he picked up the receiver, he looked back at the others. To Mrs. Tannenbaume it looked as if he was afraid to answer it. She held up her hand to stop him and walked over to answer it herself.

"Wheelhouse. Supernumerary Tannenbaume here," she said into the phone.

"Mother, were you aware of that cruise ship?"

"Oh. Hi, sonny. Yeah, I saw the cruise ship."

"I suppose you would have. It would have been hard to miss. Did you make a meeting arrangement with that ship?"

"Of course I made a meeting arrangement."

"You did? What exactly did you agree to?"

"I said we'd meet starboard . . . ah, port . . . ah . . . what's the difference? I got my point across, didn't I? But anyhow, sonny, what about the bunkers? Are we stopping in Gibraltar?"

She listened as he explained about the exchange rates. She had heard it all before. It was her idea, of course, but she did not want to say "I told you so" to her son in front of the crew, so she played dumb.

"What a clever idea, sonny. Whatever you say. You got it. Straight through the Straits."

"And, please, Mother, make proper meeting arrangements from now on."

"I promise I'll talk to every ship. Okay."

Mrs. Tannenbaume hung up the phone and the crew let out another cheer. She knew that they were not really cheering for her. They were cheering for themselves. The crew had the bridge to themselves again. They knew that Captain Tannenbaume would not bother with the bridge as long as his mother did not blow the whistle.

"Okay, people. Back to work!"

Mrs. Tannenbaume did not have to tell them two times. Swifty had a hot towel on his face before the towel had a chance to get hot. Sylvia was back at her shampoo station, doing Ski's hair. Mitzi worked the phone, calling the engine room to say her salon was back in business again. The engineers dropped their wrenches right were they were working and proceeded to the bridge without changing out of their boilersuits. When they all got to the bridge at the same time, a fistfight broke out between the engineers over who would get their nails done first. While they were fighting, Sparks slipped into the chair at Mitzi's nail station and Mitzi began working on his hands. Sparks looked just like a Dalmatian on top of a fire truck, sitting in that chair.

Mitzi took his hands in hers. "How's my Handsome Smooth doing?"

Chapter 42

KICK IT UP A NOTCH

Mrs. Tannenbaume went straight through the Straits of Gibraltar. She kept her course and speed, and not once did she make a single concession for another ship. As Ski said, marveling at her feat afterward, "The woman parted the seas. She just parted the seas, man." And she did it all simply by walking out to the wing and saying, "Yoo Hoo!" to any ship that got too close. It was a virtuoso performance.

They were now in the open Atlantic but were still in sight of some coastwise traffic coming from the north. At the moment, a tanker was proving particularly nettlesome to Mrs. Tannenbaume. It kept calling on the VHF, asking the ship on its port side (the *God is Able*) to please come to starboard. Because of its immense size, the tanker most likely assumed the smaller ship would eventually get out of the way—the tanker was big enough to saw her son's 'tween decker in half. But still Mrs. Tannenbaume kept her course and speed. When the two ships were in shouting distance, Mrs. Tannenbaume "yoo hooed" it out of the way.

Mrs. Tannenbaume could tell that Mitzi was watching her closely as she closed the bridge wing door behind her.

"You got *chutzpah*," Mitzi said.

Mitzi was doing the second engineer's hands. He was particular, like all of the engineers. He wanted a matte finish and it was coming out too glossy.

"So it's Tannenbaume with an E, huh?" Mitzi said. "You're not Jewish? So where did that son of yours get such a *Yiddisha kop*? You should have heard him talking business with the chief. He talked circles around that dopey chief. He's got *saichel*, that son of yours. He understands leverage. Leverage of all things!"

Mrs. Tannenbaume didn't know what to say. Her son Jewish? From Mitzi's mouth to God's ears. She needed him to be Jewish if he was going to be head honcho at the academy. Or she needed him to at least act Jewish.

Mrs. Tannenbaume could not help but notice that Mitzi had been talking about her son all afternoon. Could Mitzi be falling for her sonny? She loved guys with a *Yiddisha kop*, that Mitzi. Most Jewish girls just wanted a *mensch*. Not Mitzi. Her guy had to have some horse sense or she'd run all over him, the way she ran all over Putzie. Mrs. Tannenbaume had to admit that she would not mind it a bit if Mitzi and her sonny spent some more time together. Maybe some of Mitzi would rub off on him.

"So how is Sylvia coming along?" Mrs. Tannenbaume nodded her head toward the young girl, who was at her shampoo station massaging Swifty's head. "You think she's ready for more? Why not let her run things up here for you. See how she does."

Mitzi finished up with the second. "I have to admit," Mitzi said when the second was out of earshot. "These engineers are beginning to get to me. They're nothing but a bunch of whiners."

"Why not take a break? Go below and talk business with my sonny."

Mrs. Tannenbaume turned away when she said it. She could not bring herself to make eye contact with Mitzi while giving her the green light to cavort with her son, a married man. Then her eye caught Sylvia, not much more than a teenager, caressing Swifty's head like a pro. Some marriage. Her sonny might as well have married a Labradoodle for all he had in common with Sylvia.

"Maybe I will," Mitzi said, glancing over at Sylvia when she said it. "Maybe Sylvia wouldn't mind it."

Mrs. Tannenbaume raised her eyebrows.

"Wouldn't mind being in charge up here, I mean," Mitzi said.

"Oh, no" Mrs. Tannenbaume said quickly. "No, she wouldn't mind. Sylvia would like the responsibility."

"She doesn't like being told what to do, you know," Mitzi said. "Have you noticed that? She stopped listening to me a while ago. She stopped getting made-up every day. Stopped her assertiveness training. Stopped all of what I was teaching her. I think I wore the poor girl out."

"It was the doing-for-others thing. Most people don't get it. She can barely do for herself, forget about doing for others." It looked to Mrs. Tannenbaume like Mitzi was itching to get off the bridge. "Go, you."

Mrs. Tannenbaume climbed into the captain's chair after Mitzi left the bridge. It was the first time she had actually sat in the chair. The *God is Able* rose and fell on a long, slow swell out of the north, and the chair was far more comfortable than she realized.

Soon, the easy motion of the ship rocked Mrs. Tannenbaume to sleep.

Mrs. Tannenbaume woke up with a pain in her neck, which always put her in a bad mood. When she checked the GPS and saw how slow they were going, she was in an even worse mood. They had to make better speed if they were to return in time for the unveiling of that monument of the Commodore's. She had been wondering what the Commodore had meant when he said he wanted Captain Tannenbaume to make as big an impression as possible on as many people as possible. Was the Commodore setting her sonny up for a fall?

As for Sylvia, Mitzi was right. She was a hopeless student. She hadn't made herself up in days. She took anything the messman put in front of her—cold eggs, burnt toast, it didn't matter. The women in Great Neck would see right through her, that was for sure. Her sonny would have to pull off the Jewish thing all by himself. Of course, he always *did* have a *Yiddisha kop*, which is how he got to be a captain. It just had to be drug out of him, and maybe Mitzi would do that.

Mrs. Tannenbaume eased herself down from the captain's chair, called the engine room, and asked them for a few more RPMs. The chief came on the phone. "We're low on fuel. If anything we need to take *off* a few RPMs."

"You let me worry about that."

"I intend to." The chief hung up the phone without bothering to say goodbye.

From where the phone was located, Mrs. Tannenbaume was able to see directly into Sylvia's shampoo station. The second engineer was getting his hair shampooed for the second time that day.

"Yesterday he had his hair done three times. I think he has a thing for Sylvia," Swifty remarked.

Mrs. Tannenbaume thought about what Mitzi had said about leverage. Well, her son wasn't the only one who understood leverage.

She hauled the unsuspecting engineer out of the chair by his precious hair. "Do you want another shampoo?"

"Uh . . . yeah."

"Well, I want at least ten more RPMs."

"You want what? Sorry, I can't do that. The chief is the one who makes those decisions."

"So? He has to know?"

"Oh, come on. As soon as he comes down into the engine room, he'll know."

"You let me handle the chief. You just get me the extra RPMs."

After the second left the bridge, Mrs. Tannenbaume called the steward and told him to come to the bridge. She had something she wanted him to do.

Captain Tannenbaume never would have guessed that that was what the stool was for.

Not that he needed it, of course, not with his long legs. But Mitzi wanted him to use it anyway, and he'd do anything to keep that woman happy. Anything. When Mitzi said she wanted breakfast delivered to her room by the steward,

Captain Tannenbaume made sure she got it. Her mother had told her she had to have breakfast in bed aboard ship, at least once, and Mitzi said the thing with the chief didn't count—she wanted the steward to bring her breakfast. When Captain Tannenbaume informed the steward, old Stew was not happy about it, but Captain Tannenbaume had been holding a few chits on the steward from years ago, when they were on a steady run to Monrovia in West Africa. The steward fell in love with a bar girl at the seaman's center, made her his steady girl, and let the rest of the ship know it. They had a thing together for years. But one voyage the steward could not make it ashore—on account of his own cooking, ironically. Captain Tannenbaume, who did go ashore, could not resist the unfaithful bar girl's advances. When he was alone with her he discovered she had a little *he* in her. Captain Tannenbaume kept the news to himself all these years, but when Mitzi said she wanted the steward to bring her breakfast in bed, Captain Tannenbaume paid the steward a visit.

"No way," the steward said. "No way am I bringing that woman breakfast in bed. You can forget about it, with all due respect, sir."

"You remember that bar girl in Monrovia, Stew?"

The steward was trying to watch Clint. He did not answer. His eyes remained glued to the TV.

"I was with her one night. The night you got sick on your own gumbo."

Captain Tannenbaume saw the steward's eyes glaze over. Then the man's whole body went slack. Captain Tannenbaume clicked off Clint.

"He was really something. Wasn't she?"

It looked to Captain Tannenbaume like the steward was about to get sick.

"Mitzi wants breakfast delivered to her cabin, Stew."

Captain Tannenbaume waited for his answer. The glow of the blank TV screen was the only light in the lounge, and the room was silent for a long time. Finally, the steward spoke.

"Motherfucker."

"I guess I'll take that as a yes."

Chapter 43

TALKING BUSINESS

The steward told Mrs. Tannenbaume he was not exactly in the mood to do a favor for Captain Tannenbaume's mother, not after the humiliating experience of delivering breakfast in bed to Mitzi. But when he heard the favor, he felt better about it. He never much liked the chief anyway—the big Swede talked too damn much, and he was always sticking up for his little buddy, the electrician—so it was no big thing for the steward to mix a healthy dose of Benadryl in with the chief's meals.

The chief blamed his tiredness on the long sea passage and told the engineers he was suffering from a bad case of sleep debt and that they'd have to go it alone for the remainder of the voyage. With the chief out of the way, Mrs. Tannenbaume got her extra RPMs. After she confirmed that the ship had indeed picked up a couple of knots, she let the second engineer back onto the bridge so he could get his shampoos from Sylvia. The second was now getting up to half-a-dozen shampoos a day and Mrs. Tannenbaume noticed that Sylvia enjoyed giving them as much he enjoyed getting them. All the better. With Sylvia preoccupied, maybe she wouldn't notice that Mitzi was missing in action from the bridge, with no one quite sure of her whereabouts.

The swell from the west that had rocked Mrs. Tannenbaume to sleep the day before was still there. Mrs. Tannenbaume had taken to sitting in the captain's chair more and more now that Mitzi was down below talking business with her sonny. It was the perfect place to think. She was thinking now about the long swell and she wondered why the ship's ride was not as comfortable as it was yesterday. It didn't seem any rougher to her. She asked Swifty.

"It's got to do with the period of the swell," he said. "You know, the time between the swells. The time between the swells is getting shorter."

"Does that mean something?"

"Uh . . . yeah, I think so."

"Well does it mean good weather or bad?"

"Ah . . . good, I'm pretty sure. Yeah, definitely good."

Sparks, who was enjoying his morning coffee, stared out to sea and said, "You'll want to batten the hatches, then."

"Pardon me?" Mrs. Tannenbaume said.

"If Swifty thinks we're in for a spate of good weather, then prepare for the worst. And keep an eye on the barometer."

"The barometer is . . . sort of broken," Swifty said.

"How'd you break it?" Mrs. Tannenbaume asked.

"I didn't, I swear I didn't. It was the carpenter. When he needed a screw to hang the sign for Mitzi's salon, he stole one from the bracket that holds the barometer to the bulkhead. So later, when someone—"

"You," Sparks said.

"Well, okay, yeah. When I bumped into the barometer, it fell from its bracket. But it wasn't me who broke the barometer, it was the carpenter."

"Well there's always the barograph," Sparks said.

Swifty turned away sheepishly.

"What?" Sparks said.

"We sort of used up all the ink cartridges."

"Impossible," Sparks said. "I requisitioned a box of them last voyage."

"We needed the ink to color Sylvia's hair."

When Sparks gave him a look of disdain, Swifty got defensive.

"We haven't gotten a weather report since leaving the canal, have we? Why don't you tell Mrs. Tannenbaume why that is?"

Sparks turned his back to Swifty and pulled out a cigarette.

"So what's the story there?" Mrs. Tannenbaume asked him.

"Sparks broke the telex machine out of spite. Broke it right in half. And that's why we don't have a proper weather report."

"If you knew how to read the weather like a seafarer," Sparks said, "we wouldn't need a weather report. What'd seafarers do before all of these new-fangled machines?"

Toward evening, Mitzi made an appearance on the bridge. She confided to Mrs. Tannenbaume that she needed a break.

"He's energetic, that son of yours."

"You're complaining?"

"No, I guess not. So, when do we get back to New York?"

"We should be there tomorrow afternoon," Mrs. Tannenbaume said.

Mitzi was sitting in the captain's chair now and had to hold on tight as the ship rolled from side to side. "What's with the rocking and rolling?"

"Don't know," Mrs. Tannenbaume said. "Swifty seems to think the ride will improve."

"Have we gotten a weather report?"

"Sparks broke the telex."

"Want me to get him to fix it?" Mitzi whispered.

"I'm told it's broken in two. By the way," Mrs. Tannenbaume said, coming over to the captain's chair and lowering her voice, "speaking of that, there's something I've been meaning to ask you." She glanced over at Sparks to make sure he wasn't listening. "How'd you ever get Sparks to program the GPS?"

Mitzi looked over to where Sparks was. He was busy playing with his pack of cigarettes. "It didn't take much, to tell you the truth. I called him 'Handsome Smooth,' is all."

"Handsome Smooth?"

"It's what my mother used to call my father whenever she wanted something. She'd say, 'How's my Handsome Smooth doing?' She'd stroke his hair a little bit, you know, nothing much. That's what I did with Sparks. The next thing you know, he's got the GPS all set up." Mitzi looked over at Sparks. He was still looking out the window. "When he was finished, he handed me the GPS and said, 'How's your Handsome Smooth now?'"

"Come on. That was it?"

"That was it."

"What a kook," Mrs. Tannenbaume said.

"Sparks is a kook? Look around, would ya?"

Mrs. Tannenbaume did. Swifty was busy getting his facecloths ready in the coffeepot, the second engineer was on his umpteenth shampoo of the day, and the electrician was fretting over the buildup of his nail polish.

"I gotta tell ya," Mitzi admitted, "with the exception of your son, I think these merchant marines are all kooks."

"Well, Eddie wasn't a kook."

"Who's Eddie?"

"One of my sonny boy's fathers."

"*One* of his fathers? How many fathers does he have?"

"Well, since we're not sure which one of my boyfriends—Eddie, Teddy, or Freddy—got me pregnant, we just pretend he has three."

"Wow," Mitzi said. "Three boyfriends at once. I thought I was bad."

"I was a looker in my day."

"I guess you were. So Eddie was a merchant marine?"

"Yeah. Eddie was a sailor, Teddy was a tailor, and Freddy was a jailor."

"Eddie, Teddy, and Freddy," Mitzi said. "A sailor, a tailor, and a jailor. Cute."

"It was a situation, that's for sure."

Mitzi slapped her hand on her thigh. "You're something else, you know that? You got personality. You sure you ain't Jewish?"

Mrs. Tannenbaume noticed that she did not react the way she usually did whenever someone asked her if she was Jewish. She didn't stiffen up, didn't try to change the subject. She was starting to feel comfortable around Mitzi, like they were girlfriends. Mrs. Tannenbaume didn't have too many girlfriends. She just never felt like she could get too close to anyone. But Mitzi was different. Mitzi said what was on her mind, just like she did. Maybe she and Mitzi could be friends after all. "Speaking of kooks," Mrs. Tannenbaume said, "how about that Commodore?"

"Oh, gawd. What a kook. No—no." Mitzi put her hand on Mrs. Tannenbaume's shoulder, laughing. "He's not kooky—he's quirky."

"He's a flouncy is what he is."

"A flouncy?" Now Mitzi was really laughing. "What's a flouncy?"

"Someone who's full of himself. You know, always flouncing around. He's a flouncy."

Mitzi was laughing uncontrollably now. Sparks and the others were looking over toward the captain's chair to see what was so funny.

"I've never heard someone called a flouncy before," Mitzi said, drying the tears from her eyes. "Oh, gawd. That's too funny."

"And what's with his obsession with this kid who's gonna be on the monument? I've got the pedal to the metal so that we'll get back in time for the unveiling of this monument of his."

"I know," Mitzi said. "He's been practicing his speech for weeks now. Actually, he spends most of his time on his Toe Hang."

"So what is a Toe Hang, anyway?"

"Oh, gawd," Mitzi said, laughing again. "You don't even want to know."

Mitzi had a great laugh. Mrs. Tannenbaume understood why men loved her. She had it all. A great body, a head-full of hair, a great laugh. What more could a man want?

"When he's not practicing his Toe Hang, he's doing his Infinity breath. In front of the mirror."

"His Infinity breath?"

"It's a yoga thing. And get this. On his exhale, he says Edwin. EDDDDDWIIIIIINNNNNN. So to say he's obsessed with the boy is an understatement."

"Wow. I have to say, I can't wait to get back for the unveiling myself. I gotta see this Edwin with my own eyes."

Mrs. Tannenbaume and Mitzi carried on like this for the rest of the afternoon and into the evening. Mrs. Tannenbaume had not felt this good in a long time. At one point she wondered what Sylvia thought about her mother-in-law laughing and joking with Mitzi when she never did that with her, but when Mrs. Tannenbaume turned around to look for Sylvia, she was nowhere to be found. Neither, Mrs. Tannenbaume noticed, was the second.

When she and Mitzi were finally finished *kibitzing*, Mrs. Tannenbaume asked her how her sonny was doing. Mitzi said he was down below napping. Mitzi also said that she thought he was really looking forward to being admiral.

"And I'll tell you," she said, "he's just what that wacky Merchant Marine Academy needs. A real captain with a *Yiddisha kop*."

Mrs. Tannenbaume could not agree more. She could not wait to see her sonny boy in his admiral's uniform. By tomorrow afternoon, the ship would be in New York and the day after that was the unveiling.

"I'm on top of things up here. You go below and talk business with my sonny."

Mrs. Tannenbaume did not have to tell Mitzi twice.

Chapter 44

HOMECOMING

Mrs. Tannenbaume smacked Sparks upside his head. "Come on, Handsome Smooth, say something!"

They were in the radio shack where Sparks had fired up the Single Side Band radio, their only hope of getting out a May Day message, seeing as the VHF radio was out of commission. Back when Captain Tannenbaume wanted his deck officers to make meeting arrangements with other ships on the VHF, Mrs. Tannenbaume took matters into her own hands. She had been drilling it into their heads to maintain course and speed, and the last thing she wanted was for them to use the VHF to make meeting arrangements, so she cut the mic cord with a pair of scissors. The VHF receiver still worked, they just could not transmit. It never occurred to Mrs. Tannenbaume that they might one day need to do so.

The long slow swell coming from the north, the thing that Swifty knew meant *something*, did indeed mean something. A long slow sea swell is the classic forbearer of a storm. But Swifty and the mates missed it, just like they missed the significance of the cloud formations at sunset—the converging mares tails. They missed the big drop in atmospheric pressure because of the broken barometer, and they missed all of the weather reports warning of the violent nor'easter barreling down the east coast of the United States because of the shattered telex machine. So they really had no one else to blame but themselves for banging dead-up into a low pressure system off the coast of New York.

But Mrs. Tannenbaume was not interested in playing the blame game. She just wanted Sparks to get out the May Day message. But with all of the excitement of the storm—not to mention the pressure of getting out a distress message—Sparks's stutter had come back with a vengeance.

"Muh- muh- muh- muh . . ."

Mrs. Tannenbaume continued to bang Sparks over the head. "Come on, you Handsome Smooth you!"

Sparks needed to raise both hands over his head to protect himself from the blows raining down on him, which is why he kept dropping the mic. It was slowgoing, but he did begin to make some progress.

"Ay-ay-ay-ay . . ."

Mrs. Tannenbaume gave up and left the radio shack to go back to the bridge. She got there just in time to answer the telephone. It was the engine room. They were low on fuel and in serious danger of losing the plant.

Mrs. Tannenbaume hung up. "Ski, what happens if we lose the plant?"

Ski let out a long whistle. "Oh, no, we don't want to do that. Not in this weather."

So Mrs. Tannenbaume called the chief in his cabin.

"Hullo," the chief answered, not sounding very good at all.

"Chief. Get down to the engine room. Now! The engineers are about to lose the plant."

"Hullo."

"Chief! This is the supernumerary! I said go below!"

"Hullo."

Mrs. Tannenbaume hung up and told Ski to go wake up the chief. "Call him 'Handsome Smooth.'"

Ski went down below and gently rubbed the chief's shoulders as he lay asleep in bed.

"Come on, Handsome Smooth."

The steward happened to walk in just then with the chief's Benadryl. Ski looked up and saw the steward standing there.

"It's not what you think," Ski protested.

"Not my business," the steward said, backing out the door. "I'll just leave you two lovebirds alone."

Ski scrambled up and ran down the passageway after him, trying to explain that he was only doing as he was told.

Mrs. Tannenbaume was back in the radio shack now. She was not very happy with Sparks's progress.

"Duh- duh- duh- duh . . ."

Mrs. Tannenbaume hip-checked Sparks out of the way and grabbed the mic. "Yoo Hoo!"

A voice broke in over the SSB. "United States Coast Guard back to the station calling."

Mrs. Tannenbaume had no idea how to make a distress call. She did not know the ship's coordinates, or its call sign, or even, for that matter, the exact nature of their distress. She just knew that she was in the middle of a storm and wanted no part of it.

"Yoo Hoo!"

"United States Coast Guard back to the station calling. Repeat, what is the name of the station calling?"

"This is the Motor Vessel *God is Able*."

"Motor Vessel *God is Able*, United States Coast Guard. What type of vessel are you?"

"We're a 'tween decker."

"*God is Able*, what is the nature of your distress?"

"We're rocking and rolling like crazy."

"*God is Able*, do you have any engineers on board?"

"Yeah. But they're afraid of breaking their nails."

"*God is Able*, did you say nails? Are you in need of spare parts?"

"Well, we are running low on nail polish."

"*God is Able*, stand by." Long pause. "*God is Able*, do you require a pilot?"

"Yeah, but we ran out of cigarettes."

"*God is Able*, United States Coast Guard, say again."

"I say we have no cigarettes but we've got plenty of hot towels."

"*God is Able*, stand by." Another long pause. "*God is Able*, channel 16 is a hailing and distress frequency only. Please take your business to a working channel. United States Coast Guard, out."

Captain Tannenbaume entered the wheelhouse just as the *God is Able* was passing under the Verrazano-Narrows Bridge. His appearance took his mother aback.

"Sonny! You look so rested. You look like a teenager."

Captain Tannenbaume did not want anybody making a fuss over his appearance, mostly because he'd then have to account for his disappearance. "You've always told me I had a youthful look, Mother."

"But not like this, sonny. You look like a teenager. You look like—"

Captain Tannenbaume put up his hand to stop his mother. He looked around the bridge. "Where's Sylvia?"

"Uh . . . " Mrs. Tannenbaume made a show of looking around the bridge. "Oh, is Sylvia not up here?"

Captain Tannenbaume was relieved that his wife was not on the bridge. And he did not have the least interest in where she might be.

"I hope there are no hard feelings about my taking the conn from you last night."

"No problem whatsoever."

"Good."

"The rocking and rolling was starting to get to me, to tell you the truth. I'm sort of glad you took the conn. What was it that you did? Heaving up?"

Captain Tannenbaumed laughed at his mother's malapropism. "Heaving to, Mother. It's called 'heaving to.' In a storm, to ease the rolling, you put the waves directly on the bow. Then you keep just enough revs on the engine to hold her there. The ship'll pitch a little, but it's a whole lot better than taking twenty-degree rolls."

"You can say that again."

Captain Tannenbaume walked out to the bridge wing and looked around. New York. He was finally home. And he was home to stay, too. The idea of being superintendent of the academy had finally gotten a grip on him. Especially now, knowing that Mitzi was going to be his secretary. And who knew? Maybe she'd become more than his secretary. The thing with Sylvia had been a mistake—he already admitted that to himself. Thank goodness Sylvia recognized it, too. Oh, he knew all about the shampoos she was giving the second. Word gets around on a ship after all.

Mrs. Tannenbaume came out to the bridge wing where her sonny boy was standing.

"Well, Mother. Tomorrow's the big day. The unveiling of the monument. Have you talked to the Commodore? Do I get sworn in as superintendent before or after the big event?"

"The Commodore never mentioned anything about that. I guess we'll find out tomorrow."

Mrs. Tannenbaume looked up at her sonny. "Oh, sonny boy. I'm so proud of you. Think about it. After all these years, you're finally going to be accepted into Kings Point. It seems like a dream."

"I'll admit it does feel too good to be true. I owe it all to the Commodore, and I've never even met the man."

"Oh," Mrs. Tannenbaume said at the mention of the Commodore. "You're in for a treat."

"So I gather. Mitzi's been telling me about him."

Mrs. Tannenbaume felt a pang of anxiety. That their lives were in the Commodore's hands was making her increasingly uneasy. There was something about the man she did not trust. She knew that he was far too self-absorbed to advance anyone's career but his own. But at this stage in the game, what could the Commodore do to upset the apple cart? Mrs. Tannenbaume knew that the Board of Directors had approved her sonny as the next superintendent. And she knew that Mogie wanted a Jew in that position.

Oh, yes, there is the Jewish thing to worry about. She'd almost forgotten about that. Her only hope was that a little bit of Mitzi had rubbed off on her sonny after all of their time together these last few days.

What Captain Tannenbaume said next put Mrs.Tannenbaume more at ease. It was almost as if he had been reading her mind.

"To tell you the truth, he sounds a little *meshuggeneh*. Almost like he has to be the big *maccachah* all the time."

Mrs. Tannenbaume looked up at her handsome, youthful son. "Oy, sonny, you're going to be just fine."

Captain Tannenbaume missed his mother's vote of confidence. He was busy looking up at the stack. More to the point, he was looking up at the black smoke that was pouring out of the stack. It was the acrid smell more than the smoke itself that alerted him to a problem. Bad fuel. That's because it was the last of the fuel—the dregs, the sludge-like gunk that sinks to the bottom and never gets used. Unless, of course, there is nothing left to use. Captain Tannenbaume heard the phone ringing in the wheelhouse but he didn't need any engineer to tell him what had just happened.

The *God is Able* had just run out of fuel.

The ship was coming up on the Stapleton anchorage in the upper bay. For a moment, Captain Tannenbaume thought he might be able to steer his beat-up old 'tween decker into the anchorage and simply drop the hook. But such luck was not to be. A car carrier—a big, boxy, notoriously-difficult-to-maneuver ship —bore down on the anchorage from the north.

The two ships met in the middle of the anchorage in the way that two ships are never supposed to meet. News helicopters were hovering above the two ships within minutes.

The collision ruined Captain Tannenbaume's homecoming, as collisions tend to do. His long career as a sea captain was over, no one had to tell him that. And his new career as superintendent was over before it even started, and no one had to tell him that either.

BOOK III

The United States Merchant Marine Academy

Chapter 45

LIKE A MOTH TO A FLAME

I t took a while, but Mrs. Tannenbaume finally talked her sonny into going to the academy anyway. "We came this far," she said, "why let something like a little collision stop us now?"

Captain Tannenbaume informed her that there was no such thing as a "little" collision, and besides, this collision was a *big* collision. The only consolation was that nobody was hurt. Yes, the engineers ruined their nails fighting the small fire that broke out when the fuel line ruptured, but fortunately, as soon as the fuel in the line was expended, so were the flames. And yes, the fact that the second engineer singed his hair, the very hair that Sylvia so lovingly washed every day, was the height of irony, although singed hair, like blackened fingernails, could hardly be called an injury. There were a smattering of other scrapes and bruises: the chief fell out of his bunk and smashed his face on the side table (although some said he chewed up his face the day before while shaving under the influence of Benadryl), and the steward burned his hand pretty badly when his pot of gumbo came crashing off the hot stove. Then there was Sparks who, in the middle of dismantling the Single Side Band radio—the one remaining piece of electronic equipment on board—poked a hole in his hand with an awl when the two ships came unexpectedly together.

As it turned out, Captain Tannenbaume did not have much time to think about whether or not he should proceed to the Academy as planned. It had not taken long for word to get out that the captain involved in the collision in the harbor was about to be sworn in as the next superintendent of the Merchant Marine Academy, and the irony made it too irresistible a story for the media to pass up. Several dozen vans belonging to the various news outlets were camped out waiting for Captain Tannenbaume on the pier in Brooklyn. So when a fire rescue boat dropped him, Mitzi, and his mother off at Pier 1 in Brooklyn the next day, Captain Tannenbaume was more than happy to escape into the van that was waiting there to whisk him and his companions back to the academy. Much to Mitzi's dismay, she could not persuade the midshipman driving the van to drive over the speed limit, and the news reporters beat them back to the academy with time to spare.

Mr. Thompson, the gate guardsman, intercepted the van when it reached the main entrance. Mr. Thompson was under strict orders to escort Captain Tannenbaume directly to Wiley Hall, where the Commodore awaited his arrival. However, in his alcoholic stupor, Mr. Thompson jumped in the wrong van, and instead of escorting Captain Tannenbaume directly to the Commodore, he escorted Fox News. It was up to Miss Lambright to keep the reporters out of the Commodore's office, where the Commodore was busy putting the finishing touches on his speech.

The Commodore had been in his office since daybreak, and his Toe Hang was still not quite right. Miss Lambright told him it was fine, but the Commodore would not listen. He explained, again, with as much patience as he could muster, that the Toe Hang was his singular chance to become "one" with his audience. He was dead in the water without an effective Toe Hang and it exasperated him that Miss Lambright could not appreciate that simple fact.

The Commodore was also unhappy with his hand gestures. They were too choppy. In fact, the Commodore fretted over every aspect of his speech. His breathing was erratic, his eye contact with the audience was jumpy. Miss Lambright told him again that she thought everything was fine and that he was going to give a great speech, but that just upset the Commodore even more.

"If you think everything is fine, my dear, then I know that I really am out of sync this morning."

Miss Lambright left the room in tears, but the Commodore quickly coaxed her back in and asked her to comment on his pause, scan, and nod technique.

"It comes across as insincere," Miss Lambright said.

He tried it again.

"No, it still seems unconvincing."

"How can I develop any confidence in my speech with all of this criticism you're giving me?"

"I really like your Toe Hang," Miss Lambright said in a soft voice.

"You think my Toe Hang is fine? How would you know? You do not have a discerning bone in your body."

"No, really, sir—"

"Do not coddle me, Miss Lambright! Return to your desk this moment."

It was shortly after the Commodore sent Miss Lambright away that Fox News showed up. The truth is, Miss Lambright did not try all that hard to keep them out of the Commodore's office.

The reporters barged in and found the Commodore in front of the mirror doing his Infinity breath. The cameraman immediately slung his clunky camera to his shoulder and began filming. When the Commodore saw the cameraman in the mirror he froze, and if it wasn't for Mitzi, he might have remained frozen in the mirror for the entire day.

Mitzi had slipped unawares into the office through the side door and, after quickly sizing up the situation, proceeded to walk the cameraman out of the office by his ear. One look from Mitzi was all it took to make the others decide to leave the room with their colleague. When the last of the news reporters had filed out, she went back to the side door to let in Captain Tannenbaume and his mother. They stood by the door, hesitating to venture farther in without the Commodore's permission.

It took a moment for the Commodore, in his agitated state, to realize that this was Captain Tannenbaume—*the* Captain Tannenbaume. He looked at Captain Tannenbaume, then at Mitzi, and then back at Tannenbaume. He knew that the only thing standing between him and his dream of being admiral was this man standing across the room from him. The Commodore felt his throat tighten. He turned to Mrs. Tannenbaume but could not bring himself to ask if this was her son. All he could manage was a raise of his eyebrows.

"Yes," Mrs. Tannenbaume said, breaking the eerie silence. "This is my sonny boy."

The Commodore went to Captain Tannenbaume like a moth to a flame. He stood before him and, without addressing him, inspected his person. It distressed the Commodore to find that Captain Tannenbaume was so youthful in appearance. The man did not have a gray hair on his head. And his skin! How on earth was his skin so smooth after all those years at sea? To compound the Commodore's distress, he found that if he did not stand up as straight as possible, his counterpart might even be a smidgen taller than he. Captain Tannenbaume's jaw was firm and he seemed well muscled under his khaki uniform. The Commodore sensed that Tannenbaume was well aware of his superior physical attributes. *The man exudes confidence. Or is it arrogance?* Captain Tannenbaume's steely eyes unnerved the Commodore.

Well, two could play that game. The Commodore stepped an inch closer to Tannenbaume—they were now nose-to-nose—and stared deep into his eyes. He would penetrate this man's soul with his gaze, he determined. *We shall see how long he can take it.*

But Captain Tannenbaume could take it for a long time.

It was, ultimately, the Commodore who looked away first. And then his knees went the way of his eyes.

The Commodore was not expecting this. He was not expecting this at all. What with Miss Lambright's rudeness, the intrusion of the news reporters, and now this—why, his morning was not going at all as he had planned.

The Commodore broke away and left Captain Tannenbaume without ever having uttered a word.

Captain Tannenbaume walked after him. "I'm Mort Tannenbaume," he said, to the Commodore's back as the Commodore walked over to the window.

The Commodore ignored him and kept his back to everyone while he stared out the window. A deep breath, as deep a breath as he could muster, made him feel a little better. Looking out the window made him feel better too, the way a seasick sailor feels better when he keeps his eyes glued to the horizon. In the distance, by Eldridge Pool, was the monument, still under wraps, and the white bleachers the groundsmen had set up for the unveiling. The day was bright, the air clean and cloudless with just a hint of a breeze blowing out of the northwest. In his mind's eye, the Commodore envisioned the unveiling. He heard the crowd gasp at the sight of their bronze hero, the way the sun glinted off Edwin's square jaw, the gleam in Edwin's eyes. He had visualized this day for so long now that he knew precisely how it would all turn out.

But he had not foreseen all of these distractions. He had not envisioned this at all. Tannenbaume was certainly not the man he had expected. He had had no idea the man possessed such corporeal superiority. And he also could never have foreseen all of the unwanted attention Tannenbaume would bring with him that morning. Now, instead of a tightly controlled guest list, a slew of unsavory news hacks would also be at the ceremony. Who knew how many people would be there? Their very presence would surely spoil Edwin's big day.

The Commodore resolved that the man would *not* ruin Edwin's day. He would not allow it. He would personally ban Tannenbaume from attending the unveiling. And with no Captain Tannenbaume in attendance, there would be no news reporters—at least not the unwanted ones. No, he had not practiced his speech, had not worked on himself in all areas of self-improvement simply to have Tannenbaume be the center of attention. This was *his* day, not Tannenbaume's. In fact, the Commodore had assiduously planned the day so that it would be all about him. He had choreographed everything, down to arranging for a car service to take Tannenbaume back to his ship after the Commodore revealed to Mogie that the man was a fraud.

The Commodore knew he had to finesse this one, but he was off his game this morning. This Tannenbaume was clearly an arrogant man, and the Commodore knew he had to be careful. Indeed, his instincts told him it was wiser he not talk directly to Tannenbaume right this moment.

"Ms. Paultz."

Mitzi came to the Commodore's side and soothingly brushed her hand up and down his back.

"Inform Captain Tannenbaume and his mother that a breakfast is being held in their honor at this time in the officers' club. Mayor Mogelefsky is expecting them. Tell them that now, please."

Mitzi turned around, but Mrs. Tannenbaume cut her off.

"We heard him. Is the big *maccacha* going to join us?"

"Yes," the Commodore whispered to Mitzi.

"Yes," Mitzi said. "The Commodore will be joining you."

"When?" Mrs. Tannenbaume asked.

"Soon," the Commodore said through Mitzi.

"Soon," Mitzi relayed to the Tannenbaumes.

The Commodore grabbed Mitzi's arm. "Ms. Paultz."

"Yes, sir."

"Please make them go away."

Chapter 46

A CAPTAIN AND HIS COMELY CADET

It didn't take long for the cameraman to convince Miss Lambright to loosen the top button of her blouse. And then the next button. And then the next. Before long all of the newsmen were crowding around Miss Lambright's desk for a better view of her having her "official portrait" taken. So Mogie was able to walk right past Miss Lambright and the newsmen with nobody noticing him. He found the Commodore stretched out on the couch with a cold compress draped over his eyes and Mitzi sitting on the coffee table holding the Commodore's hand.

"A migraine," the Commodore was saying. "All morning practicing my speech and nothing going right, and now I have a migraine."

"But I bet your Toe Hang is as impressive as ever." Mitzi's voice was soothing.

Before Mitzi knew what was happening, Mogie had her by the arm. "You haven't seen him in over a month and the first thing you do is ask him about his Toe Hang?" Mogie tightened his grip on Mitzi's arm. "How long have you two been *schtupping*?"

"Oh gawd, Moges. Me and the Commodore? Get real. Please."

The Commodore rose off the couch, the compress wrapped around his eyes like a blindfold. Mitzi helped him over to his chair.

"I can assure you, Mayor, I *schtup* no one."

"Yeah, right. All you WASPs are hornier than a three-balled tomcat. The crack of dawn ain't safe with you people."

"Don't talk crass in front of the Commodore, Moges. He don't like bad language."

"Bad language, Mitz? You want to now what bad language is? It's talking in code." Mogie waved his hand at the Commodore. "Which is all these people do."

Mogie stuck a cigar in his mouth and circled the room before confronting the Commodore at his desk. "So where's Tannenbaume? What's he got to say for himself? It's all over the news, this accident of his."

The Commodore slowly removed the compress from his eyes. "I sent him over to the officers' club. I told him we were having a breakfast in his honor."

"A breakfast? I wasn't invited to any breakfast."

"There isn't any breakfast. I sent him there so that I could get him out of my office. There is no room for arrogance in this office."

"You mean no *more* room, don't you, Commodore?" Mogie laughed at his own joke. "Hey, Mitz. That was pretty funny, huh? He means no more room."

Mitzi ignored Mogie. She had taken the compress from the Commodore and, out of habit, began setting up the Commodore's desk with his phony work papers.

"I can't believe our new admiral just ran into a boat in New York harbor," Mogie said. "I thought you said we needed a captain who knew how to drive a boat? This guy doesn't know *gunnisch* about driving boats."

"Ship," the Commodore said. "It's a ship, not a boat. And Captain Tannenbaume's ship ran out of fuel."

"How'd he run out of fuel?"

"He didn't want to buy fuel over in Europe because it's too expensive," Mitzi said, coming to Captain Tannenbaume's defense. "You know, because of the euro."

"What a schmuck. He wants to save money so he doesn't fill up but then he runs out of gas? He's a schmuck this Tannenbaume."

"The other ship ran into us," Mitzi said defensively. "It came out of nowhere."

"The guy on the news said all Tannenbaume had to do was drop the anchor when he ran out of gas."

"It all happened so fast, Moges. Morty didn't have time to drop the anchor."

Mogie was up in Mitzi's face before the words were out of her mouth. "Morty? So you two are on a first-name basis? The two of you on a little boat in a great big ocean. I can just imagine what went on out there."

The Commodore's migraine was quickly receding now that he realized how easy it was going to be to scuttle Tannenbaume. In fact, it was looking like it would be easier than he had originally presumed. He casually walked over and draped his arm around Mogie's shoulder and pulled him away from Mitzi.

"Now, now, Mr. Mayor. You know the sway the sea holds over a woman. That a tryst occurred between a lonely sea captain and his comely cadet can hardly come as a surprise to you."

"She didn't deny it, did she?" Mogie said, looking over his shoulder at Mitzi as the Commodore pulled him away. "She didn't deny it."

The Commodore realized that Mogie had reason enough to get rid of Tannenbaume because of Mitzi alone. The Commodore also surmised that, in Mogie's mind, running out of fuel was a greater indictment of Tannenbaume's character than the fact that he collided with another ship. For the Commodore's part, it never even occurred to him that Tannenbaume's collision would prevent him from becoming admiral. In fact, most, if not all, of the faculty and staff at the United States Merchant Marine Academy had had a serious accident at sea of one sort or another. That was why they were at the academy—they had nowhere else to go in an industry that insisted on competence or, at the very least, no egregious acts of incompetence. So the best course of action to rid himself of Tannenbaume for good was to make Mogie think that Tannenbaume had serious designs on Mitzi. The Commodore had no idea what actually occurred between Mitzi and Tannenbaume aboard ship, but he guessed that Mogie's suspicion of a tryst was not too far off the mark. After all, there seemed to be no sign of Captain Tannenbaume's wife, not that that surprised the Commodore. Knowing what he knew of professional seaman, not to mention professional ladies of the night, he never really expected Captain Tannenbaume's marriage to make it past the long voyage home.

The Commodore pulled Mogie over to his desk and was about to say something regarding Tannenbaume's reputation as a ladies man when he was interrupted by the alarm clock sitting on the coffee table. He had set the alarm to help keep on track that morning, knowing full well that Miss Lambright could never be trusted to do that for him. The alarm alerted that there were only two hours to the unveiling. The shrillness of the alarm's buzzer rattled the Commodore, and he could not bring himself to turn it off. It was Mitzi who finally silenced the alarm.

"What's that for?" she said.

The Commodore did not even hear the question. He was thinking again about who would be in the crowd at the unveiling. If Tannenbaume were present, he was sure—more sure than ever now that he thought about it—that the bleachers would be overrun with reporters there to see Tannenbaume and not him. For months now he had visualized friendly faces in the crowd and now he wondered if he would get nervous when he looked out at the audience and saw nothing but strangers. Wondering whether he would get nervous made him all the more nervous. *Yes, it would be disastrous for me if Tannenbaume attended the unveiling.*

He summoned everything in his being to shrug off the great weight of inertia brought on by his anxiety. He took up where he left off with Mogie, dragging the mayor over to window, out of earshot of Mitzi.

"Mr. Mayor, I have no doubt that Captain Tannenbaume and Mitzi have formed a—how shall we say it?—*bond* of some sort. I suggest we go to the officers' club this moment and inform Captain Tannenbaume that his services will not be needed after all."

Mogie pulled himself away from the Commodore. He looked over the Commodore's shoulder at Mitzi. "So you think the two of them are *schtupping*?"

The Commodore kept his voice low and discreet. "There is a certain smugness in Ms. Paultz's manner this morning. It is almost as if she knows that she will soon be untouchable, ensconced as the new admiral's concubine. As you yourself said, she hasn't denied it, has she?"

The Commodore studied Mogie's neck vein. It told him all he needed to know.

"Let us allow discretion to be our guide, Mr. Mayor. We ought not to say a word to Mitzi, lest she tip off Captain Tannenbaume of our intentions."

Mogie was no longer looking at Mitzi. He was staring hard at the Commodore. So hard that the Commodore's mouth went dry. Had he said something to upset Mogie?

"Who died and left you boss, Commodore? I'm still calling the shots here. You think I'm a schmuck? You think I don't know that you're looking nine-ways-'til-Tuesday for a reason to get rid of Tannenbaume?"

The Commodore knew better than to respond. He allowed Mogie to stare him down.

"Let's go," Mogie said, finally. "Let's go have a look at this guy."

Mogie walked out of the office with his shoulders hunched high and his head down low. The Commodore had trouble reading his body language. Was Mogie going over to the officers' club intent on confronting Tannenbaume, or was he merely reasserting his authority over the Commodore? The Commodore signaled to Mitzi that they were leaving.

When the three of them passed through the Commodore's outer office, they found Miss Lambright sitting primly at her desk, typing. Topless. Not one reporter paid them any mind as they slunk past.

Chapter 47

YOU DON'T KNOW
GUNNISCH

Captain Tannenbaume stood outside of the officers' club with his mother. "No, Mother, for the last time, I'm not going in."

"But, sonny, they're having a breakfast in our honor."

"Mother, did you see how the Commodore greeted us? He barely even acknowledged me."

"But you're so close to being the head honcho. Don't quit on me now."

"Don't you get it, Mother? I'm a captain who just ran out of fuel and hit another ship. They don't let you run a maritime academy after something like that. I really don't know why I even agreed to come here this morning."

"But, sonny—"

"No, Mother."

When Captain Tannenbaume spun around to leave, he ran smack into Mitzi. She put her hand on his chest to stop him.

"Where do you think you're going?" she said.

"I'm out of here, Mitzi. I never should have let you two talk me into coming here this morning."

"Hey." Mitzi pushed Captain Tannenbaume again in the chest, this time with both hands. "Stick around, would you. Let's see how this thing plays out."

"I don't know, Mitz. I really don't think they want me now."

"But of course they do, sonny," Mrs. Tannenbaume said. "You're the best thing that ever happened to this place."

"Did I hear someone say 'the best'?"

It was the Commodore. He and Mogie were making their way up the pea rock path toward the entrance of the officers' club. "The best, indeed," the Commodore said as he and Mogie joined them in front of the officers' club. "Mayor Mogelefsky, may I introduce you to the *best* captain in the fleet—Captain Tannenbaume."

Mogie took a step back so that he would not have to crane his neck to have a good look at Captain Tannenbaume.

"The best, huh? What a joke. I thought we were getting someone who knew how to drive a boat. You don't know *gunnisch* about driving boats, Tannenbaume."

"*Gunnisch*?" Captain Tannenbaume said.

Mrs. Tannenbaume elbowed her sonny in the ribs. "He means you don't know nothing about driving boats, sonny."

"What's the matter, Tannenbaume? You forget your Yiddish?"

Captain Tannenbaume just stared at Mitzi. Mitzi, in a nervous voice, said, "Oh, Mort. Don't pay him any attention."

"So your name's Mort? Oh, I'm sorry, it's *Morty,* isn't it?" Mogie was flailing his arms around. "So, Morty, tell us about this accident of yours. I thought you knew how to drive a boat."

"The *God is Able* is a ship," Captain Tannenbaume said.

"Well, I guess God wasn't so able the other day, huh, Mitz? Hey, how 'bout that one, Mitz? God wasn't so able."

"It ain't funny, Moges. None of your jokes are funny."

"Well, how about this joke right here?" Mogie was pointing at Captain Tannenbaume. "The schmuck ran out of gas trying to stretch a buck. How funny is that?"

Captain Tannenbaume took a step toward Mogie, but Mitzi was there to stop him again with her hand on his chest. The Commodore pulled Mogie away. They stood next to the ship's anchor guarding the entrance to the officers' club. While they talked, Mogie never took his eye off Captain Tannenbaume.

"Look at the two of them over there. Mitzi's gaga for this guy."

"She does appear to have some affection for the man."

"How the hell is the guy so young looking? I was expecting some old sea dog."

"As was I. The sea actually appears to have done him wonders. His skin is translucent."

Mogie run his fingers through the few strands of hair left on his head. "Look at the thick head of hair on him. He looks like a damn teenager."

"He does have a baby face, indeed."

Mogie sighed heavily. He was no longer waving his arms around but was standing with his feet planted wide and his hands on his hips.

"There's no way I can have this guy hanging around here. I'll never get Mitzi back." Mogie looked up at the Commodore. "Shit. I can't believe I'm saying this, but I guess I'm going to have to go into business with you after all, Commodore."

The Commodore's knees almost gave way. His ambition to lead the Merchant Marine Academy was about to become a reality. He felt light-headed. He tried to speak but couldn't.

"Oh, look at you," Mogie said. "You look like you're about to cry."

Mogie looked back at Captain Tannenbaume and Mitzi. They were standing close together and Mitzi had her hand on Tannenbaume's arm.

"Oh for chrissakes," Mogie said. "I ain't letting them two out of my sight. We're going to have to wait until after this monument thing of yours. Then we'll turn Tannenbaume loose and have the guards escort him off the property. We'll send him right back to that boat of his."

"But the reporters," the Commodore said. "Captain Tannenbaume's presence will bring the wrong element to the ceremony. Edwin deserves better."

"Oh, quit it, Commodore. You're acting like this kid of yours is still alive. Trust me, him and all his ancestors are long gone." Mogie looked at his watch. "So when does this thing start?"

The Commodore cocked his ear toward Barney Square. "Oh, my. I hear the marching band starting up. We have to get going."

Mogie went back to where the others were standing. "Let's go. The Commodore's kid's about to be unveiled. We'll talk more after the ceremony."

Captain Tannenbaume tried to pull away from Mitzi but she still had him by the arm. Mrs. Tannenbaume grabbed his other arm and she and Mitzi dragged him with them. They followed behind Mogie.

The Commodore wanted to take one last look at his appearance before the ceremony so he took the quickest way back to Wiley Hall, cutting across Barney Square. The regiment had begun mustering in companies and battalions when the Commodore reached the square. He stopped to watch them muster up.

This was his regiment now. These were his boys. Finally, they would be getting what the Commodore knew they craved. A leader. Someone to look up to. Not just him, but Edwin, too. An icon. That's what his boys so desperately needed.

The Commodore took a deep breath. The brisk air of this perfect October day filled his lungs to capacity. He had never felt better. He saw the midshipmen looking at him. After today he would be their leader.

And he would show them the way.

Chapter 48

A TRUE UNVEILING

It was the perfect day for the unveiling of the Mariners Monument. The Board of Governors, who liked the pomp of official ceremonies, chose to sit not on the dais with the other dignitaries but in the first row of bleachers where they had a better view of the proceedings. The October sun shone so brilliantly that the widows Willowsby and Coffee needed their white parasols to stay comfortable, even with the cool breeze coming off the water. Miss Beebee chose to go sleeveless, which simply awed the widows.

Captain Cooper sat to the left of the widows. The Board of Governors had been looking forward to meeting Captain Tannenbaume's wife. The widows and Miss Beebee kept turning around in their seats, craning their necks to see if they could spot Captain Tannenbaume's spouse, but they did not see anyone who looked like she could be the new First Lady of the academy. They only saw Mitzi and a woman who looked like she could be Captain Tannenbaume's mother. Every time they turned around, the gleaming sun flared off the white parasols and sent a blinding flash of light across the grandstand. The formal parade on Tomb Field before the unveiling ceremony had not been one of the academy's best. Not one battalion managed to march in a straight line. In fact, the lines were so straggly it was difficult to tell whether it was a parade at all. The marching band was badly off-key and the Manual of Arms, per usual, was a disaster, with more than one rifle ignominiously dropped. The regiment of midshipmen was preoccupied with the same thing that had the Board of Governors so preoccupied: Where was Captain Tannenbaume's wife? They had heard the same rumors as had Captain Cooper, that Captain Tannenbaume had married a bar girl, and since nearly every cadet had been with a bar girl named Sylvia in some port of call during their sea year, they all were eager to find out if it was *their* Sylvia who had married Captain Tannenbaume.

The Commodore stood by himself under the grandstand and watched the regiment file into the bleachers to take their seats directly behind the Board of Governors. Their restlessness was palpable—they were displaying the skittishness of an unbroken steed. As for the Commodore himself, Mogie's unequivocal statement that he would get rid of Tannenbaume—and make the Commodore the superintendent—had put him in a state of grace. He was so blissful that when Miss Lambright arrived with a coterie of reporters, the Commodore remained unfazed. He had prepared for months to give this speech, on this day, and he determined that nothing was going to knock him off his game.

The Commodore knew that he never looked more splendiferous than he did that day. Raymond had worked diligently on the Commodore's service dress whites and it showed. It was as if he had etched in the creases with a stiletto knife. The Commodore had received a haircut just that morning and his hair looked as radiant as ever. Miss Lambright had mentioned at his dress rehearsal the day before that perhaps he was overdoing it with all of the medals, that he looked like the generalissimo of some banana republic, but the Commodore thought otherwise. He had personally picked each ribbon and medal out of a catalog, and he took pains arranging them for best effect. That the Commodore did not actually merit any of the medals he wore worried him not. It was the look that was important, the impression that the phalanx of medals and ribbons conveyed.

After he gave the benediction, the chaplain made a few introductory remarks about Edwin J. O'Hara. His remarks seemed to pacify the regiment. The Commodore knew that the regiment liked the chaplain. He attended every sporting event he could make, and he knew all of the boys by name, a skill the Commodore was never able to master. Whenever any of them felt the need to talk to someone, they went not to the Commodore, but to the chaplain. Today, he told them they were there to honor a boy just like themselves. He was no different from them. He had looked forward to returning from his sea year to play ball, just as they had. And up until the day of his heroic last stand on the fantail of his ship, he had been enjoying his sea year as each of them had enjoyed theirs. When the chaplain made a comment about the joys of studying *abroad* in the foreign seaports of the world, the regiment gave a loud cheer.

The Commodore, off stage, waiting for the chaplain to introduce him, could scarcely believe his own ears. To suggest that Edwin was anything like the unruly lot of boys in the bleachers was an affront to Edwin's morality. But why was the chaplain making any comment at all about Edwin? The chaplain's job was to give a benediction and then introduce the Commodore. Period.

When the Commodore finally took the stage, he took a moment to correct the record before taking the lectern. "Edwin remained unsullied until the day he died. He was nothing like these ruffians who call themselves officers in training." The Commodore flung his arm dismissively in the direction of the regiment sitting in the bleachers. "And he most assuredly was not out cavorting on his port visits as you so coarsely insinuated in your unauthorized comments up there, Chaplain." Then the Commodore poked the chaplain in his breast. "You were told to give a benediction. Your remarks about Edwin were inappropriate."

The public reprimand of the chaplain made the Commodore feel better. It occurred to him as he approached the lectern that after today he would have license to publicly scold any and all personnel under his aegis. It was a stray thought, the sort that pops in and out of one's mind throughout the day, but it was just the thought the Commodore needed to truly calm his nerves. When he took the lectern, a preternatural peace came over him.

"Board of Governors. Colleagues. Regiment of midshipmen. Alumni and guests."

The Commodore paused. He had been waiting so long for this moment that he took another second to savor it. Then he scanned the audience. He first scanned to his left, paused for a fraction of a second, and then scanned back to the right. When he finished scanning the audience, he nodded his head repeatedly.

A beatific smile came over his face. His first "pause, scan, and nod" of the day had gone perfectly.

"Welcome."

The Commodore felt emboldened by his first scan and nod so he took another moment to scan the audience. When he finished scanning and nodding his head the entire regiment nodded in unison with him. It warmed the Commodore's heart to see it. Mimicry was the highest form of flattery.

"The chaplain's remarks of a moment ago were wrong. The person we are here to honor today was not like any of you. The person we are here to honor today possessed character and high morals."

The Commodore was off-script—he knew that—but he felt he needed to set the record straight before he went any further.

"Cadet-midshipman Edwin J. O'Hara was disciplined. He was virtuous and pure. He was, to be certain, unsullied."

When the Commodore said "unsullied," he heard the regiment say the word in concert with him. So the regiment had heard all this before, was that it? Well, at least they were listening. The Commodore needed a moment to compose himself after the interruption from the regiment. Now would be the time for another scan of the audience—a way to start over.

What happened next horrified the Commodore. The entire regiment mimicked his scan technique. And they were perfectly in sync, as if they had been practicing it. Mimicry was one thing, but this bordered on mockery. The Commodore felt his face flush. He forced himself to look down and read from his prepared text:

On a fateful day in the South Atlantic in the year 1944, one of our own gave up his life so that the rest of us could live in freedom. When the German raider *Stier* emerged out of the mist and fired upon the SS *Stephen Hopkins,* cadet-midshipman Edwin J. O'Hara was ready. He had been preparing for this moment his entire young but perfect life. He fired his . . .

The Commodore realized that in his eagerness to start in on the body of his speech he was reading the text with his head down and had completely lost eye contact with his audience. He looked up and tried to catch the eye of one of the widows but they were not paying attention to his speech. In fact both widows were fast asleep.

The Commodore's first attempt at making eye contact was a total failure! And then he was in such a rush to look down at his text again that the abrupt head movement caused him to lose his place.

He felt his pulse quicken and the feeling of nervousness made him even more nervous.

"He fired his four-inch gun at the *Stier* and watched mark after mark make their round. Uh, that is—round after round make their mark."

The Commodore looked up at the audience. He did not make any real eye contact with anyone but he knew that eye contact was critical to a good speech so he looked up again. He desperately searched the audience for a friendly face but he could not find a single one.

"Young cadet-midshipman Edwin J. O'Hara finally ran out of ammunition in his four-inch gattling. Racing aft, he stationed himself on the fantail and took up the four-inch gattling. Mark after—uh, I mean the five-inch houser. And mark after—wait —round after round hit their roun—mark."

The Commodore felt the sweat running down his back. He heard the audience begin to stir, which he knew was the kiss of death for a platform speaker. He saw in the margins of his prepared text a note to remind him to use his thumb point now. He made a loose fist with his right hand and draped his thumb over his index finger.

"And here . . . "

The Commodore pointed at the audience with his thumb point.

" . . . is where Edwin J. O'Hara showed his true colors."

When the Commodore looked up and saw the regiment extending their own thumbs back at him, his knees nearly gave way. He dropped his thumb point and gripped the lectern. The regiment was mocking him outright. It was all too obvious now. The Commodore struggled to keep his composure. He had to continue as if nothing was wrong. He just had to.

He owed it to Edwin.

Knowing that his ship was mortally wounded, Edwin J. O'Hara fought on. The last five shells of his houser hit the *Stier*. The dreaded German raider sank below the waves. It was to be the last thing Edwin witnessed in this earthly world. For no sooner had the *Stier* slipped into the abyss then so, too, had the SS *Stephen Hopkins*. Cadet-midshipman Edwin J. O'Hara gave his life in sinking the *Stier*, and for his heroic actions we honor him here today.

The Commodore's eyes had been glued to his text. He had not dared look up for fear of seeing a regiment of thumbs pointing at him. His margin notes told him that it was now time for his Toe Hang. But how could he venture out from behind the lectern? How? His knees were knocking, his service dress whites were soaked in sweat.

But he knew he could not live with himself if he did not go through with his Toe Hang. Truth be told, at this point an effective Toe Hang was probably the only way for him to win back his audience. The Commodore took one more look down at his text before he left the safe confines of the lectern.

It was only twenty feet to the front of the stage, but brooking those twenty feet was the equivalent of fording a swift-moving river. His first steps were tentative, but he knew that he had to venture forth with confidence, without fear. That, after all, was what the Toe Hang was all about: the speaker leaves the lectern and strides purposefully toward the front of the stage, stops just before the edge, then moves one foot confidently forward so that his toes hang off the edge of the stage, and then glides the other foot forward and lines it up precisely so that both shoes are jutting out over the edge. A speaker cannot get any closer to his audience.

The Commodore somehow summoned the wherewithal to move with a semblance of self-assurance. He came to a stop just before the edge. He placed one foot forward with a confidence that surprised him. Buoyed by the feel of his left toes hanging off the edge of the stage, he began to slide his other foot forward. He felt a sudden elation begin to creep up his spine. He was so close now.

He heard a stirring in the audience. There was fidgeting, people were turning around in there seats. The murmur grew louder. The Commodore's foot was almost in place when a flash of white light struck his eyes.

It was from the widows' parasols. The brilliant October sunshine hit the white parasols and sent a flash of light that temporarily blinded the Commodore.

He overstepped.

The widows, by now, were moving around like little children at the circus. A second flash of light upset his equilibrium. The Commodore lost his balance. He desperately tried to recover, but the trauma of losing his balance with one foot already hanging off the edge of the stage was too great.

The Commodore's quest for the perfect Toe Hang ended in a way he could never have envisioned. He came crashing down off the stage and landed awkwardly on the soft green lawn next to his beloved statue of Edwin.

Captain Cooper rushed to the Commodore's side. Mitzi made room for the Commodore in the first row and Captains Cooper and Tannenbaume carried the Commodore to the bleachers.

The Commodore was in a state of shock. It was immediately apparent that he suffered no significant physical injuries, the only injury being to his psyche. He was inconsolable. Mitzi held his hands in hers.

Mogie marched right up to the two of them. "Hey, are we gonna uncover this monument today or aren't we?"

"Oh come on, Moges," Mitzi said. "Give us a minute here, would you? Can't you see how shook up the Commodore is over this?"

"Come on, Mitz. Everybody is waiting for the big unveiling of this monu—"

"Can't you wait a minute—"

"No, Ms. Paultz," the Commodore said, coming around now. "The mayor is right. This is Edwin's day. We must proceed with the unveiling. I always hoped to give the unveiling the flourish it deserves." The Commodore's voice broke. He waived his arm at Mogie. "Go ahead, Mayor. Give the word to Morris."

Morris, the groundskeeper, was standing next to the monument with his hand on the heavy tarp covering the statue. Mogie waved at him. "Go ahead. Let's have a look at this thing."

The Commodore's vision of the unveiling proved prescient. The sun did, in fact, sparkle just so off Edwin's square jaw, just as he envisioned it. And there *was* a gleam in Edwin's eye. And the crowd did gasp. It was a beautiful monument. Mrs. Tannenbaume, in fact, fainted at the sight of it, something the Commodore never would have predicted. The Commodore was buoyed by the crowd's reaction to the unveiling. He looked around him with pride.

Captain Tannenbaume was not even tending to his mother, so great was *his* interest in the bronze bust of Edwin J. O'Hara. And even Mogie seemed terribly impressed with Edwin. He walked up to the statue for a better look. Then he looked over at Captain Tannenbaume who was slowly walking toward the statue. The Commodore was bursting with pride. Their reaction was everything he could have hoped for. He pinched himself. He wanted to be sure this wasn't a dream, that this was really happening.

His reverie was shaken only by Mogie's outburst.

"Hey! What gives?" Mogie pointed at the statue. "It's Tannenbaume!"

The Commodore was in a state of disbelief. But then he finally saw what Mogie saw, and what had caused Mrs. Tannenbaume to faint.

The bronze bust of Edwin J. O'Hara was the spitting image of Captain Tannenbaume.

Chapter 49

THE BUTLER'S BOW

"**S**o it was Eddie."

Those were the first words out of Mrs. Tannenbaume's mouth when she came to. The longstanding mystery of Eddie, Teddy, and Freddie—the sailor, the tailor, and the jailor—had finally been solved: Edwin J. O'Hara, the cadet a young Mrs. Tannenbaume had romped with all those years ago in Durban, was most certainly Captain Tannenbaume's father.

Or, as Mogie crowed, "Tannenbaume's the bastard son of the Commodore's hero."

The news was too much for the Commodore to process.

"Captain Tannenbaume's father?" the Commodore stated over and over again as he stood in front of the statue of his fallen hero. "How can that be?"

"We had a situation," Mrs. Tannenbaume said.

"A situation?"

"You know, the hoo hoo and the ha ha."

"The hoo hoo? With Edwin?"

"I called him Eddie," Mrs. Tannenbaume said. "My Eddie was your Edwin."

"But Edwin was unsullied."

"Not with me he wasn't."

"I cannot accept it."

"But look at them!" It was Mogie interjecting this time. He had one hand pointed at Captain Tannenbaume and one hand at Edwin. "They could be brothers."

"No," the Commodore said. "Mrs. Tannenbaume is mistaken. It was so long ago. How can she remember? No, she must have been with someone other than Edwin. Some other boy, I'm sure of it."

"But look at them!" Mogie said again.

"I can prove it." Mrs. Tannenbaume said this quietly, so quietly that it made the others take notice. They turned to her.

"I can prove it was Edwin," she said again, looking directly at the Commodore. "I kept one of his uniforms. It's back home in the attic. Cadets are required to stencil all of their clothing. I remember I thought it was so funny that he wrote his name on his underwear." Mrs. Tannenbaume looked at the Commodore again, this time with a little more pity. "I have one of his uniforms that has his name stenciled on it."

The others looked at the Commodore for his response, wondering how he would accept this piece of news, but his face was blank. It was hard not to feel sorry for him. He had been so sure of Edwin's chastity that evidence proving otherwise was simply impossible for him to compute.

Mogie was the only one who seemed to be taking pleasure in the Commodore's plight. "Well, that ought to prove it, hey, Commodore? The kid's name on his pants?"

Mitzi glared at Mogie before taking the Commodore by the hand. "Let's go, sir," she said. "Let's go see this uniform."

"No, Ms. Paultz. I cannot."

"You need closure."

"Mitzi's right, Commodore. We gotta close this deal." Mogie walked over and put his hand on the Commodore's back, pushing him along. "Let's go see this uniform."

"Okay, Tannenbaume," Mogie said to Captain Tannenbaume. "Up the ladder."

Captain Tannenbaume stood firm. All he did was raise his eyebrows at Mogie.

Mogie looked up at Captain Tannenbaume. "Somebody's gotta be the boss," he said.

Mogie and Captain Tannenbaume glared at each other before Mogie walked off to the side, planted his feet, and put his hands on his hips, looking very much like "the boss." "You," he pointed at Captain Tannenbaume. "Up the ladder."

"Morty's right, Moges," Mitzi chimed in. "Who died and left you boss?"

"Look, Mitz. We're here to seal the deal. Somebody's got to do the *schlepping*." Mogie looked at Captain Tannenbaume and pointed at the ladder. "Up."

"Oh, would you listen to you two," Mrs. Tannenbaume said. "Step aside. I'll get the trunk down."

"No, Mother. Of course I'll go up the ladder." Captain Tannenbaume stared at Mogie. "I just don't like being told what to do by this guy."

Mrs. Tannenbaume remembered that the last time she tried to get into the attic the key broke off in the lock, so she went to the garage to get the hacksaw. By the time she got back, Captain Tannenbaume was at the top of the ladder.

"Here, sonny," she said. "Use this."

When her sonny got the lock off, Mrs. Tannenbaume felt her pulse quicken. Her past was up in that attic. A past she had buried a long time ago. Some things were about to come to light now, some things she had kept from her son his entire life.

Mitzi came over to Mrs. Tannenbaume and took her hand. "You've probably got a lot of memories stored up there, huh?"

"You can say that again."

"Hey!" Captain Tannenbaume shouted from the attic. "It's pretty dark up here, Mother. Where's this uniform?"

"It's in the trunk, sonny. Just bring the trunk down."

The hinges on the trunk creaked when Captain Tannenbaume opened it up in front of the small crowd at the base of the ladder. The khaki uniform was right on top. It was more of a yellowish color after years of storage, and it was brittle to the touch. Captain Tannenbaume gingerly pulled back the waistband, and there it was: Edwin J. O'Hara's name stenciled in block letters, the black ink faded to gray.

The Commodore gasped. "Oh, Edwin. How could you do this to me?"

"Wow," Mogie said. "So the Commodore's hero really is your father, hey, Tannenbaume? How does that make you feel?"

Captain Tannenbaume took his mother's hand and stood with her and Mitzi. "I don't know what I should be feeling." He smiled at his mother. "So it was Eddie."

"It sure looks that way, sonny." Mrs. Tannenbaume put her hand to her temple. "I think I need to sit down."

Captain Tannenbaume and Mitzi took her to sit on a chair against the wall in the hallway. Mrs. Tannenbaume let out a long sigh.

"He was a good guy," she said. "I'm glad he's the one."

"So let me get this straight," Mitzi said pulling up a chair next to Mrs. Tannenbaume. "Your father was a tailor?"

"That's right."

"And where was he from?"

"Bremen. He and my mother moved to Durban after the First War."

"Why'd they move?"

"There was trouble." Mrs. Tannenbaume spoke in a whisper.

"Trouble?"

"Don't you get it, Mitz?" Mogie butted in. "Her father was a garmento. He probably lived in some shtetel town in Germany. Jews weren't welcome."

Mitzi looked up at Captain Tannenbaume, who was looking intently at his mother. She took Mrs. Tannenbaume's hand in hers. "Is that why it's Tannenbaume with an E?"

Mrs. Tannenbaume lifted her face and looked at her son. She thought she saw compassion in his eyes. "I had to, sonny. It was just you and me. I had to protect us." Mrs. Tannenbaume had a tear in her eye.

Captain Tannenbaume kneeled down and draped his hand over his mother's and Mitzi's. He did not say anything, but then, he didn't have to.

"Hey," Mogie interrupted, stepping toward the three of them. "What the hell is going on here?"

"Oh shut up, Moges. You don't know what's going on."

"Well what *is* going on, for chrissakes?"

"Mrs. Tannenbaume's Jewish, Moges, don't you get it?"

"Of course she's Jewish. What the hell are you talking about?"

Mitzi and Mrs. Tannenbaume laughed together. "It looks like he got his Jew admiral after all, hey, Mrs. Tannenbaume?"

Mogie went over to the Commodore. "Will you at least tell me what the hell is going on here?"

The Commodore looked utterly defeated. "I am as bemused as you are, Mr. Mayor." He then turned to go.

Mogie held the Commodore back. "Wait. Tell Tannenbaume he's out. I'm making you the superintendent, not him."

The Commodore straightened himself up the best he could. The skin on his face sagged. Even his hair seemed to have lost its sheen. "I don't understand everything that is going on here, Mr. Mayor, but I do apprehend this much: Captain Tannenbaume is the sole progeny of the veritable hero of the United States Merchant Marine Academy. It is clear enough that I am the odd man out now. And you, sir, are on the outs as well."

Now it was Mogie's turn to be stupefied. He turned to Mitzi. "Mitz, baby. What gives here?"

"I ain't your baby, Moges. The Commodore's right. You're out."

The Commodore placed his hand on Mogie's shoulder. "It was a grand plan, Mr. Mayor. But we have been bested. No one, not even a heroic competitor such as yourself, can overcome the weight of history. It is time for us to take our leave now."

Before taking his leave, however, the Commodore decided to make one last gesture. Posterity demanded it. To the victor goes the spoils. And the vanquished? Well, the vanquished go quietly.

He stood before Captain Tannenbaume. It took every ounce of what fortitude he had left to stand as erect as he knew he must. The Commodore doffed his cap with a flick of the wrist and tucked it beneath his left arm. Then he clicked his heels and bowed at the waist.

The butler's bow. It was all that was left to do.

EPILOGUE

Morris the groundskeeper is still at the academy, still butchering hedges. The BandLeader became a millionaire as the inventor of an earpiece for tone-deaf bandleaders.

Maven did, in fact, become the Commodore's secretary. She continues to wear her tulip dresses to work.

Miss Lambright had her fifteen minutes of fame as the cover girl of *Playboy* in a spread entitled "The Women of the United States Merchant Marine Academy."

Raymond continues to do the Commodore's shirts at the Great Neck Martinizing Dry Cleaners.

The widows went on to become board members of various Wall Street banks. We know what happened there.

Captain Cooper's wife, Frank Beebee's old wife, died. He went on to marry Miss Beebee and they settled back in West Virginia. When her fellow West

Virginians discovered that Miss Beebe had married her dead brother's widowed wife's husband, they did not bat an eye.

The electrician now sells Timberland boots for a living. The yellowish nubuck leather kind.

Tibby went on to become a Tampa Bay harbor pilot. Unfortunately, he became distracted one day while expounding on the virtues of Conrad and nearly ran his ship into the Sunshine Skyway bridge. He was saved by the inbound pilot, Captain Jiso, who, seeing Tibby's ship shearing off toward the bridge, got on the VHF and said, "Wake up, Conrad." Tibby retired from piloting and went on to write a best-selling book about finding your true calling in life called, fittingly, *Wake up, Conrad*.

Ski is still behind the wheel on the *God is Able*.

Swifty went on to become professor of navigation at the State University of New York Maritime College in Fort Schuyler. His students receive straight As even though they don't know a sunline from a sunspot.

The steward is serving jail time for stalking Clint Eastwood.

Sparks retired to Snug Harbor, the retirement home for merchant mariners. He started out very popular with the retirees because he fixed all of their old analog contrivances, but he was ultimately kicked out for reading their mail.

The chief moved to Vegas where he began his second act as an Elvis impersonator.

Sylvia and the second engineer got married. They settled down in Great Neck where she opened a beauty salon. Sylvia became inspired by her Great Neck neighbors and finally started doing for others, giving free makeovers to single mothers.

Johnson's Johnson sells his wife's watercolors in retirement. He and the navy chaplain take a cruise every winter and the chaplain continues to run interference for him.

Mogie lost his mayoral reelection bid to his challenger Putzie Paultz, who financed his own campaign with money from his burgeoning dry cleaning business, now the official dry cleaners of the academy. Mogie and Jane started a Jews for Jesus synagogue. Mrs. Tannenbaume donated her papier-mâché Jesus.

Captain Tannenbaume and Mitzi got married. They had a son and named him Edwin J. Tannenbaume.

The Commodore stayed on as officer of external affairs. He continues to give his back end speech and became godfather to Edwin J. Tannenbaume.

Mrs. Tannenbaume became the sex-ed teacher at the academy. She quit St. Aloysius and joined Mitzi's synagogue. Her sonny boy offered her housing on the academy grounds, but Mrs. Tannenbaume said she no longer wanted to live in Kings Point. Her life was in Great Neck.

ACKNOWLEDGMENTS

Ronnie and Evan Weston read the manuscript from start to finish, read it with gusto, read it with all of the generosity that makes them so special. Your support has meant the world to me. So thank you, Ronnie and Evan.

Rhonda Pray read the first five chapters while overnighting at our house on the way to Buenos Aires and her encouragement meant so much to me at that early stage.

My old and good friends Scott and Keith Driscoll and Luz Lopez Driscoll gave me the unvarnished truth—as I knew they would—and their thumbs up gave me a burst of hope that maybe the book was good enough after all.

Jill Ecklund offered excellent advice on improving the readability of the book.

Jorge Viso told me, in so many words, that I acquitted myself well. High praise from Captain Viso. Thank you, Jorge.

Carolyn Kurtz also read the manuscript with alacrity and her comments were wonderfully insightful and helpful.

Thomas Pray, aka Woodbine, did not read it, but then he didn't have to. Woodbine, who has been my biggest fan, who thinks I can do anything, who flew over shark infested waters with me in the Bahamas in my ancient 1966 Cherokee Six airplane—when I barely knew how to fly the damn thing—because, as he said at the time, "I trust you." Those words meant more to me then, mean more to me now, than he could ever know. So thanks, Woodbine, for your great friendship.

My brother Jeffrey has been a fount of enthusiasm from the beginning and remains the most generous person I've known in my life.

Joe Morris is all over this book. He knows what that means. Thank you for everything, Joe.

Jaime Pineiro cheered me on from the helm of his beautiful sailboat as we traversed Biscayne Bay in the afternoon—day after glorious day—while I was writing the book.

Keith McKinney responded with memorable enthusiasm when I first told him my idea for a novel so many years ago while vacationing on the North Fork of Long Island. His words of encouragement sustained me until I began writing a full decade later.

Frank Reider also responded fervently when we discussed my book idea over lunch way back when. Frank's ardor for the book remains undiminished and for that I am grateful.

Dave King wrote *Self-Editing for Fiction Writers*, which is *the* indispensible book for the first-time novelist, or any novelist for that matter. Dave's blue pencil marked up my pages and brought my rough draft to life. Thank you, Dave. I recommend you and your book to every writer I know.

Marty Smith set me on the right path many years ago, yielding only a cocktail napkin and a ballpoint pen while we sat at the bar at my brother's wedding.

Stephen Pollan, another great and generous man, has been more helpful to me than he may know. He listened with compassion when I informed him that I wrote a novel and had certain hopes for it. That he took me seriously, that he took my call at all, I am so grateful for. He cared enough to help me out and for that, how can I ever adequately thank him? I will start by saying: Thank You, Stephen.

Stephen put me in touch with Herb Schaffner and Herb took over from there. To my great and everlasting delight Herb "got" my book. "It needs some work, though," he said. Herb served dual roles as both my editor and agent. More than that, he has been my trusted advisor on everything to do with the book business. He and his colleagues at Schaffner Media Partners are consummate pros. This book would be nothing but a yellowed manuscript by now if you had not come along, Herb. I cannot thank you enough.

Julie Matysik acquired the book for Skyhorse and was my editor, and what a fine editor she was for my book. She took great care with the manuscript, took great care with me—a first-time novelist—walked me through the whole process, answered my calls, answered my emails. Julie has been a joy to work with. Thank you so much, Julie.

Thanks to the great team at Skyhorse: Tony Lyons, Bill Wolfsthal, Esther Bochner, Nina Boutsikaris, and Abigail Gehring.

My grandmother told me that I should write a book one day and that it should be about her. Well, Nana, I did and it is. I think you would have liked it.

My mother, Betty Jacobsen, filled me from a young age with great storehouses of confidence that I could do anything I set my mind to. For that, and for her, I am most grateful.

My son, Liam, will turn six when his father's book comes out. For as far back as he can remember his father has been writing a book. Thank you for your great understanding, Liam. So sorry that you can't read it until you're eighteen.

My wife, Silvana, was enormously patient with me while I wrote this book. When a woman as beautiful as Silvana has that kind of faith in you, a guy can't help but feel like the luckiest guy in the world. I know that I am.

And, finally, to the kindred souls who have mustered over the years in the foyer between Fourth and Fifth Company, this book's for you.

ABOUT THE AUTHOR

Captain John Jacobsen, a graduate of the United States Merchant Marine Academy, spent fifteen years plying the world's oceans as a ship's officer on cargo and passenger vessels. Today, Jacobsen is a harbor pilot in the Port of Miami and the Chairman of the Biscayne Bay Pilots Association. His notes and diaries over the years inform his writing. He lives in Miami, Florida, with his wife and son.